feeding frenzy

CRIMSON COVEN

BOOK 3

ALLIE SANTOS

Feeding Frenzy
Copyright © 2025 by Allie Santos
All rights reserved.
ISBN: 978-1-965300-20-6 (Paperback)

This is a work of fiction. The characters, incidents, and dialogues are products of the author's imagination and are not to be construed as real.

Cover Art by GetCovers

Edited/Proofread by MT Editing and Proofreading Services

a note from allie

I can't believe this is the end of Crimson Coven's story! I loved writing Catalina and her psychotic vampires. These guys were seriously so fun to write. Thank you for coming along with me for the ride, it was such a pleasure bringing these characters to life.

Please consider leaving a review. Word of mouth is the biggest help to independent authors.

Love,
Allie🖤

<h1 style="text-align:center">content warnings</h1>

Murder Attempts on MFC, Violence, Mention of Past Rape, Descriptive Sex, Foul Language, Descriptive Murder Scenes, Forceful Sex Scenes, Exhibitionism, Voyeurism

Please be advised that the following trigger and content warnings contain spoilers for the story and plot of the novel.

FEEDING FRENZY is a Why-Choose Paranormal Romance. Please be advised that Feeding Frenzy contains adult content. The main characters partake in rough, bloody sex. This is the final book in this series. There are no romantic male-male relationships, but there are instances during sexual situations where males touch while with their female. They only love/crave the heroine.

Disclaimer: Vampires in this world do not think like humans, although some may try. They are instinctual, possessive, and lustful. The main male characters will own the main female character through whatever means possible.

Feeding Frenzy is set in a mythical world and all contents are purely fiction.

ONE

catalina

I SQUEEZED Asher's silk sheets under my cheek. How much time had passed of me just sobbing into the bed to the point that tears no longer flowed?

I sniffled. It had to be a minimum of a few hours. Even after letting all the negativity out, the throb in my chest hadn't disappeared.

This all had to be some joke. Some alien controlling my life was out there laughing at my misfortune.

I weakly flopped over and scooted to the edge of the bed. It even hurt to sit up. I groaned and scrubbed my face. With all the effort I could muster, I pushed to my feet and trudged to Asher's bathroom.

I nudged the door open the rest of the way and my reflection stared back at me. Messy hair, red face, blood shot eyes. Oh, God. I dropped my gaze. Best not to focus on how bad I looked.

Instead, I focused on my products nicely lined up to the left of the sink. Maddy, the human they brought to look after me, must have set them all up for me. The serum for my frizzy hair, a blow dryer, face wash, and hyaluronic acid serum . . . the expensive bottles laughed at me. All that and I looked like I'd had a fight with a vacuum, and the vacuum won.

My knees buckled and I leaned against the wall. It'd only been a night since *she* arrived, and I was drained, emotionally and physically.

I slid down until my butt was on the floor and my knees scrunched against my chest, close enough to rest my chin on.

I exhaled shakily and shoved my fingers into my hair. This was a fucking mess, and I held it together by a thread.

That female vampire—I clenched my teeth. Imogen. Her torn clothes, her ragged appearance. She had suffered away from my—her vampires. The way she broke down about being captured? No one deserved that, but I couldn't help fixating on what her appearance meant.

Would they kill me now that she'd returned? Or maybe keep me around, feeding on me only when the craving struck. My stomach churned unpleasantly. That seemed exponentially worse. I groaned and pressed my fingertips into my eyes.

The uncertainty killed me.

A touch on my shoulder saved me from drowning in the doom my thoughts evoked. Asher crouched next to me, a soft smile on his lips. His palm slid behind my neck, and I stiffened. What was about to come out of his mouth?

"I'm sorry it took me so long to come check on you," he whispered, bending low to look me in the eyes. His long golden hair fell forward, and his light blue eyes peered into mine. "Catalina."

He clicked his tongue disapprovingly. "Nothing will change, *Älskade*."

It took my sluggish brain an extra moment. I understood

his words, but I didn't believe them. It was impossible for nothing to change.

"B-but she's here," I croaked.

His eyebrows furrowed and winged down.

"Pet," he sighed. "You will never be rid of me. I told you this."

For a brief moment, elation expanded in my chest and just as quickly it was smushed under the heel of my thoughts. Did that mean they would keep me while she still remained here? I jerked my head to the side to try to get him to let me go, but I was unsuccessful. I simultaneously wanted to fight him and take off running. If that was what they wanted to do, I couldn't do anything to stop it.

"I will not stick around like a second option—"

"Catalina," he interrupted me, exasperated. "You're not understanding. *Nothing will change.* We will keep you. Imogen has no place here."

I blinked. Had I taken some sort of hallucinogen? Asher clasped my face between his large palms, pursing my lips with the grip. "But."

My stomach hit the ground. "Don't look at me with those eyes," he said huskily. "We have to tread carefully when we convey that to her. She has to get healed up and . . . the vampires she Sired: me, Jaxon, Tobias, and many others thought we were free when we believed her dead. But now?" He shook his head. "There is a certain respect that must be extended to your Sire." His eyes flicked to the side. "She's always been impulsive. She'd easily kill you," he whispered the last part. Agony flared through his eyes, forcing his brows together. "We need time. I need to talk to everyone, without her around, so we can plan." He swiped his thumb across the dampness lingering on my cheek.

"And everyone is on the same page? About me?" He knew what I was asking. Jax's love had returned, what he'd been bitter about from the start. No way would he stay with me.

"Ren is and Bastien goes without saying. Tobias will agree as soon as I get a moment to speak with him. He's been making calls, attempting to get information on how to best proceed against Wrenhaven. Jax . . ." He cleared his throat. "I haven't had a moment alone with him. If he wants to leave with her, then I will not fight him on it."

I hugged myself, as if trying to hold my insides from spilling out. Jax would leave me. He would choose her. Nausea twisted my stomach. He'd been so protective recently. In a way I could have gotten used to. I squeezed my eyes tightly shut. Every time we seemed to make headway with each other, we were ripped a hundred steps back, and there was no return this time. "Will you be patient, Pet?"

I bit the inside of my cheek.

"If I say no?" I finally whispered after a few breaths, because it hurt to try to talk past the thickness in my throat.

Red bled through his irises, and his lip curled up. He grabbed the back of my neck, drawing me to his face while he leaned down to look into my eyes. His fingernails felt like claws prickling my skin and I winced. His gaze returned to normal and his hold softened.

"Catalina." His sharp incisors flashed and he paused, closing his eyes. "Let us untangle her webs. We are yours. Just give us time."

Time? I clenched my teeth. Okay, if I took a step back and observed this like an outsider, I understood the need for time. They thought she was dead, for God's sake. On top of that, she'd been held captive and by the looks of it, tortured. But understanding didn't make it hurt any less.

"It doesn't sound like I have much of an option." Did I sound a little pissy? Yes, but I could only be so graceful about the situation. His nostrils flared with an audible inhale.

"Blood." He gripped my forearm and dragged the sweater down to unveil the bandage. Blood seeped through the thin wrap I'd found under his sink. He held my arm in a hard grip that continued to tighten. By the look of his moving jawline, he was gritting his teeth. He looked pissed. He ripped the bandage off my arm to look at what lay underneath it.

"Why didn't you say anything?" His fangs flashed with his chastising words. They extended from his gums. "Sorry, Pet, you smell so good that I can't control them." A genuine smile perked the corner of my lips. The first one since *the event*. Lifting my arm, he brought it to his mouth to slide his tongue over the jagged wounds. He licked the dried blood clean off. I closed my eyes, sighing from the relief of his tongue spreading his healing saliva across the punctures. "Fucking Tobias never should have asked you to feed her," he snapped. "She shredded your precious skin."

"I was the only human around," I said in defense of Tobias, but I didn't sound convincing even to my ears. Asher raised a single blond eyebrow at me, not even a little in agreement. A ticklish sensation spread across my wrist. The wound looked the same, no, it was smaller. So freaking weird. I focused on Asher's tight expression. He continued fussing over my wrist and muttering under his breath.

They were choosing me, or at least most of them were—I wouldn't lose them. He continued staring down at my ticklish bite marks with eyebrows furrowed. His concern seemed so poignant and real. Warmth crawled through my veins. I tossed my arms around his neck, pressing my lips to his.

He grunted, taking my full weight to the chest. I clung to him, angling my head to slip my tongue into his mouth. He softened under my touch, arms sliding around my waist to band me tight to him. I flicked my tongue against the inner side of his fang.

Asher groaned, fingers flexing into my waist and in a whirlwind of motion he was on his knees with me hoisted against him, clasping me against his chest. His cock shoved against my belly and lips against mine. My God, he tasted so good.

"I want." Kiss. "To take." Lick. "A shower." Nibble.

"My *Älskade* gets what she wants," he said gruffly against my mouth.

His fang pierced my lip, and he sucked on it. I gasped. Pleasure bloomed from the wound with each of his sucks. My eyes closed.

He hoisted me high enough for me to wrap my legs around his waist. He was moving, but I wouldn't be able to tell up from down. The shower sputtered to life. Asher's hand slid to my ass, and he lifted me a little higher. Water sprayed my back, plastering my shirt to my body.

"Asher," I gasped, pulling away from his mouth. He chuckled, turning to shield me from the spray, set me down, and started pulling the clothes off me with a sharp tug. "What is it with you vampires and ripping clothes?"

The tattered bits of fabric plopped on the shower floor with a wet splat.

"Makes getting to your delicious body faster," he whispered

against my ear, eliciting a shiver. "And you know how much I love it."

I jolted from the word. He said it so flippantly, as if it held no meaning. He clasped my face in both hands and tipped my face up. His blue eyes searched mine.

"You are all that matters to us."

Again, with the 'us'.

I hummed.

"What, you don't believe me?" His eyebrow twitched. I said nothing and pursed my lips. "Looks like I'll have to prove it to you," he purred. Asher dropped to his knees in a smooth glide.

"What are you doing?" The spray of water pelted my chest and his shoulders. He wrapped his hand around my calf. "Asher, I'm going to fall—" My complaint turned into a squeak. He hooked my leg over his shoulder, while simultaneously corralling me against the side. My shoulders hit the tile of the shower's wall.

"Trust me, Catalina," he purred. "I'll never let you fall." There was a promise in his vow that made my heart take a staggering leap. His blond hair was plastered to his shoulders as he lowered his head, burying his mouth at the apex of my thighs. He dragged his tongue up my slit. I gasped, my hips twitching up.

He repeated the motion, then rolled his tongue around my clit at the apex of my pussy. He was painfully good at teasing. Asher peeked up at me through wet lashes, a playful look in his blue eyes. Dangerous vampire. I could only imagine him as a human. Just as unrepentant as he was right now. He dragged his front teeth along my clit. I gasped, my head thumping against the tile.

Hoisting me up a little higher, he widened the gap between

my thighs. Asher grazed his blunt teeth on the bundle of nerves again. I jolted as if electrocuted.

He chuckled and the sudden invasion of his fingers sliding into my core shocked me so much I stiffened.

"Relax," he murmured against my sex.

At the order, my body listened, my legs becoming limp around his shoulders. I caught the slightest smirk on Asher's lips, and then his mouth covered my sex, sliding his tongue under my clit to flick it expertly.

I closed my eyes, feeling every bit of his skill. My toes curled and I couldn't have formed a coherent word if I wanted. I tried to move my hips up to grind against him, but he kept me firmly pinned. Instead, I grabbed and yanked at his hair with the swell of my orgasm.

Asher groaned, angling his head to slide his tongue even deeper into my core. His chin pressed against my inner thigh.

Sharp cries echoed off the bathroom walls. My whining moans would have embarrassed me as an outsider, but all I could focus on was his tongue and the spine-tingling tension taking hold of my tender core.

Asher hummed against me, thrusting his tongue in and out, incessantly, wringing every bit of my orgasm free. I could feel my channel gripping onto his tongue like it was his cock.

I whimpered, rolling my head against the tile at my back. He was so good at licking me. I floated down from the pinnacle of my release, my breaths tuning into harsh panting. Asher pulled away from my swollen flesh. I kept my hands delved into his hair, gripping onto it like it was rope.

"Sorry," I croaked and untangled my fingers.

He chuckled and gently set my feet on the floor. He stood and water ran down the shirt plastered to his body in rivulets.

I ran my hands down the dips of his chest. He shuddered at my caress and smiled down at me with soft eyes.

As I finished washing off, Asher removed his wet clothes and stepped out. He hooked a towel around his waist and turned to me with a fresh one, holding it open for me.

I leaned forward until the soft fibers touched my front. Asher swept me into his arms and carried me to the bed, tossing me on the surface. My body bounced with squeaks escaping my lips. Asher landed on top of me, his damp hair falling around his shoulders. He grinned down at me.

The loud bang of the door shutting turned our attention to Ren.

"Everyone in the house can hear you," Ren announced. "Next time, close the door." He directed the order at Asher, who just scoffed. "I brought your computer." He waved it at me and set it on the chair to the side of the door.

I glared at him. He didn't mean everyone, he meant Imogen. Before, it wasn't a problem if the door was left open, but *now* it was?

"Sorry to have bothered your precious Imogen," I said through my teeth, yanking the towel around my chest. My face burned.

"Ren," Asher groaned and closed his eyes, head tilting back.

Imogen this—Imogen that. Stop. I needed to quit that line of thought. They were useless to me and only put me in a bad mood. I yanked the towel securely under my armpits and scooted to the edge of the bed. Asher cupped my shoulder.

My lips thinned and I shoved him off me. He grabbed at me again. I took advantage of the fact that he was gentle. I slipped out of his reach again, heading directly to the door.

I fisted my hands at my side, practically stomping toward

the door. I didn't know where I was headed but fuck this. A thick arm banded against my stomach and swept me back. I yelped, suddenly airborne, then I landed on the bed with an explosive breath—again. Ren hovered at the side of the bed, lips turned down.

"What did I do?" Ren's confusion would have sounded cute, if it didn't piss me off. I slitted my eyes up at him.

"Upset her," Asher snapped.

"I'm lost." Ren scowled. Of course he wouldn't *get* it.

His eyebrows raised even higher, but why did he look like he was enjoying this? I grabbed a pillow and threw it at his face with all my might. The pillow stopped an inch from smacking into his face because he swatted it to the floor. I couldn't even have that. Frustration bubbled over and manifested into tears. I wish I was a more violent person. One that took pleasure in hurting things like them. Yet, here I was, blubbering like a baby.

"Don't," I shouted as Asher reached out to touch me. He retreated.

"Well done, Ren." Asher sighed.

"Explain it." He snarled at Asher, no longer sounding smug.

"You seemed concerned for Imogen."

"Shut it," I snapped at Asher, scooting to the end of the bed. "I'm just extra sensitive right now."

"This is because of Imogen?" He scoffed, shaking his head. "You were to explain that nothing would change. Catalina will remain under our protection. She is ours," he said it almost accusatorially.

"I explained it to her." The biting tone in Asher's voice turned icy.

"Then I do not understand the issue," Ren said scowling.

I didn't either. I really was just extra sensitive.

Ren reached for me, and I stiffened my spine, avoiding his grip.

"Come here."

"No."

By the look in his eyes, he took it as a dare. He suddenly pounced, much too fast for me to throw myself out of his way.

I tried to keep my back straight, but he leaned so close to my face that I couldn't help but flinch a little. His brown eyes studied mine.

"No?" he said it as a question, then grinned until his dimple made a showing. He kept coming. I used my heels to push off his thighs and slide back. The towel slipped free and I scrambled backwards naked.

His large hand gripped my ankle. I flipped over, struggling to get onto my knees, but he dragged me. My breasts rubbed against the silk sheets.

I fought against him, kicking frantically to free myself. A slap stung my butt. I yelped, and the crying cut off, due to my shock. The sharp sting radiated toward my sensitive sex. I stayed frozen and in silence, trying to figure out how to react.

I didn't have time to catch up to my feelings, because Ren flipped me over. I landed on my back with a grunt. He climbed up the bed, jostling me until his mouth hovered over mine. He hooked my leg up and around one hip.

"Naughty human," he said, slapping the meaty part where my ass met my leg. I jolted, my entire body tensing. Oddly enough, a swell of lust flamed to life. He lowered and claimed my lips. He shoved his tongue inside my mouth, leading the kiss with violent flicks. A touch on my jaw forced my chin up and he deepened the kiss.

I became mush under his skillful touch. Sinking my fingers into his hair, I kissed him just as fervently. One of his sharp incisors sliced into my lip and they weren't even extended. Ren sucked on my tongue. I jolted against him, hiking to grind myself against his hard body hovering over me.

He moaned and his palm settled on my hip, jerking me tighter to his body. My clit quivered and fanned the flames of my lust. Whimpering, I hooked my legs more securely and dug my calves into his back to hoist myself onto him. He hissed against my mouth and I could feel his fangs distend.

I flicked my tongue against the smooth side. Ren pulled up with a gasp. His hands moved at lightning speed to yank his cock free of his jeans.

He fed himself into my sex, with a sigh against my lips. I shuddered, arching my hips upwards to take his full girth. The stretch made my eyes cross.

Ren pumped the entire length out and then inside me. The silky shaft wrenched more moans from my mouth.

I no longer had control of my neck, and I found myself facing Asher. As Ren continued gliding in and out of me, Asher had positioned himself at my side, his golden, damp hair grazing my arm. His blue gaze devoured my features, and his thumb slid across my lip. Ren pounded into me hard, wrenching a cry from me. Asher's tongue flicked across his lower lip and his gaze wouldn't release mine as Ren continued thrusting.

"Look at me," Ren snarled, forcing my head straight. He thrust so hard that the bed jolted and the sound of our skin slapping together rang through the room.

Asher chuckled.

"The bastard got jealous." His sweet breath fanned across my cheek. "And, Pet, Ren doesn't get jealous about anything."

Ren snarled and his pace picked up. Cries spilled from my mouth with each violent thrust. I could feel him so deep inside me. He angled my head and sank his fangs into the side of my neck. I gasped, my entire body clenching up.

Asher's lustful gaze snagged mine again.

He almost seemed fascinated. He reached for my face, his fingertip hovering over my lips. Ren thrust again, the release crashed into me, and I cinched my eyes closed. Sensation coursed through every part of me. The ache throbbed through my sex, manifesting in a trembling of my legs I couldn't control.

Ren grunted into my ear and my channel responded to the jolt of his cock inside me.

"I fucking love the look on your face when you come," Asher murmured huskily. I dropped my gaze to his hand wrapped around his stiff shaft. My body reacted, tensing up with the throb of lust.

Ren grunted, pulling his fangs from my neck.

"Yes," he hissed. "Grip me with your tight little cunt." He pumped lazily. My legs wouldn't stop trembling. Ren leaned down and kissed my nipple. His shaft popped out from my sex and liquid trickled free. I squeezed my legs closed, as if I could hold their release and my need inside me.

Ren tucked his arms under my waist and scooted down to rest his cheek against my belly.

I shivered from the remnants of the pleasure fading. Asher tossed his arm across me, tucking himself under my boobs.

I sighed, nuzzling into the crook of Asher's embrace. As the panic and pain of the last few days abated, reality crawled forward. So much had been happening with me, I hadn't checked my email.

"Can I borrow your phone?" I whispered to Asher. Ren

had brought my computer, but it seemed like too much effort to get up and grab it. It was definitely laziness.

Asher leaned away to rifle through the nightstand.

Ren rolled to the opposite side, propping his head on his palm while his other hand stayed on my thigh. He dragged his fingertips up between my breasts and down to my belly button. Again and again. A shiver coasted down my spine.

"I'll make sure to order you one," Asher said as he handed me his device. I found myself staring at a picture of myself—sleeping. I peeked at him from the corner of my eye.

"Stalker activities?"

All he did was smile.

I swiped the phone open and navigated to the web browser to log into my email. Yes! Peter had finally emailed me. I grinned.

"I don't believe she's ever smiled at us like that." Asher tsked. I peeked up under my lashes to glare at him, but his attention was on Ren.

Whatever. My brother was different from them. I refocused on Peter's words.

He'd arrived and magically, somehow, he'd found Asher's contact information saved in his phone and would call me when he caught up with everything he'd left up in the air. When had Asher saved his information on Peter's phone?

"You guys really did know I would get him away."

Asher smiled.

"Thank you." I slid my arms around his neck, leaning so close until my cheek rested against his chest.

Asher hooked my leg over his hip. With a smooth twitch of his hips, he seated himself deep inside me. My sensitive sex clasped onto him. I wiggled to move on him, but his hold stiffened on my knee. The bed jostled from Ren moving higher on the bed.

"Keep it right here, Pet," Asher murmured huskily.

Ren's hand at the dip of my waist tightened and his cock prodded at my entrance. The same one as Asher. I sucked in a breath, bracing for the stretch.

"Wait," Asher groaned, and his cock throbbed inside me. I sank my teeth into my lower lip. He reached behind him, his hand patting at the nightstand. He tossed Ren something and whatever it was crinkled like plastic. Asher hadn't been talking to me. He must have tossed Ren a small packet of lube.

Ren's hands slipped off my waist, and I could only imagine him slathering the gel onto his shaft and guiding his tip into position. He prodded at my entrance again. Upon the first touch, it was so cold that I flinched, but he didn't give me a moment to shy away. He moved, sliding inside me, causing the bed to shudder.

I gasped on an exhale. The already tight fit became even more snug, making Asher's piercings pressed against my insides.

They filled me up too close to the point of pain. Ren returned his palm to my waist and squeezed.

"You have the sweetest fucking pussy," he murmured. I wiggled my hips, in a circle. The wet sound of my movement caused another throb to travel through my channel. They both groaned. Ren slowly pumped out and slid back in. I thumped my forehead against Asher's chest. He shuddered, just as affected by Ren's thrust.

"Sleep, Pet. We'll take care of you." My eyelashes had grown increasingly heavy. Each time I blinked it took a little longer for them to lift back up. I wiggled again, making their soft groans echo in my ear.

"You're doing it on purpose," Ren said gruffly in my ear. He lifted his palm from my waist and swatted the side of my butt again.

I laughed. My channel clasped onto them as if trying to grip onto them forever.

I nuzzled into Asher's neck, and he hummed. A pleased, satisfied sound. Ren grunted and ground his hips against me. My eyelids dropped shut as I settled into a satisfied, sexual fog. My eyes became impossible to keep open.

I didn't want to leave this room. Everything was too fresh, too raw. I needed to brace myself. To mentally prepare myself for whatever I would face. I had to be strong, but in my gut, I acknowledged I wouldn't play second fiddle, no matter what. I'd wait, I'd see how this panned out, but I wouldn't accept less. Or God forbid, sharing my vampires.

As selfish as it was, I wanted them all to myself.

catalina

I UNTANGLED myself from Asher and Ren's heavy limbs, scooted to the bottom of the bed, and headed to the wardrobe. With a nudge from me, the large wood doors swung open. I rifled through one of the drawers for underwear and a bra. After yanking them on, I plucked one of the many neatly folded sets hanging on a velvet hanger.

The ribbed pants flared at my ankles, and I held up the matching top. My gaze kept drifting to his shirt intermingled with my stuff. I wanted to smell like them. A silent way to claim them. I rolled my lips inside my mouth and between my teeth. I wanted Imogen to smell them on me. I plucked one of Asher's shirts and pulled it on. The oversized cream-colored, cotton fabric enveloped me.

I ran my fingers through my messy hair, but they stuck in the tangles. That was what I got for sleeping with my hair wet. I patted down the frizz as I headed to the bathroom.

I passed the hairbrush through my tangles, staring at my reflection as my hair increasingly became frizzier. I pumped some serum into my palm and worked it through the long strands, taming the mess. With a shake of my head, the tips of my hair fluttered around my waist. Wavy was the best way to describe it. Neither curly, nor straight, almost like it wasn't sure what to be.

I hadn't felt a need to pretty myself up before. I sighed and leaned on the sink with my head bent forward.

Imogen was really messing with my mind. She'd only been here a short time and I was getting ready like it was armor, but I couldn't help but feel threatened. They'd been together for years.

I groaned.

Everything would be fine. Asher said so. And the way he and Ren touched me last night, the whispered words—I believed them. Time, just a bit more time and they would be all mine. I straightened with a huff and turned on my heel. I shoved my feet into my slippers near the door and closed it behind me with care. Sunlight spilled into the hallway where it opened to the staircase. I descended, sweeping my gaze over the foyer. There was no sign of blood anywhere. Like that night had never happened. If only it *was* a nightmare.

As I entered the hallway leading to the kitchen, the clatter of plates reached me. Once I rounded inside, Maddy stopped what she was doing and hurried to grab my hands. I blinked up at her worried face.

"I heard about her showing up."

My lip twisted.

"From who?"

"Tobias, when he called me to deliver blood," she whispered. "He seems all high strung about it."

"Oh." That was all I could come up with. She studied me, but I worked to make my face blank.

"You're not okay."

I tugged my hands until she let go. Going around her, I sank onto the island stool.

"That's an understatement." I sighed, clasping my hands on the smooth surface. Maddy leaned forward with the island digging into her stomach.

"Do you think they'll act different around you?" Maddy murmured. My stomach clenched into a tight ball. They'd been different already, but all I offered her was a shrug. What else could I say? They were tiptoeing around her feelings, and completely disregarding mine? That I was a shit person because she'd obviously been held captive and hurt yet I still wanted to pitch a fit?

I groaned and dropped my head back, staring at the bright lights embedded into the ceiling.

"Enough about this ridiculous situation. How's Sydney?"

"Oh, she's great! A little upset that I didn't bring her today, but I want her nowhere near Imogen. My parents are too old, so her aunt from her dad's side agreed to keep an eye on her for me when I can't be around."

"That's good." She should keep her away from vampires.

"No choice," she sighed. "Anyway, are you hungry?" She turned, grabbed something behind her, then slid it across the granite counter. I caught the edge of the plate with my pointer finger.

Chilaquiles. My mouth immediately watered. Tortillas cut in squares coated in a tomato-based sauce and beans on the side.

"I asked . . ." A strange expression crossed her features. "Um, I feel like I asked someone about your favorite foods after you didn't give me a clear answer, but I can't remember." Her lips squeezed together. "Maybe I didn't ask someone."

She continued hemming and hawing while I stared at the food, trying not to let my emotions brim over the edge. The only person that could know I loved this breakfast food was Peter. If she didn't remember him, one of my guys must have compelled her to forget about him. They were always three steps ahead.

I cleared my throat and blinked away the sheen. My parents died when I was too young and to my shame, I didn't remember much of our time together. Other than this—my favorite meal mom would make. After they passed, my aunt had taken us in. She'd been a good enough guardian, if a bit distant, because she had her own kids. Overall, she provided the basics, which was a roof over our heads and frozen meals.

"I followed the instructions on my notes app, down to every little detail, so hopefully it tastes good." She reached to hand me a fork.

I wordlessly took it and stabbed it into the *chilaquiles*, then dipped it in some beans. It smelled just as I remember. I hadn't cooked this in so long, but Peter still remembered I loved it. I really didn't give him enough credit. The savory taste spread on my tongue, literally bringing tears to my eyes. Just as I remembered.

The little bits of tortilla crunched with my chewing. I preferred them a little less stiff, but for a first time, Maddy did amazing.

She watched me with her eyebrows raised, waiting.

I put my thumb up and scarfed some more down. So freaking good. It didn't take me long to clear the plate. I scooted it away from me and leaned back.

"I'm stuffed."

"I don't think I've ever seen you eat something so fast."

I smiled sheepishly.

She looked over my shoulder. "They'll be rising soon."

I followed her attention to the thin window lining the top of the wall.

The sunlight was extinguished and only the faintest purple hue of the dusk hinted.

Clipped footsteps echoed down the hall, lighter and unfamiliar. There could only be one pair of footsteps that I wasn't familiar with.

My stomach turned and soured. She was barefoot and in Jax's shirt. I was going to vomit. Her willowy figure seemed even slighter because of his clothes. Her long, pin straight hair hung around her shoulders.

As she approached, it almost seemed like a glide. She stopped right beside my stool.

"Off, human," she flicked her hand, shooing me away like a fly. My spine straightened. Blood and dirt no longer stained her face. Had Jax bathed her? A sharp hurt stabbed my chest. I breathed in and out slowly. "Hello?" She snapped her fingers in my face. "Where did they find you—wait, I do not care." Her hand wrapped around my throat.

"Stop," Maddy cried, while I struggled to drag in a breath. Imogen's fingers dug into my throat. Her sharp nails digging in hard.

"Freeze." Imogen snapped her fingers at Maddy. "I'll feed on you, once I drain this one, do not worry."

With a sudden rush of motion, Imogen's head was yanked back. I followed the grip to Ren's wide shoulders looming over both of us.

"Ren," Imogen hissed. "Release me."

"Not until you release my human."

"Your human?" She mocked, her eyes wide.

"We keep her. No discussion." Ren yanked her head back even more. Imogen bared her teeth and shoved me back so hard I went flying. Someone caught me and upon impact, air puffed from my lungs. I peeked over my shoulder.

"Asher?" I whispered.

He squeezed my hip.

"Oh!" Imogen exclaimed, dragging my attention back to her. Her eyes narrowed in on me. "You are the one that fed me." She licked her lips. "You tasted delicious." Her eyes flashed red, but Ren dragged her back by her hair and shoved her away from where I stood. Imogen caught herself, her eyebrows high on her forehead.

"You're not touching her," Ren announced, leaning a hip against the island. He seemed at ease, but fire played along his fingertips.

Imogen huffed, staring at the flames with a sneer curling her lips. Tobias's clipped steps entered. He was dressed in loafers, slacks, and a cable knit sweater. By the look of his damp hair, he'd showered.

His gray eyes assessed the room.

"What have you done, Imogen?"

His voice held no inflection, as if he was used to asking the question. Imogen smirked and crossed her arms.

"I was only trying to feed on the human."

Tobias's frown deepened.

"Do not touch her, Imogen. She is off limits."

"You too?" She whirled. "My saintly brother wants a woman?" Her head fell back and laughter exploded from her mouth. "A lot has changed while I was captive." She wiped invisible tears from the corner of her eyes.

"I put the best courtesans in front of you, and nothing, but *this* human made you falter?"

The way she stared at me made me want to huddle into myself and die, but I stared at her in silence, gripping Asher's arm.

"Well, if you lot are so possessive of your blood-whore, I'll give you time to get used to the changes that will happen. You." She waved over Maddy. "Come here to feed me."

"No," I retorted, struggling to keep my voice even. "Maddy is not a meal."

Asher's grip on my hip flexed. Imogen stilled and slowly turned to face me. Stunned and shocked that I would dare to speak.

"Excuse you?" She stilled preternaturally. It made the hair on my body rise. She was creepy.

Asher tsked and gripped the back of my neck. His fingers pressed into the column, like a warning.

"We've allowed her free reign, Imogen. We enjoy the little human's outbursts." His thumb rubbed the side of my neck. I lowered my eyes to the floor. How humiliating. When he said I would need to give them time, I didn't know it meant that I would be reverted to a simple blood-whore.

Tobias cleared his throat.

"Imogen. I've contacted Alistair. He's opening the department stores for you tonight." Tobias focused his gray eyes on Maddy. "Madison, take her to Crimson Nights once she finishes with her purchases. Imogen, this human can escort you to feed to your hearts content."

"Yes, Mr. Crimson." Maddy tugged the apron tie from behind her back and pulled the fabric off. She hung it on the hook next to the stove.

I opened my mouth to say something, to say no, but Maddy shook her head slightly.

"And do not kill this human. She is our housekeeper." I relaxed at Tobias's order. At least Maddy wouldn't die while with the crazy bitch.

"Fine," she huffed, crossing her arms. "You will have to brief me, once I return. Especially about that parasite, Bastien—"

"It didn't take you long to get back to your charming self," Ren drawled. He seemed almost derisive, but she didn't react like it was abnormal.

"Have you done away with him?" she continued like Ren hadn't spoken.

My lips thinned and I couldn't control my eyebrow's furrowing. "Oh, the human is glaring at me." Imogen's eyebrows raised and the corner of her mouth tipped up. "Go ahead, speak up, human. I can tell something is just bursting to come out."

"Keep Bastien's name out of your mouth," I said the words quietly, without too much force behind them. Asher exhaled, oh so quietly, near my ear. He said something in his language, and it didn't sound good.

"You new-age blood-whores are another breed."

Everything happened in the blink of an eye. Imogen lunged at me. An arm banded around my stomach and pulled me back. I flinched, peeking through my slitted eyes. Ren, again, had a hold of her hair which stopped her midway toward me, while Tobias held her arm. Everything went scarily still.

"Fine." She huffed. "That disgusting emaciated blood-mad vampire doesn't deserve my time."

Bastien? He was the furthest thing from emaciated. She yanked herself free of the two vampires and shook her hair out.

"You." She snapped her fingers at Maddy. "Let's go." She strutted out, her hips swaying provocatively.

That was hot. Maddy mouthed as she left, her gaze flipping from me to my vampires.

I had to agree.

Their footsteps retreated; the hollow thump of the door slamming echoed down the hall.

"She's left," Tobias announced, his tone sounded unsure, weak.

"You," Ren snarled, lunging toward me, his strides wide and angry. "We let you get away with things, but remember, you are human—weak." His lips raised in a snarl again.

I flinched, clamping my lips into a thin line. My eyes filled with tears. It dragged me back to when we first met. When he'd been so cruel.

I deflated, feeling helpless. Talking back wasn't me, being bitter wasn't me— jealousy caused all of it. A tear trekked down my cheeks. Tobias was suddenly in my space, clasping my hands in both of his. I stared up into his smokey gray eyes. "Imogen's presence must be hard for you."

Understatement of the century. "Asher explained everything he said to you. Do you understand we are yours?"

I pursed my lips and hesitantly nodded. He must be talking about Asher's spiel about needing time.

"I am working on finding a safe location for her to go, but she doesn't want to be alone." He grimaced. "I would go with her, but I do not want to leave you. My selfishness is causing you pain." He closed his eyes and sighed. "Imogen is part of a past life. Having her around, puts all of us on edge." I peeked at Ren's angry downturn of his lips from the corner of my eyes. "Ren and Asher are remaining patient because of me.

Nothing will change your position in this Coven or with us—"

"Why wasn't I part of this conversation?"

Tobias didn't turn to the voice behind him, but I leaned around him to glare at Jax. He stood near the kitchen exit, mouth pressed into a thin line. No one responded to him. Jax glared at Asher.

"Everyone knows your choice," I said in the most even tone I could muster. He scowled and a line appeared between his eyebrows.

"My choice?" He sneered. His fangs had descended at some point, and they flashed. "I wasn't given one."

"Your choice is clear with the shirt she was wearing." Petty of me, but I didn't care. "Where did you sleep last night?" Even saying the words caused my stomach to twist like my intestines had been grabbed and yanked.

His eyes thinned. He suddenly appeared feet away from me, too fast for me to track, and shouldered Tobias to the side. I gasped, stumbling back and hitting Asher's chest. Ren had a hold of Jax's shoulder.

"I won't hurt her," Jax spat, yanking free of Ren. "You fuckers don't think much of me, do you?" He stepped in front of me and reached over my shoulder to shove Asher. "I expected more from you."

"Jaxon, you haven't left her side."

I stiffened.

Jax hissed and grabbed Asher's shirt and yanked him, leaving me squished between them.

This was not the type of twin sandwich I enjoyed. The cotton of Jax's shirt pressed against my cheek. His sweet scent enveloped me. For a split second, I teetered forward, toward him. No, I had to snap out of it, Jax did not deserve my care anymore. He'd crossed the line. He had what he wanted now, anyway. Why was he kicking up a fuss?

"Get off him," I snapped at Jax, shoving him. He didn't budge, so I wiggled out from between them to face all of them. I pointed at Jax. "I'm done with you."

I didn't like what this jealousy was turning me into. My lower lip warbled and Jax stepped forward, but I put a palm up.

Asher's eyebrows furrowed and he collected me to his chest. I breathed him in. He was my Asher, the one that always looked out for me, in his oddly psychotic way. I didn't want to lose them to Imogen or to age.

I was ready to be with them. For good. I couldn't let her take all of this from me, especially if they were serious about choosing me.

Taking a deep breath, I lifted my eyes to Tobias, resting my temple against Asher's chest. His shirt was open at the front, so my face rested against his skin warmed by my blood.

"Turn me into a vampire."

Desperation burst the words free. I'd been playing with the idea for a while, but I hadn't had the guts to ask them. Was it a fear of rejection? Highly likely, but now that the words were free, it was easier to breathe.

This was the only way we would have nothing between us, and Imogen wouldn't be able to kill me so easily.

My announcement caused every single vampire to still. Tobias exchanged a look with Ren. That cautious look wasn't the reaction I expected. I pulled away from Asher, taking a step back.

I rubbed my sweating palms against my thighs.

"I mean . . . if you guys were serious, and Imogen showing

up doesn't change anything. I want forever with you." I breathed in shakily. "I don't want to lose you."

Too much happened to me, and I wanted to fight for what I had with them. I never belonged before—more importantly, I'd never felt safe. I would hold onto it with both hands.

"Catalina," Tobias started. He went quiet. My gaze bounced from one vampire to the other. They all looked like a stiff wind could topple them over.

"What is it? Spit it out." My stomach hurt. I hugged myself like I could keep the pain at a manageable level.

"You can't be turned," Ren announced, obliterating my bloom of hope.

Tobias's jaw flexed.

"It's impossible. Female turn rate is in the low twentieth percentile," Tobias said, taking a step toward me.

Asher wrapped himself around me. He tipped my chin up to look into his eyes.

"And if you did survive, you would be blood-mad," he whispered.

Like Bastien.

What. My lips were so numb I could only mouth the word.

I . . . couldn't be turned into a vampire?

"Oh."

"*Älskade*." The corner of Asher's lips turned downward. I could hear the pity in his tone. My face heated, and I extricated myself from his arms.

"I need some time," I croaked, shaking my head as he moved toward me again. I peeled my eyes wide to keep the tears from spilling. I needed to get away—now. The closest exit was down to my room.

I sped to the metal door and slammed it shut behind me.

IMOGEN NEEDED TO LEAVE. I pressed my fingers against my temples, moving them in little circles. Tobias's gaze was unfocused, so I angled my glare on Ren.

"You were too harsh, Ren."

Ren's jaw bunched.

"With a careless moment, Imogen will snap her neck. I'd rather be harsh, when coddling could mean her life."

"I'll make sure she doesn't approach Cat." I raised an eyebrow at Jax. "Imogen must have caught on, because she made sure to get up while I was still weighed down by the sun."

I scoffed.

"Sure, that's why you're stuck to her like glue."

"What is that supposed to mean?" Jaxon was suddenly in my face. I smirked and poked his shoulder.

"It means you don't look like you're having a hard time keeping *an eye* on Imogen." I sneered. I had hoped my Pet could sway him to her side, but as always, he fell for that toxic bitch. "Have you already fucked her?"

He jerked back as if I'd slapped him. "Because if you did,

keep away from Catalina." My jealous Catalina would fall apart. It would be difficult for her to detach from him, I'd seen the way she looked at Jax. I'd encouraged her softness toward him, but it'd been in vain.

"I have nothing to explain to you," Jaxon snapped.

"Wrong, we have every right to know if you hurt her."

"Your *Älskade*," he spat. "Because you care for her, it does not mean you get to have the single claim on her. That's your problem, Asher, fixation. You'll lose interest. Sure, you've held on this far, but." Jax shook his head. "Knowing you—"

"Now you're defining me by my past?" I scoffed. "You think because I was a whore I do not understand devotion?" I leaned close to him. "That makes me more of an authority on it, I know the difference between meaningless fucking to what I feel for Catalina. Unlike you, you think you're so enamored by Imogen, she treated you like scum at her feet. Only using you to do her bidding—"

Jaxon stiffened and in a flash his palm lashed across my jaw. The sting left as fast as it came.

"Did you just slap me?" I clasped my face with my fingertips, almost expecting blood. Jax seemed as shocked as I did, so to get rid of that stupid look on his face, I swung my open palm toward him. His head jerked to the side.

Ren shoved both of our chests, forcing us a step back.

"Enough," Tobias shouted. The shock of it dragged our attention to the oldest of us present and the one that was supposed to be levelheaded. He seemed conflicted, so I said as much.

"How can I not be conflicted, Asher? Imogen, with all her flaws, is still my sister." Tobias's fangs flashed and he scrubbed his palm over the top of his head. "She is about to lose a lot."

Tobias faced my twin. "Jaxon, what will you choose? Are you going to remain by Imogen's side?"

Jaxon's eyes narrowed and his lips thinned.

"If I am reading your mind right, Jaxon. You've made your decision."

My twin's eyes closed and his expression rippled.

"What decision?" I asked when Tobias didn't elaborate. "What is your decision?" I was ignored. I gritted my teeth.

"I read Imogen's mind. Wrenhaven was not gentle with her. The things he did . . ." Tobias's mouth twisted. "We need just a little time. I will explain myself to Catalina. I will take on the repercussions of this decision."

A ring came from his pocket. Tobias fished his phone out. He had learned how to handle the device quickly. Usually, I'd be the one to handle vampire relations, but I'd been distracted since Catalina came into my life.

"What's your plan, Tobias?" Ren grunted out, arms crossed.

"I am gathering information on Wrenhaven. I will not allow his mistreatment to go unpunished."

"We need to move it along. There is only so long I want Imogen around Cat."

"I do not like her in pain either, Ren," Tobias said and strode into the hall as he put the phone to his ear.

"I need to speak to her," Jaxon announced and took a step toward the door.

"Why?" I blocked his path.

"I won't explain myself to you," he sneered at me. "*Du gör mig verkligen förbannad.*" I narrowed my eyes. He never explained himself to me, but I fucking knew how his mind worked. All he'd ever wanted was that bitch back.

He shoulder checked me as he walked past me.

"Unbelievable," I muttered. "She doesn't want to see you, *bror*."

"Too fucking bad."

Was that how it was?

I gritted my molars. Not if I had anything to say about it.

"Where are you going?" Ren shouted.

As I followed Jax, I yanked my shirt over my head and shoved off the slacks, tossing them at Ren.

"To make sure he doesn't cross a line." I became invisible and headed right for him. I yanked his shoulder before he touched the door. He whirled on me and his fist flew toward me, but I ducked in time and became invisible.

Jax sneered as his eyes scanned.

"Cheap of you, brother."

"*Fy åt helvete, bror.*"

catalina

THAT WAS why they kept saying I would live a long time at their side but never mentioned turning me. I'd sat midway down the steps and the hard surface was uncomfortable and making my butt go numb.

I thought they were being considerate about my past with vampires, not that it was literally impossible for me.

I couldn't have forever with them, just extra decades, if I drank their blood.

My lip trembled, but I forced myself to my feet to descend the rest of the way. I left my slippers at the entrance of the basement living room. My door was ajar. Doubts festered liked a fresh wound with Imogen here. I nudged the door the rest of the way open.

Bastien's flowing white hair moved like a wave. He stood and took a step toward me. The chain rattled. They'd installed chains to the wall above my bed. They were the same color and blended in well.

His head tilted and his eyebrows furrowed. Seeing the concern on his face punched through the wall I'd erected around me, and I ran to him. He swept me to his chest and his palm rubbed against my back.

Another gut-wrenching sob escaped.

"Shh, Little One," he croaked.

"It hurts." I sniffled. Then I froze.

Bastien spoke?

I had to be hallucinating.

"You can talk?" I gasped, pulling back enough to look up at him.

His expression rippled and there was none of that awareness that he'd been staring at me with. I untangled myself from his grip, and he kept hold of my wrist. I pressed my palms into his hard stomach.

"Sit down, you're making me nervous looming like that." His huge body followed my guidance.

He only stared at me, his gaze focusing for a spilt second.

I speared my fingers through my hair. He watched me through pensive, expressive eyes. Each day he seemed more aware, and I was noticing he got the clue about things faster than normal. He was reacting less immediately than usual . . . but only when he was alone with me. "You can understand me, right?"

Bastien stared steadily, and I held my breath. Finally, he nodded.

"I knew it," I breathed.

Bastien cocked his head and then tipped it forward toward me.

With the speed of snapping my fingers, the awareness fled his gaze.

Bastien gripped my hip and dragged me close, until I stood between his widespread legs. His palms slid up my sides, stopping at my hips with a squeeze. He set his cheek on my breasts, nuzzling me.

His fingers delved under Asher's shirt I wore, and his cool hand slid up my side.

Their temperature tended to change, if they didn't feed after a while.

"Don't rip it," I breathed and pressed my palm over the back of his large hand. Mine was laughably tiny over his. I pushed it down until it spanned across my belly so I could yank the shirt over my head. It landed on the edge of the bed. My bra landed on top of it. Bastien hummed, his thumb rubbing against my belly button. He made me breathless. I hooked my fingers into the hem of my undies and pants and shoved them down my ass. They pooled at my ankles.

Bastien ran his nose over the swell of my breast, and he hummed against my skin. His shoulders moved with his inhale. His red eyes flicked up to mine.

He sank his teeth into my nipple, and my knees gave out, with a smooth motion, he pulled me onto his lap with my legs spread around his thighs. He pulled me close, until I was flush against him. Chains rattled with the movement of his arms.

I slid my palms between the split robe and smoothed my hands over the steel-like skin as I pushed the robe back to expose his shoulders. My fingers played across the thick muscles that twitched at my attention. His cock flexed under my ass, and I pushed up a bit to pull the tie from his midsection. The end flicked against my wrist with how hard I yanked it free. I settled on top of him, feeling his hard shaft nestle against my core.

His head tipped back with a groan. Slickness throbbed from my sex, making me glide against him.

I groaned, moving my hips to grind down on him. I sank

my fingers into his hair and arched my spine. He held me up as he leaned me back, so his mouth covered the tip of my breast. He sank his fangs into the soft flesh. He sucked, causing lust to flare to a painful level. A shiver coursed down my body, and my pussy throbbed from the need to be filled.

"Bastien," I moaned. His hands flexed against my back, clasping me so tight.

He held me with such possession—almost verging on desperation. In a sudden movement, he pulled his fangs from my flesh. Droplets trickled from the wound, painting my skin. Bastien's bright red eyes scanned my face. He stood with me in his arms. I squealed, scrambling to hold onto his shoulders. He tossed me on my back, high on the bed.

I popped onto my elbows. Bastien was already prowling up the mattress, his gaze focused on me, and very aware. A smile curved his lips, edged with madness.

"Bastien?" I whispered.

"Yes, Little One?" Again, his voice sounded rough.

I licked my lips.

"How can this happen? They said being blood-mad made you irreversibly ill."

He stiffened and shook his head side to side. I pressed my fingertip to his shoulder.

"Bastien?"

He hissed, eyes on me. He grabbed my waist and flipped me to my stomach. I grunted upon landing. I didn't have a chance to get my hands under me, because he grabbed my hip and yanked me up, presenting me to him.

The bed jostled with all our movement.

"Bastien!" His thickness slammed into me. I gasped. His hips pumped, and he slid his cock in and out of me with a smooth glide. I was so wet. His thighs hit the back of mine with a loud smack. I curled my fingers into the bed sheets. He rammed into me again and again, rutting me hard.

Bastien took hold of my hips and lifted them even more. It changed the angle, and the tip of his cock nudged something inside me that immediately made my legs shake. I cried out as he continued to batter against me with hard slaps. It took all my strength to hold myself on my elbows and not fall onto the mattress like a noodle.

The orgasm rammed into me, and I screamed into the bedsheets, bucking. My channel squeezed around him with repeated throbs, but he didn't stop. My legs shook so hard that I couldn't control them.

His fingers dug into my hips and the smooth glide of his cock came with the suctioning sound of moisture. I sank my teeth into my lower lips, going limp in his arms. Bastien placed a palm under my belly and my torso lowered while he hiked me higher. The angle prodded his tip deep inside me and catapulted me into another spine-tingling orgasm.

Nonsensical sounds spilled from my lips, and I couldn't control them. I yanked at the bedsheets like a crazy person. My channel's sensitivity made me a twitching mess. Yet, the smooth glide of Bastien taking me didn't abate, his pace remained hard and commanding. My arms gave out completely and my cheek pressed into the mattress.

My belly clenched. The growing swell working through my nerve-endings sucked the oxygen from my body.

"You're going to break her," a voice snarled. I peeled my eyes open to see Jax standing at the side of the bed. He swayed forward.

Bastien's grip tightened on my hips, and he bared his fangs at Jax.

I kept my gaze on Jax. He stared at me with hints of anger lightening through his intense, blue lapis eyes that flashed red for a brief moment. His knees perched on the bed and his hand lifted, but just as suddenly he dropped his head, clenching his eyelids closed. Regaining his composure, he backed up a few steps. The edges of my vision faded, and the orgasm washed across my body. My toes curled, and I became weightless and although I could hear the muffled sound of my cries, I couldn't have controlled them.

Bastien's cock seized violently inside me, filling me up so much, his cum dripped out.

When I came back to earth, I lay flat on the bed with Bastien beside me. We lay diagonally and he had his palm on the small of my back.

My heart raced so much that I could hear it in my ears, drumming away ominously. I stretched my arms up, a small tremble coursing through my limbs.

"Come here," Jax ordered, expression stiff.

I glared up at him. Why was he still here?

"No thanks," I said and stifled a yawn.

"Catalina," he said, not sounding happy. I rolled to the end of the bed to get away from him, but Bastien reached for my ankle right before I rolled off and yanked. I bounced on the mattress with a huff and my hair spilled over the edge of the mattress. Bastien dragged my legs wide open, and he fell on me, his tongue lapping at my sensitive, wrung out sex.

I met Jax's eyes over his head. Bastien's fingers on my thighs flexed. Tension seemed to radiate off him.

"Go away."

Bastien's shoulders flexed, the thick muscles bulging. His mouth settled over my entrance. His tongue flicked up my slit, lapping up our combined juices. I squealed, writhing under his tongue. A shudder worked down my spine.

Hands wrapped around my wrists, and I was yanked away from Bastien, my body sliding off the bed in a move so fast it made me nauseous. Jax cradled me to his body, huddling me close.

"No," I shouted as Jax carried me away. Chains rattled, mingling with violent snarls. Jax slammed my bedroom door shut, effectively cutting Bastien off.

I shoved at Jax's chest, writhing to get away from his oversized body. He wrestled me over to the white couch and dumped me onto the cushion.

I landed with a huff.

"What the hell!"

"Why are you fighting me?" he snarled.

"Because I have nothing to say to you." My tone held no inflection, just pure disinterest.

He stiffened.

My body felt warmed up and limber. I felt good. Forget Imogen and her negativity. My vampires were mine, even if I wouldn't have Jax . . .

My hand found its way over the sharp stab in my chest. I lifted my chin. I'd get over it.

"Well, I have things to tell you," he said through gritted teeth. He usually looked pissed as a default, but right now? I could make a good case saying he needed some anger management classes. Were there any of those for vampires?

"You're going to hear me out." His words were laced with a

threat. Bastien's snarl echoed from my bedroom. "But I need to show you something."

Suddenly, his back was to me, wide shoulder's hardly moving as he strode toward the exit.

"Why?"

No response. I sighed and scanned the room. A silk robe rested across the end of the couch. I tugged it on, as I hurried up the stairs.

"Jax," I called, reaching the kitchen. He stood diagonal from me at the furthest point, holding open a door I'd never noticed. I approached, frowning. As I neared him, I recognized why I'd never spotted it before, because the wall dipped into a small nook and hidden to the side was the door. I peeked into the dark hallway.

"What's down there?"

"The vehicles."

I mouthed my 'ohhh' my attention still on the dark, spooky looking hall. They mentioned the garage was behind the house, this must lead to it.

"Listen, Kitten."

I put my hand up and amazingly he shut up.

"You always talked about her like she was some—" I stopped myself and took a deep breath. There was no point in spitting all my frustrations at him. "You have your Imogen back." I forced through my tight windpipe. "What do you want?"

Jax raked his hand through his hair, mussing and making it stick straight up.

"What do I want?" His nose scrunched. He shook his head and sliced a hand through the air. "I want to explain *why I've been by her side.*"

I was being a petty bitch. I exhaled slowly and took a step away from him and the door. His eyes softened. He looked so worried it made my chest hurt.

"Jaxon," Imogen shouted but her voice sounded far away. "Where have you gone?"

I narrowed my eyes at his stiff face.

"Yeah, go *Kitten*," I flipped my hair over my shoulder.

A hand wrapped around the back of my neck. "Let me go, Jax."

"This is not over."

FIVE

I SIGHED and tipped my head back. Difficult female. I thought vampires were stubborn—this human girl gave any female vampire a run for their money. This wouldn't be easy, and I hadn't made it easier with my big fucking mouth. Asher called it 'lacking impulse control'.

The rest of them believed I deserved her ire, because I'd *chosen*. I clenched my teeth—I hadn't been given an option. They'd written me off so easily. Just like my human. I'd hurt her …

No, I shouldn't be blamed for my initial reaction to Catalina. My yearning for her fostered anger. How could I crave her? That question was all that swirled my thoughts. She'd been an unknown human, stepping where she shouldn't, causing things to shift. I hadn't understood the difference between her and Imogen. Or how it felt to be cared for. Of not being on edge, of no pain.

I hadn't known.

Catalina could not punish me for my ignorance. The thought was tinged with desperation, but I kept my desires sealed. I would not let her see my devotion to her—as much as I wanted her, she could not know the power she held over me.

Kitten wasn't malicious. She was soft. She was the opposite of Imogen. She was what I wanted. I hadn't known having Catalina could be so addicting.

If Imogen knew, she'd rip her to shreds, especially after the rejection from Ren and Asher.

Upon discovering Tobias also valued the human, she'd been close to ripping Kitten's throat out, so I'd gripped her shoulder to stay her, but if I would have known Catalina would look at me with such cold eyes, I wouldn't have.

"Earth to Jaxon Crimson." Catalina waved her hands in front of my face.

"What I needed to tell you." I cleared my throat and lowered my voice, so the approaching Imogen couldn't hear. "I will stay after Imogen leaves."

Catalina raised her eyebrow.

"You don't want to leave the guys."

I frowned, shaking my head, but before I could tell her it was for her, she continued, "I mean, I get it, you guys have been together for a long time. You didn't expect all this drama."

I scowled, confused.

"Jaxon." Imogen's footsteps echoed down the hall leading into the kitchen. Catalina's lips thinned.

"I don't get why you're telling me. We're done. Plus, I don't need you. I have a better version of you anyway."

I internally recoiled, while my body remained stiff as stone. She shrugged. "As for the others, you have to talk to them about how you guys will handle the separation. Leave me out of it."

Her words rocked through me with acute pain. A shroud

crept over my thoughts. Her mouth was moving rapidly, but I struggled to focus on her words.

If Imogen knew my doubts. Of the insane, illogical, weak urge to collect the human to me, she would kill her.

Yet, I was being punished for wanting to keep Catalina safe.

"Can you explain it to me?"

"What?" I said, harsh. Her lips thinned but she didn't flinch or recoil . . . almost like she was used to my outbursts.

I didn't like that.

"What did Imogen mean about Bastien looking different before?"

The switch in topic restarted my sluggish brain. Imogen was talking about the time Bastien escaped and was gone close to a month. Ren was the one who found him.

"He looked nothing like he does now. Bastien was emaciated, not even a shadow of himself. He was unrecognizable. Drained and skeletal."

Her eyes widened and fear flitted through them. She took a step back.

"How long ago did he disappear?"

"About four years ago. That's an estimate. When Ren brought him back, Bastien was as he looks now. We've tried to figure out how—" I shut up. Her chest stopped moving and her heart stuttered. I collected her hands in mine.

"Breathe, Cat," I said with more force than I intended, but humans needed oxygen to breathe, she could hurt herself like this.

She coughed, dragging in breaths with each rattle. "What is wrong?"

"N-nothing," she said, but her eyes were wide and spooked.

I frowned, scanning her features. I couldn't figure out what feelings she grappled with.

"I promis—"

"Jaxon," Imogen called out again. It was close enough for Cat to become stiff.

I clicked my teeth together and released her hands.

I couldn't collect her into my arms as I craved.

The look on her face crushed me. Like I'd betrayed her.

I avoided looking in her eyes. Every second I stood here, while she stared at me accusingly, chipped at my resolve.

But I couldn't pull her into my arms without endangering her. Imogen would not kill this human. Even if it meant I could not have her.

"You should go," she said, hollow, fixing her eyes on the floor. I gritted my teeth and turned, walking down across the kitchen and through the hall with clipped steps. Imogen stood in the middle of the foyer with bags surrounding her.

"There you are." She grinned at me. "We really need to get more servants. Can you work on that for me?"

I inclined my head, but she was already striding to the stairs. "Be a dear and bring my things." She snapped her fingers toward the bags sitting where she'd been standing.

I stiffened, but she was already halfway up the stairs. The compulsion of her direct order forced me to collect her bags and trail after her.

She'd begun to set up the third floor for herself and once that was completed, she would have me fuck her. All that had held it off was that Imogen needed her area perfectly to her style. Her compulsion to 'redecorate' had saved me insofar, but it would not hold off. I had to speak to Tobias.

Asher's words from earlier echoed. A meaningless fuck. I could tell the difference now.

Something needed to be done quickly. Kitten was a jealous sort and based off everything I'd learned about her, if I fucked Imogen, she would never willingly touch me again.

I stepped into the disarray of the prior second living room.

"Jaxon," she clapped, "I purchased us each a coffin to sleep in. They should be delivered in a few weeks."

And she would not be here.

"Jaxon." Her warm hand touched my cheek. She'd fed recently. "My loyal Jaxon. You've remained faithful." She slipped her hands around my back, petting my spine. I gritted my molars.

"Yes," I forced out.

"You seem so cold now, my child." Was she doubting me? Fuck, she couldn't. Catalina wouldn't be safe.

I hissed a breath out.

"You left me." Appealing to her pride would be the only way to get her thoughts away from my behavior.

She squeezed her arms around my waist once more.

"Not by choice." She sighed and stepped away. "I can't wait to go through all my new things." She flounced over to her shit. I scrubbed my face with my palm and looked over my shoulder at the exit—fuck, I wanted out.

All these new emotions would be the end of me.

catalina

I BURIED my head under the pillow. I hadn't slept a wink. Even when the shutters dropped and then opened a few hours ago, I still didn't move.

Hopefully, Asher and Ren got the clue to leave me alone after I'd ignored them when they came to check on me.

Cobwebs seemed to cast a net over my thoughts. Disbelief, fear, and confusion all battled to be at the helm of the volatile emotions suffocating me. Jax answered my question and rocked my world in the process. The date lines up and the description. There was no other explanation.

Bastien was the Pale One.

That's why he'd never come for me after I'd freed myself. He'd been chained to a wall. He couldn't have come for me.

Everything I believed I knew was a lie.

The door creaked and I stilled, closing my eyes. For show, I let out a small snore.

"I can tell you're not sleeping." Asher sighed. His footsteps echoed closer. "Pet, you have to get out of bed." I ignored Asher. He'd go away like he had before. I just had to hold off.

"I know Jaxon's hurt you—"

A hysteric laugh burst free, and I sat up, dashing the tears away.

"Yes, he did," I choked out. And Bastien. The realization of who he was came out of left field. My blood-mad teddy bear vampire was the creature that dragged me into a hillside cave and fed on me for weeks. The one that had pinned me under him with the rise of daylight. The reason I'd resorted to eating bugs.

The crawling little legs . . . nausea lurched through my stomach. The overwhelming sensation of suffocation.

Asher's lips pursed, eyebrows furrowing. His blue eyes scanned my face.

"You need air, socialization, food—" Asher's eyes widened, and he perked up. "I know just the thing that will make you feel better."

"No thanks to the orgasms, Asher," I said sarcastically.

I couldn't believe those words exited my mouth, but my mental state wasn't in the right place for freaky time.

"Nonsense, orgasms make everything better." Asher batted away my words. "But that's not what I have in mind right now. You're coming with me." He was suddenly at my bedside, he grabbed my arm and hoisted me up.

"Asher," I whined, yanking to be let go. No use though. I stumbled after him as he toted me to the door. Good thing I'd taken the time to go through my self-care routine this morning —night, ugh, it was so confusing to refer to the start of my day being dusk. I'd been trying to pull myself out of my funk, but showering, straightening my hair, and all the other self-care routines I had, hadn't worked.

I trudged down the steps, staring at Asher's silky hair as he guided me through the foyer. He'd tied his hair up in a short half-ponytail while the rest hung around his shoulders. He peeked back at me with a fang-y grin. It would never cease to amaze me how different the twins were.

He led me into the kitchen and across it toward the door where Jax and I had our argument. This time, I stepped into the hall. The sconces were on, illuminating the well-lit hall. There were no windows, and it stretched to a dead end. Except it wasn't a dead end, it took a sharp turn to the left. The floor started to decline, the hall remaining the same the entire way.

I huffed on a breath. The garage was far, and from the feel and musty scent of it, underground. Double French doors came into view. Shrouded panes didn't allow me a peek inside. Asher pulled the doors open with a dramatic flourish.

"Ta-da."

I side-eyed him and finally turned toward the garage. But it was much larger than I imagined. Like so much larger. It looked like an underground mall garage, except there were so many luxury cars. I gawked at the row along the furthest wall. *One*. I kept counting. *Ten*. And that was only the first row.

There was maybe a twenty-yard distance between the French doors and the first row. I took another step forward. The mass amount of money in here was mind-blowing and I couldn't wrap my head around it.

A car revved out of the third line-up and rounded the pathway between the other rows. The flashy bright-red car roared toward us. I gasped, stumbling back, but it squealed to a stop a foot away from me.

I squinted against the fluorescent light reflecting off the shiny windshield. The engine hummed and then hissed from being shut off.

The door popped open, and Ren's large body emerged.

"What is going on, Asher," I asked, completely confused.

Ren tossed the key up and down, his focus not leaving me.

"You will be taking a bat to the car Jaxon purchased for you," Asher said.

"What?" I said sharply. "Jax bought me an Audi?" I scoffed. That was why he was bringing me down here before Imogen arrived? I stopped myself right there. He'd gotten it for me before she came, so it was meaningless. I wanted nothing from him. I scowled. "He has no right to buy me anyth—"

"Whoa, whoa, don't bite my cock off," Asher chortled, his fangs fully out. He scanned my face and clasped both hands together with the slight widening of his eyes, he said, "You're so pretty when you're angry."

I narrowed my eyes, lips thinning.

"This is just your first car, inconspicuous enough, beautiful, and fast."

"Asher," I snapped. He smirked.

"Beating things is cathartic," Ren offered. "Do it."

I struggled to wrap my head around their words. My head was beginning to throb. I rubbed my temples.

"That's wasteful."

Asher blinked, still just waiting.

"I'll make it worth your while."

"But let me guess—I have to beat the car." I rolled my eyes.

Asher swatted my butt. I yelped. The swat stung. I rubbed my left cheek. "Ouch."

He grinned and raised an eyebrow.

Ren cleared his throat.

"How about, if you do it, I won't go find the first human I encounter and torture them in front of you?" The corner of

Ren's lips curved up. Fifty-fifty chance that he'd follow through with that threat. His eyebrow twitched up. Maybe more like ten-ninety.

"Take the bat," Asher said, wiggling a metal bat at me. Where had he pulled that out from?

"Now," Ren barked. I lunged for the handle and gripped it.

"Psychotic fucking vampire," I whispered under my breath.

"What was that?"

"Nothing," I said just as quickly. As soon as Asher released his grip on the bat, the heaviness dragged the tip to the floor with a loud thud. It was heavier than it looked.

I wrapped both hands around the base and hoisted it up with a grunt. I experimentally swung, but it was clumsy, and the tip crossed about an inch from Ren. He raised an eyebrow like he was daring me to swing again.

"Sorry." I cleared my throat, my face flushing.

Arms suddenly pressed against mine, the large muscles corralling me. Ren no longer stood in front of me. Damn vampire speed! More than the others, he seemed to love spooking me.

"You look scared of it, Kitty Cat." His gruff, rumbling voice caressed the shell of my ear, eliciting a shiver. Ren pulled me back more securely, his hands wrapping over mine. Lust bloomed to life, warming my stomach. He enveloped me entirely. He smelled so sweet, but not in a cloying way. I sank back against him. His hands stiffened over mine, and he swung the bat with me holding it. Our bodies rocked with the sway. I bit the inside of my cheek to stop the moan.

"To make any sort of dent, you need to swing." Humor touched his tone. "Or do you need me to fuck you first?"

My lips thinned.

"You don't seem any less affected," I grumbled, leaning back into his hard shaft.

"That's what you do to me," he murmured gruffly.

His hips gyrated forward, driving his steel into my back. Butterflies erupted through my gut.

"This wasn't what I was thinking," Asher drawled. His voice ripped me out of the lusty haze.

"I got it," I croaked, straightening. I wiggled free of Ren, taking the weapon with me. The bat tilted, but I heaved it up with a grunt. I rested the tip against the hood. It clanged against the metal as I dragged it until I was positioned outside of the passenger side.

God, I am so sorry for doing this to the pretty car.

I took a deep breath and swung, hitting the windshield. The dull thump echoed in the garage and vibrations traveled up my hands. I'd only chipped the surface.

"A little more oomph, Pet." I didn't bother glaring at Asher, but his tone, that condescending tone! All of them had this tendency to talk down to me. I could acknowledge they knew more than me, that they were overall advanced. How could they not? They'd lived decades—no, centuries. But right now, it did nothing more than flame my frustration.

I gritted my teeth and, clenching my abdomen, I swung with every bit of festering anger. The thud was accompanied by a crunch, little flakes of glass hit the floor, too small for me to see.

For all that, there was only a slight shattering of the windshield. The blunt force seemed to have only scratched it up.

"One sec," Asher called and appeared feet away, popping a car open. The third along the first line of cars, a sleek foreign car, and riffled through. He appeared in front of me and slipped glasses onto my eyes. The brightly lit garage became dim. "I can heal you, but I don't want those pretty browns injured."

"Uh, thanks." He stepped away, clearing the view to the car. I lifted the bat, and this time, I swung at the side mirror. Glass shattered and fell on the cement like raindrops. The hollow thump wrenched through my wrists.

But that kind of did feel good.

"Stiffen your grip," Asher called. "And pull the bat all the way back until it's over your shoulder."

I did what he recommended and swung again. This time, it hurt less. A thud accompanied each of my hits. I wasn't a violent person—more of a runner than a fighter, but as I drew back to hit the side window, some of that frustrating tension clinging to my shoulders melted away.

But with every hit that shifted the bunched nerves at my neck, it loosened the ball in my throat. Bastien was the Pale One. The glass webbed. Bastien did things—no, he raped me. I had to face it head on. My next swing spread the cracks in the glass. Gritting my teeth, I continued pounding into the car. A wave of tears spilled free. He'd sodomized me. He'd been this *thing*. Unrecognizable to the protective Bastien I knew, but did that exonerate him? The glass ruptured in a loud crash, yet I didn't stop hitting.

Jax was another topic entirely. My heart hurt, and more embarrassingly? My pride. He'd chosen another woman. But none of those negative feelings had anything close to the utter devastation at the fact that I'd lost him.

My fingers were beginning to numb, but that didn't stop me either. So much fucked. Up. Shit. Happened. With each word, I slammed metal against metal.

I thought the Pale One had been after me, but if they'd had Bastien locked up, then someone else was trying to kill me. I blinked to get rid of the tears blinding me. Crying had likely already ruined my mascara.

"Catalina, stop," Asher's voice finally ripped through the tornado of emotions battling inside me.

What? I staggered back, panting. The tip of the bat thumped on the cement. A dull throb radiated down the column of my neck and into my shoulders. My breaths puffed out and sweat beaded at my temples. I yanked the glasses off my face.

Shattered windows, the side mirror hung on by a wire, deep dents littered the surface—I'd done a number on the vehicle.

The suffocating pressure in my chest had abated. I exhaled slowly, swiping the back of my hand against my damp cheek. Tears continued to trickle free.

"Cat," Asher said gently and lifted my hand, his tongue laved across the bleeding nicks scattered across my arm, collecting the blood. Ren strolled around the car and met my eyes, nodding like a proud father. Asher hummed, bringing my attention back to him. "Good as new."

"What have I stumbled upon?" The English accent held a stiffness, no, a chastising edge. I whirled to find Tobias behind me. I craned my neck to look up at him.

"Love, you have the look of a racoon."

Tobias lifted the bottom of his sweater, giving me a peek of his hard abdomen.

"That has to be expensive," I sniffled, moving away from him. He caught the back of my neck to hold me in place and he swiped the sweater across my face until the tears were gone. By the fifth swipe of his sweater, I tried to pull away.

"Stop struggling, I have erased most of that charcoal."

A snort escaped. Erased.

"How tender," Imogen's obnoxious voice invaded my ears. My smile evaporated while Tobias watched me. He frowned. I sheepishly turned away. Considering she was his sister and all that jazz, he didn't need my utter hatred for her blasted at him.

Jax stood slightly behind her, his arms crossed over his chest. Fury flickered over his features for a split second. Then he wrenched his eyes away from the car.

My cheeks heated under his glare. What?! No, he didn't deserve my attention. So what if I destroyed the very nice vehicle he'd gotten me? I sighed. I really shouldn't have done it. Damn my soft heart.

Imogen hooked her arm around Jax's as they strolled closer.

"I'm thirsty," I mumbled, and I shoved past Jax, making sure I smacked into his side. Agony jostled my bones, but I bit my tongue hard to keep my cry in. No one stopped me. It made sense, they wouldn't get close to me while she was around. But I felt all their eyes on me as I left.

I waited until I was through the door to rub my shoulder. I bit back my whimper and squeezed my sore arm. It felt like I'd run into a concrete wall. Hurrying back through the long, bland hallways, I arrived at the kitchen. I shut the door behind me and beelined to the glasses in the pantry. Then headed directly to the water dispensary on the fridge door. The glass filled up quickly. I chugged down the water as Maddy rounded the corner with a box in hand.

"You okay?" she whispered, peeking over her shoulder.

I nodded and thumped the glass in the sink.

"Thanks for organizing all of my stuff in Asher's room."

Her frown deepened. "Of course, let me know if you need anything else."

I nodded tersely and walked past her, aiming to get back to my room to shower.

"Wait!" her muffled voice echoed down the hall to me just as I stepped into the foyer, right before I reached the stairs.

Colors caught the corner of my eye, and I backed up, struggling to process what I wasn't sure I'd seen. "Crap, I was trying to warn you that she made me put them up." I didn't respond to Maddy, she disappeared down the hall as I stood frozen before the frames.

The large, centered portrait was one I'd never seen before. It had all of them: Crimson Coven, and right in the middle, was her. They stood all around her in various poses. Ren with his arms crossed and a fearsome look on his face. Asher sprawled on the floor, back propped on the chair she sat in and with a cruel twist of his lips. Jax stood behind her, serious as always. They each looked like they had a broom shoved up their ass. The only one missing was Bastien. Beside the canvas was the portrait of Imogen I had seen before.

I scrunched my hair through my fingers, staring up at the obnoxiously large image hanging in the foyer. She was so full of herself. I gritted my teeth, holding back from dragging a ladder in here to yank the atrocious portrait down.

"They've stayed together because of me."

I startled, whirling with a gasp. Imogen stood behind me, her eyes practically glimmering as she stared up at the images.

I kept my mouth shut. She didn't speak for a few seconds. If I sidled to the side and hurried up the stairs— "I'll allow your presence."

What?

Still, I stayed quiet, studying her features. She looked so much like Tobias, except her nose was thinner and her cheekbones fuller. They had the same brown shade of hair and piercing gray eyes.

"They will grow tired of you, eventually. Then I can snap your neck," she spoke so calmly it gave me chills.

"They won't," the words came out rushed and slightly defensive. The corner of her lips twitched. She had the reaction she wanted. I bit my lip. *Great job, Cat.*

"You'll see, they will get used to the idea of your death. Just as they became used to becoming a Coven." She clicked her tongue. "Do you know how difficult it was to wrangle them together?" Her eyes turned to me, weighing on me. I stiffened my spine, so I didn't stumble back. "Yet, you enter to profit over the months of negotiations it took me to create us."

Her finger swiped across the bottom of the portrait. She studied her fingers, but I could see nothing on the fingertips.

"Human number two," she shouted.

"Coming," Maddy shouted from down the hall, sounding harried. She rounded into the foyer, her eyes downcast and her hands laced in front of her. She had on her apron and a splatter across the front of the pale cloth.

"Dust the portraits. A speck is unseemly."

"Yes, Mistress." Maddy dipped her head and backed away, likely to get the cleaning stuff.

I thinned my lips.

"Oh, does that anger you?" Imogen said it so low I could hardly hear it. Her eyes widened innocently. "My apologies. Humans are lowly creatures—"

"We're not your servan—"

"Catalina," Jax snarled, cutting off my angry shout. His eyes scanned me so briefly and he stormed to Imogen's side. I took a step back. "You left," Jax said to her.

Imogen seemed to shrink upon herself when they were around. She was feeding this whole 'poor me' act. Tobias and Jax were eating it up. Seeing his absolute support of her ripped at my heart.

Good thing the other two weren't, they knew her toxic ass would love to hurt me.

"You guys started arguing." She shrugged. "So, I left."

Jax's entire focus remained on her. My stomach twisted and turned like he'd reached inside me. I crossed my arms and turned to face her head on.

"You won't be able to." I twitched the corners of my lips up just slightly—mockingly. Her head tilted. "Take them from me, I mean."

"Leave," Jaxon hissed, suddenly in front of me. He grabbed the back of my neck and shoved me toward the stairs.

I gasped, managing to catch myself before I toppled onto the hard step.

I glared at him as I backed away, catching Imogen's smirk from the corner of my eye. Sneaky bitch.

I stormed upstairs and slammed Asher's door behind me. I sank my fingers into my hair. The Pale One hadn't been hunting me.

That begged the question, who wanted me dead?

Who had the motive? Any vampire who hated Crimson Coven . . . but we'd been careful, no one knew that I wasn't just their Pet. Imogen had shown up too conveniently. As soon as I thought it, I couldn't let it go. Was this some elaborate play she'd concocted? Had she even been held by that Wrenhaven

Sire? Coming out and accusing her didn't seem like the smartest plan, but who could I talk to about it?

My gut was telling me this wasn't just my overactive imagination. But how to prove it? These were baseless accusations that could easily be brushed away by thinking I was jealous.

Either way, I needed to prepare a get-away bag and stash it somewhere, in case they refused to see the truth.

I STEPPED out of the steaming bathroom with a towel wrapped around my body and came to a screeching stop.

"God, Ren! You scared me."

"It was explained to you. Keep away from her. Do not incite her."

I wasn't a fan of his tone. He continued coming at me and I shrunk back. My back flattened against the wall. "Yet, you never listen."

"She keeps pushing my buttons."

"She's wily, that's what pleased me about her."

I wasn't like that, even a little. I dropped my eyes to his lips. Would they become tired of me?

"Then she was right." I raised my eyes to study his chocolate brown ones. "You'll grow tired of me."

He cocked his head.

"She's trying to get into your head. And she's succeeding."

"How can it not?" I scrubbed my face with my palm. "All I do is think about your past, about her presence, about how careful you all are being, all while convincing myself that you will stay with me—"

One more step had him flush against my front. I sucked in a breath, my palms falling on his broad chest.

"I will."

The heaviness in my chest doubted it. I rubbed my palms against the cotton of his white shirt. I needed a release. I needed to lose myself.

"Can I . . .?" I tugged at his shirt.

He continued to just stare at me, so I took it as assent. Inch by inch, I exposed his tatted chest. Once I had it above his nipples, he swiped the shirt off the rest of the way. My attention fastened on the defined muscles. I couldn't get over how fake he looked. Literally so perfect, and that ink only made him hotter.

"Like what you see?" His voice took on a huskier tone. My sex pulsed in response.

"Yeah," I breathed. I really, really did. I licked my lips and ran my fingertips up his left side, over the koi fish and cherry blossom trees. He watched me, his artfully mussed hair falling at his temple and forehead. Sexy vampire. I slid my fingertips down until I hooked my fingers into the waistband of the cargo pants.

His thumb pinched my chin, and he guided my face up to look in his eyes.

"You have skill with distracting me."

The corner of my lips twitched, and I pulled my face from his hand and lowered to my knees in a smooth drop. His zipper smoothly glided down with my descent. I tugged the pants, spreading the flap wide. His cock bobbed free; the tip had already begun to bead with red-tinted pre-cum. I licked my lips. He tasted good here too.

Peeking up at him under my eyelashes, I flicked my tongue across the tip. His lips parted with a heavy exhale.

I gripped the base of his bobbing cock. Warmth radiated from the thick shaft. I squeezed, causing him to grunt. More droplets of cum accumulated at his tip. My mouth watered and I leaned forward to pop his tip into my mouth.

His abdomen flexed with the flick of my tongue. With my free hand, I traveled it up to graze across his happy trail. The thin line of dark hair was soft and oddly alluring. I rubbed my fingertips against it.

Tipping my chin up, I relaxed my jaw and took more of him between my lips. The corner of my mouth stretched, and I angled to fit him better.

"Take all of me." He groaned deep and loud. "Just like that."

Moisture gathered between my legs, dampening my undies. I worked my mouth over him until my lips touched my hand where I gripped the rest of his girth that I couldn't fit. A mix of cum and my spit coated his shaft, making the glide smooth. I rubbed my tongue against the steel of him to gather more of his taste. His hips jerked forward, but he didn't take his eyes off me as his eyelids lowered.

I set a steady pace of gliding my mouth up and down his shaft. "What a good little human." His throaty voice caused my channel to pulse. I lost myself in licking him up, in his taste and those sounds he made that were maddening, driving my desire to a painful pinnacle. I squeezed my thighs together to assuage some of the pressure I needed, but it was a poor substitute to his cock.

This was about enjoying him . . .

And a small, worried part of me wanted to prove to him that I could be whatever he wanted, if he only stuck by his decision to stay with me.

Sigh, I definitely had issues.

Ren moaned and his hips thrust, driving his tip against the back of my throat. I gagged, and he erupted.

I swallowed each jut from his cock, drinking him down like the delicious vampire vanilla smoothie he was.

I hummed around him, not releasing his softening shaft. I swirled my tongue around his tip and caressed the cock with eager flicks. His grunt was accompanied by a throb of his steel as it regained its former stiffness.

"More," he grunted. He pulled me up into his arms. My legs wrapped around his waist and in the same motion he slid into my channel. The towel slipped off me and pooled on the floor.

My whimper cut off my shout. Ren pinned my back against the wall and thrust into me, once, twice. I gritted my teeth but sounds struggled to escape. He withdrew his cock and slammed into me again.

"Moan for me, Kitty Cat."

"What if she hears us?" I gasped, mostly mocking his comment from yesterday.

He rammed his hips against mine so hard my teeth rattled. The thrust wrenched free a moan.

"I don't fucking care. She can't do anything to me." The extra emphasis on 'me' set off alarm bells.

Did that mean she would do something to the others? Ren chased my worries away, sliding into me with frenzied thrusts.

I ate up every second of it, swallowed by his lust.

catalina

THE COLD CEMENT of the bench reached through my clothes and coiled around my bones. I shivered, rubbing my arms. Nights were becoming freezing, and my damp facemask wasn't helping, but I'd needed fresh air after trapping myself in Asher's room.

I'd gotten a few chapters done of the Historical Romance I was working on. Nothing would come of it, but I didn't care. It was an escape from my reality.

I tugged the fluffy robe tighter around me. Upon further inspection of the wardrobe, I'd discovered some new items had been added, soon my stuff would overtake Asher's. Slowly but surely, I was collecting a semblance of a life but how long would I be able to keep it?

Something tickled my leg, and I yanked away, eyes widening on Binx.

"What do you want?" Binx rubbed his head into my leg. Jax could only show affection as a cat it seemed. I raised my legs on the edge of the bench, away from him, and dropped my chin on my knees.

He turned back into a human. The change was sudden and honestly, frightening. Jax appeared kneeling in front of me. He suddenly clasped my face, thumb against one cheek, and pointer finger gripping the other. He squeezed gently, but it was enough to block whatever words were trying to escape my lips.

"What the fuck is on your face?" Although the words were aggressive on their own, his tone was oddly soft. His accent thickened his voice.

I knocked his arm away, and his grip slid my facemask down, so the eyeholes were no longer in the proper place. Damn him, he'd ruined a perfectly good treatment.

My facemask was cold to the touch, the white sheet clung to my fingertips. I glared at him. If I didn't start taking care of myself, I'd start breaking out. I wasn't lucky like them, blessed with their immortal skin, nor would I ever be, unlike I'd thought.

"A facemask," I kept my response simple.

"Humans." He shook his head disapprovingly.

"What do you want? Why are you skulking around." I swept my gaze around the garden. "Aren't you scared the big, bad Imogen will see you with me?" I lowered my voice dramatically.

"Funny," he hissed.

"Thanks."

His nostrils flared and red spilled into his irises, overtaking them. His palms gripped my thighs, jerking them flat on the bench. His eyes returned to normal. "Don't touch me." I was used to this—arguing with Jax. A small thrill traveled down my spine.

"Don't tell me what to do, human," he gritted the words.

"I will when you're invading my space." I shoved his shoulder.

"If you do that again, you will not like the consequences." He glared back.

The elation bloomed, turning to desire.

"I'm so scared," I deadpanned. Wanting to rile him up. Wanting him as passionate as he *had* been with me. Since Imogen showed up, he seemed too careful, too unlike himself. The red overtook his eyes again and he grabbed my hips. With a twist of his wrists, he had my body bent over the bench. Before I could hoist myself up, his grip on my waist yanked my knees toward him. My palms scrabbled for purchase, and I managed to grip onto the edge. Fabric ripped as he did away with my pj bottoms. He tilted my hips high enough, so they hovered off the hard surface. Suddenly, he slammed his girth inside me. I yelped at the sudden invasion. He withdrew, dragging need from my channel, until it dripped down my thighs. His hand left my hip, but amazingly, he didn't jostle me. His now freed palm slapped over my mouth just as he slammed back inside me.

My shout was muffled.

"You won't throw me away."

I cried out, the rough words reached through my chest, even though I didn't understand them. Did he mean now? Or like in general? Was he intending to keep both of us? Would he want to have his undead cake and eat it too?

His next thrust was so hard his balls slapped against the back of my thighs punishingly, forcing thoughts to fade until there was only hunger.

Deep, guttural groans came with each of his thrusts. His fingers squeezed my hip, flexing. Like when he'd taken me in front of all those vampires. His touch held desperation. But I didn't get why he was acting like this. He was choosing Imogen.

The palm on my mouth pulled my head back, forcing me into an arch. Electrical pulses fired through my nerve endings, causing my thighs to tremble. Numbness crept up from my toes. The wet sounds of his thick shaft sliding in and out of me threw me over the edge. My pussy gripped onto him with a vise-like grip, wringing my channel with the ecstasy of my release. His cock spasmed inside me. Jax moaned, but he didn't stop pumping his hips in a slow glide.

The swell tapered off and my arms trembled from holding myself up. Jax lowered my knees to the hard surface. I dropped my head, panting.

His hard drag of breath reached my ears. The sound of it irked me. How dare he sound breathless? How dare he touch me? *How dare he make me want him?* I flexed my fingers against the groove adorning the edge of the bench, still not strong enough to push myself upright.

"You have to fuck me from the back to make yourself feel better?" I spat out, glaring down at the ground. "Can't accept that you want human pussy. A weak, spinless, human." My lip trembled the slightest bit, so I bit it. He brought this nasty, edgy side out of me.

Instead of saying anything, he grabbed my waist and settled me on the seat, straightened my shirt, and leaned down to kiss my forehead.

Then he was gone.

"Jerk," I hissed into the quiet night. Jumping to my feet, I tugged the hem of my shirt down, but it didn't cover anything.

I stormed into the house, the cold air chilling my ass, while I kept the front of my shirt so low that my boobs strained for freedom.

Tobias raised an eyebrow, pausing on the stairs as he descended.

"What happened to you?"

"I don't want to talk about it," I shouted and beelined for Asher's room.

LOUD INTENSE THUMPING lulled me from my nap. Last morning I'd spent hours into the day typing away, so a nap had been sorely needed. I stretched my arms up and yawned.

The nightstand was empty, but a little worn card poked out from the drawer. I plucked it out. Maddy must have cleaned. If one of the vampires would have seen the card, their nosiness would have led them to questioning why I had Alistair's card tucked away in the drawer under the restocked lube. I tucked it into the drawer even though at this point, I didn't need it. I stared at it enough to have memorized the number.

Thumping from outside persisted. It was a low, gritty echo that had to be extremely loud if I could hear it from in here. I rolled onto my feet, stretching my arms behind my back.

I slid into my slippers by the door. I frowned; the door had been left ajar. Pulling the door fully open, I winced from the assault of noise. What was going on downstairs? I rubbed my exhausted face. The hem of my PJ shorts tickled my thighs as I stepped into the cold hallway.

I descended into the foyer slowly. I scanned the area. My grip on the banister tightened. It vibrated under my palm, going to the rhythm of the bass. Not only was the music different, but either new lights had been installed, or the bulbs were switched to red ones. At the base of the stairs, I had a clear view into the living room.

My heart stalled.

A nude woman gyrated on top of a man. I could only see her dark hair flutter against her bare back, and the knees of the male who gripped the couch cushion with his hands fisted. My pulse raced. Those loafers—no. The edges of my vision became hazy.

I staggered forward and yanked the girl's shoulder. Not thinking, because if I had been, I would have known it was a bad idea. The woman whirled and snarled at me, flashing sharp fangs, but I was already looking at the male. Red hair—not one of mine. I backed up, but before I stepped out of range, the woman grabbed my arm near the elbow.

I gasped, flinching from her tight hold, but she didn't let me go. Her breasts bounced with her sudden movement, and I got a flash of the male's cock inside her.

"Let me go." I tugged fruitlessly.

I swept my attention around. More vampires in various states of undress. On the floor was a couple, a male holding another male to the ground by the neck as he thrust. The other settee had a female's legs spread wide eagle while a man went down on her. Moans and groans reached through the thumping music. My attention fell on Asher standing near the wall with stiffness radiating from him. Thank God he was dressed, but what was all this? He faced the wall as if it held the answers to the universe.

"Asher," I shouted. My voice was drowned out by the music, but somehow, he heard me. He turned so suddenly, and his eyes widened.

"Asher," I croaked.

"Let her go," he snarled at the woman holding onto me, but he didn't step closer, he remained near the wall, scraping his hands through his hair.

"You should have said you would bring food, Ash, just like the old days." Her grin widened and she pulled me closer, breathing in deep. Kind of uncomfortable since the man had begun to gyrate up into her. His eyes were on my face, half-lidded and intrigued. He was a big male.

"Let me go," I said through my gritted teeth.

"She smells mouthwatering," she said, her eyes flashing red. She swayed forward. An arm wrapped around my belly and at the same time a hand lashed out to smack her across the face. She yelped and let me go, blood sprayed on the male inside her and his eyebrows twitched up as he smirked at my savior. I huddled back into the hard body at my back and peeked up at Ren. Thank God.

"Thank you," I said, choked. He always showed up when I was in deep shit. Kind of like when Bastien—

I rubbed my eyes, pressing my palms into my eye sockets. When I removed them, everything around me was still the same. People were fucking, but the woman Ren backhanded had unmounted the redhead. He sprawled back, his dick still out. I averted my eyes, my face flushing.

What was it with vampires and orgies? And in Crimson Manor?

Imogen. That weird bitch. I wiggled free of Ren's surprisingly loose grip and hurried to Asher's side. He stared down at me, eyebrows furrowed.

"Let's go, Asher." I grabbed his hand and tugged, but he was like a boulder.

"No," Asher said through gritted teeth. The response sucker punched me in the gut, and I flinched. His expression became even more stiff, unrecognizable.

I scowled, shaking my head, so confused. A few days passed and he chose *this*?

"You're unbelievable," I spat. His head jerked back like I'd taken a bat to him. The ball in my stomach pulsed and the nastiness spread, spilling into my words.

Ren settled his palm on my hip, he leaned down to speak near my ear.

"He can't."

"Bull! If this was what he wants. He should have just told me." I pressed my lips into a thin line. So hurt. The music cut off suddenly.

"If you liked all this so much, I would have gotten out of your way." My shouted words lashed out, aiming to hit him. There'd been comments about him being a former 'sexual service provider'. Every time it was mentioned there was a level of derisiveness to it. I had no problem with the profession, but I believed he only wanted me. In all the times he'd disappeared, had he been fucking Imogen?

Heaviness in my stomach pulsed, causing my chest to feel like rocks were accumulating in it. I couldn't breathe.

Asher continued to stare at me with dead eyes.

"Out." I whipped my head toward Tobias's shout. His stone like face turned into a sneer. The flurry of movement became dizzying with how fast everyone moved. The only one that seemed to be taking his sweet time was that red-headed male. He slowly zipped up his dick and strolled out with a smirk.

Imogen inched inside the living room, yanking all of my attention to her. She did this.

"You," I shouted and ran faster than I ever had. I shoved her, but she didn't even budge. Her eyebrows rose.

"Why this violence, human?"

An innocent, *fake* expression.

It pissed me off even more. My hands trembled at my side. Clatter and cursing erupted down the hall. Moments later a grinning semi-naked female vampire staggered around the bend with chains in her cloth-wrapped hand. She tugged again and Bastien entered, yanking at the chains with a snarl. They weakened him, otherwise he would have done away with her easily.

"I let this big guy loose," the female vampire laughed. "I kept hearing the clang of chains. When did Bastien go blood-mad?"

Ren yanked one of the metal legs off the coffee table and swung until the jagged tip sliced into her chest. She gawked down at the pole sticking out of her. Then her body disintegrated until she was ash. I clutched my chest, gawking at the pile of dead female. Ren tossed the broken metal piece to the floor. Bastien was suddenly next to me, feral red eyes focused on Imogen, lips fixed in a sneer.

"Mood killer," Imogen drawled, but her attention hadn't moved from Bastien. She blinked, studying him. "You didn't look like *this* last I saw you."

Bastien snarled at her, angling in front of me.

Imogen sniffed and tipped her chin up.

"Savage." She derisively sneered, but still she scanned him. My metaphorical hackles raised. Even though Bastien had been the one to hurt me, I didn't like the insult toward him.

He may not understand the degrading words, but I did.

I swung to look around at the others, but none of them said anything . . . like they were used to her talking about Bastien in such a degrading way.

My stomach rose in my throat.

I fucking hated that.

How could they just allow it? They were supposed to be a team. I whirled so fast it caused my vision to swim.

"Don't talk about him like that."

"Oh, I did not mean anything by it, human." Her eyes rounded, and she blinked as her face crumpled. She just had to tack on 'human' it was her thing, a little jab of reminder in front of them. Just another way she showed her underhandedness. I turned to the guys, and they seemed visibly uncomfortable. Tobias smoothed his frown.

"Calm yourself." He lightly pressed on my shoulder, skillfully inserting himself in between us.

I clenched my teeth.

"I was treating Asher to a night of fun. The kind he truly likes."

I was practically frothing at the mouth at this point, but I continued to fight off the tears.

"We leave for a few hours, and you do this, Imogen?" Tobias stared at his sister. I whipped my attention to him accusingly.

"You let this happen."

"Catalina," he started, hesitantly.

Imogen scoffed and lifted her chin, that stupid confused innocence fading.

"And you've been holding Asher back."

Tears flooded my eyes. I gritted my teeth so hard I could feel them close to shattering. "He likes variety. Not your weak—"

"Enough, Imogen." Tobias's voice held no room for argument. The low, hissed threat sent a chill down my spine.

"No, enough of all of this!" I jabbed a finger at him.

"Of what, human? Fun?" Imogen smirked.

"Shut. Up," I retorted.

"Leave." Tobias was showing fang at this point.

She sniffled and lightly touched her nose with the back of her finger.

"Imogen, things have changed in your absence," Tobias said.

"But it hasn't even been a century," she cried out. "It was so easy for you all to forget me? Did you all forget I am the one who brought us together?" She dropped to the couch in a dramatic sprawl, sobs wracking her shoulder.

"Enough theatrics. I'll deal with you later." Tobias sighed.

"Fine," Imogen shouted shakily and left the living room. "I have errands to run anyway."

"Wait," Ren snapped. "Release him."

Her eyes widened slightly, but seeing Ren's deadpanned face, she sighed. "Do as you wish, Asher." She lifted her nose in the air and left the room. He staggered forward. Was that her special ability? Keeping someone in a spot?

Asher reached for me, and I smacked him away. He almost seemed hurt. He stormed over to Tobias and hissed words out so low I couldn't hear them. Bastien touched my spine, and I stiffened. I shuffled away from Bastien's crowding. Ren had joined their conversation. Looked like I wasn't needed here anymore.

My heart gave a wretched little skip.

I believed they cared for me. Nothing like love, but some

fondness . . . and I believed they didn't want me hurt, and I counted on that.

I cleared my throat, pointedly.

They stopped their low conversation.

"You should be resting." Asher strode to me; he brushed my hair over my shoulder. I looked up at him and then focused on the little dip at his throat. Looking at them kind of hurt.

I rubbed the sore spot the female vampire had gripped and the sting radiated up my limb. It didn't help detract from the pain in my chest.

"Catalina?" Tobias murmured, attention turning to me. I'd taken the time to mull everything over and determine how to bring up my decision, but now I struggled to get words out.

I licked my lips to try again.

"I'm causing you guys problems." I crossed my arms, pressing my lips into a thin line. Tobias didn't have the right to look as concerned as he did. The softening of his lips and eyes shouldn't get to me the way they did either. I felt sick to my stomach, so I bit the inside of my cheek hard. The pinch forced back the tears wanting to explode from my chest. I hurt so much.

"It is something we will resolve in time. Just keep patient—"

"I'm hurt," I shouted, Tobias's words boiling my frustration over. Absolute silence from them. "And me, I can't share like you guys." I licked my lips. "It's best for me to go, for all of you and for Imogen." I barely contained my sneer at saying her name. Asher opened his mouth. I knew where his tirade would go. "I know," I said forcefully. "Since you guys can't compel me, you can't just let me go, but you never said I couldn't go to another Coven."

Asher snarled. I flinched, but didn't cower.

"You care for me. I know it, you all do. If you don't want me in pain . . ." I couldn't help the break of my voice. Asher took over my vision, and his jaw feathered. "Let me go to another Coven." Asher scoffed, taking a step back as he shook his head. The other's seemed similarly stunned. I had no clue silence could feel this loud.

"You're out of your mind." I whipped to look at Jax standing at the entrance of the living room, an unholy look in his eyes. I stepped back and hit Bastien's chest.

"I contacted Alistair." Lie, but they didn't know that. I was planning to do it once I got to my bedroom.

"You what?" Ren's low hiss sent chills down my flesh.

I sensed they respected each other when interacting at Calliope's place. The anger gracing their features though, had I made a grave miscalculation? Maybe I shouldn't have shown that specific card yet. I licked my lips. Jax's appearance dragged it out of me.

"You need to rest before you continue spouting more nonsense." Asher huffed, taking hold of my arm. I wiggled out from his grip and forced my eyes up to his.

"I know what I'm saying. I'm taking myself out of the equation. I will go—"

"You're not going anywhere," Jax snarled. He encroached on my space, and I shrunk backwards. I expected anger from Asher but not Jax. I squared my shoulders and lifted my chin.

"I don't like Imogen," I shouted back. "Something is off about her, and I think she's lying to you guys." I lifted my chin, not backing down from my death-defying words. Again, the silent stillness sent chills down my body. Now they all formed a half circle, staring at me. Bastien pressed his palm into my shoulder, curling his fingers into my muscle. He would cause tears to spill, if he kept it up. I had the desire to lean into him. Which was fucked up beyond belief.

I breathed hard, collecting my thoughts. They still hadn't said anything as they studied me.

My theory about her hovered on my tongue, but a pitying twist rippled on their features.

"I understand you are not well since her arrival, Love." My words sucked right back down my throat.

"There is no need to be jealous—"

"I'm not just jealous!" I cut off Asher. "She's manipulating you," I forced out. "I know you guys don't see it, but she is."

Bastien paced behind me with thudding steps. His agitation worsened with every second. The others didn't think he was there mentally, but they were wrong. And putting aside my confusion about him, he seemed to hate her with a passion. We agreed on that.

The front door opened.

All of their heads whipped toward it eerily.

"If it's Alistair, I'll kill him," Ren's chilling voice sent a shiver down my back.

Maddy sashayed past with grocery bags swinging. She inclined her head to us as she passed and gave me a confused look, before she disappeared. She'd definitely quiz me later. Suddenly, Jax had my arm in a rough grip, forcing me to my toes.

"I'm setting up a meeting with Alistair," Tobias announced, his gray eyes piercing me.

"To discuss a Coven switch?" I asked hopefully. Maybe a little sarcastically.

"You're not going anywhere," Jax snarled. He manhandled me to the staircase. I fought it, fruitlessly. I shot Asher a pleading look and he shook his head, his lips turned down with displeasure.

"I am not with you on this, Pet. You forget you are ours."

"Contact your Progeny. Have them set up a meeting with Alistair at the club," Tobias rattled off orders as he stormed up the steps in front of us, leading the way up. Everything was moving so fast.

Jax let up on his grip and my feet flattened on the floor sending a dash of pain to my calves.

Tobias stood before Asher's bedroom, holding the door open while Asher's fingers flew over the screen tapping out what he said to his Progeny.

Jax forced me through the door and to the bed with a hard push. I sprawled with my limbs akimbo. Asher was suddenly next to me, clipping a set of fuzzy cuffs from me to the bed.

"Wait!"

I yanked, but it was too late, the latch closed.

"I can't have him doing your bidding and breaking you out," Ren's words were filled with irritation. He shoved Bastien out the door. I cried out, jolting forward, fighting against the restraint.

"Let me out!" I shouted.

"It's for your own good," Asher said, determinedly.

"And Alistair's," Jax's threat rang lower and threatening.

I gritted my teeth, stopping my useless yanking against the cuff.

Jax slammed the door.

EIGHT

tobias

I STUDIED my sister lounging on the couch of the space she had claimed. Clothing was littered across the room. She'd done extensive shopping—she had not changed in our time separated. Misery marred her expression. She looked from me to Asher, and then Jaxon.

Ren had gone to prepare the car and idled at the front. Once I was done with our conversation, I would head to my meetings.

"I can't handle it," she shouted. "If you will not kill her, make her leave," she ordered, sniffling again. "I tried to accept her presence, but she thinks she's better than me." She sprang to her feet. "Did you see the way she looked at me?" She scoffed, shaking her head. "If we kill her, everything can go back to normal."

"No," Asher hissed. Imogen turned beseeching eyes to Jaxon.

"Jaxon, please,"

"No."

Something turned cold in her gaze. I had not seen that

before, and it was because Jaxon never denied her. He went along with whatever she ordered.

"She's not going anywhere—"

"Shut up," she hissed, her eyes flashing. As her Progeny, Asher had no choice but to be silent. She smoothed her hands over the skirt of her dress.

"I am going shopping, and I am taking that human servant with me." She stood, but I did not take my eyes off her expression. Her pride had been injured.

They have chosen. That is fine. Her thoughts slipped into my head, and they weren't clear, it was as if hearing them through a thin veil. That was how I knew she was not using her ability to reflect her thoughts to me. Imogen walked out the door without a backwards glance at any of us.

A chime went off and Asher lifted his phone.

I was glad I no longer dealt with communications. Asher had returned to his rightful role. He was certainly more apt at managing the virtual requests. He could whine about the work, but I was done with carrying his duties while he was wrapped up with Catalina. And now that she was mine, I did not need a distraction from her.

"The meeting is set with Calliope and then Alistair." Asher sighed. "She's refusing to meet at Crimson Nights. She wants us to go to Saphire Lounge and she's demanding I be present." Asher frowned. "I wanted to stay and keep Catalina company."

"I will stay with her," Jax said, crossing his arms.

"I don't know about that," Asher scoffed. "You're likely to piss her off more than anything."

"Well, at least she'll have someone protecting her."

"Ren should be the one staying." I knew well why Asher said this, but it wasn't possible to leave him behind.

"Ren has to go. He has the best chance at getting through to Calliope. Tobias will read her mind. We have no choice." Jaxon paused.

"We shouldn't be long," I added. I had the same concerns as Asher, but we needed to take care of how we handled my sister. She was vengeful, so we had to figure out how to break her away from us, and the first step was meeting with Calliope.

"Fine, then once Imogen leaves, we will go." Asher turned to Jax. "And contact us as soon as she returns."

I only nodded. Taking all this care was necessary.

Imogen already caused so much damage, and my little human could no longer handle it. I prayed for a little more time, but it had run out.

And the fact that a mere human, one so sweet and gentle, could even make us consider choosing her, when we'd only have a measly few centuries with her, showed how much we had changed.

Imogen would not and had not been handling it well.

I would find a place where Imogen would be safe and protected—and away from Catalina.

catalina

I STARED up at the ceiling, swinging my arm side to side as it dangled in the cuff. I didn't think they'd put up such a stink about me leaving. Honestly, wasn't I doing them a favor? They were obviously torn, their precious Imogen returned to take center stage, and I wouldn't get in the way.

I dashed away the trickling tears with the back of my hand. Ridiculous, demanding vampires. None of my arguments had been heard, but I would not stop until I proved my point. My exit would benefit them.

The door creaked as it opened.

Maddy poked her head in.

"Maddy," I gasped, sitting up straighter. "Can you get me out of these? My back is on fire."

She grimaced. "Sorry, I was ordered not to. But I did bring you a tea." She lifted the little plate with a teacup. The bed dipped as she perched next to me. She raised the plate, and I took the little handle. I wasn't the biggest tea person, but I was damn thirsty.

I gulped some down and struggled to hide my grimace at the bitter taste.

"I should have added some sugar in it, huh?"

"Maybe a little." I cleared my throat and drank the rest of it and set it back on the saucer. "Can you tell one of the guys I need to speak with them?"

"They're not back yet. I think only Jax is here." She fidgeted with her hair.

"Nevermind." I grumbled. Jax didn't make the list of anyone I wanted to see right now. Not that I wanted to see any of the others since they locked me up in here, but I could tolerate the others at least.

"Do you know where they went?"

"I think they went to Crimson Nights." Maddy eyed me.

Ouch. I grabbed my aching throat.

My lip trembled, and I sucked in a deep breath, but upon my exhale, a sob exploded out.

They'd gone out?

I cinched my eyes tight, but tears tricked out from the side.

These relationships would lead nowhere, *but they wouldn't let me leave*. If I went to another Coven, maybe to work for them. Could that work? If I were completely honest, I preferred Alistair to any other vampire I'd met. At least he seemed fair from what I'd witnessed, and he'd saved my life during that hunt. And he owned a mall, maybe I could work in a shop, instead of as a feeder.

"Earth to Cat." Maddy snapped her fingers near my face. "What was it with them earlier, they looked like they were about to rip heads off?" Maddy brushed her hair back, looking around nervously, as if keeping an eye out for them. I squeezed my cuffed hand into a fist. The tingling was so severe, it was beginning to spread to my other hand like some phantom pain.

"I asked to change Covens."

She gawked.

"You have bigger balls than I thought. I mean, don't get me wrong, you were already with all of them, so I thought a lot of you, but that?" She whistled. "Their nature would rather kill you than give you up. I can tell you that much."

"I learned that, thanks," I said dryly and wiggled my cuff. "How do you think I ended up like this?"

And here came the tears again. I really needed to get out of these cuffs, my entire body was becoming numb.

Her lips thinned and then her eyes suddenly widened. She looked down at the teacup, horrified.

"I am so sorry, Catalina. She compelled me to forget."

She was blubbering so fast I couldn't make sense of her sentences. Her change in demeanor gave me whiplash.

"Maddy," I shouted. Her sobs quieted. "What's going on?"

"The tea had a paralytic drug."

What? I could only blink, but that heaviness to my limbs I believed was numbness became more intense. I tried to move, and it took all my effort to hold my head up.

"I am so sorry," she cried. She stood from the bed stiffly.

"Don't go," I choked out.

"I can't help it." Tears trekked down her cheeks. She slammed the door shut behind her. I breathed harshly as I dragged myself upright. My stomach felt unsteady. And it was so hot.

"Jax," I shouted, the panic in my voice obvious. "Jaxon!"

A scratch at the door froze me. It sounded like someone

dragging their nails down the wood. The hair on my arms stood and I scooted to the edge of the bed.

The door swung open with the hiss of fabric moving. A wide skirt rustled through the entrance.

Imogen . . . She closed the door. My body gave out and I slumped against Asher's headboard.

I licked my lips nervously, digging my fingers into my palm. She took another step closer.

"I fucking knew it," I said. I couldn't lift my head.

Imogen clicked her tongue.

"I'm sure you know everything."

"Condescending bitch," I slurred.

Her eyebrows raised.

"I'm sorry, what was that?" She tilted her head like she would be able to understand me better.

"Ffff-k yhou." My tongue felt especially heavy. She gripped my ankles and pulled them, spreading me on flat on the bed. My head flopped to the side. I followed her with my eyes as she approached until she stood over me with a grin.

"Would you look at this?" She clicked her tongue disapprovingly again. "Let me help you with that."

I couldn't even turn my head up to look as she gripped my forearm. I could feel it being lifted, but I had no control over my movement. My heart pounded a mile a minute. The cuffs clanged against the headboard. She jerked on my arm and excruciating pain traveled through my fingertips.

Tears flooded my eyes, and my scream was muffled behind my lips. A loud pop came on the heels of mind-numbing agony. A ringing filled my ears. I couldn't move, but all I wanted to do was huddle into a ball. She patted my now free hand and it sent agony spiking up to my elbow.

"Don't worry, the dose was just right." She grinned down at me and smoothed my hair back. "You should be able to talk soon."

She settled on the edge of the bed, staring down at me with cold eyes.

"You have been quite the thorn in my side." She sighed. "Like a cockroach, refusing to die. A car didn't take you out, a vampire I sent confused another female for you, and the mercenary I hired didn't succeed." Her laugh held a bite to it.

I knew it! She'd been behind the attacks. "Such accusation in your eyes. As if you weren't the one invading my territory. Truly, it was a surprise how well you wrapped the stupid males around your fingers. It was quite disappointing." She let out a deep sigh and returned to petting my hair back. Her face remained serene as she studied me. "What surprised me most was how you turned Jaxon and my brother from me." She clicked her tongue. "But don't worry, they'll get over you quickly."

My lips began to tingle.

"You like talking don't you," I said, slowly enunciating my words. My jaw and lips felt weird, but at least I could move them now.

"Quite," she said smiling. "You know what else I like?" She leaned closer. "Screams."

Her hand settled on my wrist, and she put weight on it. Stabbing agony splintered through my bone. I screamed so loud my ears rang. She didn't let up on her weight, just continued to pulverize what was left of my fractured arm. My scream cut off with a grunt and a crunch reached my ears.

Nausea rolled through my stomach and the room spun. She

lifted her hand off my injury. She smacked my cheek hard. The sting reached my temple.

"Don't pass out on me now. I want to savor your pain."

"Stop," I croaked. "Please."

She threw her head back.

"You broke much too easily—so disappointing." She chortled. "Come now, make it fun for me." I blinked with effort. "How about I tell you just what you've attempted to take from me? Hmm?"

My sight blurred.

"Do you know how hard it was for me to get them to agree to be in a Coven? They were always squabbling." Her perfect eyebrow twitched in the same manner I'd seen Tobias do it.

"Even my saintly brother tried to convince me to stop my games. He always tried to grab onto the human ideology of morals." Her eyes glazed slightly, her thoughts taking her far away from the bed. "Yet, you have taken him from me too." Her gaze refocused. "They replaced me with such ease. I expected at least five centuries of pain."

She seemed honestly upset.

"They thought you were dead. Why would you leave them in the first place?"

"Boredom." She peeked at her nails stained with blood. "I wasn't planning to return. I was having a great time in France, but when word reached me about their new little pet, curiosity had the best of me." She shrugged. She was answering all my questions because she was going to kill me.

Please, God, all I asked was that Peter be left alone once I was out of the picture.

I focused on her face. Pride. This was all about her

wounded feminine pride. She wouldn't let me live, and she'd make me hurt with whatever time I had left.

"You were always like this, weren't you? Manipulating them into being with you. Using them against each other—hurting them," I said between my teeth. "Pathetic."

She hissed, her sharp fangs flashing. She slammed her hands on the bed, corralling my head. My heart jumped, but I gritted my teeth, waiting for the death blow.

"You don't think it's going to be that easy, do you?" She wrapped her palm around my knee and squeezed.

Bone crunched and bile rose up my esophagus. The door exploded from Jax ramming through. His eyes scanned my body and all I could do was eye him from my limp position on the bed.

The shock of his appearance stopped the vomit from making it out.

"Cat—"

"Do not move, Progeny," Imogen ordered. Jax immediately froze.

"Let her go, Imogen." His nostrils flared.

I gasped. I didn't expect this. Not even a little.

Imogen's eyes widened dramatically, and her palm landed on her chest.

I managed to roll my head to keep them both in my sight.

Jax remained stiff with his eyes peeled wide.

"If I let her go." Imogen sashayed over to him, her finger grazed across his chest. "What will you do for me?"

Jax's jawline flexed. His eyes flicked to the side, but he didn't look at me. His head rose higher.

"Anything."

Imogen went eerily still.

I thought he wanted to be with her? They kept her things here like a shrine. I had truly believed they wouldn't have given me a second thought if she'd been around. My story would have ended when I was dragged into Crimson Manor on day one, especially at the hand of the vampire currently speaking up for me, except now he was trying to bargain for my life?

"I'll tell you what," she announced, suddenly reanimating. She clapped her hands together and flounced over to the lounging chair near the door. The wooden legs dragged across the floor with an obnoxious squeak. She placed it about a foot away from me and patted the back cushion. "Take a seat here, Jaxon. Only observe. No matter what, you will not move an inch once you sit." His teeth clicked together, and he jerkily approached the chair and dropped into it.

Imogen turned her attention back to me. She rounded the bed to stand on the opposite side. Now the bed sat between her and Jax. I kept my attention on her. She was a snake poised to strike, and I was her victim. She leaned over me, her face hovering an inch from my nose.

"They stayed together because of me. They are *mine*," she repeated.

The thickness in my throat throbbed.

"Doesn't look like it to me."

That pissed her off even more. Her hand settled on my thigh, and she squeezed it until the sharp nails ripped into my skin. My stomach turned over and my chest began to tighten. Sweat beaded at my temples. It hurt so much. I gritted my teeth, but I couldn't contain my whimper.

Jax hissed, but the sound faded behind the ringing in my ears. Finally, she let up on the pressure. I gasped, watching her bring her blood painted fingertips to her lips, licking away my taste.

"Mmm." She grinned, showing her bloody teeth. "If I didn't want to hear your screams, I would just drain you," she spoke conversationally as she hooked her finger into my shirt. She yanked and ripped it open, baring my lacy bra. A flush warmed my face.

Her eyes grazed over me with a sneer on her lips.

"I don't get it. You're nothing special."

I struggled to swallow. How degrading.

"I will enjoy this." She dug her nails into my skin. Searing pain burned my flesh.

I screamed.

TEN

I COULDN'T STAND THIS. My Kitten thrashed in agony, and all I could do was watch. I focused on moving my fingers on the armrests, but it was no use.

I exerted all my energy trying and trying. Still, I couldn't save her. I sucked in a breath.

Imogen propped herself on one arm, leaning over Cat's bared stomach.

Blood trickled down her side, painting lines across her flesh. Her soft tan flesh that should be worshiped, not shredded.

Imogen carved into her skin, but from this angle, I couldn't see what it was.

"Stop," I croaked. Gritting my molars, I fought to stand, to morph, to twitch even, but there was no use. My body betrayed me, but I didn't stop struggling to free myself. Her cries wouldn't allow me to. Panting breaths left my mouth.

Imogen had locked me in the basement while I checked on Bastien. Meanwhile, she enacted this bullshit plan. It was all a fucking ruse. The metal door had almost succeeded in keeping me sequestered.

I'd torn through the door and was up here as quickly as I could, but I should have stopped before slamming inside. If I had only taken a moment to *think*, I could have called the others—

Cat made me weak and desperate. More than I'd ever thought I *could* experience.

I stared at a red droplet traveling down her side. I could do nothing. I was helpless.

My stomach pitched.

The echo of her screams remained in my ears, refusing to release me.

Watch her suffer, Jaxon, my love. And just know, you did this. Imogen projected her thoughts at me using her ability. Blood filled my mouth with how hard I bit the inside of my cheek.

I met Catalina's damp eyes. She stared at me. Agony in their brown depths. I didn't break eye contact.

"Please. Imogen." The words felt ripped from my throat.

"Just for that, I will make you play. Jaxon, follow directions clearly." Fuck. "I want you to grab her hand and break her fingers one by one. Nothing more, nothing less. Then you will sit back and watch her writhe."

No.

"No." Even as I said it, I leaned forward, reaching for Catalina's hand. Hurting Catalina would destroy me. I didn't want to do this.

She'd carved *whore* into her stomach. Deep enough that I could see the layer of fat. "No." My voice was unrecognizable.

She tensed.

My chest felt like it was being crushed under boulders and more kept being added.

"And once she's dead, we will fuck on her corpse." I wouldn't have a choice if she ordered it of me.

I wanted to rip her blackened heart out from pure revulsion. Imogen shattered Cat's bones, so much that fractures of bone punctured through her skin. I gnashed my teeth.

Gore never fazed me, but the vision before me was too much for me to handle.

REN

CALLIOPE'S PROGENY led us into a chamber located toward the back of Saphire Lounge. Secluded and far from prying ears. As I entered, I rapped my knuckles on the wall. Even sound proofed. I felt special. Her Progeny moved to the side and inclined her head. Calliope had them trained well. A quick sweep of the area showed this door to be the only entrance. Calliope lounged on a leather couch, her legs crossed as she sipped her bloody drink.

How she liked her theatrics.

She'd already made us wait longer than necessary. To the point that the Alistair meeting had to be postponed.

"Welcome, gentlemen," she drawled, lifting the wine glass to her lips. Blood sloshed from one side to the other, leaving a thin layer of residue behind. She waved a hand around as if we couldn't see the chairs neatly pulled out around the table. She'd upgraded her interrogation room.

Without compunction, I sprawled in the too-small wooden

chair. The legs creaked under my weight. Tobias carefully took his seat beside me, meanwhile, Asher was already strolling around the chairs until he was at the far end of the couch. He reclined on it in a lazy drape. She did not like that. The corner of my mouth twitched.

"What was so urgent you needed a meeting with me again, Crimson Coven Sires?" The slight bite to her tone told me everything I needed to know.

"You're still bitter about my threats," I mused. Her shoulders tightened.

"Whatever do you mean?"

I raised an eyebrow. Her temper visibly flared.

"It was in my home," she sneered. "You were a guest in a Coven Sire's home and you—"

"Come now, Calliope," I mocked. "You're putting on airs after everything we've been through?"

She straightened, leaning forward.

"You uncouth swine! I—"

"We come to ask a favor," Tobias interrupted what was surely about to be a scathing comment. I smirked.

That was nicer than I'd put it, especially since it wasn't a request.

"What do you need from me?" Her eyes narrowed suspiciously.

"Now—"

"Take Imogen in."

Tobias shot me an exasperated look I ignored.

Calliope's eyes widened.

"You lot have officially lost it. Imogen is dead."

"She is not."

Her eyebrows furrowed. "Are you going to elaborate?"

"There was a mistake, she was on vacation," Tobias offered.

We all went silent, not elaborating.

"Without telling any of you? You all believed she was dead." Her eyes narrowed. "Something's fishy here."

"Enough hypothesizing," I said, trying to keep my tone nice and even. Tobias held a palm up in my direction.

"What we mean is," he said emphatically. I didn't have to read his mind to know he was telling me to shut up. "We come to you asking a favor. You have a strong, loyal Coven that trusts you. You would be doing us a great service."

Now he was blowing air up her ass.

"I don't know if this would be a good move for me. She has many enemies. What if they come for her?" She shook her head. "I need to think of my Coven."

I tapped my finger on the surface of the armchair. As true as that was, my patience wore thin—nearing catastrophic levels. Calliope eyed me. She'd increasingly grown stiff with each glance she sent me. The shuffling in her seat grated on my nerves.

"Will you take her in?" Tobias repeated the question. He'd made a strong case. Our alliance for her taking Imogen into her Coven. Without us, Imogen was as strong as Calliope. She could handle her, so she wouldn't step out of line.

Calliope's eyebrows raised high on her forehead.

"You know what a big ask that is. Imogen has always been unpredictable."

"I'm sure she will eventually create her own Coven. She just needs safe harbor."

"Away from us," I tacked on to Tobias's sentence. I was

ready to be done with that cunt. The only reason I hadn't taken her head off was because I'd have problems with Tobias. Killing both of them could fix the issue.

Tobias raised an eyebrow at me. I grinned, unrepentant.

"I would like to see you try."

Stuffy vampire.

I only shrugged. Tobias returned all his attention to Calliope.

Her pink tongue wet her lower lip. She would say no.

"What if we offer you the ring?" Interest finally sparked in Calliope's eyes. The corner of her lips moved the slightest bit. We had her. She'd been wanting that ring for ages. We'd held onto it because, if it was in the hands of another Coven, it would put ours at a disadvantage.

"Your precious ring?" She tried to hide the excitement, but I clocked it a mile away.

"You would never use it against us. If you do, we kill you, or one of our Progeny kills you. We'll set precautions."

Not only would we kill her. We'd take out Freya, the vampire who would take her spot as Coven Sire. In essence, inheriting all of Calliope's assets.

"I am unsure . . ."

"Stop playing difficult." I bristled, leaning forward to brace my elbows on my knees. The corner of her lips finally turned up.

"Deal. But I need to ask something from you." Her eyes settled on Asher.

"Now, now, sweetheart, I always knew you had a thing for me but I'm a new vampire. I belong to one female now—"

Calliope scoffed with a sneer.

"I need you to talk to someone."

Asher looked over at Tobias. His eyes slightly thinned. He focused on reading Calliope's mind.

"Do it."

If Tobias agreed, he would have reason for it. Calliope looked over at the male standing near the door.

"Bring her."

He only nodded and exited.

"One of my people was taken." She turned her attention to Asher. "You know her."

He hummed. "And what do you want *me* to do?"

"She's been shutting everyone out. Get her to tell me who took her."

"And her Sire?" She could be ordered to spill instead of tiptoeing around her.

"Died a century ago. She pledged loyalty to my Coven." She turned away from me and back to Asher. "She's refusing to open her mouth. She cringes and hides from everyone. We found her bound in shackles, weak and without blood. She would have turned to dust if we hadn't gotten to her. But she's always liked you, Asher, so I'm banking on her lowering her guard and Tobias can read her mind to see if she's lying."

"Why—"

"Let's get this over with. If she's going to take Tobias's pain-in-the-ass sister, I'm all for this," Asher interrupted me.

The door creaked with the entrance of a thin female. She didn't seem to be paying attention to anything until she focused on Asher. Her eyes slightly widened, and she was suddenly clinging to Asher. His lips thinned and then he smoothed his expression. His hand dropped on her shoulder, and he maneuvered her until she sat on the couch. She let out a deep, wrenching sob. Red tinted tears left lines on her cheeks as she sniffled.

Asher patted her shoulder, using it as an excuse to keep her at a distance. I had no doubt she would toss herself at him again. Maybe I should take a picture and send it to Catalina. Then she could come sleep in my bedroom.

Tobias frowned at me. I sighed.

"What happened, Daniela?"

"My name is Ruby," she said through sobs. Asher grimaced.

"Ah, that's right, I remembered, I was just testing to see if you could hear me over that sobbing." He smirked and all the crying tapered off as she stared up at him with mooning eyes. A load of bullshit. He never remembered women's names. "You're safe now. Nothing is going to happen to you." His coaxing words were lies. Her shoulders relaxed a fraction. Her eyes remained glued to Asher like he was her savior.

"C-can I switch to your Coven?"

"Ruby," Calliope hissed.

"I don't think you can protect me." Ruby curled forward, hugging her legs. The crying started up again.

Tobias cleared his throat. Calliope's mouth shut and she plastered a fake fucking smile on. Asher scratched his temple.

"We can discuss that after. Who took you?"

"I d-didn't know him." She shuddered, rubbing her arms.

"Did he tell you what he wanted?"

"He wanted to know about the lounge and my job here. He would . . . he would . . ." She hiccupped. He lost her again.

"What did you tell him about my lounge?" Calliope's voice lowered threateningly. She was about to lose it. I leaned back to enjoy the show.

Asher gripped one of her hands and squeezed. "Focus, Daniela—"

"Ruby," Tobias corrected.

"Ruby. Can you tell me anything about the male that took you? Hair color, eyes, anything at all?"

She seemed calmed by his touch. She sniffled in and nodded frantically.

"Um, he—he was tall, a deep voice." She licked her lips. Was it the same male that was after our Cat? "He was—"

"Wrenhaven," Tobias snarled, standing.

A sudden boom rocked the walls. The male still standing by the exit shoved through, leaving it open behind him. A cacophony of screams echoed, mingling with the stampede of footsteps.

Calliope was already up and through the door.

Ruby gripped onto Asher's arm, sobbing.

"Please take me with you, he'll kill me." She sobbed. Asher gently shook her off, leaving her on the couch, curled into herself.

"We need to get back home," Tobias said. I followed after him with Asher at my back. We wove through the maze until it spit us back out at the main bar floor. A vampire smashed face first into Tobias. Blood leaked from multiple lacerations on her body. That was the only look I had before she was gone.

Chaos erupted in the Saphire Lounge. Vampires worked to tamp down literal fires dispersed throughout. A male dressed in military grade garb, slammed his stake into the chest of a female vampire. Blood smacked my cheek from the exit wound at her back. By the sluggish movements, the male was human, and he'd missed her heart.

"My shirt," Asher whined from next to me, his fingers rubbing frantically on the red stains. "This is limited edition."

"Let's get out of here."

Tobias and I were on the same page. A similarly dressed figure flung a stake at Tobias with speed and skill that a human would never have achieved. Tobias caught it before it slid into his skin.

"Close call." Asher smirked. Tobias tossed the stake at me and avoided another blow. We closed rank, placing ourselves back-to-back.

The attack came from vampires and humans. In the madness, they were visually indistinguishable until they fought. This attack was coordinated and meant to confuse.

A broadly built one came at me, slashing with impressive speed.

I slammed my hand through his chest and ripped out the heart. The attacker crumpled into dust. I flicked some of him off my fingers. In a swift crouch, I swiped the long metal pike he'd been stabbing at me. I rubbed off some of the blood from the tip with the bottom of my shirt. Nice and sleek.

"A little help here," Asher shouted, ducking and weaving from the stakes being stabbed at him.

I slashed the pike-like weapon into one of his attacker's throats. Blood burst from the carotid vein being punctured. That one was human.

Still, they kept coming and we hacked, slashed, and ripped.

"They keep spawning," Asher huffed.

The drag of the coming day made my movements sluggish.

A stake sliced into Asher's chest, missing his heart by a hair. He staggered and ripped the wood out. "Ow," he huffed.

I plucked the attacker coming at his back. I grabbed the neck and squeezed until blood and meat burst under my hand.

"Shit," Asher hissed and snapped the human's neck he held. He swayed and pitched over.

"Help," Calliope screamed, making a beeline toward us.

"You best get out of here, it's the end of this place," I mused. She bunched the front of my shirt. I would have slapped her away if her eyes weren't shifting side to side wildly. I extricated myself from her hold.

"No. Please you have to help me," Calliope screamed. I scooped Asher up and tossed him over my shoulder.

"It's over, Calliope. You lost the place," I said, arranging Asher's legs to the side so he wasn't hitting my cock.

"No!" she screeched. I raised my eyebrow.

"Leave this place or you'll end up dust." Her eyelids were struggling to stay open. Soon she would give in to the sun as Asher had.

Tobias matched my stride. We stepped over bodies and limbs.

"Leave Jax a message letting him know we will not be home tonight," I said to him. He rubbed his face.

"Done already," he said, low. "We need cover."

Tobias swept his gaze across the madness. The bludgeoning continued. I would have gladly stayed to participate, if the drag of the sun wasn't coaxing me to get to shelter.

"Asher's Progeny lives on the east side, let's go there."

I nodded. "We'll have to go on foot."

Pieces of wall crunched under my boots. I climbed through the hole and into the night. It spit us out to the side of the building.

"Round to the back," Asher slurred, but I was already on the path. I kept my focus on any approaching threats.

"Wrenhaven must also be behind the attack on Crimson Nights." Attacking us and now Calliope?

"You know what that means," Tobias said.

This was war. "A vampire world in strife will never allow Catalina peace. They will come at us, ruthlessly."

My lips thinned. What was worse, war could be fought in many ways. I preferred a violent one opposed to the political upheaval all this would cause.

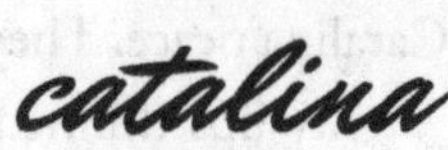

catalina

HOW LONG HAD she been hurting me? My vision faded around the edges. Every breath I took sent fire down my body. I hurt *everywhere*. Jax held my limp hand.

He took hold of my thumb.

"I am sorry, Kitten," Jax croaked. My lip trembled. I kept hold of his blue eyes. My body hurt so much.

I couldn't have stopped the screech if I tried.

Jax's face crumpled. He grabbed the next finger—I think. I couldn't distinguish between them because everything hurt so much. Snap.

My ears rang, turning my screams muffled.

A choked sound escaped Jax.

"Please, just kill me," my voice trembled. Red spilled from the corner of his eyes, leaving a faint redness along the path it traveled to his chin. He grabbed the last fingers and, with a crack, finished the job.

Bile rose. The sour taste settled on my tongue, and I gagged. Vomit made it's escape.

"Turn her head, she'll choke," Jax snarled. Imogen only laughed that tinkling laugh. Everything sounded far away.

I weakly coughed up, liquid trickling from the corner of my mouth and the nasty taste mingled with blood.

Asher was going to be pissy about his sheets.

"Kill me," I slurred. His face was a blur. Good. The look on his face almost hurt as much.

A clang broke through my ragged panting.

The shutters trembled and descended. It would be morning soon.

Imogen stretched her arms up with a yawn.

"Time for bed, we can continue this in the morning," she announced cheerfully. She clapped her hand on my already stinging cheek.

I wouldn't last much longer.

"What did you do to the others?" Jax barked.

She looked at him, hand on her chest.

"Nothing at all. I would never harm them." She almost sounded offended. "But you have nothing to worry about. They are otherwise occupied. Now, sit pretty and do not move from that spot. You are not to release her. Or touch her." With that she turned, the length of her skirts fluttering around her ankles as she disappeared through the open door.

"Catalina. I'm compelled to do as she says." Like humans were to vampires. Just how Asher had stood by the orgy.

I struggled to move my heavy head. The taste on my tongue was awful. I clawed back to consciousness.

"Is that her ability?"

"No, it's because she's my Sire."

I hummed. I floated on a bed of nails. Pinpricks across my

body hurt like I was being stabbed with mini swords. So many things were broken. So much of *me* was broken.

"I shouldn't have—" his eyes shuttered and his nose scrunched from how hard he closed them. I pried my eyes open. He looked so off. So dejected. So defeated. I shouldn't feel sympathy, but I couldn't help it. I didn't want him in pain.

"Tell me something?"

"Anything," he said it like a vow.

"How did you meet her?"

He went quiet and I waited, because what else could I do? Finally, he spoke.

"Asher sold his body. I thieved." His lips twisted bitterly. "Until I tried to steal from the wrong group." He paused. "She appeared like a vengeful goddess."

Ouch. His eyelids began to lower. "That's what I thought when I first saw her. I was close to death, the stab wound to my throat caused me to slowly bleed out on the dirty street. As I lay there, half dead, she arrived. I believed she was my savior. She offered me strength by turning me and I wanted the same for Asher, so she changed him for me."

He struggled to keep his eyes open.

"All she wanted was to use me." He went quiet. "I realize it now, Kitten. I fought this crippling urge to make you mine . . ." His voice faded and he fell into his vampire slumber.

The sun had risen. Now that he was no longer aware, body-wracking sobs exploded from me. I lay in sweat, vomit, and blood, hoping for death.

TWELVE

catalina

I ROLLED over in my bed and stared at the ceiling . . . I could move! Had it all been a nightmare? I popped upright and almost smacked right into Bastien's face.

"Bastien," I cried and threw my arms around him. A sob wracked my body, and I buried my face in his chest. "Bastien," I repeated. Even though I was in the dream world, my body still kind of hurt, like it felt the shadow of what had been done to me.

I pulled back to get a better look at him. Haziness at the edges of my vision made it difficult to see my surroundings.

Bastien's red eyes weren't wild or blank.

"Can you understand me?" my voice cracked.

"Yes, Little One," his voice vibrated in my chest it was so deep, immediately the sound of his voice called my rapid pulse.

"Help me. Imogen won't stop." My voice cracked.

He sneered, tensing under my hands.

"Imogen?" he hissed and the awareness faded from his eyes.

The walls were suctioned into a black hole. Wait, no, not yet—

"Kitten," Jax's voice floated into my consciousness, ripping me fully from the dream.

I blearily blinked. I tried to sit up. But fire blazed up every inch of my body, narrowing in on the pain from my stomach. I dropped back onto my back with a whimper.

Imogen leaned around the doorsill with a grin.

"I'll be right with you. Just handling a few things," Imogen said and disappeared again.

I cinched my eyes shut. I hadn't died in my sleep.

"Kitten," he hissed again.

"Mhm, leave me alone," I whined. That blessed sleep felt too good. There was no pain there.

"Catalina. Look at me." He snarled, "Catalina!" The panic in his voice dragged my eyes open, but it felt like weights were tied to my lashes.

I turned my head toward Jax.

"What?" I said, moodily.

"You need to try to get out of here."

"Let me sleep," I slurred.

"No," he hissed. "Do not sleep."

Whatever. Everything would be fine . . .

"Tell me about what hurts."

I sighed and pressed my lips into a thin line. Was he trying to be funny with me right now?

"Everything," I said dryly.

"Catalina, get up."

"I can't, Jax," I said sadly—defeated. I was just a human. Weaker than them. Even if I could move now, I didn't want to. I whimpered, "Sorry for being a weak human."

Jax closed his eyes, becoming very still.

BASTIEN

I SNARLED, ripping into my skin. Bloody jagged wounds opened up to my wrist. I had wasted time. My anger had catapulted me into mindlessness once again.

I had no way to determine how long I had been indisposed, since I dream walked. The chains weakened me. I would not be able to free myself.

There was another way. Gritting my teeth. I stood and swept my attention across the bedroom. That device on the edge of the counter . . . I had seen Tobias use it.

My vision blurred.

"No," I snarled. *Do not lose focus*.

I lunged for the electronic communicator. I clumsily swiped it open. This seemed like a speaking telegraph of some sort. The upside-down images prompted me to flip it. I studied the surface and pressed on the little button with the word 'contact' under it.

The madness crept over my thoughts. The odd device faded in my vision. I clicked on the first name listed. Asher.

The thing beeped on the other end. I held it an arm's length away.

"Who is this?" The device spoke at me. It worked like a Reis telephone.

"Return," I snarled more than said. I struggled to control my vocal cords.

"Who is this?"

"Come back," I hissed, clutching my head as I bowed forward.

"Bastien? How the—What the fuck is going on—" The voice became unintelligible.

My human! My gums burned, prompting my fangs to burst free. I clenched my hand, shattering the device as the madness overtook me once again.

catalina

"PLEASE," the crack in his voice forced me back to the present. Jax's voice wouldn't let me rest. I wanted to shout at him, but I just had no energy for it. Couldn't he leave me in peace? "I beg you, Kitten, *wake up*."

The desperation coating his voice ripped me to the surface and I fought to open my heavy eyelids. At this angle, with my chin lolling closer to my chest, my gaze fell on Imogen near the door. She stood frozen.

She suddenly moved to the end of the bed.

"You beg a human?" Imogen hissed. "You lower yourself to one?" Her infuriated gaze was on Jax.

"Let her go," he responded.

"You beg?" she spat. "*You* begged this maggot?" She appeared at my bedside. A fist flew at my face.

My nose cracked and blood flooded my mouth. Tears came like a torrent, and I cried out. Using my non broken leg, I tried to scoot back, but she grabbed my foot and crunched it in her fist.

My scream came soundlessly, and everything faded.

"Kitten," Jax shouted from somewhere much too far away.

I must have lost consciousness for a second. Pressure settled over my chest.

"How could they want a worthless human?" Her poisonous words didn't even touch me. I was already floating away. Pressure on my chest made it difficult to breathe.

I forced my eyes open to find Imogen sitting on my chest. Her eyes glinted with a frightening sheen. I choked on blood even as it leaked from the corner of my mouth.

"Jax, tell her she's worthless." Another slap that made my ears ring. Vomit rose again.

"She's worthless," he gritted out.

"Don't be cute, Jaxon." She hissed and gripped my chin, forcing my neck to twist to the side. "Tell your little human."

His wide eyes flicked side to side like pinned prey.

"You are worthless." The words sounded ripped from him.

"That no one could want her," she continued.

"No one could want you." Even though it wasn't him, my agonized brain just felt pain. Tears spilled from the corners of my eyes.

Her clawed hands wrapped around my throat and her other one yanked the top of my hair, so my head straightened.

"I want to see life flee your eyes."

Her hand joined the one around my neck and her fingers pushed into sensitive skin, cutting off my oxygen.

"Imogen," Jax snarled. "Let her go. I'll do as you wi—"

"Quiet." He shut up at her order.

My heart stuttered and my lungs seized. I thrashed under her, but didn't manage to budge her.

A cell phone rang, breaking through my choking gasps. She did not let go. The ringing fell away then started up again.

She snarled and lifted one hand. The slight movement allowed me to suck in a breath. She fished inside her corset and lifted the phone to her ear. Her eyes widened and a sneer curled her lips. She shoved the phone back in her bra.

"Looks like our fun is over."

Imogen's eyes met mine. In a sudden move, she rammed her hand against my side. A loud crunch took my breath away and I could only whimper. Pure, searing agony blinded me.

"No," Jaxon bellowed.

She turned her head as if listening for something. My next breath wheezed, and an alarming about of blood spread on my tongue.

"Bingo, I managed to rupture her lung." Her grin spread. "None of you will be able to heal her from that in time."

I coughed, spraying blood across her face. She looked down at me in disgust and swiped the back of her hand across her cheek, smearing red across it. Imogen lifted off me and moved to peck Jax's temple.

"You should have stayed faithful." She clicked her tongue. "I best not see any of you with another female. You are welcome to try and save her Jaxon. It will amuse me to watch you try." With that, she was gone.

I coughed again. Liquid continued to trickle from the corner of my mouth. There was so much pain. I whimpered. If that bitch wanted me to suffer a slow, painful death she succeeded. My vision faded.

A palm brushed my hair back.

"No, Catalina." Jax's face swam before me. He sounded so heart wrenchingly desperate.

I watched him through swimming eyes, my blinks became more and more difficult.

A copper taste coated my tongue.

Jax, I mouthed and hacked up more blood. His fangs sank into his wrists, and he shoved his wrist against my lips.

"Please," he croaked, looking at me, his shoulders bunched as he hunched over me. "Drink. Quickly." Tears traveled down his face, and the red-tinged liquid dripped onto my cheek.

"I can't," I struggled to say. It sounded like nonsense. I gurgled up more blood, no longer able to keep my eyes open.

I was so lightheaded.

"Please, hold on Kitten. Please."

asher

I DROVE the car onto the sidewalk, scraping the bottom, but I didn't give a single fuck.

I hadn't had time to explain myself to Tobias or Ren. I would have had to return for them, but I'd shot Tobias a text. He had to have seen it on time, there was no other choice. Hitting the brakes, I careened to a stop in front of the gate, the wheels fishtailed, and the bumper slammed into the brick wall framing the gate. Bastien calling me should have been impossible, but it was something to worry about later. I shoved open the car door so hard it cracked and dangled to the side.

Movement caught my eye. The gate swung open, and Imogen flounced through with a huge grin on her face and blood splattering her porcelain skin. I was in her face within seconds, my hand lashing across her face.

"What have you done?" I snarled. She clasped her cheek and then looked down at her palm with her eyes wide on the blood staining her palm. My nails had caught her cheek, ripping her open.

"Do not move, not one inch."

My body stiffened. I struggled against the invisible compulsion gripping my body.

"Free me," I shouted.

Her lips quirked.

"No. I want you here, suffering. Knowing that you can do nothing as she dies in the arms of Jaxon."

"Imogen," I snarled. "Free me."

"I saved you from the slums you and your brother came from. I made you a predator. And this is how you both repay me? I would kill you now, but I want you to live with knowing you will never escape me. Both of you will suffer. And it all starts with the dead bitch upstairs." She began to walk away. I tried to turn, anything, but it was no use.

"No," I roared as her tittering laugh disappeared. Helplessness ate my insides. "Catalina!" I tried to move my fingers, but nothing.

I staggered forward so suddenly I almost tipped face down on the cement. Catching myself, I was up at the front house and zooming into the foyer.

A deep, soul-wrenching tormented bellow echoed from upstairs. I was in my room within seconds. My veins went cold. Jax huddled over the bed, clasping Catalina to his chest. Her legs spread limp under him, her spine curved up where he held her to him, but her head . . . it lolled—lifeless.

No. Impossible. I blinked. No, she couldn't be dead. Imogen was just trying to set me off. But why wasn't she moving?

I was shaking my head as I approached.

"Pet?" I croaked.

Jax turned and hissed at me, his eyes blood-red. He clutched her tight to his chest, backing away like he was guarding a meal. Her body flopped in his arms.

"You're going to hurt her." His arms tightened around her even more. If he continued like this, he would split her frail human body in half. "Release her—now. We can help her, brother," my voice lowered cajolingly. Jaxon didn't back up when I approached this time.

Red faded from his eyes and a stricken look crossed his face. His eyebrows furrowed and he looked down at her. "I-I tried to give her blood. I tried." He trailed off. Her face was smeared with blood to the point of it being unrecognizable. My nose burned and the pressure spread to my eyes.

I gingerly touched my face.

I had not cried since I was a human. I slowly slid my arms under her body, taking her from Jax and propping her up more securely.

"She's not going to die," I said, resolute. She would not die. I nodded, agreeing with myself.

Jax dropped to the chair beside the bed. He fixed his attention on the wall across from him. He didn't move.

"You will be okay, Pet," I said to her, smoothing her hair.

Her death wasn't an option. She would beat the odds and turn into a vampire. I would not be able to survive her leaving me, I would not want to. Bruises littered her body, and her body was broken down—weak. I lowered her onto the mattress.

"Catalina," I whispered near her ear. "You will be okay. I will take care of you." I stretched out her arms at her side. "We'll get you cleaned up."

ASHER HAD NOT RETURNED for us in the car. It was supposed to be a minute long wait, but time stretched more than it should have.

"Something is wrong."

Ren grunted, standing at the threshold of the duplex.

"Darius, give me your car keys."

"Yes, Sire." Darius hurried away, and was back within seconds. He tossed Ren the keys.

"Let's go."

I followed Ren to the truck, and he revved it on. The tires bumped and bounced across the asphalt.

"Did you bring your phone?"

"No," Ren answered. And I'd left mine in the basement room. I ran my hand through my hair. Asher wouldn't disappear like this without reason. Ren cruised beside Saphire Lounge and our vehicle was gone.

"He would not have left us unless Catalina called," I said.

Ren grunted in agreement, and he sped onto the main road.

With the way he drove, he had us at back at the manor in record time.

"Fuck," he muttered.

The vehicle we'd taken to Saphire Lounge was half on the embankment.

"What has Asher done?" He pulled up behind the mess Asher made. A few bricks had chipped off the wall and lay scattered across the asphalt.

Ren was already out of the vehicle, and I was only a step behind him. Upon entering through the wide-open door, there was silence. Ren slowed, and then climbed up the stairs to where we'd cuffed Catalina.

"That's right, you are going to be just fine, *Älskade*," Asher's cooed words echoed from his open door.

I entered the room a few steps behind Ren. He seemed to be speaking to a sleeping Catalina.

"She doesn't have a pulse," Ren sounded confused—lost.

She wasn't dead. Impossible. Ren's thoughts slammed into me, mixing with my own horror and disbelief. Fire played along his fingertips. Jaxon hadn't moved an inch. Like a statue, he stared at the wall, catatonic. No thoughts came from him.

The scent of her blood lingered in the air. A pile of rolled up sheets sat on the floor at the end of the bed. Even though they were bunched up, her blood stained the material.

I returned my attention to Catalina. My shoes felt glued to the ground. I took a step, and then another until I stood beside the bed. Asher sprawled against her, on the side Jaxon sat frozen, he caressed her damp hair. She wore a silk red slip that matched his pants. He picked up her palm and pressed it to his cheek.

"Once you wake, I'll get you the best blood I can find," he

cooed at her. Her face didn't twitch. I reached out and glided my finger across the bridge of her nose. No breaths left her lips or nose. Her chest did not move in the way I'd become used to. Bruises bloomed on her face as if they'd been painted on.

Asher moved and the mattress bounced. Her head flopped to the side and blood trickled from the corner of her mouth. I staggered back, as if a physical blow had landed on me.

I did not understand.

Think.

I doubled over. *I must think*. God. I hissed out a breath.

"You'll be a sexy little vampire won't you." I focused on Asher's voice. "Maybe blood-mad, but we can find a cure."

She would turn?

"You gave her blood?"

"I found her with Jax. She was already out, but there was blood on her lips." Asher touched said lips with the tip of his fingers. He turned to look at me, and his eyes were slightly glazed, as if he'd lost grip of his mind.

I turned to Jax.

"Did you feed her blood before she died?" My voice sounded breathless even to my ears. "Answer me," I bellowed, but Jax did not even twitch. I gritted my teeth.

"*She* did this," Ren's voice ripped through the room. "Where is that slag," Ren snarled. "You can fucking read minds, why did this happen?" He almost burned a hole in the ground with all the pacing. Fire lined his hands.

"She fooled me." My lips felt numb. "She fooled us."

"Not me," Asher snapped. "I let you convince me to talk Cat down. To harbor that bitch."

"Why are you so calm?" Ren was suddenly in my face. He shoved me and I staggered a few steps back. My lips thinned. It was my fault. I'd caused this. I gritted my teeth. "Tobias, she will not get away with this. You understand?"

I side stepped him to get Catalina back within view.

Imogen had done this. I'd fooled myself. Made myself believe she was hurt and had truly been distraught.

Imogen had tricked me. She, more than anyone in this world, understood how to shield her thoughts from me, but I had not expected such a vile, repulsive trick.

I sneered.

But she would not fool me again. Imogen was done.

She must have had Wrenhaven torture her for the believability. She'd accused him, but the attack on Saphire Lounge—all of this was connected.

I had been blinded.

"Where are you going?" Asher shouted at Ren, but he was already gone.

Ren left the room. He would hunt her down.

I slowly made my way back to the end of her bed and dropped on the mattress, every bone in my legs giving out on me.

"Isn't it interesting how this little thing ripped our hearts out?"

I studied Asher as he caressed her, talking and cooing at her like she would understand. "Somehow, we love her."

Awe filled his voice. We weren't meant to love, so when we cared for something, the devotion that came from that could not be matched.

This clenching in my chest whenever I saw her, or how I wanted to hold her at all times. This was not normal. I had been with my Coven mates long enough to see their hunger for her was just as strong as mine.

Obsession bloomed to more, until she had her little fingers deep inside us and around our cocks.

I studied her slack features. The little half-moon eyes smiling up at me. I did not want to live in a world she did not exist. I would not.

"We have to prepare—"

"For what exactly?" Asher whirled on me. I thinned my lips. "We are not staking her," Asher snapped. Jax still did not react.

"We are not," I said in agreement. We would keep her with us even if she was blood-mad.

She had to make it. She would beat the odds and turn into a vampire, even if bruises littered her body and her bones looked out of place.

I settled in to pray for the first time in a long time.

SIXTEEN

ALL OF IT WAS CONNECTED. Whoever attacked did it knowing we had come to Saphire Lounge. I had no doubt Imogen had a part, but who informed her we would be here? There were too many options: Calliope, Alistair, anyone under Calliope—too many enemies crowded closer and closer. And the percentage only grew.

"I don't know anything," the snarled words dragged me back to the male bound by shackles before me, he kept eyeing the brass knuckles I'd slipped on over a protective glove. I'd had them specially made—with more steel than brass in the mix.

I stared back. I had no desire for levity.

He wore the same garb as the rest of the attackers. I'd found him huddled in one of Saphire Lounge's storage closet.

Blood dripped off him at a steady pace. His face was a broken mess from the damage my brass knuckles inflicted, but he'd given me nothing. No information, no details. I flexed my hand into a fist. I could tell he hurt, because he took gasping breaths every other second. But as much as he tried to act nonchalant, the fucker was tense and hurting.

"Where is Imogen hiding?" I repeated.

"I don't know what you're talking about," he croaked. He spat blood on the floor.

I grinned, flashing my fangs.

I swung again and again and again. A layer of his cheek skin hung off his face. His eyes flickered side to side. He was clearly in agony.

With each of my attacks, he became limper, until the chains wrapped around his torso were all that held him up. He coughed and a gurgle of blood trickled from the corner of his mouth.

They would suffer. Each and every one that had even the slightest part in hurting my female. I sneered at the pathetic creature struggling to keep his eyes open.

Cat was much too soft for this world. Everything vampires were not, and now she lay on a bed—

I wrenched my thoughts away from my weak human. As it had every time, a suffocating pressure compounded on my chest.

The door creaked open. Only one person had entered since I'd arrived at Calliope's, dragging this piece of shit behind me.

"You've been at this all night. You need to hunker in for daylight," Calliope said hesitantly.

I whipped my head around to face her. She stepped back, her eyes wide as they scanned me. She feared me.

As she should.

"I set up the bedroom closest to this room—"

"I'll sleep here," I responded. I would be unaware to the world regardless. A cement floor would do nothing to me. Once I woke up, I would resume my investigation.

I would rip him apart with my hands. Little by little. Until something useful came from him. And if not, I would use the violence to distract myself from the suffocation eating me alive.

I SWIPED my bloodied hand on my similarly bloodied jeans, then turned Asher's doorknob. I would have nudged it with my foot, but blood stained them too.

Slowly entering, I found everyone in the same position they had been in before I left last night. No one had moved. My steps echoed across the room, until I stopped a few feet from *her*. I kept my attention fixed on Asher.

"What have *you* been doing?" he sniped, derisively dragging his eyes down my body. His arm hovered above her stomach as if to protect her from me.

"Trying to find answers," I spat back at him. Unlike all of them.

"We all have different ways of coping, Asher," Tobias intoned. His eyes were closed, head resting on the headboard, and hands laced over his stomach.

Was that what we were doing? *Coping*. My lips twisted bitterly.

"Still hasn't moved?" I grunted, jerking my chin toward Jaxon. "You could be helping me hunt." I kicked his chair, and it screeched on the ground, but he did not react.

Asher was the only one that kept talking. Jaxon and he should switch spots. I raked my fingernails against my scalp.

The squeeze in my chest wrapped around my neck like a noose. What was this *feeling*?

"You're worried," Tobias answered, eyes still closed.

"Stay out of my head."

Tobias said nothing in response. I'd take it as an assent.

"Her bruises are disappearing!" Asher exclaimed.

I wrenched to look at her. That pressure in my chest pulsed, forcing me to take a breath.

I scanned her limp body. My hand lifted, as if with a mind of its own.

"Do not touch her with all that blood on you."

I clenched them into fists and studied her tan, silky skin. Even stretched out, her leg held an unevenness. I'd broken enough humans to understand Imogen shattered her bones internally. I scratched at my chest and breathed in hard. The purple staining her face turned yellow, then disappeared. The slice across her eyebrow became smaller. It was so slow that it took a while, but I stayed fixated on staring. We all did.

Asher yanked up her sleep gown, exposing matching underwear and her belly.

Whore was scribbled across her skin. The edges of the injury split wide. Imogen had gone deep into her skin until the edges curled.

I breathed in again, and this time my shoulders shuddered. I hadn't looked at her since I'd first seen her bloodied, broken body. I hadn't seen *this*.

A snarl left my lips, instinctively, violently. I would make Imogen suffer at my hands. How vile—

They were disappearing.

She wasn't decomposing. At this point she would have had to be decomposing, but she wasn't. There was no putrid, dead body smell.

My legs gave and I dropped to my knees. Another breath

exploded from my mouth. The compounding force on my chest pulsed like a living thing. My fangs exploded out from my gums.

She was not gone. I had a chance to find a cure to blood-madness and bring her back to me.

catalina

A FEVERISH BURN coated my flesh, narrowing in on my gums. It hurt as much as the pit in my stomach.

I jolted upright with a scream, slapping at the fire ants stinging my flesh.

"Cat?"

I whipped my head toward Ren. Everything burned. It felt like I was crawling out of my skin. I whimpered. Ren stared at me from a foot away. He was the only one in . . . I was in Tobias's bedroom.

"It burns." As soon as I focused on the ache, it flared painfully. My eyes watered and I whimpered. "Ren, help me." I clasped my face like rubbing my jaw would abate it, but it did the opposite.

His eyes widened, but he still hadn't moved.

I huddled into myself, hugging my stomach. Every inch of me burned as if fire ran through my veins. He was suddenly leaning over me, his face near mine. His brown eyes were wider than I'd ever seen them as they scanned mine.

He smelled so good. I licked my lips and narrowed in on

Ren's throat. That was where the scent radiated pungently. Such warmth. I wanted it inside me.

Once I had the thought, I lunged at him, wrapping my arms around his shoulder, clinging to him like a monkey. My gums stung and I attached my mouth to his throat. Liquid aphrodisiac burst onto my tongue.

"Argh!" Ren grunted, stiffening. He tasted so good. I moaned, squeezing my thighs around his waist as he straightened. He jolted back, taking me with him. The burn subsided to the sweet taste traveling down my throat. I gulped again, savoring his blood.

What was I doing? I was conscious of my actions, but I didn't want to stop. I just wanted to drink. It was the only way to soothe the agony in my throat.

My fingers speared through his hair, and he moaned, hands flexing on my hips.

Yes. Yes. Give in.

He stopped trying to shove me back and his hands settled, squeezing as he moaned. That same fire flared to my sex, blazing a path down. I arched my hips, grinding on his abdomen.

"Catalina?" The gasp yanked my eyes open. Asher gawked at me, and it was enough to pull back the cobwebs masking my will power. I ripped through them, focusing on Asher's shock. What was I doing? Sweetness spread on my tongue, but it came from Ren's throat. I reeled and ripped my mouth away from his neck.

I dropped to my feet, agilely, and stumbled back until I fell on the bed and crawled until I huddled against the headboard.

"What was that?" I gasped with horror. "I am so sorry, Ren." I didn't know what came over me. Red painted the sides of his neck, along with the deep imprints of all my teeth.

"Catalina?" Asher repeated but this time with awe. He slowly approached, stopping a few feet away. I put my hand up, as if I could stay him. The bed bounced under my cringing body. I kept trying to sink into the headboard like it could hide me away.

"Asher?" I rubbed my finger above the skin covering my aching gums. The area felt sensitive.

Asher wore silk lounging pants. I looked down at my night gown. We matched.

"Did you do this," I muttered, disgruntled as I waved a hand from my clothes to his. I caught a peek at red staining my fingertips and I gawked at the blood that had come away from my mouth. I looked back at Ren and the bite marks under a thin layer of blood. "W-why did I bite you?"

Ren seemed to have become a statue. He only stared.

My thoughts raced. What was happening? Why had I bit him? Why had I liked the taste? Asher moved forward again.

"Stay back," I shouted, choked. "What's happening to me?"

"Your eyes didn't stay red." So, we're ignoring my question?

"Why would my eyes stay red?" The burn had been assuaged the slightest bit, but that wasn't the only pain. I pursed my lips and something sharp stung the inside of my mouth. I curled my lip up and gingerly touched my teeth. Why was my tooth sharp? I gasped and slid my finger to the other side. Another slight protrusion. The pad of my finger stung suddenly. I flinched, drawing it away from my mouth. Using my tongue, I felt my teeth. I'd felt this sharpness. It was an awful lot like fangs before they extended. My stomach dropped and I lifted my wide eyes to Asher.

His shoulders moved with a breath. He grinned so wide it looked like it hurt.

"Tobias," Asher shouted.

He appeared moments later. "He's still not responding . . . Catalina?" He scanned my face, devouring my features. He was suddenly leaning over me. On instinct, I flinched, and when I peeked through my lashes, I was off the bed and cringing against the wall. I seemed to have flown to the other side of the room.

My knees became weak, and I used the wall as a perch. Slowly sliding down, I sank onto the floor.

What happened? Although a haziness coated my memories, they slammed into me full force. Imogen had killed me. I scoffed, shaking my head. Jax begging was the last I remembered. She killed me and I turned. Wasn't I supposed to be blood-mad?

"I'll get blood bags and order a feeder," Tobias announced abruptly, hurrying away.

"I changed?"

Jax had managed to get me to drink his blood? But I'd been throwing up. I couldn't have swallowed. Blood—*mmmmm*. A burn in my gums intensified and my mouth was suddenly crowded.

Asher knelt before me, awe in his widened eyes.

"H-how?" I thought I was supposed to be blood-mad. "You th-aid I couldn't be a vampire. This makes no th-ense—"

"Calm down, Pet,"

Calm down? *Calm down*!?

I shoved my fingers through my hair, pushing it back from my cheeks. I'd turned into a vampire. I pressed my hand to my chest. What happened to my heart? My heart didn't beat at the normal rhythm. It felt sluggish under my palm, giving one pump every minute or so.

"Did you guys lie?" I threw out accusingly. Ren stepped

beside Asher. They stared at me with as much confusion as I felt. "If you didn't want me to be a vampire, you could have just said so."

My body felt different—and I hadn't breathed?

I sucked in a breath and the plume of sweetness entered my nostrils, wrenching a moan from my mouth. That burning returned with a vengeance. With my next blink, I had Asher flat on the ground with my legs wrapped around his waist as I bit into his throat. I sucked down another mouthful of that sweetness I couldn't get enough of. He moaned, his body jerking under me. My hips ground down, applying pressure to the need between my legs. My eyes slowly closed, and I drank more.

His taste spread on my tongue, assuaging the burn. I whined against his throat, rubbing myself over the hardness under me. I took another drag from Asher. A sharp shout left him, and his body jerked so hard he bucked like a horse.

I breathed in again and a tart, salty smell, just as good as the one in my mouth filled my nose. The warmth in my belly allowed me to pull back.

Asher panted under me, unmoving as he watched me make my way down his body until I pressed my nose over the waist of his pj pants. I yanked the hem down. His cock bounced free. A fine layer of slightly pink cum coated his cock. That was what smelled so good.

I flicked my tongue across the bobbing, wet tip.

Asher groaned, his hips jolting up and forcing his tip between my lips. My fang sliced the side of his cock. Blood touched my tongue. I gasped around him and fitted my mouth lower, until the piercings on the top of his cock knocked against my teeth. I sucked, tasting both the salty and sweetness of his essence.

He choked on a cry.

I rubbed the flat of my tongue against the bottom side of his shaft. I sucked again, dragging blood from the small cut.

So suddenly, his cock pulsed and then he exploded on my tongue, giving me more of him. I moaned, swallowing every drop he offered. He continued to pulse, filling my mouth again, until it overflowed and spilled from the corner of my lips. I bobbed down to collect what escaped. His tip shoved against the back of my throat and his piercing clinked against the back of my front teeth.

Asher's hips bucked and he shouted. I slowly lifted my head, studying his flushed face and his heaving chest.

"Fuck," he grunted, gripping the base of his cock and squeezing. His eyes cinched shut and he gritted his teeth. I dropped my attention to his straining cock. More beaded at his tip.

Then I was attached to it, licking it away.

Asher hissed out a breath and the salty, delicious smell ratcheted up another notch. I wrapped my mouth around the tip and another jut of release coated my tongue. My eyelids lowered and I hummed. He tasted so good.

Asher whimpered, yanking my eyes up to his slack features.

"Holy, *ffff*uck." He almost seemed in pain.

I pulled up so fast he jerked. I hovered my hand over my mouth.

"I'm th-orry," I croaked. Fortunately, my palm hovering over my mouth covered how I couldn't stop licking my lips.

"I brought the blood bags," Tobias announced, entering with his arms hugging a sleek container with bags in it. He slowed and scanned my position over Asher's drained cock. Ren watched us with utter shock. He'd watched all of that. My eyes dropped to the bulge in his pants.

I ripped my eyes away before I went mad and attacked him too. Clearing my throat, I tugged the front of Asher's pants over his cock.

"Th-orry," I repeated and fell back on my ass.

"Oh, *Älskade*, you never have to apologize," he croaked, his arm flopping over his face. Asher remained laying on the floor, taking a few breaths every other few seconds. Practically panting by vampire standards.

I gingerly touched my fangs. A slice opened on the tip of my finger.

"How do I make *th*em go away?" My face warmed. I pressed my palm to my cheek.

Ren knelt beside me and cupped the back of my neck, guiding my face up to look at him.

"Stop clenching your jaw like that. It's like turning your head. Think it and do it." I glared at him. Very helpful. Still, I focused on my teeth so much that my face ended up scrunching.

"It-*th* not working," I cried. "And I can't th-top li-th-ping."

The corner of Ren's lips quirked. I glared up at him and he quickly smoothed his expression.

"It's fucking adorable," Asher remarked unhelpfully from his sprawl on the floor. He folded his arms under his head, watching me hungrily. I took a breath. That sweet scent emanated from all of them. Focusing on Asher, my gaze dropped to his growing bulge.

"You're going to be the end of me," Asher hissed and his cock throbbed under his pants. I licked my lips, cutting my tongue on a fang while I was at it. The sting was enough to distract me from his blood.

"Close your eyes and think about how it'd feel for them to go back into your gums," Tobias offered.

I closed my eyes, imagining and imagining. If I took a breath, maybe it would help ground me, like when I was human. I sniffed again and the delicious scent filled my nose, flaring the burn to life. I lunged at Ren. Tobias pressed his finger against my forehead, stopping me an inch from Ren's throat. He slowly pushed me back. The moment was enough to force me to hold my breath.

"I don't mind," Ren glared at Tobias.

I curled my legs up and hugged them.

Tobias crouched and pulled one of those bags out. Blood sloshed inside the clear bag. Using his teeth, he ripped the edge off the bag and held it out to me. My hand trembled and I pinched the spot next to the hole. It was so weird the way it swished in the bag. Licking my lips, I brought it to them.

It was just like drinking prune juice.

Before I gave it more thought, I fit the ripped edge against my mouth and gulped it down. The taste hit me. I recoiled and spat it out. My eyes widened. Blood spattered all three of them. They looked shell shocked as they gawked at me. Except for Asher, he wouldn't stop chortling.

My mouth flopped opened and closed. I looked back down at the bag. What was wrong with me? Why did it taste so gross?

My mind was a mess. I clenched my eyes shut.

"Love?"

Gray eyes hovered so close. The color of the one that hurt me. I flinched, ending up against the wall, feet from him. My hands flattened against the wall, and I slid down it until I was on my butt again.

Tobias's eyebrows were furrowed, his hand still outstretched.

"I . . ." He looked a lot like Imogen. His jaw flexed, seeming to understand my unsaid words. His hand dropped to his side, and he took a step back. I ran my tongue against the back of my teeth. Shoving to my feet, I stalked from one end of the room, to the other. Their heads comically followed my path.

I stretched my jaw side to side. My teeth felt bigger, but that was an illusion, it was just my brand-new fangs.

"Why did you lie to me?" I took care with my tongue and enunciated my words.

"No one lied to you."

"You thh—ssaid no female could be turned. That if they somehow managed, they'd end up blood-mad." I pointed at myself. "Explain this?"

"We are just as shocked as you." Asher sat up, stretching his arms up.

They'd cleaned me up, and by the matching set, I would bet everything that Asher dressed me in the silk night gown. Honestly, I was surprised he'd put underwear on me.

"If you all thought I would turn and be blood-mad, then what?" My eyes widened and I whirled on them accusingly. "You were going to keep me here, trapped and contained like Bastien." I scoffed. "What? Just let me sit on the sidelines as you found a different—"

"No," Asher and Ren said at the same time. Tobias remained quiet and in the background with his expression stiff.

"We would try to search for the cure again."

"Right," I snorted. "You could have done the same with Bastien."

"Bastien *called* me." Asher was off the floor and approaching me. The urgency in his tone . . . Right, they hadn't heard him talk like I had.

Asher frowned.

"You're not shocked?"

"He spoke to her," Ren said so sure, coming to the right conclusion.

"Why didn't you say anything?" Asher questioned.

"Like you guys tell me everything." I shrugged. Bastien didn't come searching for me because he'd been trapped. When vampires shared their blood, they could find the human that drank from them. It had never been because I was somehow immune to their ability. It was because Bastien had been locked up.

But now as a vampire, no one would find me. Not even the three in front of me.

I rubbed the back of my neck. Pounds kept compounding on my shoulders. They dropped under the weight.

"My body feels heavy," I stretched my arms experimentally. It felt like weights were attached to my wrists.

"It's the sun, Love." As if on cue, the shutters clicked with their decent. I swayed, then nothing—

catalina

THE VIEW from my window left a lot to be desired. I ran my fingertips along my windowsill. Crimson Manor stretched up intimidatingly. If only I'd known. The edges of my vision blurred. This was a dream.

I whirled and faced Bastien. He sat on a large recliner that had not been in my room when it existed. His ankle was crossed over his knee.

I pressed flush with the wall as I eyed Bastien. His white, long hair smoothly rested around his shoulders as if he'd artfully arranged it around himself. No robe, no nudity, instead, he wore slacks that had a neat crease down the pant legs as if ironed. His white button-down had a few buttons opened at the collar, allowing me a view at his golden skin.

"Little One." His voice seemed to vibrate inside me. Why did he sound so pleased? He grinned at me, his long, sharp fangs fully on display while his red eyes studied me. "Come now, we do not have much time. Free me before they wake."

"How are *you* awake?" His dark eyebrows flicked up and he stood slowly. He stuffed his hands in his pockets. He seemed so unfamiliar to me, yet I wanted to run into his arms. The shirt moved over his wide, muscled chest.

"Why do you back away from me?" He frowned. "I will never harm you, Beloved."

I squeezed my lips tightly together.

"How are you awake?" Even now, in this dream world, I struggled to move my mouth.

"Although the sun's will is a heavy burden, if you work at it, you can—"

He staggered back and gripped his temples.

"I do not have much time—" His words turned to snarls and he whipped his head toward me with a snarl. Showing me the Bastien I knew.

He came at me.

Wake up.

Up. Up. *Up.*

My eyes struggled to open. I stared at the ceiling. It felt like I was drugged. It was dark in here, except for a night light coming from the bathroom. It was enough for me to see. I sluggishly turned my head to one side and Asher's limp body rested at my side, while Ren was on my other. We were still in Tobias's room and the shutters were still down.

My plan was still the same as before I turned. Heading out of here, but now that I was a vampire . . . did I still need to be part of a Coven? Were there rogue vampires?

Questions I could ask Alistair.

I rolled to my side and my arm flopped on Ren. He didn't twitch. Using him as a perch, I gripped his arm and pulled myself up with effort. I gritted my teeth and managed to topple off him and land on my knees.

Weight tried to force me back to the ground. I trudged

forward, shaking my head. It took three tries to turn the doorknob, but I finally managed. Then came to a stop. The sun was no longer high in the sky, so it didn't spill across the middle of the hallway. At least there was no direct sunlight.

I staggered to Asher's door. Moving was getting a pinch easier, but weight still shackled me.

I froze at the entrance. Jax sat in the same spot, his head hanging forward. He was deep in his day sleep. Leaving the door cracked, I dashed to the wardrobe. The clothes swung side to side. The bottom drawer, where my pjs were housed, was semi-cracked, with clothes peeking up from the top. I shucked the silk nighty, pulled on leggings, a bra, and a hoodie. And then dug my hands behind my sweaters, where I'd shoved the backpack.

I hooked it on my back. My skincare! As soon as I thought to go to the bathroom, I was already halfway there. I gawked at my reflection. Right, I no longer needed it. I looked like me . . . but smoother? At least my face. Just like the rest of their skin, smooth, almost poreless. Yet, my hair frizzed. I frowned at myself. Guess that didn't come with the newly-fanged vamp package. Plucking my frizz-resistant hair oil, I staggered from the room. The low cast of the sun had all but disappeared. Pressure lifted from my limbs and no longer hindered my stride. I had run out of time.

Running down the stairs, I dashed through the hallway.

The clink of gears reached my ears, then a hum as the shutters moved. I had to get out of here. Even though I wasn't human anymore, they could wrap me in chains and keep me here. My steps could hardly be heard with how fast I moved toward the kitchen. I was across it, through the hall, and past the French garage door next. Metal still littered the floor from the car I'd taken a bat to.

I ran to the sleek sports car closest to the exit ramp. I would feel bad about taking it with me, but they had a garage filled with them. Hopping in, I revved it to life, dropped my bag in the passenger seat, and without giving it a chance to warm up, pressed on the accelerator.

I sped up the incline, taking a sharp turn away from the main garage. A large door blocked my exit. I yanked down the vizor, but there was no button to make it rise. My sluggish heart squeezed, causing my pulse to jump. With each throb, my gums began to sting, like me panicking caused the borrowed blood to burn through me much faster. I only caused more hunger by panicking, but I couldn't help it. Sounds of birds chirping, the rustling leaves . . . I could hear it.

I stepped on the gas pedal. There was no other choice, I had to break through, hopefully it wasn't strong enough to stop the car.

I flexed my hands on the steering wheel and squeezed my eyes tightly shut. God, please let me make it. My fangs popped out and I gritted my molars. Metal ripped in a screech as the hood of the vehicle took out the garage door. I peeked through one eye as the tires bounced over wreckage. Taking a sharp turn, I peeled out until I burst onto a side street.

The scent of exhaust and rubber permeated my senses, stinging my nostrils. I coughed. I preferred not breathing.

Zooming past the house, I drove through the streets until I reached the first freeway. I sped up. Getting as far as possible was the goal, then losing this car. Maybe I could take a bus out of town, but I needed money. I sank my teeth into my lower lip.

My sharp incisor split into my lip. A hiss exploded from my mouth at the sharp stab.

I flicked my tongue over the blood. Nowhere near as good as Ren's blood. The base where my fangs pushed out from my gums throbbed. I focused on the next exit sign and just drove.

Forty miles away from Crimson Manor, I slowed to get off the ramp.

I had to stop somewhere I could make a call. Pulling into the first shopping center I came across, I parked. I left the keys in the ignition and hopped out. I wouldn't be able to take it with me anyway. It could tie me to them, and I didn't want to be found.

The hum of voices and chatter melded into a cacophony of overwhelming sounds. I grabbed the car door to brace myself and cinched my eyes shut. A call first, focus on making the call.

I used to distract myself from oncoming panic attacks, so this would be easy. Sucking in one breath, I coughed at the inordinate number of smells singeing my nose. I stopped breathing again.

The noisiness tapered away. I'd grounded myself.

"Miss, are you okay?" I whirled to face an old man. His eyes widened and he reeled back a few steps. A sour scent overwhelmed my nose. I'd spun around too fast. He backed up until he was almost running away.

If I'd taken care of how fast I moved, I could have asked to borrow his phone. I made a beeline for the closest store. A restaurant. A kid around Peter's age stood behind the podium playing on his phone. I came to a stop in front of him. He didn't look up until I cleared my throat.

He jumped and his phone shot out of his hand. I managed to catch it in a smooth motion. His eyes widened on mine and immediately dropped to my breasts. I quirked an eyebrow, waiting for him to look back up at me.

I flicked at the buzzing near my ear. Was that a fly? As much as I swatted, the sound didn't go away.

The guy rounded the podium and stood in front of me. The buzzing grew. I frowned, eyeing his flushed face. It wasn't a fly; it was his heart. As soon as I figured it out, the rapid beat thrummed rhythmically. My eyes dropped to the fluttering at the base of his throat.

A faintly spicy scent reached my nose.

"Thank you for catching it." He took the phone from my lifted hand. His fingertips touched mine and he breathed in audibly. "A table for one?" Interest piqued his eyes, and he looked over my shoulder then returned to me with a little smile.

I hummed my assent, rubbing my fingertips against my gums over my skin.

"Can I use your phone?" I made sure to keep my hand hovering over my mouth to block my fangs.

"I'm sorry, we don't have any that are for customer use."

"No," I burst out, then clamped my lips shut. The guy eyed me hesitantly.

Could I compel him to let me use it? Would that make me a bad person? I pursed my lips.

I brushed my fingers through my hair, and the frizzy, wavy locks flowed around my shoulders. His eyes fixed on my boobs again.

"Please?" I lowered my chin, trying to look as harmless as I could.

Desperate times.

His nostrils flared the slightest bit, and he swayed toward me.

"Okay," he breathed, holding it out. I snatched it and quickly dialed Alistair's number.

The line rang . . . and rang. Right when I was about to give up, he answered.

"Yes?"

"Alistair Blackthorn?" Silence on the other end. "This is Catalina Herrera." Still silence. "Crimson Coven's Pet," I whispered lower. The guy didn't give me a weird look so he must not have heard me. "We met at Calliope's weird party."

"Ah, yes," he purred. "I never thought I would hear from you."

I licked my lips. I could do this.

"Can you come get me?"

Silence, then a chuckle on the other end.

"Hmm, I don't think so. Your males left me quite a few scathing voicemails. My Coven, along with my manhood, were threatened if I took you in. We were supposed to reschedule our meeting, but they haven't returned my call." He was a chatty one. I tapped my foot on the floor and lifted a finger toward the guy eyeing me questioningly. He was beginning to get impatient.

"Please—"

"I have no desire to endanger my cock—"

"I-I'm a vampire now," I whispered.

"Where are you?" His tone changed. I put the phone on speaker.

"Where are we?"

The guy rattled off the address.

"Did you get that?" I said to the phone.

Alistair hummed.

"I will be there momentarily."

"Thank you," I breathed in relief. He didn't respond, so I lifted the phone to look at the screen. He'd already hung up. I pursed my lips and handed it back.

"Uh, thanks." He side-eyed me. That spicy smell coming from him disappeared. As he rounded behind his podium his whispered words seemed shouted at me, "Weirdo hot girl." He shook his head.

I pursed my lips.

"Can I get a booth?"

He waved me through the entrance. "Take any available." He was already back to playing on his phone.

I selected the booth at the furthest corner, where I had my back fully to the wall. I slid onto the bouncy faux leather. A server approached.

"Can I get you anything?" she chirped, cheerfully. I smiled, close-lipped, in case my fangs chose to make a showing.

"Coffee and pancakes please and that's all." She typed on an electronic pad, presumably sending the order over to the kitchen.

"Coming right up." She left, and I was alone. I laced my fingers together and squeezed my hands.

My gums burned . . .

I scrubbed my palms over my face and groaned. Well, I had what I wanted. I was a vampire, but of course I was some screwed up version of one. Human blood didn't entice me a bit. But vampire blood? My gums pulsated.

catalina

"CATALINA HERRERA."

I jumped, banging my knee under the table. I'd been so absorbed in blocking out the clanging coming from the kitchen, the conversations of customers, and the crying child across the restaurant that I hadn't noticed him. Alistair slid into the booth opposite of me. I slowly let out the breath I'd held and took care not to breathe through my nose. Wouldn't want to try to eat the vampire I had to rely on.

I turned toward the waitress's footsteps as she approached with my food.

"Here you go." She set the plate of pancakes and steaming coffee in front of me.

Her gaze settled on Alistair and her eyes slightly widened, her body visibly reacting. Sure, Alistair was attractive, but I had too many Crimson males on my plate. I was good. My gaze fastened on the pounding at her throat. I fixated on it.

Alistair tapped the back of my hand, and it ripped me out of the alluring sight of the pounding at her throat. Only the knowledge that I wouldn't like the taste held me in place.

"Let me know if you need anything," she said, but my attention was already on the food before me. I couldn't take a breath yet, but steam floated off the top of the coffee. Would it taste as good as I remembered? I licked my lower lip and grabbed a fork and stabbed it into the pancake. The tips clicked against the plate with a loud crack. A fissure opened up to the edge of the ceramic. I pursed my lips and scooped some pancake with the prongs.

"You shouldn't do that," he drawled.

I stuffed the fork into my mouth and it clinked against my now sharp incisor. I winced, but clamped my mouth shut. The food rested on my tongue like sawdust.

My stomach turned. I frantically looked around for a napkin.

Alistair sighed and tugged a folded piece of cloth from his pocket. He held it out for me. The material was smooth against my fingertips. I winced apologetically and turned to the side to spit the food out.

"Uh, thanks," I croaked and bundled the sullied cloth on the plate. I cleared my throat and lifted my chin. "What will you want from me?"

He leaned back, lacing his hands on top of the table.

"What is it *you* want from *me*?"

"Safe harbor. To get my questions answered."

His eyebrows raised.

"Perfect. I have a few questions myself." He went quiet, studying me. "Why don't we start here, how did you turn without becoming blood mad?" He cocked his head.

I pursed my lips.

"I don't know."

"Does it have something to do with you being immune to compulsion?"

"I don't know," I repeated with more frustration. He hummed. "Can a vampire be without a Coven?"

"Sure. But I do not recommend it." He grinned. "Strength in numbers. If you're a lone vampire, anyone can take you out without repercussions, but if you have a Coven, you have the Sire's protection."

"Oh." So many decisions to make.

"Many things to think about," he said and checked his phone. "I can house you until you decide."

Relief dropped my shoulders. I wouldn't have to sleep in a bus station tonight. I nodded and was already standing.

Alistair raised an eyebrow up at me.

"You'll have to learn the art of blending in."

I laughed nervously, shuffling from foot to foot as I looked at the mess I'd made on the table.

"Can you let me borrow money?" I asked sheepishly. I could feel the blood I'd fed on rush to my face.

His eyebrow lifted and he pulled out a worn leather wallet. After rifling through it, he tossed a hundred on the tabletop. "Thanks."

Alistair wasn't so bad. I trailed a few feet behind him. With each step to the exit, thoughts pounded against my skull. Was this the right choice? Maybe I should go back to Crimson Manor? This would be my fresh start, but did I want that?

The glass door clanked shut, and I followed Alistair. He headed directly for the SUV parked along the curb.

I rubbed my eyes. I didn't know what I wanted, but I was already down this path. At the very least, I could take a moment away from *them*. Their demanding presence—their overbearing tendency to steam-roll me.

I grimaced. That was what this boiled down to. I was hurt. And I wanted to do the same to them by taking myself out of their equation. And I knew that would hurt them because they cared for me.

Alistair opened the back door and waved me forward. I came to a screeching stop. Familiar leather seats. A knee moved and then Tobias came into view.

"Get in here, now, Catalina," he hissed. Oh, he sounded pissed. My fangs extended and I clicked my teeth at him.

I whirled and now faced Asher with his eyebrows drawn down, eyes slitted and lips twisted. Turning to make another run for it in the opposite direction, didn't work either. Ren sneered at me.

I was trapped.

That was why Alistair was so accommodating. And while he was at it, he was getting information out of me.

"You liar!" I whirled on him. "I take back all the positive things I thought about you."

"They would have savaged my Coven with theirs. I couldn't risk my people." He winked. This duplicitous—I threw myself at him, hissing and yanking at his shirt, trying to reach his throat.

Arms banded against my stomach, and I was pulled away. I smacked at the arm and tossed an elbow back.

"Fuck," Asher grunted in my ear.

"She's spitting mad." Ren sounded too happy. I stiffened and turned my glare toward him.

Ren lifted his hands, as if he were turning himself over. But that stupid godforsaken grin didn't leave his face. Before I threw myself at him, I cinched my eyes closed. This was much more aggressive than I'd ever been. I didn't like it, but my God, they brought it out of me. I went limp in Asher's arms and when he softened, I pulled free, smacking his roaming hands away.

"Catalina," Tobias snapped from the car, sounding more cross than I'd ever heard him. I clamped my mouth shut and glared at all of them with my arms crossed. "In the vehicle."

"No," I said stubbornly and began to walk.

"Pet," Asher snapped. I yanked my arm away before he grabbed it.

Alistair watched with a smirk on his face. I took a beat, breathing in through my nose before I could remind myself not to. Sweet, sweet blood.

Blood flowed in their veins. The one they stole from others to keep alive, but there must be some chemical change when it goes into vampire bodies, because human blood wasn't delicious like vampire blood. My body tensed to spring.

I gritted my teeth. I could do this. Stay still. *Stay*!

I flung myself at Alistair, the closest vampire. My fangs burned to sink into his throat. I bunched his jacket and hauled him down. His throat was *right there*.

Hands plucked me away from him. Thrashing, I managed to land a headbutt backwards. Whoever held me grunted. I flailed toward Alistair, but he was already feet away from me. I turned my attention to the arm around my belly. Shoving at it was useless.

"Ren, let me go!" He continued dragging me to the SUV parked at the curb.

"Shh, Pet, you're calling too much attention to us."

"Had she been trying to feed on me?" Alistair's eyebrows raised.

"Don't be ridiculous," Asher scoffed from somewhere behind me. I was too busy pushing against the edges of the car. My arms were spread, braced against the open door, while my feet braced against the bottom edge.

"In. Now," Ren snarled in my ear. He swept my legs out from under me and shoved me in, face first. Tobias caught me before I face planted.

Ren swatted my ass. I yelped more from the shock than it hurting. Ren pushed his way in, making me crowd against Tobias who curled his arm around my torso.

"Don't," I bit out, pulling from his arms and plopping down on my butt with my arms crossed. Asher slipped into the passenger seat and turned to look over the middle console. "You're not going to be able to keep me forever. I'll fight you, and this time, I'll hold my own."

Silence as they all exchanged looks. Tobias sighed. He was likely listening to their thoughts.

"I'll kill Peter if you try," Ren said, so casually. Of course they would threaten Peter. That was how they got me to do what they wanted last time.

"I'll kill myself," I gritted my teeth, holding his gaze. He stiffened. "I'll slide something right through my heart. Be nothing more than dust."

No smugness in sight. I had him. I raised an eyebrow. "Stop threatening my brother."

His lips thinned. A beat, then another passed.

"Fine," he hissed.

"Fine," I hissed back, my fangs popped out in the same breath.

Ren's tense face relaxed, and he gripped the back of my neck, pulling me to his lips.

"You have no right being this sexy."

I smacked my palm on his face and used it to push back from him. He gawked at me, but I only crossed my arms again.

"We need you," Tobias murmured. I didn't turn to look at him. Every time I did, I thought of Imogen.

"You seem fine without me." The corner of my lips twitched. "Why don't you go look after Imogen, if you *need* someone." Tobias stiffened beside me.

"You are the one we want." I slowly turned to look up at Ren. I forced myself to look unimpressed.

"Words. Words. Words. From you guys, it means nothing."

Ren's face slowly became red. He was going to blow, but I didn't care.

"Please, Pet." Asher's eyes widened earnestly. "We need your help. Jax is unresponsive."

"He's deep in his mind. He thinks you're dead," Tobias interjected. "He's suffering." It was a slap to the face. My lip warbled, but I quickly stiffened it.

"He's not my problem. None of you are my problem," I ripped the words out from the hurt balled inside me.

I gritted my teeth.

"I'm going to fuck the tantrum out of—"

"No," Tobias cut off Ren.

Ren and I stayed glaring at each other. He bristled.

"We're done forcing you, Catalina," Tobias said it like he was pissed. I laughed.

"She's fucking laughing now?" Ren snarled out.

Tobias shoved open the door and held it for me.

"What are you doing!" Asher shouted.

"We are not disrespecting her desires any longer." I jumped

out of the car. The sound of shuffling came from behind me, but I took another few steps.

"Please," Asher croaked. I slowed. "Don't leave us." Another pause. "Don't leave me." The raw whisper reached deep into my chest.

I took another step away and clenched my hands. I could disappear. Leave them behind . . . I wanted to. Then why couldn't I move my feet?

Their faces rifled before my closed eyelids. I didn't doubt that they cared for me. It was never that. It was the kowtowing to Imogen. I slowly turned to look at them. Every inch of them strained. Ren steadily stared at me—waiting. Tobias had his back to me, his shoulders tight.

"I did wrong by you. By our Coven," Tobias said. "I should have taken Imogen somewhere else as soon as she arrived."

"You should have," I managed to push from my tight throat. An ant crawled across the cement, a piece of food in its mandibles as it struggled up the incline.

"Do not blame everyone else for my mistake." Tobias paused. "If you order me to, I will leave Crimson Coven." I whipped my head toward him, but he still had his back to me, so, so stiff.

"You should have told me Sire's can order their Progeny and force them to obey."

"An oversight. I would apologize for that, but you will never be placed in such a situation again."

"Have some sympathy for us. We have not navigated being a human or human emotions since we were one," Ren said.

"Sympathy? That's funny coming from you."

Ren scowled and leaned against the car. Their please filled my head, mingling with guilt. Jax thought I was dead?

I sighed and slid into the backseat. Ren took a seat on my other side, forcibly scooting me to the middle seat. I tried to elbow him, but he dodged it. Asher clapped Tobias on the shoulder, and it jolted him to life. Asher went to the passenger side while Tobias slid into the driver seat. He pulled away from the curb.

"I left the car over there." I pointed at the vehicle as we passed it.

"You wrecked the—" Asher cut himself off and groaned. His phone was already out, fingers flashing over it. "Talia will drop it off later."

I shrugged.

"I'm staying on a trial basis." They didn't respond to that. I scooted to the left to get some space from Ren, but he was once again flushed to my side once I managed to get distance. "You need to apologize to me."

"For what?" he grunted.

"Are you serious?" I scoffed. Asher's head whipped back and forth as he followed our argument. "How about being a dick, throwing me around, almost draining me, *burning my stuff*?"

"No, I don't feel apologetic about burning down your house. It brought you closer to me." What a twisted load of bullshit. He was always like this: unrepentant, demanding, casually cruel. The burn in my gums became unbearable. I lunged, sinking my teeth into his arm.

He hissed, but all that faded away as I sucked in a mouthful of the sweet blood. On the first swallow, the fire in my gums and belly abated. My knees perched on the edge of the seat, while I held his arm to my mouth. I'd moved so fast that I struggled to comprehend it.

There was no resistance from him. I dragged in another pull of blood. Nectar filled my mouth, and a moan hummed in my throat. Warmth flooded my system, settling in my belly. My eyelids lowered and I floated on a cloud of bliss. On my next swallow, I breathed in, taking in his scent.

Ren groaned, his palm settling on the back of my head to keep me to his arm. He didn't need to force me into it. I wanted to drink my fill.

"What the fuck is this?" Ren croaked, and his hips shifted. "Being bitten shouldn't feel like this." His words were veiled behind a muffled curtain. I breathed again so I could taste him at full capacity. A throb pulsed through me. Heat flowed through my veins. Maddening lust. I pulled up, yanking my fangs from his arm. The wound continued to leak. I sank my fingers into his hair as I tossed my leg over him to straddle his waist.

I pressed myself so tightly against him that my front was flush to his and I struck again, sinking my fangs into his throat. The layer of skin gave under the sharp incisors with a satisfying *pop*. He jolted up, driving his hips up, so his cock ground against me with the layer of jeans between us. Blood flowed into my mouth. I settled on the bulge, my hands slid over his body, traveling between us.

I slipped my finger into the waistband of his jeans. With a quick jerk, I ripped the seam. His cock bobbed free, the wet tip grazing my hand. I wanted him in me. Now. I yanked at the hem of my pants and a rip traveled down the side. With a quick jerk, my bottom half was bare. Pulling free of his throat, I hoisted myself up to perch on his tip, staring down at his parted lips. His eyelids were lowered so much that I only saw a sliver of his brown eyes.

Ripping clothes was definitely simpler as a vampire. I hovered above him, his tip pulsating at my entrance. Blood trickled from his bite wounds, but I especially liked the one at his throat.

Their biting kink was really beginning to make sense. I was mesmerized by the blood slowly traveling down his neck. I licked my lips and leaned down to tongue the droplet before it bloomed into his shirt.

Ren hissed a breath out. He tasted so good, and I loved his sounds. His thighs tensed. Before he could beat me to it, I sank onto his shaft. He eased inside me. My channel fluttered around him, clasping onto him. I moaned and nuzzled my nose into his throat. I inhaled, savoring him, then sank my fangs in again. This time, much gentler. He grunted, jolting his hips upward to drive inside me.

A burst of blood filled my mouth, and I hummed, attached to his throat. I moved my hips in a gyrating grind on him while drinking him. He muttered nonsensically and it was music to my ears. Lust was a breathing, living thing inside me and he fed it so easily.

I slid my fingers into his hair, tugging at the strands and scratching my nails into his scalp as I gripped strands. I didn't let up grinding on him. His cock filled me up, prodding at my cervix with each writhe. Ren jerked under me, the thrusts as uneven and frantic as mine. I drank more from him. Liquid spread on my tongue, and I drank every bit of it. I lapped my tongue against the bite wounds and Ren hissed.

He took hold of my hips and slammed me down. Again and again until the steady rhythm of our flesh meeting filled the car. Fire blazed through my sex and the growing sparks exploded. I cried out against his throat. My hips moved frantically. As if my body had a mind of its own. Ren shouted and his throat vibrated against my lips.

"Yes," Ren hissed. He pounded into me so hard.

I cried out with each demanding thrust, and it threw me over the edge.

My channel gripped him greedily—draining him. His release warmed my core. He jutted his hips upward again, releasing more into me. I wound my arms around his head, riding out the wave of pleasure.

Bliss.

Orgasms were already phenomenal, but holy shit, this sensation wrecked me, like every nerve ending had been set aflame. Electrical pulses shocked my system. The sudden passionate swell abated, like the lull of the receding ocean.

I went limp in his arms. Ren petted my spine, running his hand from the top of my head down to the small of my back.

The burn had been satiated.

I wiggled on top of him. We were so wet. I pushed up and a gush of moisture dripped down the insides of my thighs.

"Clean me off," he said gruffly. His hand wrapped around my neck and guided me down. My knees settled on the floor of the car and Ren spread his legs. His shaft glistened with our mingled need.

I wanted his cock in my mouth. Wrapping my hand around the thick base, I smoothed my hand over the steel shaft, gliding it up and down the wetness. The tip pulsed, red and straining. I leaned forward and ran my tongue across the little hole at the tip of the mushroom head.

His taste filled my mouth. The same sweet and salty taste

mingled with another taste. Mine. I hummed with him in my mouth.

Ren groaned and I peeked up at him to see his face slack jawed as he stared down at me. His eyelashes pointed downward, so they seemed longer from this angle. Cleaning the rest of the liquid from his tip, my fang grazed against his shaft.

I shied away, but he forced my head back down.

"Bite me," he ordered.

I widened my eyes up at him. That sounded like it would hurt.

"Bite m—" I angled my head slightly and sank my fang into the shaft. This time, there was no pop. His blood flooded my mouth, and I curled my hands into fists at his thighs. I sucked, drawing more blood into me.

He shouted, fisting my hair in his hands. I pulled up slightly, giving him a second. His chest moved in a harsh breath again.

There was a perk to blowjobs. I didn't have to breathe anymore. I grinned.

"What's with that evil grin?" Ren murmured, swiping his thumb across my lower lip.

"You taste good."

"Insatiable, needy, Cat." He blinked slower, then his head lolled.

"Ren!" I shouted, propping his neck before he tipped to the side. "Asher, what's wrong with him?"

A hand settled on my shoulder, and I followed its guidance, until I crawled to the side. Asher leaned over the center console. He gripped Ren's hair, forcing his head up.

"Be gentle," I croaked. Had I killed him? Asher let Ren's

head go and he tipped to the side, forehead thumping on the window. Horror struck me. "I killed him!"

I clasped my face and tears had already begun to drip down my face. I shuddered on a gasp. "Why are you laughing?" I cried, shoving Asher's shoulder so hard he pitched back. It only sent him deeper into a laughing fit. He managed to catch himself with a palm to the shoulder of the seat. "What have I done?" I cried, my hands hovering near my mouth.

"He's not dead," Tobias said, meeting my eyes in the rearview mirror. There was an odd tone in his voice.

I whirled on Asher who finally calmed enough to swipe the corner of his eyes.

"He needs to feed, Pet." Another coughing laugh.

I sank my fangs into my wrist.

"What are you doing—no!" His shout came too late. I'd already shoved my leaking wrist to Ren's mouth. Once my blood smeared against his lips, his throat worked. He swallowed and on the third, he clasped my wrist to him.

"Okaaay, nevermind," Asher drawled.

"What?" My slowed heart lurched, but I kept my wrist up to Ren's lips. "You guys need to stop with the cryptic stuff."

Tobias's hands flexed on the steering wheel.

"It's not supposed to taste good," he said.

My lips twisted. My confusion must have been plastered on my face, because Asher said, "Vampires do not feed on vampires."

I blinked, struggling to wrap my head around Asher's comment. "It's seen a little like cannibalism."

I gasped, jerking back so fast my back hit the door and pulled my wrist from Ren.

"You're scaring her," Tobias snapped and yanked Asher to sit down. "And stop popping your head up. I don't want to get pulled over. It's a waste of time."

Ren stretched his neck side to side with a groan.

I settled in the seat beside Ren, watching him while I wrung my hands.

catalina

THE BED DIPPED under my weight. Jax's eyes were closed. He hadn't moved from the chair he'd been in since I ran off.

I poked his chest, but he didn't move.

"Jax?" I said it low at first but repeated his name louder.

Not even a twitch.

I grabbed his arm and shook him.

"Jaxon Crimson."

Asher settled in the bed next to me until his thigh was flush against mine.

"Whatever happened left a mark on him," he said. I scrunched my nose and looked at my hands on my lap. "Want to tell me about it?"

"Not really," I mumbled. I squeezed my hands tight together. I sighed. "Nothing you wouldn't expect. She broke my bones. Laughed about it. Ordered him to do some things to me." I rubbed my intact fingers. The remembered agony was shrouded behind a foggy layer.

"Did she force him to fuck her in front of you?"

My heart jumped and my fingers curled into a fist. I turned to look at him, my eyebrows furrowed, and fangs extended from the gum.

"Since she's been back, did she do that to you . . .?" I trailed off.

His eyes widened.

"I did nothing with her. Nor did Jaxon. But it was coming. That's why the others and I paid a visit to Calliope. After her little stunt, forcing me to watch the orgy, it would have headed that way, if we did nothing."

The crippling fear that prickled over my nerves made me want to lash out. I'd thought being emotional was supposed to go away with becoming a vampire, not feel more intense. I forced my fangs back in and licked my lips. I needed to distract myself before I crumpled on the ground at the idea of Imogen forcing the twins to do things they didn't want to.

The encroaching freak-out faded into the background much faster than I'd ever been able to calm myself down and I compartmentalized it.

So, I felt things stronger, but I could distract myself easier, got it.

"And what did you need from Calliope?"

"A favor."

I lifted an eyebrow. That wouldn't fly anymore. Asher pursed his lips and nodded. "We wanted her to take Imogen in. Then there was an attack on Saphire Lounge." An attack right when they met up with her?

"Imogen must have planned it." It was too perfect. All of it was. She'd had Maddy drug me, then shown up while all the guys were gone. It was definitely a plan. Maddy's part in the situation hovered on my lips, but if I told them, what would they do to her? She hadn't been at fault. Maybe I could wait a bit before telling them, and allow their trigger-happy selves to relax a little.

"Of course she did. I should have never let my guard down." I stiffened, for a moment wondering if I'd spoken about Maddy aloud, but no, he was talking about Imogen.

I could throw it in his face. Yes, Asher shouldn't have let his guard down, but he'd been too busy trying to keep the peace. Both with getting me not to run out of here like a bat out of hell and with Jax's mercurial behavior. It couldn't have been easy for him thinking that Jax would leave with Imogen. I'd believed it, and I was sure he had too.

Jax hadn't made the assumption any less probable with how he followed after her like a puppy. "If we'd had you instead, maybe we would have an easier time with all these emotions. We became used to feeling nothing. Doing nothing but satisfying our whims and accumulating power and wealth."

"The wealth is kind of great." I shrugged. Silver linings, right?

The corner of his lips twitched.

I hadn't moved my attention away from Jax's stiff features. His eyes were closed and by what Asher told me; they'd been closed a while. Asher theorized it was because Jax was sinking deeper and deeper into his psyche.

Was he thinking about losing Imogen? Now that she'd done this, it was clear the others would not stay at her beck and call. Did the realization break him? He'd lose something—either his Coven or his woman. If I were him, I wouldn't want to wake up either.

Thinking about Jax caused the boxed compartment I

stuffed my emotions for him into to start opening. I refused to look at it. I didn't want to poke it with a stick. If I paid attention to it, I would crumple into my sadness.

Once he woke up, he was bound to leave. I rolled my lips inside my mouth. There was the crux of it, I didn't want that. The box in my chest pulsated. I pressed my palm to my gut. It felt oddly like nausea, but yet, not. So weird. I hadn't had time to really take stock of the changes to my body.

No longer was I crippled by the attacks that seized my lungs. Just like when I had their blood, but better and permanent. My hearing, sense of smell—everything became advanced. And the blood. My fangs extended from my gums.

Asher raised a blond eyebrow at me.

"That's kind of embarrassing."

"Blood-boner, Pet?"

I was not a fan of the smirk. I rolled my eyes and turned back to Jax. I'd tried talking to him and then shaking him, now we sat just staring at him. It was kind of strange, sitting here in front of him after he'd snapped my fingers like twigs. He didn't *want* to, sure, but still, the memory was alive and well. As was his pain-filled voice. I didn't doubt he had a small, tiny soft spot for me. He'd given in to the lust between us well enough.

A soft rap at the door and Tobias came in slowly. "Any luck?"

"No," I said, frustrated.

Tobias's eyebrows met in the middle. His gray eyes were focused on the side of Jax's head.

"What is it, Priest?" Asher was suddenly alert, standing as he turned from his twin to Tobias.

"He thinks he's dreaming." Tobias blinked and his

eyebrows raised. He turned to me. "He's with you." He scratched his temple with one finger. "Sitting on your lap—as a cat?"

"I am so confused," I muttered.

"He doesn't want to wake up. He's . . ." Tobias's eyes narrowed. "Happy?" I pursed my lips and scanned everyone's faces. They all seemed put off, like they'd lost something.

"Vampires can dream?"

"No," Asher answered, and his lips twisted. Based off the look they sent each other, they knew what was going on already and it shocked them. I crossed my arms.

"Enough with the cryptic. Don't leave me in suspense."

"Bastien has him trapped in a dreamscape and Jax doesn't want to leave it."

Asher was already halfway to the door.

I hurried after him and grabbed his arm.

"What is it?"

"I'm paying a visit to Bastien."

I puffed out a breath and pushed before him. Bastien couldn't hurt me anymore, but he didn't seem to remember what he'd done while in the dream he pulled me into, or was that a trick?

I fisted my hands at my sides and hurried downstairs. Ren's wide shoulders were already at the threshold. Had he been listening to the conversation? The metal door was propped to the side, dents bending the middle. The wood where the hinges had been were shattered and splinters littered the ground. Ren disappeared.

"We haven't come down since he called me," Asher said from behind me. I purposefully made my way down the stairs slowly. I stopped on the final step and looked up at him over my shoulder.

It must have been after Imogen tortured me. *He'd saved me?*

Asher's lips moved but I couldn't make out what he was saying over the rushing in my eardrums.

"Pet?" His inflection tilted higher at the end like he found me funny. I tore myself out of my thoughts and refocused on him. "Not even two nights a vampire and you're already beginning to lose yourself to your mind." He dropped from the step to stand over me. "Is everything all right?" He was worrying about me when I should be the last thing on his mind, considering his brother upstairs. That wasn't fair to him. I licked my lips and forced myself to nod.

"My mind just wandered." I cleared my throat. "So, what happened at Saphire Lounge?" I tried to keep the accusation from my tone. They hadn't known what planned, so it wasn't their fault. But then again, they'd allowed that bitch in here.

"It was a massacre. We had to hunker down nearby before the sun rose."

"All planned," I muttered. Imogen was meticulous. I hurried through the door. The first to catch my attention was Ren. I followed his focus to the bed.

Bastien reclined against the headboard.

"Took you all long enough." He wore a too tight sweater that strained over his shoulders. I could practically see the muscled divots in his stomach and shoulders. "Hello, Little One."

I pursed my lips and didn't say anything back. Scanning his features, I hunted for any resemblance to the corpse that kept me captive. The emaciated creature had nothing in common with the filled-out male in front of me.

"Are you wearing my clothes?" Tobias asked without inflection to his tone. That was why the too-tight clothes looked familiar. On Tobias's slighter form, they fit loose.

Accusations, hatred, tears—all of it pounded through my mind. Did any of it matter anymore?

Bastien's head cocked, and his attention hadn't swayed from me. "What is on your mind?" It sounded like speaking hurt him with how raspy and deep his voice was. So odd having him speak to me.

Which was super ironic, because this was the version that had control.

"Thank you for calling Asher," I forced from my throat. I licked my lips again. The corner of his lips twitched. The chains around his wrist rattled as he swung his legs over the end of the bed to stand. Even from a distance he towered.

"I believe I should be the one thanking you."

"Me, why?" My eyebrows furrowed. His lips twitched.

"All in time."

I scowled at the cryptic comment. So annoying.

He rattled the chains pointedly.

"Release me." He smoothed his hand down his chest. "And get me some clothing that fits." Great, he was just as demand-y as the rest.

"What did you do to Jax?" Asher interjected. Right, that was why we were down here in the first place.

Bastien messed with the sleeves of the sweater, rolling them up to his forearm so they no longer touched the raw section at his wrists. It looked like he'd already tried to get them off.

"Jax told me what he did to you, so I trapped him in his

mind," Bastien said it toward me but then fixed his attention on Asher. "And you should be thanking me. He was headed down a self-destructive path. If I hadn't trapped him in his mind, he would be out there, fruitlessly hunting down his Sire. And if by chance he found her, what do you think he'd be able to do against Imogen? *His Sire.*"

The answer was nothing and everyone knew it, by the silence Bastien received.

"If trapping him helped get all of you down here." Bastien shrugged. I thought when humans were turned into vampires, some switch went off in their head that just made them callous and cruel, but I felt *almost* the same.

A little blood-thirsty. I would still do anything and everything for Peter. Maybe I'd become just as violent, with time. But what made the most sense was that they were all as messed up in the head even before they became vampires, and becoming a vampire only enhanced those negative aspects. I rubbed my temples. Trying to make sense of vampires would only drive me crazy.

"What did he do to you, Love?" Tobias turned his body toward mine, but he didn't move forward. He'd behaved cautiously since I first flinched from him. He wasn't the one who hurt me, but he'd been convicted. He took another step forward. I didn't move away, and he stepped close, until he stood before me. I didn't want to reiterate what Jax was forced to do. I didn't want to have to defend him either and I knew I would have to. He hadn't wanted to do it.

"He broke all of her fingers at Imogen's orders," Bastien said.

"He what?" Ren said low and tense. I sighed.

Asher gripped my hand and lifted it to his lips, kissing my

knuckles reverently. "Let him out of his mind," Ren's insistence seemed off. His lips curled up at the corner and his eyes took on a far-off look.

Bastien sighed and sat back down. His mouth seemed tighter at the corners.

"I will not."

"Let him go," I forced out. Bastien turned to me and his long white hair moved like a rustling curtain. He scanned my face.

"Are you sure?"

Was I? No, but I still nodded.

"As you wish," Bastien intoned.

"Catalina," Jax bellowed so loud that it reached us in the room.

"I should get hi—" Asher cut off with Jax's sudden arrival.

Jax was suddenly in front of me, his shoulders heaving.

"You're alive," he whispered. Taking my face in his hands, he angled my chin up toward him. His hands skimmed down my neck and touched my shoulders, then down to my hands. "I . . ." He shuddered.

Jax's hands were ripped away. Two forms blurred, exchanging blows. Ren hit Jax so hard something popped. Jax grunted, stumbling back as he palmed his nose.

"Fuck," Jax hissed.

"You broke her fucking hands," Ren snarled. The words hit Jax, and he staggered back. When Ren came at him again, he didn't fight back. He fell to his back with a grunt, taking the flurry of punches at his face. Jax's blood sprayed across Ren's cheek.

I kept holding my breath, because, if I didn't, I'd lunge at them and start feeding.

I gritted my teeth.

Ren held him down, pounding his fists into his jaw with repeated swings and Jax just took it. I struggled to comprehend the violence. I'd never seen them go at each other like this.

Blood leaked from Jax's lip, nose, and eyebrow. A laceration opened on his cheek upon the next hit landing. Ren was going too far.

"Ren!" I screamed and grabbed his arm. I strained and managed to at least get him to look at me. "Please stop."

My eyes continued to drift to the blood splatters. My mouth watered, but I continued not breathing. This confirmed it though. I was still not a fan of violence.

Asher shoved Ren back a step, keeping himself between them. I pinched my nose. A burn had begun in my gums, but I couldn't tear my eyes away from Jax. He lay on the floor in a puddle of his blood. His face had been turned into a bludgeoned mess.

Delicious, sweet blood. I closed my eyes tightly.

"How uncivilized," Bastien commented, lacing his hands on his stomach as he stared derisively down at the two of them. "Now." Bastien paused, he shook his head with a groan. His lip curled and his red eyes flashed up to pin me. The calm, analytical Bastien disappeared. He'd returned to staring at me fixatedly and not speaking. His fangs had extended, and he lunged toward me. The chains rattled around him.

"Bastien?"

He snarled.

Tobias moved and he snarled, beginning to pace the little he could with the amount of give of the chain. He reminded me of a caged tiger.

"Kitten?" Jax stood and swiped the back of his hand across his mouth.

All the blood. Such delicious, sweet blood. It plunked onto the floor with a rhythmic drip. I couldn't help but fixate. Jax swiped the back of his hand across his nose again and blood smeared on his skin. Lickable—

"I have to go." I clamped my hand over my mouth and ran upstairs.

catalina

I SANK onto the stool and placed my elbows on the edge of the granite counter. I sucked down a breath for the first time in a while. The smell of blood lingered in my nose. I closed my eyes, stopped breathing, and fisted my hands. Attacking Jax after Ren pulverized him like that was a line I wouldn't cross.

"Catalina?" My hair fluttered around my shoulders with how fast I turned. Tobias reached for me. Those gray eyes . . . violent, gray eyes. My stomach turned over.

Tobias's hand hovered but didn't touch me. His lips thinned and he withdrew with a frown. It must have been written all over my face.

"Sorry." I placed my hand to my chest, even though my heart wasn't pounding like it used to. He slowly moved around my stool and pulled out the seat next to me. He sank down and set his hands on the counter. He moved with such care; I could tell he did it to not spook me.

I settled next to him. And the more he just stayed quietly studying me, the more my shoulders relaxed.

"You fear me. You fear Bastien."

"It's not fear," I said defensively. "Where are the others?" Was it a method to distract the conversation? Sure was.

"They're giving us a moment."

I only hummed.

Tobias opened his mouth to speak about three different times, but nothing came out.

"Do you still want me?" The vulnerability in the question took me a second to wrap my head around. Tobias's expression was fixed and stiff. Like he braced himself for my 'no'. "I see how you flinch from me." He paused. "You blame me. Rightfully. If I hadn't asked for her to stay, we wouldn't have had this—" He scrubbed his hair. "Catalina. I regret my decisions."

A muscle jumped in the side of his sharp jaw.

I reached for his hand and lifted it in both of mine. His gray eyes met mine, blank, cautious.

"I know you're not her, consciously, I know it. Just for the foreseeable future, give me a heads up if you come up behind me. Your eyes . . ." I licked my lips. "They're the same as hers." And it brought on a searing agony through my stomach. A phantom pain from where she'd carved into me.

"It's not your fault," I finally pushed out. I understood more than anything the love one could have for a sibling. "You gave her the benefit of the doubt, as you should have." He avoided my eyes. I licked my lips. "You rely on your ability. You trust it. She knew that and took advantage."

Finally, he looked at me. "All of this." I waved my hand around my face. "It's a lot." As quickly as the fear had come, it disappeared. He wasn't his sister. "I have a question about being a vamp."

He inclined his head, encouraging me to continue. "I

thought vampires couldn't feel, but everything seems enhanced." I pressed my palm to my stomach.

Tobias leaned until the edge of the island pressed into his back. I sat straight in the stool and still had to lift my chin to stare into his eyes.

"Your negative emotions are emphasized," he began. Bloodlust, hunger, jealousy, irritation. Check and check. "They drown out all other emotions and if it's not that, then it's hunger. Think back to your past. It's almost behind a hazy curtain, yes?" I slowly nodded. "As time passes, it becomes more difficult to hold onto those memories and the emotions that come with them. Vampires do not love because we *cannot*." He brought his hand up, lifting it toward me. Slow enough that I could have turned my head away. His fingertips grazed my cheek.

"It is not easy to pull those softer emotions from vampires, but once you have, they will bond to someone for eternity. We call the one that returns that piece of ourselves a 'Beloved.'" The corner of his lips twitched. "You reminded us what softness felt like."

"Beloved." I frowned. "Is that some sort of magical thing?" I thought they said magic didn't exist. There also weren't any other creatures from stories that existed from my understanding —all the myths came from vampires.

"If you're asking about predestined, or a tether to tie us to you, no. But you were the one that forced us to *feel*." His lips twitched up higher, wrinkling the corners of his eyes. "I supposed there is a magic in that, if you prefer to think of it that way."

"Will I forget how to love?" I frowned. I couldn't imagine losing myself and no longer caring about Peter.

"No. Asher and Jax had each other. You note how they have loyalty to each other? They are also a reminder of each other's humanity. This is why they *feel* much easier than the rest of us." He paused. "You have your brother and *us*, if you choose to stay by our side." He stopped and his eyebrows furrowed. Suddenly looking unsure. I slid off the stool and stood, craving his arms.

"More like you're stuck with us." Asher entered into the kitchen, rapping his knuckles against the broken metal door leaning against the wall. All four of them came in, with a shirtless Bastien bringing up the rear. "Tobias, Bastien was infected when Ren trapped him in a cell with a blood-mad vampire." The way he spat it out was how a kid would tattle.

"What?" Tobias hissed, straightening.

Jax moved fast and appeared in front of me. Blood stained his face, but there no longer seemed to be open wounds. He cupped the bottom of my jaw, turning my head side to side.

"Jax—"

He dropped to his knees and yanked my shirt up. His face was level with my stomach. Blue eyes scanned my skin.

He released a gust of oxygen from his mouth and dropped his forehead to my belly. His golden hair rustled. I slowly lifted my hand and sank my fingers into the strands. He shuddered, arms slipping around my waist and hugging me tight.

I remained frozen from shock. He looked for what Imogen had done to my stomach.

"What?" Tobias's eyes flashed red, and he yanked Jax's shirt. The cotton ripped and a low hiss left Jax. He released me and stood to face Tobias with a curled lip. Although Jax was taller, Tobias looked like he would tear his throat out. And I didn't doubt the damage they'd inflict on each other.

"Tobias." I lifted my hands in a staying motion. Someone

pulled me back from my arm, and I looked over my shoulder to Bastien shaking his head. I pressed my lips into a thin line.

Tobias shoved Jax back, turning to meet my eyes. He looked haunted. I dragged my attention away from him, suddenly feeling so exposed. He'd likely seen Imogen carve '*whore*' into my stomach through Jax's memories. Bastien squeezed my shoulder. I leaned back into him.

Every muscle in my body tensed. What was I doing, taking comfort from the star of all my nightmares?

"Are you well, Little One?" His gruff question soothed the fear that clutched onto my throat. I hadn't moved an inch. I bunched the fabric of my pants in my fist. Squeezed once, twice . . . my shoulders loosened and with it, the urge to take off running.

"Why would you do that to Bastien?" I asked Ren, figuring distraction was the best course of action. Ren crossed his arms, not seeming even a little sorry.

Bastien's lips twisted. "Imogen's orders, I presume."

"You did not hide your plans to leave the Coven," Ren said.

"I was searching for a cure," Bastien snarled.

"And she wouldn't have benefited if you left."

"So, she had me infected." Bastien scoffed with disgust. "I managed to behead the poor blood-mad sod, but he bit me in the struggle." Bastien crowded into me, but he wasn't groping at me like usual. After a beat, his arm snaked around my waist, and he pressed a kiss to the top of my head.

I struggled to swallow. The big, gentle male confused me. For the life of me, I couldn't connect the Bastien I'd come to care for with the creature that kept me trapped.

"If it's truth telling time, I have something to add." I flexed my hands.

"The Pale One I told you all about, the one I thought was hunting me?" They watched me with such focus, not rushing me. "It wasn't him. Imogen has been behind everything."

"She had a vampire trap you?" Tobias narrowed his eyes.

I shook my head. I wasn't explaining this properly.

"No, he couldn't have been the one hunting for me." I licked my lips and spat it out, "The Pale One is Bastien."

Silence.

Bastien's arm slipped off my waist.

"The bastard who kept you captive was him?" Asher's expression twisted with confusion.

"You mentioned he got out once and then he returned looking closer to this?" I motioned behind me at the large, healthy male vampire.

"Ren was the one who found him," Tobias said in agreement. Ren both caused and saved me from it. If he'd never followed Imogen's order—no, I needed to stop. The past couldn't be changed.

"You were there," I said in awe, connecting the rest of it. They'd mentioned Ren was the one who found him but I'd been so wrapped up in who Bastien was, I didn't focus on the vampire who pulled him away from me. "He'd had me pinned a-and you pulled him off me." Leaving me bleeding, for another human to find me and call for help. "Do you remember me?"

Ren's arms dropped to his side.

"I wouldn't have paid attention to a human. I was too stunned at Bastien's change." Ren stepped back, head shaking.

"We believed he'd gorged himself and that had been what began to heal him from the blood-madness. But with each new feeding we gave him, he did not advance," Tobias said.

"That was where he was that entire time we searched for

him? With you." Jax's phrase at the end became less of a question.

I nodded. Asher was in Bastien's face, and his quick movement forced me back a few steps to get out of the way.

"You were why she was so scared." Bastien didn't flinch at Asher's accusation.

"What did I do?" Bastien murmured, eyebrows dropping down over his red eyes. He fixed a piercing look toward me. "What did I do to you?" The question almost sounded angry.

I put my hand on Asher's shoulder and wiggled between them to push him back.

"He doesn't even remember, leave it be. We have someone else to worry about." Asher's jaw line bunched, and he took a slow step back. He grabbed my elbow, keeping me to his side.

"So, if it was never the blood-mad male after you. Imogen is behind it all," Tobias said.

I nodded curtly.

"She had a lot of fun gloating about everything she'd done while she broke me. She also gloated about having someone run me over." She'd been trying to kill me for a while now. "I feel like I should get an award for surviving this long," I said wryly.

"We'll be bringing her ashes to you," Ren vowed. That would mean they would hunt her down. My heart jumped in my chest in a slow agonizing squeeze.

"No. We need to stay far away from that psycho." I shook my head hard. *We*. The word echoed in my head. Were we a 'we'? I stepped back. "You know what, there's no *we*. Jax woke up. It's time for me to go," the words flowed out quickly, almost panicked. I was too comfortable.

All five of them became preternaturally still.

"You're not going anywhere," Jax snarled.

"You don't have a say in anything." I whipped my head toward him and shoved him as I backed away until I faced all of them. They stood across various spots in the kitchen. "Am I supposed to wait until you disappoint me again?" I whispered.

I closed my eyes. Everything became so silent I could have heard a pin drop.

"We'll remove the issue," Ren announced. I met his brown eyes. He crossed his arms. Irritation flickered over his face, but he stayed in place. "The one who keeps hurting you." His eyes focused on Jax.

"You're acting like you never tossed me around or burned my life belongings." There was a desperate edge to my voice. Because . . . because they were convincing me.

"We settled that," he said, smiling so wide his fangs and dimples showed up. He was right. He took accountability in the car. I licked my lips.

My eyes bounced from one to the other.

"Fair," Bastien added, nodding. "If you do not want Jaxon here, he will be forced out of the Coven."

Jax remained silent, like he was too stunned to speak.

Asher sighed and rubbed his temple.

"If this is what you want, Love, we agree."

"What the fuck is this?" Jax snarled. "I'm not going anywhere." The three that spoke studied him. Tension crawled up my shoulders. Asher continued rubbing his temples.

"I . . ." I licked my lips.

Jax's eyes widened with alarm. He was suddenly standing in front of me. His chest heaved once and then again.

"You can't do this," he whispered. "I can't leave. I won't." His nose flared. He slammed his palms against the wall near the sides of my head. He shoved his nose into the crevice of my neck, eliciting a shiver to life.

"I need you," he whispered it almost accusingly. I clenched my hands at my sides. He felt too good. His nose rubbed against the column of my neck.

He'd make me melt into him. I needed a clear head. I shoved him back and ducked to the side.

Jax grabbed my forearm. My throat closed up and I just reacted—whirling, I sank my teeth into his arm.

I breathed in through my nose, the taste of his sweet nectar exploded on my tongue. I moaned and held onto the underside of his arm near his elbow. I ran my tongue over the bite wound to collect blood. I sucked again.

Jax groaned, staggering back, until he sagged against the wall. I followed, holding onto him.

I yanked myself back so fast, I almost fell. My reflexes helped me catch my balance. Jax stared at me, eyes so wide. He panted. My eyes dropped to his hard bulge.

I dabbed my tongue on my lip to collect the rest of his blood.

"I'll bring you her ashes," Jax said, still breathless.

"What?" I shook my head hard. "No. Just leave it be." I just wanted peace.

"She won't let it be, Pet. Especially if she discovers you survived."

"That will anger her more," Ren added.

"Tobias, tell them." Maybe he would be on my side. Sure, it would be more of a selfish reason, but that was fine with me if the outcome was the same. I whirled toward him. His gray eyes scanned my face.

"I agree. She needs to be stopped."

He'd just agreed to kill his sister. "She's crossed too many lines," he continued. I wasn't sure if he was trying to convince me or himself.

"Nothing will happen to us. She's outnumbered," Asher murmured, tucking my hair behind my ear.

"More like two against one." Ren met Tobias eyes. "She's your Sire. You three cannot be anywhere near her."

"In case she orders—" Jax went quiet. He knew exactly what she could order.

My stomach did not feel good. All I wanted was for her to stay away from me. I didn't want to even look at her, but their words rang true. I knew she wouldn't stop coming for me if she discovered I was alive.

She was an older vampire too—much stronger.

"Shh," Jax said, cocking his head. "Do you hear that?" Everyone went silent. The tapping started up again and all of us turned toward the sound coming from across the kitchen.

Tap. Tap. Tap. In quick succession. I started toward it, but Asher stopped me with a touch to my shoulder and approached the door leading to the garage.

Asher's nose flared and he gripped the doorknob. He pulled it open. Maddy toppled face-down on the tile. Asher moved out of the way before she fell on him.

"Maddy!" I hurried forward and helped her turn her head to look at me. Her eyes widened on me and tears flooded them, spilling down and over the duct tape wrapped around her mouth. The muffled talking was intelligible. I couldn't roll her over because her arms were tied tight to her ankles. She'd been trussed up like a turkey until she couldn't move. I dropped to my knees beside her to hunt for the tab end to lift the tape. I smoothed my fingers along the textured surface until I reached an abrasive bit and used my nails to peel it up.

"This is an excessive amount of tape," I muttered, unwinding it from around her head. Finally, at the final layer, I stopped. "It's stuck on your hair." Instead of tugging the tape and her hair along with it, I pulled off the final layer from the other end across her mouth.

She gasped, tears continuing to spill.

"A little help would have been nice." I eyed Asher balefully. He'd watched as I struggled. I moved down to the rope and took hold of it with both hands.

"Why would Imogen leave her tied up here?" Asher asked, eyes narrowed.

"I'm so sorry, she ordered me to bring you the drugged tea." She shuddered, crying until she hiccupped. With a quick yank, I ripped the threads binding her. Her arms and legs flopped out and she groaned. The position did not look comfortable.

"You're right, it doesn't make sense."

I brushed at the bits of fibers that flew off the rope and clung to my shirt. A palm pressed into my spine; I looked over my shoulder at Jax. He hooked his hands under my arm and hoisted me to my feet. He brushed his hands over my clothes. I could only study him in shock. What had happened to Jax and who was this?

I caught Asher's smirk, and he quickly smoothed his face. Maddy bumbled to her feet. I was about to make a comment to Jax about his weird behavior, when Maddy lunged toward us.

She moved in a lagging motion, as if she were under water. I stepped in her way as she lifted a sharp metal stake and swung it so hard it sliced my shoulder open. I hissed, flinching. Shock kept me in place and holding my stinging arm. She swung again, aiming behind me, toward Jax.

I gasped and put my foot out to trip her.

Ren caught her by the wrist, he squeezed until she cried out and released the weapon. It clanged against the ground.

"Don't hurt her," I shouted.

Ren's lips tightened.

"I will not take chances with your safety again."

"Ren! Please," I cried. Jax wrapped an arm around my waist.

"If she is at fault, she dies."

"Fine, but it wasn't her." They'd see, this was another stupid move of Imogen's.

"Look at me." The push of Ren's compulsion forced her eyes up, so she faced him. Maddy's lip trembled. I tried to approach but Jax held me tighter.

Maddy's shoulders tensed and since she faced Ren, I couldn't see her expression.

"Wh-what happened?" she croaked.

"Why did you attack?"

"I don't know what—"

"Tell me." The force of compulsion thickened his voice.

"Imogen ordered me to kill Jaxon Crimson," her voice took on a low, sleepy tone. I knew it.

"I release you from Imogen's compulsion." Her body went limp, and she dropped to the ground. I hurried to her side, crouching.

"Maddy? You okay?" I whispered.

"I didn't want to do it," she choked out.

"How sure can we be that—"

"Stop it," I grated out between my teeth and glared at Jax. "Let's get you cleaned up in my room."

"You're not going anywhere with her."

"Ren, stop!" I smoothed my palm down Maddy's hair. "We might have to cut this off." I told her. I didn't spare them another look as I guided her to the hall. She wouldn't stop shaking.

"I'll keep an eye on her," Jax said to the others. I whipped my head around to glare at him. "I'm not leaving you alone."

"What has happened in my absence?" Bastien's question reached me, as I hurried down the hall with Maddy. I turned all of my attention to her. She wouldn't stop shivering.

TWENTY-TWO

bastien

MUCH HAD HAPPENED in my absence.

"Ordering for you to be infected is too far." Tobias had fooled himself where it came to Imogen, but the veil was beginning to lift.

They knew as well as I did that it would have made her maddened had I left. Imogen enjoyed having her nails in me. I had gone along with it, from boredom, and the concept of a powerful Coven. It was becoming clear that we had joined her for that reason. Other than Tobias and Asher, who were webbed in by familial ties.

Asher continued looking toward the door. Anxious to return to our Little One as I was.

It was a visceral urge that gripped onto my throat. Her presence addicted me, but she seemed raw and on edge.

"Give her a bit more time." I tapped my fingers on my thigh.

What had they done while I'd been incapacitated? Fooled around uselessly.

"Enough with the assumptions, Bastien," Tobias snapped.

"What's he thinking?" Asher asked. The whore was always much too nosy for his own good.

"He believes we have done nothing with our time."

"They are not assumptions," I offered. "You *did* nothing." The edges of my vision blurred. I pressed my palm to the wall to brace myself. If I lost it to my alter ego, there would be no doubt they would shove me into chains again.

"What did you want us to do? We thought gorging you with blood would heal you, but nothing sufficed. There *is* no cure. If you didn't find it with all your experiments, we would have even less of a chance," Asher spat.

"Then explain *me*?" I bared my teeth, pointing at myself. They became silent. "There is a cure. I was simply missing a key component. A component to protect the cells from the virus, one to repair the cells."

Catalina was the answer.

"Is that why she tastes—"

"Clue me in here, you two," Asher glared.

"I believe Catalina carries the gene marker I searched for."

Asher stiffened and he looked toward the hall.

"If that's the case, no one can ever know. She would be a target."

"More than she already is," I agreed, thinking of her feeding on Jax. Feeding on another vampire had always been taboo. Some claimed it was cannibalism. Her blood should not draw us in. "Our little human upstairs has something special."

"And you plan to poke her up with needles?" Asher hissed.

I narrowed my eyes at him.

"I would never endanger her." She meant my life. She was my savior and my Beloved.

"Asher, he will need to test her blood to even see if it is still different now that she's a vampire."

"Of course it will be different. She's a whole different kind of vampire."

Considering she finds human blood repulsive as they informed me downstairs, that was not a far-off hypothesis.

"Why does she fear me?" Her hesitancy wasn't lost on me. It was as if she fought with herself when she was around me.

"You had her trapped in a cave. You starved her. And sodomized her when she tried to escape," Asher snapped.

I jolted as if struck.

"She was a terrified asthmatic female when she came into our lives."

"I do not recall," I struggled to speak. My fang punctured my mouth. Hurting Catalina was not something I could understand.

"She obviously does not blame you," Tobias interjected. "Anymore."

I struggled to collect my thoughts.

"Do I . . ." I stopped speaking. For once, I did not have an explanation.

"Nothing. Do nothing and say nothing." Asher pinned me with his gaze. "This is pissing me off, so I'm changing the subject." He sighed. "How did you know how to call me?"

I worked my jaw side to side. The youngling was angry with me?

I fished out all that was left of the rectangle device from my pant pocket.

"I observed you using this."

"You've been regaining your mind since she arrived, haven't you."

"Yes."

"There's where my phone went." Tobias snatched the piece from my hand. Half of it crumbled until all he held was a small corner of plastic. I had been unsuccessful putting it back together after I crushed it.

"There's something else you should know. Not only does she feed on us, but her blood calls us as much as it did while she was human, more so."

My vision fluctuated.

I snarled at Tobias. Mine. My human. I hissed a breath out.

The violent, mindless beast continued to live within me. I wrenched back control and tugged my fingers through my hair.

"She won't be safe here, anymore," Asher said to Tobias. He opened his mouth, but a sharp ringing broke through the room, interrupting him.

"We have a situation, Sire," the small voice on the other end of the call reached my ears. I turned toward Asher as did the rest of them. *"Imogen is here with a Council representative."* I tensed.

"We'll be right there," he hissed.

These males had been with Imogen and allowed her into Catalina's space. A mistake I would not have made. Unlike them, I saw through her madness from the beginning but had cared more about what she could do for me.

"You three need to stay away from Imogen," Ren ordered.

I turned my attention to the footsteps approaching. And the rest of them became silent.

"Where is she?" Catalina asked, curling her fingers into a fist. "I heard you say her name and don't lie to me."

"She is at Crimson Nights," Tobias said.

Asher gripped her arms and pulled her close.

"You should wait here."

"No!" Her eyes widened and her heart jumped. "I'm going with you," she announced, her chin lifting stubbornly. Such a beautiful female. Her eyes flicked side to side. She did not want to be alone.

catalina

MADDY KEPT RUBBING her palms against her jeans and readjusting herself next to me. She'd insisted on coming with us. I tried talking her out of it, but she refused to budge. Perspiration beaded at her temples and her eyes continued to flick side to side.

I had no doubt if I breathed in, I would smell her fear. As it was, the rush of her heart pumping echoed like the softest buzzing to my ears.

I sank my nails into my thigh. Fabric tore, and I relaxed my hand, so I didn't break into skin. The SUV bumped onto the drive and Ren pulled up to the curb behind Crimson Nights. I'd never been to the side of the structure. Brick buildings stretched around us. Lights from a sign flickered in the distance. Nightclubs surrounded the area, but all that would point to Crimson Nights being a nightclub was the line stretching from the front doors.

Considering all the explicit activities on the dance floor the last time we were here, I had no doubt they compelled whatever humans did make it through. A sleek car pulled up next to the

SUV. Bastien, Jax, and Asher hopped out. They all scanned different sections as they surrounded the SUV. Bastien had glasses blocking his red eyes. He pulled my door open and leaned his forearm against the top.

Ren shut the engine off. All the vampires seemed on edge and quiet—introspective.

Tobias turned his torso to look at us in the back and the leather seat creaked.

"Maddy, you remain in the vehicle with Cat." This was news to me.

"What why! I want to go with you!" Panic vised around my chest.

"No, Catalina," Tobias said sternly. "If anyone remembers you from the last time you were here, there will be questions about your differences."

"Imogen cannot know you live," Bastien agreed, and he cupped the side of my neck.

Well, that was true, but I didn't want to be stuck in the car without one of them.

"Could one of you stay?" I asked in a small voice. Bastien and Tobias shared a look.

"I have not shown myself in decades. I will stay."

I deflated with relief.

"Let us get this over with," Tobias spoke like he knew exactly what awaited them inside. They left too quick for me to track. The metal back door slammed shut.

"Will they be okay without you?" I couldn't tear my eyes away from where they'd disappeared. I would never forgive myself if I asked him to stay, and they'd needed Bastien.

He nodded once, I couldn't tell if he was looking at me or through the window behind me.

"If Imogen is with a representative and they are here, where there are many vampires present, they are likely serving us with a summons."

"What's that?" Sounded ominous and by the twisting of his lips, he was not happy about it.

"I do not know how to explain it." Bastien frowned, removing his palm from my shoulder to place it on the side of the door. His shoulders rippled under his borrowed t-shirt with each of his movements.

"They're getting summoned before the Council. Imogen likely put a claim against them," Maddy offered, side eyeing Bastien. Discomfort bled from her posture.

"And that means . . . ?"

"We cannot kill her as we planned." His teeth flashed with his grimace.

"It basically puts U.S Alliance eyes on Crimson Coven." Maddy fidgeted. I followed his gaze to the scuffle at the corner of the building. Two men shoved each other, shouting loud enough that their cursing reached my ears.

"Something is not right," Bastien frowned. The shouting grew louder.

"Go," I whispered.

"No."

A loud bang echoed all around us. The buildings were so close together that the sound continued to resonate.

"I'm getting you out of here." He cupped the bottom of my elbow.

I bunched his shirt.

"You have to check on the others, you have to! What if it was a trick?" Panic made my voice rise a few octaves. "Please, go fast."

"I—"

"Bastien!"

His teeth clicked together. He looked over his shoulder.

"Please!"

"Do not move from here," he hissed. "I will be back in moments."

I nodded.

He slammed the door and disappeared. I slumped against the leather.

"Something is happening in there," Maddy muttered, hugging herself. "I have a really bad feeling."

A sharp scream stung my ears. Maddy straightened and peered out her window. I followed her gaze to the high-pitched shouts. Past the large garbage containers, within the ally, a male threw a woman against the wall, shoving her against it. She fought against him as he pinned her hips with his.

"We can't just watch." I yanked the door handle open. I didn't like conflict, I ran from it, but she needed help. And now, I could actually hold my own—or at least not die so easily.

"No!" Maddy shouted, grabbing my arm. I yanked out of her grip. "Wait."

"I have to help her."

I dropped my hand from the door handle. Her heart pounded so fast it sounded like it would burst from her chest. I understood the fear in her eyes. It was the same suffocating sensation writhing inside me, bidding me to remain in the vehicle.

"Wear this with the hood up," she handed me her sweater. She was right. No one could recognize me. I pulled it on as Maddy spoke, "If something happens to me, please protect Syd, my parents are old and can't care for her." She took a deep, raspy breath. "She knows about vampires."

As she spoke, I shoved my head through the sweatshirt, pulling it on in time to watch Maddy yank the door open and run out.

"Maddy," I shouted. A loud engine roared closer and closer.

Gunshots exploded through the windshield in a rapid-fire. Someone was shooting the SUV. I ducked, taking cover. Finally, the sounds tapered off. Using the lip of the car door to hide behind, I poked my head out and crept to the tail end of the SUV. I reached for a shiny bullet laying on the bumper. Upon my finger touching it I hissed, yanking my hand back. I flicked my hand like I could shake away the fire blazing my fingertips. I blew on the burned tips. Pure silver.

I needed to get away from the SUV, before they started shooting it up again. I reached up to pull the strings of the hood to cinch it closer to my face.

Across the street, Maddy huddled near the large garbage bin with the crying woman. She was alive. Thank God.

TWENTY-FOUR

"AND YOU'RE DROPPING this on us so casually," Asher drawled, crossing his arms where he leaned against the wall with Jaxon. They'd taken point furthest from Imogen. We couldn't allow them near her, so I hovered close to where I could rip her heart out, if necessary.

"I am simply an unbiased representative." Gil Cain folded his arms on the table. Roberta, Sire of the Cain Coven would serve as one of the Council members during the trial. It meant he had all of the protections. If anything happened to him, every Coven involved would be investigated.

With Catalina's situation, we couldn't allow that to happen.

I'd seen this happen before, when Tobias had received a summons to serve as a Council member a few decades ago. The U.S Vampire Alliance contained a database with all Sires and the selection of Council members were on a rotation, fortunately, our Coven wouldn't be summoned to do that bullshit for another few decades based off rotation.

Tobias rifled through the packet Gil handed him. Unbiased representative for now, soon he, along with the other ones in this Council, would vote to determine our fate. And if we did not like it, it would pit all vampires against Crimson Coven Sires, turning us into sport.

He raised an eyebrow at Imogen perched right next to Gil. She had a stupid, smug grin that made me want to choke her until her throat popped.

This was the bitch that hurt my Beloved. She may have driven us into a corner, but we lived forever, eventually, I would be able to come for her and end her wretched existence.

She'd always been this way, impulsive and silly. Having Catalina had opened my eyes to just how much.

"This is ridiculous, Imogen," Tobias said sharply, pulling me from my thoughts. "You want absolutely everything we've accumulated."

"None of it would exist if it weren't for me." She leaned forward. "It began with me, and it will end with me."

Gil cleared his throat, and he typed on the computer in front of him.

"Are you writing that down?" Imogen huffed.

"I am an unbiased observer." And peacekeeper. He would have us stopped, if we attacked her or vice versa. I was not fooled. He likely had some device on to ensure his safety. If we attacked—it would lead to vampires coming for us in droves.

I narrowed my eyes at him.

I would do anything for my Coven. The one I never wanted to lose. The female I would always remain beside. Even if it meant biding my time for bloodshed.

"How did you convince Wrenhaven to torture you?" I asked.

Imogen clasped her chest with an offended gasp. "Gil, I

would like this uncalled accusation chronicled in my claim."
She flicked her hair over her shoulder.

"Wrenhaven?" Gil interjected, raising an eyebrow. "This is
the first I'm hearing his name was involved."

"He is not," Imogen sniped. "We had the slightest
disagreement, and we handled it ourselves." Lies. They worked
together. Wrenhaven likely knew everything and worked to help
her, but to keep his hands clean, she would feign ignorance.

It worked in Imogen's favor, but in a moment's notice she
would turn on him to save her hide.

"This is a conflict of interest. We may have to find another
for the trial," Gil's fingers flew over his phone screen.

"Why would it be a conflict of interest?" I narrowed my
eyes.

"He's part of the current Council."

"He needs to be removed," Tobias hissed. He hadn't looked
in Imogen's direction, since we entered the private area Talia
had cleared out for the meeting before our arrival.

Imogen hissed and stood, slamming her palms on the flat of
the table.

"You understand how the system works, Tobias. His service
had come up, but an investigation will be conducted. If there
has been collusion, he will be removed."

"Are we done here?" Imogen straightened and smoothed
her palms down her dress.

"We're done here." Gil pushed his chair back as he stood.
"Your presence is required in a fortnight, location to be
disclosed via electronic means on the day prior. You are allowed
fifteen witnesses." He shut the laptop and tucked it under
his arm.

"We don't have to do this," Imogen said, her eyes widening

slightly. "Would you like to return to my side, Jaxon?" Jax didn't turn to look at her. "What about my little brother?"

Tobias's lips thinned and he took a few steps toward her until he was an arm's distance away.

"You are nothing to me." For the first time since we'd entered, her smirk faded. Her steady gaze didn't leave her brother's. She snapped out of her thrall.

She snarled.

"I should have drawn out her pain."

Tobias hissed, shoulders becoming tense.

Gil stepped between them. "You can't attack her, or you will immediately lose your case. You will be booted from the Alliance. All vampires will come for you."

Having a target on us would mean lack of safety for Catalina. If she were to live surrounded by death. . .

Tobias flicked his eyes toward me. His lips thinned and he stepped back. He agreed with my thoughts.

"Your welcome here has expired."

She only smiled at him.

Gil followed Imogen out. That stiff-assed twat. I'd shove a stake up his ass, if he ever crossed my path once this was over.

"This is fucking bullshit," Asher gritted out.

"It was the only way she knew how to stop us from coming after her. She knew her death was imminent." Tobias kicked the chair out and dropped down, ungracefully.

"What are we going to do now?"

"What do you mean, Jaxon? There's not much we can do." She fucked us over before we could drag her ass into the sunlight.

"She can't get away with this." Jax scowled.

"Not forever," Tobias agreed. "We have to play this smart."

The heavy door swung on the hinges allowing in chaos from outside of the soundproof room.

"Sires, we have a problem," Talia said, face splattered with blood. "Humans are raiding."

"Details?" Asher asked Talia.

"Men burst through the door with guns and started shooting everywhere. It's a massacre. They're calling us terrorists, but, Sire, they're using silver bullets."

Another attack framed as a hate crime.

It was a repeat of Saphire Lounge, but this time, we couldn't leave, we had to protect our people.

"Fuck." Jax shoved his fingers through his hair. "That bitch must hav—" He stopped talking.

"I need to go find Cat." Jax grabbed Asher before he could do what we all verged on doing.

"I will go," I said.

Asher acquiesced. I would be the safest bet for Catalina.

A loud, wall shaking bang echoed down the hall.

"This is fucking bullshit," Asher hissed. "Imogen made sure to be with Gil, he will vouch for her."

I was already through the door, on a hunt for my female. The attack reeked of Imogen, but we had to find a way to prove it, and Imogen never left stones unturned—it was something I used to admire her for, now I wanted to rip her head from her body for the inconvenience.

JUST AS I was about to lunge into the hiding spot with them, a truck careened around the corner of the street and the engine revved as it pulled up next to the SUV. People spilled out in military looking garb. They flooded into Crimson Nights through the same entrance my vampires entered.

No! I gasped, stepping forward to follow, but gunshots started up again. I dropped onto my butt, covering my head. Holes burst through the bumper, and I screamed, getting on my stomach.

The shooting cut off and this time, when it started up again, I wouldn't be able to avoid it. Asphalt scrubbed against my jeans with my roll to the side. I pushed into a crouch. I peeked out and sprinted toward the little alleyway across from where Maddy and the other girl hid. I didn't want to lead attention to them.

I huddled against the wall, shadowed by the tall buildings. There were no lights, so I would be hard to be detected. I pressed my back against the wall. I just had to wait for one of my vampires to come get me. Vampires and humans spilled from Crimson Nights in droves.

One shot through the heart and vampires were dust. I gawked at the pile of ash feet away. The poor female vampire had been running away when the bullet sliced through the air and right through her. She crumpled into herself, her body shriveling slowly into itself.

Screaming and snarling erupted from the side of the building near the destroyed vehicles. Ren tossed bodies, ripping through humans with ease. He scanned the lot.

"Cat," he roared. I tried not to pay too much attention to the mangled humans he left behind. I sucked in a breath to shout for him.

Ren avoided another bullet and sank his fingers inside a chest. I followed the line of the gunshots.

The shooter hiding behind the large truck diagonal to the back entrance crouched lower, angling the barrel toward Ren. No! I was already moving, so fast that it made me dizzy. He didn't see me coming, because he was focused on shooting Ren.

I threw myself on the large back, slapping my palms over his face. He immediately straightened, taking me with him. I hooked my legs around his waist and sank my fingers into his face harder and harder, until he let go of the machine gun. It fell onto the bed of the truck with a loud thud. He hissed and jabbed his elbow back. My fangs erupted from my gums. I grunted, sucking in a breath.

Grabbing onto his hair, I yanked to the side to offer me space to bite him. I sank my fangs into the side of his throat. My teeth met resistance of the thick vest he wore. He bucked and turned, slamming my back into the truck. I yanked to the side and tried to bite him again. My fangs sank into his throat. He gasped and he staggered. His blood flooded my mouth.

This one was a vampire. His taste flooded my mouth. It was nowhere close to what I was used to. I let it leak out from the corner of my mouth. I sucked blood from his wounds and his head fell forward, with a moan.

I slackened my grip and yanked my mouth from his skin.

The vampire ripped out of my hold and turned to punch me in the face.

I whimpered, cupping my stinging lip.

The vampire came at me again and I moved to the side with a flinch. His first slammed into a wall, causing dust to plume and a crack to shatter through the stone. My eyes widened on the fist coming for me again. It moved in conjunction with the stake.

I put my hands up to protect myself, but the attack never came.

I peeked through my fingers. Bastien held the back of the vampire's neck. He took hold of his hair and pulled back. Skin from his neck stretched and continued to stretch until it began to tear. My stomach lurched. I could see inside his throat. Bastien ripped his head off and blood splattered across my face. I gawked as the body crumpled into itself, turning to dust.

Bastien cupped the side of my head, and I had to crane my neck to look him in the eyes. I held my breath, not wanting bloodlust to take over.

"You okay, Little One?" I nodded hesitantly, still not able to articulate anything. Bastien turned in time to catch the vampire coming at his back. I yelped at the thud of his body hitting Bastien.

"Where's Maddy?" I shouted over the noise. Snarls, screaming, and gunshots exploded through the night. I shoved past Bastien, but he stayed glued to my side as I hurried to the alley she'd hidden in.

Red splashed the ground, and I followed it to a body leaning to the left of the garbage bin. It was that girl she'd hidden with. Her eyes were open, staring up at the sky sightlessly. Her throat was ripped through, like she'd been shot repeatedly in the neck.

"Maddy?" I shouted over the chaos.

"Catalina," Bastien murmured in my ear, his hand on my shoulder guiding me down the alley. A wet cough exploded off the walls. I ran toward the sound until her feet came into view. There was so much blood. I dropped to my knees beside her torso. Blood seeped into the fibers of her clothes, all dripping out of her raw, open neck. She'd been shot. She took a gasping breath, her eyes flicking side to side.

"Maddy?" I struggled to push the words out. She would not survive this. I sank my fangs into my wrist and pushed it against her lips, but they didn't move. Her eyes were peeled wide—scared.

She coughed up the blood.

"Syd." She gurgled. "Please." She mouthed the last word. Tears dripped on her face. I'd been too late. I pressed my palm to my stomach like I could contain the hollow sensation. She had Sydney. I sniffled in, still holding my wrist against her mouth insistently. *Come on, drink.*

"She's dead, Little One." Bastien wrapped his arms around my torso, holding my arms to my chest. He stood me on my feet, but I couldn't feel anything.

"We can't leave her," I croaked. What if I did manage to get her to swallow my blood? What if she would turn?

"I'll send someone for her. We have to get inside before human authorities arrive." The finality of his statement forced my lips together.

catalina

"YOU GUYS DIDN'T GIVE up on me!" I shouted, pacing back and forth. She would be okay, right? I sat on the cushion of the rounded couch across that Pepto pink room, where one of the vampires placed Maddy.

Her body hadn't moved from the bed. She lay so still. Asher sank next to me, his palm rested on my back. He patted me in soothing circles.

"Cat, this happens with humans—"

"Stop trying to pacify me," I shouted, getting back to my feet to pace. "She mattered, she wasn't just *a human*." Asher looked chagrined.

Ren gripped my arm and dragged me toward the room. I stumbled after him as he shoved me inside, guiding me until I faced Maddy's limp body. A bandage was wrapped around her neck, covering the injuries.

"What are you doing?" I hissed, fighting to get out of Ren's grip. Tobias shoved Ren back and broke his hold on me.

"Being rough about it will get you nowhere."

"She's in denial. And *that* will not help her."

I glared up at him. Bastien was suddenly in front of Ren. As the two biggest males, watching them glare at each other shouldn't have looked as intriguing as it did. Ren shook his head and put his hands up.

"Breathe in her scent, Catalina," Tobias said gently, bringing me back to him. I licked my lips and shuffled closer to the bed. Maddy had been cleaned of all the blood, I wasn't sure who did it, but Talia ordered it before she left to collect Sydney.

I breathed in as Tobias asked me to.

A putrid scent slapped my senses. I gagged and clasped my hand over my mouth, holding my breath again. It was a mix of rotting cabbage and spoiled milk.

It hadn't worked. I couldn't change her. Her body was already decaying. I could tell in the dip of her cheeks and the hollow of her eyes.

"That's cadaverine, skatole, indole, putrescine, and hydrogen sulfide. Bacteria create it during decomposition," Bastien said, his voice coming from right behind me. "It will only become worse with each hour that passes."

My lip trembled and I closed my eyes, turning into Bastien's arms. He rubbed my back, and I let a sob out into his chest.

"Sires, we handled human law enforcement," a female voice called from the threshold of the room. Handled was a pretty way of saying they compelled them all.

Bastien stiffened and he suddenly snarled toward the interloper. He pulled me into his side, backing us up until he was flat against the wall. His eyes held none of that sharp intelligence that was usually present when his mind was. I held onto his arm.

The female vampire with multicolored braids disappeared as fast as she had arrived. I peeked up at Bastien and his head still swiveled around. I wasn't sure how long he would last this way. Some 'moments' stretched longer than others. I hooked my arm with Bastien's.

"You should rest before the girl arrives," Tobias murmured.

I smiled wryly.

"Vampire, remember?" Resting did nothing for me.

"There's a bath in there and you should take Bastien in there while he's . . . like this." Tobias waved a hand. "There are too many vampires around you and it's not a question about 'if', but 'when' he will attack one of them." I remembered how crazed he'd been when I first encountered him. He'd not allowed any of them near me either.

"Okay," I muttered. I hated how defeated my voice sounded. Jax frowned down at me and he turned to guide me to the bedroom. Bastien trailed after me, my grip not loosening on him.

Asher no longer lounged on the round couch. Jax lead me to the door across from the pink room. Upon opening it, I was surprised at how normal it looked. Just a simple bed with a ruffled bed skirt and a quilt.

I pulled Bastien inside with me and peeked over my shoulder. Bastien's red eyes were fixed on me. This side of him, instinctual, and rash, held a soft spot for me.

"The shower is over here." Jax turned right and through a rounded alcove. I followed the sound of the sputtering shower.

The floor to ceiling mirror reflected my blood-stained clothes. So much blood. I slowly lifted my hand to the smear across my cheek.

Steam filled the bathroom, fogging up the mirror. I squeezed Bastien's hand.

Perhaps I was giving in much too easily. He'd sodomized

me, and that remembered trauma would never fade. I wouldn't be okay with that . . . but why did I want to keep hold of his hand. I should be running the other direction. Now that I was a vampire, I could run—yet I stayed.

I could attribute it to a fear of Imogen, but she didn't know I lived. And as defective as these males were, they wouldn't betray me. They may hunt me down and search for me until they found me, but I didn't believe they would harm me anymore.

"All ready," Jax said, flicking water from his hands. "I'll get you a change of clothes."

"And for Bastien too, please," I mumbled, still half lost in my thoughts.

I let go of Bastien's hand to shuck my ruined clothes. I stepped one foot into the bath before turning back to the still clothed vampire who hadn't taken his eyes off me.

Wrapping my fingers into his hem, I studied the clothing stained with gunk that would never be fully rubbed out of the fabric. Instead of struggling to take it off him, I tore it, baring his chest. The shirt fell to the ground. I reached for his pants and unhooked the loop. With a little shove, they pooled at his ankles.

I ran my fingers over the divot of Bastien's chest. He made this rumbling sound, shuddering as his eyes slitted shut. If I continued feeling him up, then we'd run out of nighttime.

I stepped into the shower, making sure to scoot closer to the water pelting into my hair, so Bastien fit with me. Water splashed my face. I just stood there, allowing the spray to fall over me and the pinkened liquid to swirl down the drain.

I sank my fingers through my hair, but palms settled on top of mine, taking their place.

"Bastien?" he hummed in answer. His mind had returned. I let my hands drop to my side and embraced his long, strong fingers rubbing into my scalp. Soap dripped down my chest. I let him wash me off. The soothing rub of his hands calmed my racing thoughts. It felt good to have him touch me.

"You seem more comfortable with the Hyde version of me," Bastien murmured. His deep rumbling voice vibrated in my chest.

"The irony isn't lost on me," I said wryly. "This Jekyll version of you—I don't know him."

His palm settled on the side of my neck. His hand was so large he could probably wrap one hand around my entire throat.

"Your heart stuttered."

"You do have your hand around my throat."

"I would never hurt you." He grunted. "I'm yours to command."

And butterflies shouldn't go off in my stomach at his dark promise.

"For such a big guy, you're a softie, aren't you?" I said wryly.

He laughed breathily.

"Only for you, Little One."

I didn't doubt it one bit, after watching him tear someone's head off.

"I have the clothes," Jax announced from the bedroom. I shook myself from the thrall of our intimate conversation and shut off the water. I plucked the towel from the cubby to the side of the shower and wrapped myself in it, quickly stepping out and into my sneakers.

Bastien didn't say anything. A good thing because he made me feel fluttery and unsteady.

I shuffled to the bed, where Jax had placed the pile of clothes.

Asher opened the door in the middle of me pulling on sweats and a long-sleeved shirt. The scratchy material sucked, but beggars couldn't be choosers.

"The girl is here," Asher said, brushing my wet hair back. I tossed the towel I'd scrunched my hair with.

Stepping out into the main room that webbed into all the bedrooms, I scanned for her, but there was no sign. Steps echoed from down the hall. I hurried around the couch as Talia entered with Sydney right behind her.

Sydney didn't look at me, she stared straight ahead with a blank look on her face.

"Release her from this." I glared at Talia. She turned the compelled girl and tipped her chin up.

"Sydney, return to yourself."

The young girl gasped, her wide, frightened eyes flaring.

"Wh-where am—Catalina?" Her wide eyes went from Talia to me.

"Hey, Sydney." I grabbed her hand and tugged her to the room beside the Pepto one for some privacy. I didn't want her to have to fall apart in front of everyone. Jax moved to follow me, but I put a hand up, staying him. I wouldn't want some stranger watching me while receiving bad news. She didn't know me well, but at least she recognized me.

"Where's my mom?" She looked around, nose wrinkling.

I closed the door in Jax's face and turned to Sydney. She slowed, looking around the room, with her arms crossed. All of the walls were painted black and there was a plush couch circling a center table with built in shackles. She settled her eyes on mine.

"Weird," she whispered but I could hear her from my position across the room. I should have returned her to the bedroom Bastien and I had been in, it was the most normal looking one.

"Your mom told you about vampires." Her eyes widened and her heartbeat picked up. The thud, thud, thud, of her heart pounded in my ear.

"I don't know what you're talking about," she said it so quickly her voice melded together. I pursed my lips. Now she avoided my eyes. And I could see the pulse in her throat.

"Sydney," I murmured. "She asked me to look after you." I struggled to find the words. What did one say to the person that lost everything. Once upon a time, I'd been in her shoes, but at least I had Peter to look after, he'd kept me going, because I knew he couldn't survive without me.

"B-but why? Where is she?"

"Sydney." I slowly approached. She backed up.

"Spit it out," she shouted, her eyes welling. She knew, some part of her had to know.

The doorknob jiggled.

"Catalina?"

"Wait out there," I shouted. Thank God, I'd locked it.

I returned my gaze to Sydney. She swiped the back of her hand across her eyes.

"Who?" Her eyes filled with tears.

"We don't know."

"A vampire?"

"A gunshot wound."

"D-did they turn her?" Her eyes widened and she hurried

toward me and grabbed my hands. "Those Crimson vampires she worked for? She's okay, she's a vampire now, right?" Her shoulders dropped, visible relief on her face. "That's okay, she can be a vampire," she said it under her breath, like she was talking to herself.

"They tried," I whispered. She didn't seem to hear me. Then she went quiet, and her legs gave out. I crouched next to her. Her head dropped forward and she sobbed.

I pressed my hand on her back and watched the young girl sob. Tears gathered in my eyes and trickled down my cheeks.

Sydney swiped the back of her arm across her face.

"Why are your tears pink?"

"I'm a vampire." I sniffled.

"Vampires can cry?"

I could only nod, joining her in another bout of tears. She would go through all of the emotions. I had to let her. She let out another wrenching sob.

"The people that hurt her will pay."

"Promise?" She hiccupped.

Her arms wrapped around me, and she sobbed into my chest. I patted her back, letting her cry the next bout out.

Eventually, the loud, gut-wrenching sobs tapered off and in between were shoulder wracking hiccups.

"I know it wasn't the vampires she worked for. She talked about how they helped her." Sydney sniffled and dashed the back of her hands across her nose. "She loved one called Talia, but my mom never let me meet her."

"She knows who you are." I smiled softly. "Do you want to see your mom's body before she's buried?"

"She wanted to be cremated." She hiccupped and sniffed in

hard. I nodded slowly and stood, holding my hand down toward her. She reached for me, and I pulled her to her feet.

I didn't let her hand go as I guided her to the pink room. The door was already open, and Talia sat at the edge of her bed, combing Maddy's hair back.

Sydney pulled free and leaned over the other side of her mother. I swiped my fingers across the few tears that escaped.

"You're a sensitive little one," Bastien murmured into my hair. He kissed the top of my head and straightened.

"Let's get her home," Asher murmured. Talia stood from the bed, giving Sydney privacy with her mother.

"Sydney will stay here with me. I'll make sure she's safe."

I turned to look at the young girl not letting go of her mom's hand.

"Please call if she needs anything," I said with effort. Talia finally looked at me and nodded.

"I will call my Sire, if I need to contact you." I didn't pay any attention to the slight bite in her tone. There was a bit of possessiveness to how she spoke about Asher, but there were more important things to worry about.

REN TURNED the SUV onto the main road Crimson Manor sat upon. We'd all packed into one vehicle, which was how I ended up wrapped up in Asher's arms, reclining on his lap. Light flickered in the sky. The orange hue a striking difference from the dark backdrop. I straightened, leaning forward.

"What is . . ."

"Fuck," Ren hissed. Ren stepped on the gas. The inky fog

came closer and closer. The top floor of Crimson Manor was on fire.

Smoke plumed into the sky and dark smog coated the house. Fire engulfed the garden and sputtered out of the broken windows.

My hands began to shake. Again?

"My things," I whimpered. There goes everything I'd collected since the last time, but this round hurt just a little less. "My laptop," I shouted. I crawled over Asher's lap to press my palms to the window. Yellow and red flames flickered from the top of Crimson Manor. *Everything I'd collected.*

My lip trembled. The car jolted to a stop.

A door snicked open and closed, in the same breath.

"Where are you going?" Asher shouted. "Ren!"

All I saw was his back as he disappeared through the gate. I yanked at the door, but Asher kept it closed.

"You're not going in there."

I kept yanking even though I knew Asher wouldn't give in. "What is he doing?"

The siren of a fire engine spilled through even the closed doors of the car. A sudden slam rocked the SUV side to side.

Ren, soot covered, slipped into the SUV and shut the door. He put it in drive and peeled around to race away from the burning building.

"Why would you do that?" I screamed, shoving at his shoulder.

He lifted something and the light of the fire behind us glinted off the metal from my laptop. My lip warbled.

"You shouldn't have done that." I smacked his shoulder again. Ren only wiggled the laptop toward me. I finally took it, hugging it to my chest. "If you do something like that again, I swear to God," I whispered.

Arms wrapped around my waist, and I was tucked against a chest. I looked up at Jax. He smoothed his palm down my arm in a rhythmic pat.

I nestled close to him. What sucked the most was, if we had stayed home, we would have been roasted in the fire, especially if it had happened while the sun was out. The attacks kept coming and closed in on us.

And the guys. I studied them all one by one. They seemed stoic, but it was that very stoicism that told me they craved ripping into throats.

Ren revved onto the freeway.

"Where are we going?" Tobias asked.

"A different property," Asher answered.

"That we have thanks to my insistence," Ren drawled.

"And what about the pile of ash?" I asked wryly.

"One of the humans we have on payroll will handle everything with officials while we sleep. They'll package anything that was not destroyed," Tobias said.

"Already texted Talia to get one of her people on it," Asher offered. That would have been Maddy's job if she was still alive. My nose burned with restrained tears.

Jax readjusted me on his lap, so my head nestled on his shoulder. I closed my eyes tightly and breathed his scent in. A slight burn stung my gums, but I restrained my urge to sink my fangs into him and drink.

"Where are you driving to?" Tobias asked.

"You'll see," Asher intoned ominously.

catalina

I POPPED UP IN BED. A very comfortable, large mattress. I pushed onto my hands, squeezing the plush, flower-embroidered comforter. All I remembered before sunrise dragged me under was Ren putting the car in park in the paved driveway.

A sheer canopy surrounded the king-sized bed placed smack in the middle of the bedroom. I scooted to the edge. Dark brown chestnut colored wood covered the floors. A pair of slippers rested to the side. The exact same as the ones I had back at Crimson Manor, except this pair looked brand new.

I slid the new slippers on and shuffled to the window facing the bed. I moved so fast the sheer black curtains fluttered. They were the same as the sheer of the canopy. Shoving them to the side, I had a clear view through the large, arch-top window framed in black iron.

The same iron framed the lamps interspersed across the sprawling lawn and emitted a soft, yellow light. Past the boundary of them sprawled unending darkness. I inched closer to the window and looked down. The drop was steep. Bone shattering steep. I breathed out and my breath caused fog to condense on the surface.

It looked so quiet and spooky out there. I turned to survey the rest of the bedroom. An archway to my left led to a pristine white bathroom—no door, while the only door was to the furthest right side of the room, on the other side of the bed.

Where were the guys and why was there a pile of clothes next to the door? My heart somersaulted and I hurried to the pile so fast my surroundings blurred. I dropped to my knees. Please, no ash. With my throat excruciatingly tight, I shuffled through the bloody and ripped pile of clothes.

My shoulders lowered, it looked like they just took their clothes off. I exhaled in relief and climbed to my feet. My fingers were a hairsbreadth away from the iron door handle when it clicked down.

"Jax," I breathed in relief. He quirked an eyebrow. I threw my arms around his waist. Jax tensed and after a beat, his arms pulled me tighter to him. I closed my eyes. I wasn't sure what I was thinking. That they burned and one of them managed to drag me in here. Or that I'd lost one of them—I didn't know, all I understood was the gut-wrenching drop of my stomach upon seeing the clothes.

"You okay, Kitten?"

"I'm just happy to see you." I pulled back to peek up at him. His eyebrows lowered. "What?"

"You're . . . happy to see me?" He sounded almost offput by my statement. I pursed my lips. Was that bad? I drew back a little more.

"Uh, sorry." I guess it was a little weird. I hadn't allowed myself to be soft toward Jax recently. Or maybe affection just made him uncomfortable.

"No." He caught my hand. "I've never had someone happy to see me." His expression turned chagrined, and the slightest pink flush rose up his neck. "I mean—"

I slid my arms around his waist again, flushing myself tight to his hard body.

"Where is everyone," I asked, muffled by his shirt.

"Getting everything settled." I was glad I didn't have to take charge of anything like that. A perk of being around centuries old vampires that knew how to handle themselves. Not being relied on to keep things together felt really fucking good. I'd always had to worry about someone. I still did—Peter—but it wasn't as hard anymore. I had them.

The simple phrase '*I had them*' shouldn't drown me with such relief, but I couldn't help it.

"I'm here to feed you."

As soon as he brought attention to blood, a burn infested my throat.

I pulled back so I didn't sink my teeth into him. Liquid sloshed and my gaze dropped to the blood bag in his hands. I curled my lip, dropping my arms. I was not a fan of human blood. It didn't satiate the cravings or taste good.

"No thanks." His gaze followed mine to the bag in his hand.

"This is for me." He tossed it on the bed, and it bounced once before the bag settled, blood swishing side to side. Jax grabbed the hem of his shirt and pulled it up in a quick drag. He bared his chest, allowing me the full view of his long torso.

My fangs burst free, and I slapped my palm over my mouth. My eyes dropped to the golden hair trail leading to the waistband of his jeans.

"I don't . . ." A burn in my gums overtook my words. He looked absolutely delicious. He strode directly toward me. "We should get someone else in here. I don't know if I can control myself."

He did not, in fact, stop. He crowded me until my legs hit the bed and I sprawled onto my back.

Using my heels, I slid up on the bed, still trying to get away from him. He placed his knees on the edge of the bed and crawled up. I was trying to keep him safe, for God's sake.

I licked my lips, and a cut opened on my tongue. My blood was nowhere near as delicious.

"Jax," I breathed, my eyes wide as his face hovered over mine. I scanned the chiseled line of his jaw.

"Yes, Kitten?" he said gruffly, his accent thicker.

"Are you sure?" I wasn't sure what I asked about. Choosing me, turning from Imogen, feeding me—maybe it was all of it.

He ran the back of his hand up my jaw until his thumb petted my cheek. There was such warmth and affection in his lapis blue eyes. There had been the slightest hint of it before the urn situation—or because of this elusive 'ring' they mentioned to Calliope that day she had us come to her place for that dumb test, but I didn't buy that for Jax. He'd been holding on to the idea of Imogen.

"If you change your mind again." I pursed my lips, shaking my head.

"Feed, Kitten." Jax scratched a thin line at the base of his neck. Blood welled to the surface. I dragged him down, burying my fingers into his hair and pressed my mouth flush to the cut. Upon the first taste, need roared through my veins.

I hooked my arms more securely around his head and opened my legs to cradle him on top of me. His hips gyrated forward, and I snaked my legs around his waist until his shaft rubbed against my core. We simultaneously groaned.

His neck craned to the side allowing me even closer. Every part of the front of my body touched him. I moaned, running my tongue against his skin. He jerked his hips up, driving into my sex.

My fangs burst out and I sank my fangs into his neck. His skin popped satisfyingly, eliciting shivers from me. The rub of my nipples against his chest felt so good, even with clothes between us.

"Fuck. You feel so good," he groaned in my ear. A hot flush worked though my sex. Even his husky voice made me wet. I gyrated my hips in a circle. The motion rubbed me against the hard seam of his jeans. I cried out against his throat. A bit of his blood trickled out of the corner of my mouth. I pulled back to lick my lips.

Warmth traveled through my veins. He felt so good and tasted even better. Jax's chest moved up and down in a sharp movement. He cupped my jaw, staring into my eyes.

"Gorgeous, female." The blood I just took from him filled my cheeks. Jax wasn't sweet like this.

"What have you done with Jax?"

He chuckled.

"What have *you* done to him?" The heat on my face didn't get any better. I opened my mouth to say I didn't even know, but his lips caught mine. His tongue delved into my mouth and caressed with demanding sweeps. We kissed with the desperation of two lovers coming back together. Tears trickled from the corners of my eyes.

His thumb swiped across the dampness. He hovered over my lips, his sweet breath mingling with mine.

"What is it?" He smoothed his finger over the fresh tears.

"I didn't think we'd get to be like this anymore," I whispered huskily.

Jax's lips turned down and I could see some explanation brewing. But with him, I didn't want the words, I wanted his actions. Only that would make me believe him. I threw my arms around his shoulders, dragging him back down to my mouth and sank my fang into his lip. Attaching myself to the bleeding wound, I sucked. He moaned, his hips jerking with such force it pushed me higher onto the bed.

He tasted so good. I licked his lip and pulled back burying my mouth into the crevice of his throat. I sank my teeth into him again. He gasped and every bit of his weight settled on me and it felt so good. I pressed my heel into the bed and rolled us with a grunt.

Jax's eyebrows raised at me, now sat on top of him. I grinned down and moved my hips in a gyrating roll over the thick shaft.

His jaw slackened, eyes sliding shut. Meanwhile, a tremble worked over my sex, driving me close to madness. I tipped my head back and did the same movement. Jax's palms slid under the oversized shirt, and he yanked with a quick tug, pulling it off like it was paper. The simple bralette I'd been loaned had been a tad too small, so my flesh pushed out against the thin fabric.

Jax wet his lower lip, gaze fixed on my body. He hooked a finger under the strap and tugged. It ripped, splaying open and leaving me bare to his gaze. I shrugged off the scraps of fabric. Jax groaned, his head falling back.

"You're driving me fucking crazy," he hissed. His voice was some far-off buzz in my head. All I could focus on was the column of his neck stained with red. I dropped over his throat and sank into the fleshy bit where his muscle met the base of his neck. The muscle flexed and more blood spilled into my mouth. Jax echoed my moan, and his searching hands dipped into the waistband of my borrowed sweats. He yanked the fabric, and it tore with a satisfying rip.

I slid my hands down his hard stomach and pulled free the button of the jeans. Jax lifted his hips, scooting me high off the bed as he jerked his jeans down. He did it so fast, and now I rested against him, without anything between us.

The steel length of his shaft pressed against my sex. I gasped, gyrating on instinct. A thrill ran up my spine and I moved my hips again. My slippery sex moved against him with ease because of how wet I was. Jax groaned, gripping my hips in his large palms. Sitting on top of him, I stared down at his slack expression. His eyes were slightly glazed, his lips damp and plump from our kissing. The muscles of his chest strained. He was unfairly sexy.

I wanted another bite. I leaned down and sank my fangs into his chest. One suck and I lifted, staring at the leaking wound. Blood dripped down his chest and toward his abdomen in a delicious trail of sin. I leaned down, keeping hold of his gaze and licked the blood. His cock throbbed under me.

Just one more bite. Right above the one I'd already made, I sank my teeth in. That delicious pop exploded in my ears like a rush of adrenaline. My sex throbbed and I gyrated harder on his shaft. The slickness between us grew with each second.

"Mark me, Kitten," Jax murmured breathlessly. He lay back, watching me from half-lidded eyes. I didn't need an invitation, but it made me feel better about my perverse craving. He'd noticed it. My face flushed with blood, but I was too far gone in my lust. I sank my fangs into his shoulder.

Another spine-tingling pop.

I gasped, my sex throbbing. I was already about to come, only from biting him. I panted, gazing at the puncture wounds bleeding on his body. Vampire blood was different to human blood. It seemed to move slower upon his skin. Taking its time, as it painted him with trails.

Lifting a little, I gripped the base of his shaft, holding him poised for me to slide onto him. His eyes flared wide and I sank down on him. He grunted, entire body jolting, like I'd stuck him with electricity. He flexed and caused more blood to spill from the punctures in his chest. My channel squeezed his shaft.

He moaned, panting and bucking under me. His lips were parted, offering me flashes of his fangs. He let go for me. I whimpered, bouncing up and down to feel every inch of him.

We moved in a frenzy. A gyrating pile of need.

"*Snälla. . . bara sådär. . . min älskade. Jag behöver dig. Alltid,*" he continued muttering until it was a string that I couldn't pick out word for word, but whatever it was sounded sexy.

My channel pulsed around him, gripping him and tossing me into a mind-bending orgasm. Stars sparked behind my closed eyelids. I couldn't stop moving on him, grinding, taking, claiming. He shouted and bucked under me. His steel throbbed, releasing jut after jut of cum into my sex. I didn't know how long I was suspended in the air. My senses returned from the swell, and I sucked in a few breaths.

The magnificent orgasm still caressed my senses. I couldn't tear my eyes off him. I loved watching him fall apart. He finally looked so free. My heart turned over in my chest. His eyes slitted open and the corner of his mouth twitched.

My fangs nicked my lip. I'd punctured myself.

"Kitten," Jax grunted. He pushed up, those delicious hard muscles on his stomach flexing. He leaned up and the angle changed the position of his cock. He captured my gasp with his mouth.

His shaft pulsated inside me. He groaned and shuddered, wrenching another aftershock from me.

His body jolted like he'd been electrocuted. He sucked my lip into his mouth with harsh drags. But instead of scaring me, I leaned into him. The tug from his mouth warmed my belly. He pulled back, wound my long hair around his hand, and angled my head to the side, baring my throat to him. I couldn't move with how tight he grabbed my hair. I panted, waiting. So suddenly, he struck his fangs into my throat.

I screamed, gripping his shoulders hard. My hips wouldn't stop moving. I thought I'd never feel this staggering pleasure of being bit again, but his bite felt just as good, if not more so.

"Jax," I whimpered, grinding down, taking every inch of his cock. Pleasure emitted from my neck where he fed from me and from where he claimed my sex. Thoughts evaporated.

I couldn't tell where he ended, and I began.

I rode the wave of release, while his cock seized inside my channel.

"Catalina. Fuck," he muttered gruffly against my neck. "Kitten," he groaned. He continued muttering more in his language, but I was lost to the aftershock throbs of his spasming cock flaring mine to life. The orgasm settled into a lulling pleasure. Jax released his hold on my hair and dropped onto his back with a loud gasp.

I flopped onto my back, my head hanging off the edge of the bed. His cock slipped from my sex, releasing liquid down the inside of my thighs. My hair fluttered around me in a wavy mess. His hold had been what kept me upright, because I'd become boneless.

"I should be the one calling you Kitten," I mumbled. "Or Binx." Every inch of my body had electricity running through it, in overload. His taste lingered on my tongue and the side of my neck felt sensitive.

God, I felt like I rode a wave.

"You can call me whatever you want, Kitten."

I grinned up at the ceiling. I'd expected him to take off running, but he lay on the bed, our legs tangled with each other.

The door slammed against the wall. I peeked through my slitted eyelids and lazily met Bastien's red eyes. He tensed at the threshold.

"Bastien? Are you okay?" I would get up, but I couldn't seem to move my body.

A change flickered over his features incrementally, like he fought to keep the madness at bay. Ultimately, it won.

He was suddenly on me, his fangs sinking into my shoulder. I yelped, more from shock than pain. His knees thumped on the floor, lowering his position and allowing him to nuzzle into my neck. I sank my fingers into his long hair. His hands slid across my body, and he palmed my breasts in his big hands. I arched my spine toward his touch. Jax moved and the bed bounced. Hands not belonging to Bastien pried my thighs open. I was achy and wet.

"Jax, w-wait." He did not wait. A tongue licked the inner side of my thighs. He licked up, closer to my sex, then repeated the motion. He was cleaning our need. Bastien sucked another drag from my neck, wrenching my mind into a blissful fog.

It felt like a crime to be this turned on. Bastien palmed my breasts, and his tongue flicked across the wound. In the same breath, he bit me again.

I screamed, closing my legs around Jax's head. His mouth fastened on my pulsating clit. He flicked his tongue against it.

My toes curled. I didn't know where I ended, and they began.

"What the fuck!"

Bastien yanked his fangs from my neck. He whirled, hissing. I rolled to my side, avoiding kneeing Jax in the temple, and sat up to face the door.

Jax's palm smoothed down my back, petting me.

Asher stood at the threshold, slack jawed.

I followed his gaze down my body. Blood from my neck trickled between my breasts.

"I want in," Asher hissed. He tore his shirt off, so quickly, and then his pants were shucked to the side, in the next moment. Moving that fast had to be a skill. I barely saw more than a blur.

My eyes dropped to his swelled shaft. A vein throbbed along the side of the piercings. I was off the bed before my thoughts caught up with me.

asher

CATALINA WAS A DELICIOUS MORSEL. I was utterly, wholly obsessed.

Her dazed focus on my cock caused it to throb. I gripped the base and squeezed. Precum beaded at the tip. She came at me so fast that she struggled to stop. She caught herself on my chest, but her momentum was so hard that my back slammed against the wall. She dropped to her knees, her entire focus on my cock—her tongue flicked out to lap the liquid at the top.

A shiver worked through her body. That ecstasy on her face was about to make me come.

Her hand wrapped around the base of my cock. The contrast of her tan flesh to my blood-filled cock caused more liquid to rise.

She lowered and wrapped her mouth around the tip. Her fangs scratched the side of my shaft, her teeth clicking against my Jacob's ladder piercing. I moaned and clenched my hands hard, forcing my release to wait. She ran her tongue along the side of the shaft, collecting blood and precum. My balls drew up to my base. Son of a bitch, I wasn't going to last long.

She lifted slightly, and so suddenly, she sank her fangs into the side of my cock. I shouted, falling against the wall. She sucked once and I could not handle it. I burst, my need painting her cheek. Catalina wrapped her lips around me and took every bit of my release as cum jutted from me with wringing throbs. I couldn't hear with how hard I came. The haze lifted and I found myself curved forward and my hand buried in her long hair from the force.

I wheezed and stared down at her in awe. Her mouth gave a final tug, and she ran her tongue up the shaft as she pulled her mouth away. She swallowed and looked up at me, her pink tongue taking the cum beaded on her lip.

She swiped her finger across my undead little swimmers on her cheek and popped her finger in her mouth, licking it clean with a hum.

I slid down the wall, until I was on the floor. Jaxon raised an eyebrow at me as he buttoned his jeans with a smirk plastered on his face.

Bastien watched from the bed, gaze on her. His mindless side was in the driver's seat, based off the intense focus on her. When he was normally himself, he could mask his obsession—for the most part.

"I came to fetch you." The pressure in my chest forced me to take another breath. She'd made me fucking breathless. "I have a surprise for you."

Catalina's eyebrows furrowed and she looked leery. I couldn't blame her. She crossed her arms over her luscious breasts.

I reached over and grazed my finger across the swell. Her mouth parted and an almost dreamy look crossed her face. I curled my fingers behind her neck.

"Wait." She pulled away, managing to get free. I huffed. A downside to her becoming a vampire. I hadn't thought there would be one, but here I was, hating my inability to pull her around. "I need clothes."

We hadn't had any deliveries yet. Maybe Baron had something she could wear—no, I didn't want another's clothes on her.

While I'd been mulling what to do, Jax strolled up. He yanked his shirts over her head. I knew it was his, because it was basic as fuck.

She sputtered her hair out of her face while Jax scooped it out of the clothes. It fell around her shoulders, the tips fluttering around her arms. We'd get her bundled in all new clothes, but this would do until then.

The way he touched her, so carefully, as if she was made of porcelain, fascinated and excited me. I wanted him to have her sweetness too. The corner of my lips twitched. He'd not removed his gaze from her.

I fucking knew it. No, more like *finally*. I was tired of his stubbornness. It was bound to ruin everything and this time, I refused to save him. But she didn't flinch from his touch. Getting to my feet, I dragged my pants up and tucked my drained cock behind the fabric.

I caught her hand and pulled her from the bedroom. She followed behind, slightly stumbling, but I didn't stop hurrying down the hall. I wanted to show her the new office. While she'd been in bed, leaving me out of the fun, the rest of us were trying to get the estate in order. Making call after call and coordinating duties with Tobias. It'd swallowed up all my time, or I would have been with her sooner.

I'd placed a call to Talia to keep me updated on the club.

Baron would fill the spot of Maddy. She was equipped enough —as long as she didn't give Catalina a difficult time.

I'd already expressed to her the severity of the punishment if she stepped out of line. Extradited from the Coven, or death. Depending on what Pet wanted.

Baron was one of the few humans Jax turned into a vampire.

When Imogen arrived at the manor, I'd sensed problems a mile away. At the beginning, I hadn't known what would happen to the Coven, all I knew was Catalina was mine. And since Imogen had seen the inside of the manor, I no longer wanted Cat anywhere near there long term, so I'd begun to search for an estate with Ren. But to do that, I'd needed help, so I'd reached out to the one vampire that wouldn't betray me for the sole reason that she hated Imogen. But the problem rested in her little obsession with Jaxon.

Good thing Ren had been in agreement to find a new place. Tobias had been wrapped up in revenge and Jax had been fighting himself.

Catalina gawked at the high ceilings. Hopefully she liked it. I'd thought of her when choosing it. She slowed, taking in her new home.

Putting her on the deed would save this place if Imogen managed to get her way and everything was split during the trial. In preparation for that, Tobias had begun to switch most of the monetary assets so they were under Catalina's name.

TWENTY-NINE

THE HALLWAY EXITING the bedroom was long and winding. Other doors littered the halls, but they remained closed.

"There are so many rooms."

"All empty other than beds," Asher announced cheerfully. "Yours is the only one fully furnished." He kept pulling me after him, but fortunately, I'd gotten him to slow down.

"How big *is* this place?"

"This is the fourth floor. There are three levels with this same layout, barring the room I'm about to show you, and then the first floor, which is different."

My bare feet padded across the smooth wood surface of the floor. The slap, slap, slap of my feet echoed down the bare, unfurnished hall. A dead end came up, and at the sharp right there was a narrow staircase. I only had a peek of the steps, because he pulled me past them and into the adjacent hall, heading directly for the two doors facing us. They were wider than all the others I'd seen, but just as tall.

He peeked over his shoulder to grin at me.

An antsiness hovering over my psyche spilled through my veins. Excitement. Genuine excitement I had not experienced in so long—or maybe ever—at least not at this level. Asher's grin was infectious.

"This is your new office," he announced and yanked down the handles to push the doors open with a flourish. The flush-mount ceiling fixture smack in the middle of the office was wide enough to cast soft light over the entire space. The brightness flared and then dimmed again.

"It's adjustable." Asher stood by the door, fiddling with the round knob. "Now that you're a vampire, it'll be easier on the eyes. Not going to lie, this one was Ren's idea." He pursed his lips, chagrined. He stopped messing with the dial and left it at a lower setting.

I grinned and bounced onto my toes to throw my arms around his neck. They'd put thought into the room. He laughed, arms banding around my back. Just as quickly, I let him go, wanting to scope the room out.

"No way," I breathed, staring.

Now this, *this* was definitely my style.

Unlike the rest of the house, the wood floors were a lighter gray, and the walls were a cream shade, including the floor to ceiling bookshelves . . . and the ladder with wheels at the base to reach the higher points of the shelves.

Although I wrote, I'd never collected books, it would have been too difficult to tote them around while on the run. As it was, the small number of items I took place to place was difficult to handle.

Writing had always been an outlet I could sink into, and

second to that was reading, but I seldom had enough time for it. But not now that I had forever.

Emotion clogged my throat, and I squeezed Asher's hand. He grunted and I loosened my grip sheepishly. I peeked up at him under my eyelashes. He studied me with a soft expression.

"I love you," the words spilled from his perfect, pouty lips in a rush. His eyes widened and pink flushed the bridge of his nose and spread to his cheeks.

I struggled to spit words out, but I could only gawk.

Asher grimaced, his eyes shifting side to side. I'd never seen him so discombobulated. It smacked me out of my daze, and I threw my arms around his neck again. His arms slowly slipped around my back and his nose nestled into the crook of my neck. He breathed in audibly.

The thick knot in my throat didn't allow me to say anything. I attributed it to fear and emotions. I squeezed him tighter, and he mimicked my grip.

"You keep rubbing against me like that, I'm going to fuck you before I show you the best part," he said gruffly.

Thank God, I was about to fall apart in Asher's arms.

"All you think about is sex." I rolled my eyes, trying to make light of the heavy moment. He seemed more relaxed now that we moved away from the topic.

"You're much too delicious not to," Asher grumbled and turned me in a circle to face the wall beside the doors. There was another floor to ceiling shelf, but this one had a row with books already neatly organized.

"Those . . . I wrote those." Blood flooded my cheeks. "How did you find out my pen name."

He grinned.

"You guys had me investigated?" I asked sharply.

"Just some light invasion, Pet, nothing to get your panties in a twist over." I glared. "That aunt of yours was nothing more than a figure head." He tsked. "You've been relying on yourself for much too long."

I raised Peter. I'd been all he could rely on.

"I don't blame her for needing to focus on her family," I mumbled, walking over to the shelf. Asher leaned his shoulder against the side of it. He plucked one of the books from the shelf.

He wiggled his eyebrow up and down, waving the man chest cover toward my face.

"I'm a little jealous, but I'll let it be." He sniffled in sharply.

"Pft." I plucked it from his fingers and tucked it back in place. I turned away from the probing glances. I felt raw and flayed open. I licked my lips and took my time taking in the rest of the room. Asher didn't stop watching me, and it made me more self-conscious than I anticipated.

No windows.

My tastes swung more along the basic spectrum. Neat, simple, and elegant were good descriptors of my fashion sense.

Deep burgundy accents littered the room. The chair behind the desk, the abstract rose painting on the wall. I ran my finger along the smooth surface of the cream-colored desk.

"You will no longer have to worry about a thing. We will take care of you."

The words felt like he'd reached inside me and squeezed my stomach. I used the desk as a prop for my suddenly weak knees. The part that couldn't rely on anyone for so long writhed inside me, frightened. But the much larger part in me that craved belonging, swelled.

"Stop," I muttered, not facing him. His thumb rubbed my cheek.

"How long have you been planning this?" Jax's sharp voice sliced through my musings.

When I turned, Jax stood an inch from Asher, not looking happy. Asher didn't seem bothered by his brother's ire. He lifted his hand to inspect and pick at the cuticle.

"While you were up Imogen's ass," he drawled.

Jax stiffened. The bunch of his arm, the cording of his neck. He was going to hit Asher. I moved forward too quickly. My head spun, but I managed to catch Jax's fist, before it slammed into Asher's face.

"Do not start fighting in here," I chastised. "You ruin one inch of this office and I'm—" Jax raised an eyebrow. "You won't like what I do." I poked my nose higher in the air, but instead of looking intimidated, Jax only smiled. He tapped the tip of my nose.

I scowled up at him, pouting my lower lip out.

"Are you two good now?" Asher's eyes seemed too bright.

"Yes."

"Trial basis."

Jax and I spoke at the same time. I glared at him. "Mighty sure of yourself, bloodsucker."

"Determined."

"What have you done with my twin?" Asher gasped, pressing his hand to his chest.

"Don't get too excited," I mumbled, tossing them a warning look and backed away to continue taking in my new desk. My laptop sat on the surface, ready and waiting for me.

"When did you have time to do all this?" Jax asked, pacing the room as he took everything in.

"Ren helped and we tasked a vampire we knew would have nothing to do with Imogen. Talia was too busy to burden with all this." Asher turned to me. "You'll meet Baron later; she helped us get everything organized."

"Baron?" Jax snapped, multiple expressions sifted over his features, all of them negative. He turned toward me and was next to me in the next second. He took my hand and yanked me to face him. I caught myself before smacking nose-first into his chest.

"I didn't fuck her."

I blinked up at him. "Ever."

"Uh, okay," I said hesitantly.

His lips pursed.

"I have never and will never care for another but you, Catalina."

I frowned up at him. He seemed desperate to make me believe it.

"You're seeming more suspicious with your passion, Jaxon," Asher chortled.

"You should not have chosen her to help," Jax snapped.

"I had to work quickly." Asher sobered up, his lips twisting.

"Some more explanation would be nice?"

Jax let my hand go after a quick squeeze.

"She's someone I turned." I knew that bit.

"What are you trying to get at here, Jax," I asked wryly.

He ran his palm over his face. More than anything, his reaction put me on edge.

Asher tossed his arm over my shoulder.

"He's nervous," Asher whispered exaggeratedly into my ear. Jax sneered at Asher. "I had a talk with her. She knows to be on good behavior."

They both looked chagrined.

"Fine," Jax muttered.

Asher was right, this was definitely a new Jax.

"I want to see the rest of the house."

"Your wish is my command," Asher said, hooking an arm with mine and pulling me from my new office.

THIRTY

I TOOK my time trailing after Asher as he showed me the third and second level of the new place. He'd accurately described it. The floors mirrored the first one. The only difference was the spot where the library was on the top floor didn't exist on the rest of them. I couldn't help but compare the houses. The one I'd become used to, that had started to feel like home while this was a monstrosity.

The narrow staircase spiraled down. I reached the base of the stairs, and it spit us into a slim hallway. Asher continued forward, arms swinging at his side.

"I prefer this location," Jax mused from behind me.

"Right? Secluded, less windows. Getting the mechanical shutters installed was one of the first things I had Baron do. Cost a pretty penny, but I'd rather spend it all than let Imogen get her bitchy hands on it."

"How did you get the money withdrawals past Tobias?"

"All of you were too busy—"

"Got it," Jax snapped, interrupting him.

"Do you need Tobias's permission or something?" I wondered.

"Or something, Pet." Asher slowed, and it allowed me to catch up to him. He threw his arm over my shoulder. "All our assets have been combined for decades. Just another attempt for Imogen to get us under her thumb."

"And you just realized that?" Jax drawled.

"Of course not," Asher huffed, almost offended.

And what Imogen wanted from Jax, she got it. I peeked over my shoulder. Jax's eyes weren't focused. The trauma bond he'd had with Imogen was for him to unpack. I couldn't do it for him. He was coming to the realization of just how toxic and manipulative she'd been. Or more accurately, he'd known, and that was what he struggled with, the fact that he never should have gone along with so much of it.

"I need to check in with Tobias about something," Jax muttered and was then gone in a flash. He'd been in a dependent relationship. That was what Jax struggled with—I based this assumption on nothing more than a guess. I could totally be wrong. But theorizing about it helped me feel better about his past.

Men's minds, even vampire males, were something I didn't want to begin taking apart. The hallway leading from the base of the staircase ended and opened to the left. This was one similarity to the other house, the foyer, except it stretched more in a rectangle than a square.

The front door was wide open, and the sconce light caught the little knocker. I approached and using a finger, lifted the bat knocker and released it. Metal clanged against metal. Unlike the one at Crimson Manor, this bat was upright, and its little wings were spread out upwards.

I pursed my lips.

"I'll be right back," Asher muttered and crossed the foyer, walking down to the left exiting hall. From the opposite direction Asher went, soft chatter reached my ears. I focused and made out Ren's deep voice echoing from the opposite side. He'd saved my computer, and he'd gotten this place with Asher. I passed a small living room area and hurried around the bend of the second threshold and stepped into a huge kitchen. His back was to me as he spoke to Tobias and Jax, they were deep in conversation.

I was hyper-focused on Ren.

"We need to have Talia vet another human to work here—"

I threw my arms around his waist, clinging. His body stiffened and his hard abdomen flexed.

"Cat?" he said, a slight question in his tone.

His palm covered my wrist, and he squeezed. Not letting go of him, I shuffled until I was in front of him with my arms still around his waist. My neck craned to look at him.

Ren's eyes flicked to the side then returned to mine. He seemed almost uncomfortable with my show of affection. I dropped my arms, but before I could back away, he pressed his palm to the middle of my back and forced me back to him. I grunted from the force he plastered me to his chest. He avoided looking down at me.

I rolled my lips into my mouth, keeping my smile from blooming. I'd interrupted whatever conversation he'd been having with Tobias.

"Son of a bitch," Asher hissed. I whirled to see him storm through the entrance beside the fridge in a huff. He beelined right to the fridge. He yanked open the door and pulled out a blood bag and collected a glass cup from the cabinet to the side.

He yanked open the packet with his teeth. I didn't watch him pour it in, because my attention was on the doorway where a woman stood with her mouth hanging open. Fangs poked out, framed by her bright pink lipstick.

Her long curly hair swayed around her shoulders.

"Jaxon," a woman cried out. She clapped her hands together and flounced forward.

Her bright pink dress fluttered around her knees and her tall heels clicked on the cream tile. Those pumps were to die for.

She charged right toward Jax. He grabbed my bicep and yanked me away from Ren so I was between her and them. Just in time for her to smack right into my forehead. She hissed, cupping her chin, and in the process hit me with her elbow.

I winced.

"Catalina," Jax gasped. He cupped my face and smoothed his thumb across my lower lip. I sucked it into my mouth to lick up the blood from my fang slicing into my lip. Tonguing the area, I didn't feel the cut anymore.

"Be careful," Asher hissed. She flinched, her nose wrinkling.

The woman, dark haired, willow-y and painfully beautiful, stared with her lips parted.

This must be Baron. Her eyes flicked to me and then to Jax.

"I was just going to say hi." An accent thickened her voice. She huffed, eyeing Jax over my shoulder. I cleared my throat.

"Catalina." Her big brown eyes focused on me, she threw her arms around me, squishing my boobs against hers. She pulled back, keeping hold of the outside of my arms. "Please do not misunderstand, young vampire. I saved myself for Jax, and he only tossed it in my face." Her eyes narrowed at him over my shoulders.

"How is that my fault?" Jax snapped. "Let her go."

Baron dropped her hands and crossed her arms with another exaggerated huff. She dropped me with the speed of a vampire doing as their Sire ordered.

Ren bunched the back of her curly hair and yanked her back another step. She stumbled on her heels.

"Do not touch her."

Baron put her hands up and tried to pull away, unsuccessfully.

"Apologies," she mumbled. "I did not know you were serious, Asher; you are never serious about these things. Especially females."

I touched Ren's arm. He let her go and crossed his arms, not looking like he'd just yanked her around. She patted her hair down with a frown. Her brown eyes focused on mine, and she pursed her lips.

"I mean no disrespect," she said, her eyes wide and flicking side to side. All of her earlier energy tamped down.

"Don't even worry about it, they're being dramatic." I flicked my gaze from one too-stiff vampire to the other. "Asher told me you helped find this place. I love it."

"Yes." She perked up. "I did . . ." She continued to ramble on. She smelled pretty good. Not as good as their blood, but something that would do. I couldn't look away from her throat. Was she stepping close to me? A hand yanked me back and I bounced against a chest.

"Be a dear, Baron, and purchase some more items for the house and some clothing for everyone," Asher ordered, sounding rushed. I shook my head to snap myself out of the craving.

"I will compile a list!" She clapped and turned to me. "I will show you when I am done." Her heels clicked as she rushed away.

I waited until she was gone to exhale and buried my face in my hands.

"Why am I like this?" I mumbled.

"I might have an answer for you," Bastien said. I whirled to him, where he stood at the entrance of a different area connected to the kitchen. He wore fresh clothes, and his slacks were attached to shoulder straps, keeping the pants up. "But I need to take a look at your blood to confirm my theory."

"What's your theory?"

Bastien scratched the bridge of his nose.

"That you are a predator to vampires." I only blinked, because what the hell? Me as a predator was hilarious. "We all know about evolution. Vampires are apex predators. It would make sense for the gene to mutate. But I do not think it was quote, unquote, 'nature' which caused this."

"Hunters," Ren added and by his tone, I could tell they'd already talked about this.

"Hunters? Like Vampire hunters?"

"Before we got rid of them, they'd been collecting vampires, trapping them and experimenting on them," Bastien said.

"And you think they created me?"

"Not necessarily you, but a gene that developed and evolved with time, making you, for lack of a better phrase, a vampire's predator." I could only gawk at Bastien.

"So, my blood heals vampires like yours heals humans?"

"That's my theory." But if that was the case.

"Am I able to compel you?" I whirled and stepped in front of the closest vampire. Jax stared down at me. "How would you do this?"

Asher pressed against my back and leaned down until his lips brushed against my ear. "Relax, look into his eyes, and push your order at him."

I rolled my shoulders and looked into Jax's lapis blue eyes, making sure to *feel* my desire behind the order. "Shift into Binx."

"It's called morphing," Jax offered. Damn, it didn't work.

"What about humans?"

"If you can't compel vampires, why would you be able to compel humans?"

I pursed my lips.

Asher chuckled against my ear.

"Maybe you're wrong?" I said to Bastien.

He still watched from a few feet away, rubbing his chin pensively. He shook his head.

"Jaxon, are you absolutely sure you were unable to feed her your blood?"

"I am sure, she didn't swallow anything."

Bastien nodded slowly.

"The gene must have been in her already," Tobias murmured. "It makes sense. Her immunity to being compelled. Her taste, her scent."

"So, I was never human?" They were beginning to confuse me.

"You were human, you simply carried a gene." A gene that would have been passed down.

"Why didn't my parents turn when they died?"

"I believe it has to be activated by vampire blood or being bitten. I am not . . ." Bastien trailed off, a slight glaze crossing his red eyes.

I touched his bicep. He shook his head and focused on me. "What was I talking about?" He palmed his head.

"That I was essentially genetically engineered, and my change was activated."

Bastien hummed, straightening, as if he'd never hunched forward.

"You attract your hunt. The way humans are attracted to vampires."

"Why don't I have any neat ability?"

"Genetics can be influenced by other sources." He shrugged those large shoulders, and the suspenders stretched over his shoulders flexed. "Once my lab equipment arrives, I'll be able to further my study."

A ding prompted Asher to pull his phone out. His jaw fluttered and he looked up at Tobias and slightly turned his head.

Tobias's eyes narrowed.

Asher pressed a kiss to the top of my head.

"We'll be right back, Pet."

Ren and Tobias had already disappeared.

"Wait—" The rest of my sentence was cut off by an arm banding around my stomach. I grunted from the force of being smushed to a chest. Bastien jerked me back so quickly it gave me whiplash. I yelped and shoved at his arm, but he snarled in my ear.

"What are you doing?" I huffed. Jax was gone too. I struggled in Bastien's embrace, but he only gripped onto me tighter. I gritted my teeth and smacked at him. Bastien jolted. Ha, now that I was a vampire he'd feel it. I wiggled until I turned in his arms.

I shook my head.

"You're Jekyll one minute, and then peekaboo, here comes Hyde. No warning, no nothing." He didn't react to my comment.

"Bastien," I shouted. He shuddered and closed his eyes, leaning all his weight forward until his forehead rested on my shoulder. His fists perched on the kitchen table, corralling me between them.

I gripped his shoulder and shook him a little. "Bastien?"

His arm wrapped around my waist.

"That was an unfortunate lapse." He cleared his throat, straightening as he smoothed his palm down his chest. "Did I harm you?"

"I'm fine—"

A shout echoed from the foyer.

My slowed heartbeat jumped. What was it now?

catalina

THE CHATTER of unfamiliar voices came from the foyer. I let go of Bastien's hand and ran toward the sniffling and arguing.

"And you thought to bring everyone *here*?" Jax hissed.

"I am sorry, Sires," Talia's strained voice echoed to me. "I didn't know what to do." She sounded so lost. I hurried through the threshold and came to an abrupt stop.

A group of five hovered near the door, covered in soot.

"We had no choice," a short female vampire with blonde streaks in her hair said, her voice trembling. Jax snarled at her.

She screamed and ran behind another taller female with long flowing hair and brown skin. In her flurry, she bumped a smaller figure who stumbled to the side.

"Sydney?" I said, frowning, hurrying to help her straighten. I smoothed her messy hair back from her cheeks. Bits of ash floated off her. "What happened?"

Her lip trembled but no tears came. She opened her mouth and closed it. I turned to look at Talia who had her lips pursed and stared at the ground. Asher and Jax stood in front of her, glaring.

"What's going on?" I turned to Tobias who stood near the wall.

"Crimson Nights was burned down." I returned my attention to the soot covered group.

"It's not Talia's fault. We didn't know where to go and the sun is going to be up soon," Sydney whispered.

I fixed a glare on Jax. Raising Peter had created a mother hen of me when it came to kids.

"She could have exposed our location to Imogen by coming here," Jax snapped, angling his glare at them. Talia dropped her head.

"We will leave—"

"Let's just stop for a second," I said, stepping back. "You guys aren't going anywhere."

"Pet—" I whipped toward him so fast I gave myself whiplash. Asher shut up. Everyone's attention focused on me. Other than Sydney and Talia, a lean man stood huddled with three others. A quick scan told me they were all vampires.

"It is close to sunrise. So, instead of kicking your Progeny out, we should probably fix up some rooms."

"Catalina, having others—"

I shoved my elbow into Jax's stomach.

"And you two over there, stop being secretive."

The back-and-forth between Ren and Tobias toward the corner of the room shut up.

"Where did Baron go?" I scanned for her, but she'd disappeared to make a list. "Baron!" I shouted.

She was the only other person around that knew the layout of the place and knew where all the stuff was.

"You called for me?" Baron's voice echoed from down the hall. She rounded into the foyer and slowed. "Oh my, visitors." She grinned.

"Baron, can you get everyone set up in a bedroom?"

A heavy sigh came from one of my vampires, but I ignored them.

"There are no furnishings—"

"Where are you sleeping?"

She pursed her lips. It was obvious she wasn't exactly a fan of my suggestion.

"I will figure out something for tonight." She inclined her head and then turned her brilliant smile over to the group. "If you all follow me to the second floor."

The four vampires turned to look at Asher questioningly. He met my eyes and then scratched his temple.

"Fine." He sighed. He turned back to the vampires waiting for his order. "Go. You are not to contact anyone."

They exhaled simultaneously and scurried to follow Baron, shooting me curious looks as they passed.

"You turned them?" I asked Asher.

He pursed his lips. "Ex lovers?"

He blustered, shaking his head.

"Assssher?" I glowered.

"I don't remember," he mumbled, miffed.

"I think that's the last thing we should be talking about," Talia said sharply. She shot a glare toward me.

Jax hissed.

Talia flinched and hugged herself.

"She has a point," I said. I'd allowed myself to get distracted. But to give myself credit, I wasn't trying to be difficult, it was a simple question. I cleared my throat. "Crimson Nights was burned down?"

Talia didn't look at me.

"Yes, they were hit a few hours ago." At least she answered.

"Imogen is a real piece of work." I grimaced. "Since it was a direct attack, can the Council do something about it?"

"The cameras didn't catch anything. And like last time, they made it seem like a hate crime," Talia said.

"If we start accusing her, she'll claim its retaliation." Tobias ran his hand through his hair.

"So, there's nothing we can do?"

A hand settled on my shoulder. Tobias shook his head.

"Not yet. We can attempt to find a witness that will prove her culpability, but Imogen never leaves witnesses."

The vampire justice system was as broken as the human one.

"That's bullshit." I scowled. Tobias's eyebrows twitched.

Talia cleared her throat, and she faced Asher.

"We caught a vampire skulking around, but he's not talking." Talia sniffled. "We have him in the trunk wrapped up in tons of chains."

"Perfect." I could only describe Ren's grin as wolfish. He was through the open door within moments, Jax on his heels.

"Asher, we lost vampires," Talia croaked. She eyed me. "Maybe we should speak in private."

"Treat Catalina the same as you would me."

"Yes, Sire." She lowered her head. "Again, I am sorry for showing up here."

A scuffle sounded outside.

"Catalina, Pet." Asher gripped my arms. I looked up at him. "You should go. You're not going to want to see what they do."

I scowled. I opened my mouth to argue and Ren and Jax entered, dragging a struggling body between them.

A sack covered his face. He thrashed between them, wiggling side to side frantically, the chains around him rattling.

I watched them drag him away.

Then I turned to Asher.

"I'll be writing." I hurried upstairs.

ASHER

I BALANCED on the two back legs of the chair. Tobias leaned forward, elbows on the dining table, hands buried in his hair. Everything was in danger of going to shit. We'd taken a vote and unanimously decided to keep the trial date from Catalina. She would know nothing. We needed her to stay safe and out of the way.

Imogen's goal was to cripple us. She knew what the night club meant to me. But the anger I expected wasn't as searing as I anticipated.

Tobias's gaze remained unfocused.

"What are you mulling over?" I asked.

"We need to set up precautions."

"Should I get Amira on Imogen?" She was a good spy and in all the years she'd been watching Calliope, she'd not been caught. "She has the best chance of finding her." Her ability to track never failed.

"Yes, do that," Bastien said from where he hovered near the fridge.

"I'll call her and pull her from Calliope."

catalina

I FINISHED TYPING out my email to Peter, asking him to call me on Asher's phone as soon as possible. He had a life back in Mexico, but at the very least, I merited a call. I puffed out my cheeks. That wasn't fair of me. He had classes, and his girlfriend, and things kids his age did.

Things I didn't have a chance at experiencing, because I'd been too busy worrying about him. Worrying about my aunt getting angry at one of us and sending us away. As hard as all of that had been, I wouldn't trade it because if we'd gone to the system after our parents passed, there was no assurance that we would have been able to stay together.

It was sad how much I spent my life worrying and in fight or flight mode. No wonder I'd needed so many little routines for myself. Baths, skin care, painting my nails, all of it allowed me to shut my brain off and focus on myself.

It was difficult to break the habit though. My brain kept swirling around the idea of one of the visiting vampires killing me. I didn't know how, and I knew my vampires would never allow it, but it was a worry, nonetheless. So, I'd stashed a stake under my mattress. Just in case.

I clicked send on the email and leaned back. The cushioned chair reclined. I smoothed my palms along the soft fabric of the arm rests. I'd taken a moment to look up some of the stuff they'd set up in here, and when I saw the price tag of the chair, I stopped looking.

I rubbed my hands over my face. I would blame my scrambled brain on my sleeping situation, but to be completely honest, once the sun rose, I knew and felt nothing until sundown, when I woke up. My body no longer felt the effects of sleep, good or otherwise.

A creak caused my eyes to fling open. Tobias studied me from near the door. I'd not paid any of them a thought when I woke up this morning, I'd headed directly to my new office.

"How are you, Love?" He slowly approached. I leaned forward and slumped against the desk, dropping my cheek on my arm. He perched on the desk a few inches from me. He slowly reached out. I followed the progression of his hand coming toward my head. He was giving me time to back away from his touch.

I didn't move and he gently tucked my hair behind my ear.

"You don't have to be so cautious," I said, half-muffled from how I laid against my arm. His lips twitched.

"We do not deserve you." He sighed, sounding almost sad. "But you will be taken care of for eternity."

"Don't promise something you can't be sure about," I mumbled.

He chuckled.

"You don't understand, Catalina. You've earned us and you will never be rid of us."

A hot flush flooded my chest, forcing me to take a breath. The sweet scent of his blood filled my nose, and I stiffened, holding my breath. But it was too late, the damage was done. My fangs stretched from my gums and a burn pulsated my throat. I straightened, smiling sheepishly.

"I am your meal for the day, Love."

I blinked up at him as he tugged the sweater off, leaving him half naked.

"Do you guys have some 'feeding Cat' rotation going on?" I snorted. The idea was ridiculous.

"Yes, we do." He folded the sweater and carefully set it behind him.

I scoffed, but everything except his lean muscle faded from my mind. He was compact strength to the point that I could see the dips and curves of his torso. A line cut the edges of his stomach and with him curved, I could make out the faint outline of his abdomen.

He pressed a finger under my chin and forced my face up. I looked into his gray eyes. "Are you okay with me feeding you?" He went silent and a little dent formed between his eyebrows.

In answer, I stood and slid my arms around his neck. He was so smooth and taut. His carefully parted hair sat in place. He never applied product in it. He was blessed with silky, perfect hair. I ran my fingers over the moles littering his shoulder. My eyes fastened on his throat. The smooth column called my name. Unlike humans, his pulse didn't jump under his skin. Too much time between each beat of his heart.

I pushed to my toes to reach his shoulder and pressed a kiss to his skin on one of his moles. A shudder worked over his shoulders. He slid off the edge of the desk. His arm lashed around my waist, and he pressed me flush against him. I craned my head to look into his gray eyes, tracing a path to his upturned nose. The arm banded around me tightened and he lifted me, turning me to perch me on the edge of the desk. It allowed me to reach him without straining so much, especially since he leaned down and pressed his palms into the desk, corralling me.

I sank my teeth into his shoulder. Blood flowed to the surface. The sweet taste spilled into my mouth. My fingers tightened into his back, and I pressed myself to him, stretching my mouth to cover the puncture wounds. I moaned, licking every drop of blood he offered me. I widened my legs, pressing my inner thighs against his hips.

Tobias ground forward, rubbing his hardness into the apex of my thighs. I slid my hands higher, until I slipped them into his hair. I speared them into the neat strands. He tasted so good. I moaned and he jolted against me with a guttural grunt.

Pulling back from his neck, I licked the punctures so they would heal faster and pressed kisses to his shoulder, up his jaw and to his lips. I slid my tongue against his and he matched my energy. I turned my head to twine my tongue around his, while I dropped my hands down to his waistband. The slacks were easy to unlatch.

His cock bobbed free, bouncing against my hand. I clasped onto the shaft and squeezed. He groaned, hips gyrating forward. I forced my fangs back into my gums.

Lust had taken hold of me, along with the furious need to see him lose control. Them losing it was an image I'd become addicted to. I slid off the edge of the desk and dropped to my knees.

I peeked up at him. His mouth was parted as he watched me with hungry eyes. I gripped the base of his cock. The tip beaded with liquid and my throat burned. I took him into my mouth. The salty taste coated my tongue, and I lapped the silky underside. Tobias gasped, his head falling back. I repeated the motion and with each one, he jolted on my tongue. I breathed in to smell his sweet blood.

My fangs burst free and pierced the side of his cock. He shouted, sagging forward, his palms slamming onto the desk to prop him up. I sucked blood from his cock and Tobias hissed, his hand bunching my hair. I couldn't stop if I wanted. His sweet blood filled my mouth. I sucked again and he throbbed in my mouth. I forced my fangs back in and flicked my tongue against the puncture wounds.

"For God's sake, Catalina," he said, breathless. "I-I can not stop—"

His hand stiffened in my hair, and I could tell he had tried to pull me away from his straining cock, but I didn't let him pull me away. His shaft jolted and cum pooled in my mouth, mingling with blood. I closed my eyes, swallowing every drop of his release.

I was so into licking his shaft, that it took me a moment to register how he panted. I slowly lifted off him. He watched me with wide eyes. I smiled sheepishly, dropping my hands to my lap. He closed his eyes, shaking his head.

"Unbelievable," he muttered under his breath. His blood warmed my veins, and I studied Tobias still leaned over, with his palms propped on the desk.

"Tobias?" I said, concerned.

He straightened and staggered back a step. I hopped to my feet to grab his arm.

"Are you okay?"

He huffed out a laugh.

I studied his pale features, and the pinched aspect to his lips. "Have you fed?"

"Not yet, I will get a blood bag—" I lifted my wrist to my mouth and sank my fangs into the thin skin. I offered it to Tobias. Blood trickled down to my elbow in the seconds he stared.

"Hurry or it will close—" I stopped with a grunt. He took my wrist and covered it with his mouth. As soon as his lick flicked across the bleeding wounds, his eyes flashed red, and he took hold of me with both hands. He grunted against my arm, sucking hard. The ticklish sensation warmed my belly. His eyelids lowered and he moaned. My eyes dropped to his hardening cock. On the third slurp, he squeezed my arm and pulled back abruptly. His shoulders moved with harsh breaths.

"Your taste has only enhanced," he said, voice roughened.

"I feel like I should say thank you."

He snorted and my eyebrows flew up. I'd never heard him make that sound. He cleared his throat and yanked his pants closed then plucked the sweater off the desk. With a quick jerk, he was dressed.

"Right, well." He cleared his throat. "Come down, so I can introduce you to our temporary inhabitants."

I leaned forward and pecked his lips.

"Yes, Priest," I said cheekily.

The corner of his lips twitched.

"Ex—" I mouthed the word at the same time he did. He clicked his tongue, shaking his head, exasperation all over his face.

He caught my hand, and I swung our arms between us as we walked through the halls and down the stairs. Once on the first level, we crossed to the right of the foyer and entered the kitchen.

Three vampires sat at the tall dining table, staring at the red liquid in the wine glasses. A smiling Baron stood across from them, her arms crossed. All of their eyes flung in our direction as we entered. They looked at my face, dropped to our clasped hands, then to Tobias. They seemed especially focused. I followed their gaze.

The front of his hair stuck straight up. He looked recently fucked. I pursed my lips and reached up to smooth the hair sticking up.

"Catalina," Baron said, sounding pleased. She flowed over to me. "Let me introduce you to everyone. This is Damien, Violet," she said, motioning to the vampire with blonde stripes in her hair. "And Laney." She pointed at the last girl. The girls wore very pink clothes, while Damien had on a too big shirt.

"Hi—"

"Thank you so much." Laney stood so fast the chair scratched the ground. She laced her hands together and cleared her throat. "For letting us stay."

"Kiss ass," Violet muttered. She lounged in her chair. I caught Damien's wince.

"I am so sorry about her." Laney glared at Violet. "We won't be a problem at all."

"Sit down," Violet hissed at her. "And you don't need to apologize for me." Laney's lips twisted and she dropped on the chair.

"You know what Sire said," Laney murmured at Violet.

"Sire?" I sighed. "Asher talked to you." I didn't need to ask him to know. I clicked my tongue. I looked up at Tobias. "He's such a busy body."

His lips twitched.

"That's why he's the contact person."

"Well, then. As I was saying. We are not going to have feeders here. There are enough blood bags to satisfy your thirst." Baron turned to me, but my attention was still on Violet scrunching her nose at the wine glass. "Your things should be delivered soon."

"I thought you needed me to check the list?"

"Asher confirmed it already." Her eyes widened. "Do you need me to cancel the order?"

"Not at all, he knows what I like." And he had great taste.

"He knows what a lot of people like," Talia said, standing near the fridge. I whipped to look at her, lips pressed together. My stomach dipped to the floor. I scanned the faces looking at me. They were all Asher's Progeny.

Footsteps shut everyone up.

"Pet," he exclaimed with a grin, walking toward me. I couldn't relax my stiff posture. His hand on my shoulder slid off.

"Asher," I said wryly, trying to keep my cool. Talia really did not like me. Baron glared at Talia and Laney had dropped her eyes, while the rest avoided looking at us.

I wasn't stupid, I knew he had a large body count, but she didn't need to be cruel about it.

"Pet." His lips thinned, and he scanned my face. "What is it?" He sounded so serious.

I sidled close to him and slid my arms around his waist. "You're mine?"

He nuzzled the top of my hair. "For eternity, *Älskade*."

THIRTY-THREE

I CLOSED the pliers around his finger and the gush of blood and crack of bone came with my squeeze. His blood spurted onto my drenched shirt. The chained vampire jerked against the chains binding him to the chair. He was limp and the chains were all that held him upright. Vampires could not regenerate appendages, but if he spoke up, I'd do him a solid and keep his fingers so he could have them sewn back on. Eventually, they could heal up.

"Are you going to talk?" I asked him.

The bastard sneered at me, blood still covering his face. I'd removed all fingers from his left hand, but he was pissing me off to the point that I would chop off both hands.

I lifted his arm, studying the finger bone sticking out. The cut had been clean through. I turned toward Ren, waving the last finger at him.

"Any new ideas?"

Ren was just as bloody as me. He'd taken his turn first and beaten the vampire until every bone broke in his body. Then we waited for him to heal before I had my turn. The door slammed shut and footsteps thudded on the tile. Bastien entered, carrying a large box. He placed it on his table.

"Keep your activities to that side of the room." Bastien flicked the finger away that had flown to his worktable, across the room. "You will contaminate my study."

He sliced the box open and rifled through the contents, setting things next to his other materials.

"We can just kill him," Ren said. His calm words didn't fool me, he was pissed the fucker wasn't talking.

"I can make him talk," I said, resolved. I scanned the drooping body. "We can cut off his dick, see if that will give him incentive."

His body stiffened.

Gotcha.

"No," he croaked, whimpering.

Ah, something I could work with.

"Do we have sharper pliers?"

"You're being generous." Ren laughed.

I smirked and moved forward.

A hesitant knock came from the door. "Can I come in?" Catalina called.

"Hide that," Bastien snapped.

"Fuck," I hissed. I shoved a rag into his mouth and pulled the binding hanging from his neck over it so he couldn't spit it out.

Ren tossed a large tarp over the area to cover the blood and gore. She would smell the mess, but at least she would not see it.

We had it all covered in time for Catalina to stride through. She slowed, frowning as she swept her gaze across Bastien's lab.

"Why are you guys looking all suspicious—ah." She cleared her throat, looking at the blood the tarp wasn't long enough to cover. Catalina's eyes widened. "I don't want to know what you're doing to that vampire, huh?"

"No," I responded.

She grimaced.

"I'll stay curious." She turned to Bastien. "Tobias let me know your stuff to check my blood out arrived."

"Yes, it did, Little One." He patted the bench to the side of his worktable. She propped her luscious ass on it.

"Oh, and, Jax, Asher was looking for you. He wanted to know if you got the guy to say anything."

"Right." I cleared my throat and went in search of the others. Ren deviated to kiss her forehead and then trailed after me as Bastien set up his syringe.

Fuck, I would like to switch spots with him. Being near Catalina allowed me a peace I never could have anticipated. Being around her was like how I imagined being around the sun was. It had been so long since I'd felt it's touch but the warmth that spread in my gut whenever I even thought of her didn't seem possible.

I'd believed Imogen was my Beloved, but I'd been wrong. What I had felt was a manifestation of what I believed it would have felt like. Now I understood how I could so easily fall to Catalina. She was my true match. She completed our Coven.

catalina

BASTIEN CAREFULLY SET ASIDE a rounded dish. I knew absolutely zero about science beyond the words mitochondria and nucleus. His large body leaned over the desk. He'd tossed the box toward the large tarp covering the vampire they had tied up. I forced my attention away from the pooling blood. I meant what I said, not knowing was best.

I had a soft heart—I acknowledged I wouldn't be able to handle whatever mess was under there. It wasn't like I could stop it; the vampire had been a part of the plan to burn Crimson Nights down, I wanted him to spill.

I knew how losing everything felt. And answers were needed. Imogen was behind all of this, but it had to be proven.

"Genetic mutations and recent scientific discoveries have come a long way. So much has changed in the decades I have been trapped." He lifted the needle, drawing back the plunger. "So much has changed, yet so much has remained the same." A small smile played along his lips. "Humans never know when to quit."

"You can say that again," I muttered.

"Humans never know—"

"I didn't mean that literally." I laughed. Bastien cocked his head studying me. A small smile crested his lips. His red eyes scanned my face.

"I am not sure what you mean." He frowned. I pressed my lips together.

"You have a lot to learn."

Bastien grunted. "Yes, I will learn quickly. Asher ordered that device for me." A computer rested toward the other end of the metal table. "Hold out your arm."

He slid the needle into the bend of my elbow. He tugged the tube connected to it. Oh, so slowly, blood traveled up the tube and slowly began to fill the bag.

"This will take a while, but I need to take additional blood to check if there are antibodies matched in the ones I found in mine. Then I will combine it with human and then vampire blood to see the reaction." He seemed so in his head about all of this. Intelligence brightened his eyes. He liked doing this stuff.

"Is that all I am to you, Bastien, an experiment?" He excitement was oddly cute.

"Not at all." He straightened so quickly; it jostled the blood in the bag.

"I don't know, it sounds like it." A muscle jumped in his jaw, but his expression remained non-aggressive. Messing with him was fun. A flustered Bastien.

"You are not an experiment—"

My smile stretched the corner of my lips.

"You are laughing at my expense," he said, nodding.

He cupped the back of my neck and tugged my chin up to look at him. He studied me with blood red eyes. They no longer made me want to run the other direction. He hadn't known what he'd done. "Naughty, Little One," he said gruffly against my lips.

I smiled. He grunted and caught my mouth. He glided his tongue against my fang and groaned.

"If I do not finish now, I will not be able to." He sighed and straightened. He fiddled with the bag and my dark-red blood swished side to side.

"I heard you beat Asher on how many Progeny you have. Is it really that many?"

"I like experimenting." So that was a yes.

He raised the needle from my skin. A single drop of blood formed. Bastien lowered his head and swiped his tongue across it. He hummed.

"And what makes me taste good to vampires?"

"That you're a predator. Your food source is us. It was an attempt of hunters to take us out, but I believe it's morphed and yours behaves like an antibiotic, attacking the virus." He wagged the bag of blood at me. "There will be answers soon."

"Can I stay and watch you work?"

"You are always welcome where I am." Bastien cupped my jaw and kissed my forehead. Butterflies flooded my stomach. Such a sweet talker.

"Can you hand me your computer?" He slid it toward me, then returned to drawing a vial from the blood bag. He removed the tube and sealed the cap onto the edge of the clear bag. He left the vial on the little stand and took the bag to the mini fridge where he'd stored more bags of blood.

I logged into a streaming account I'd created this morning.

"The fastest way to learn about changes." I typed away. "Is to watch recent media." Bastien returned to the edge of the desk and began to assemble some metal thing—a microscope?

I scooted over to his side and angled the screen of the computer toward him. So, as he worked, we watched a show.

That was how Ren found us.

"What is this trash?" He raised an eyebrow.

"Hey!" I scowled.

"It's not terrible," Bastien drawled, shrugging. I elbowed him.

"Admit you love it."

Bastien suddenly bowed forward. A piece of hair slipped from the tie pulling it back and caressed his cheek.

I reached out to touch his shoulder. He whipped his head toward me with a snarl and lashed his arm around my waist with my back to his front. He dragged me to him, hissing at Ren. The vial of blood in the little stand tipped over and began to roll. Ren caught it before it shattered.

Bastien sank his fangs into the side of my neck. I gasped, the rush of endorphins hitting me like a truck. I could feel every inch of his body pressed up against me. His hard shaft shoved against my back. Bastien removed his fangs from my neck and slammed them into my shoulder. Liquid dripped down my collar bone.

Ren's eyes flashed red, and he was in my face, burrowing into the side of my neck and biting. I screamed, jolting between them.

Clothing tore, and my shirt was gone. A cock pressed against my ass and then lower, seeking my core. He gripped the back of my neck and smushed my cheek against Ren's chest. Bastien thrust, seating himself deep inside me. I grunted from the quick thrust.

Ren braced me, hooking his arm under my knees and spread me wide. I cried out at the change of angle. His other hand went to his jeans, and he yanked. He guided himself to my sex.

He worked his tip inside me. My channel throbbed around Bastien, and the fit became tighter than it already was. I was so wet I easily took them. I hissed a breath out between my fangs. I hadn't noticed when they'd popped out.

I sank my fingers into Ren's shoulder, writhing between them as Bastien continued thrusting. He sank his fangs into my neck again and licked up the side, lapping up my blood. It felt so good.

I shuddered, my body trembling. Ren groaned and when he opened his eyes, the red had faded. He pumped into me, not withdrawing as much as Bastien. I sank my teeth into my lip and opened a gash with my fang. Ren leaned forward, caught my mouth and soothed the sting with his tongue.

An orgasm crashed through me and my channel throbbed around them, as if trying to take them deeper. I cried out, riding the wave of release.

I ground on them, frenzied with lust.

They didn't stop and I took every thrust—happily.

I FORGOT the room was connected to the kitchen with only a slab of door; a thick, sound proofed one, but it'd been left cracked open.

Damn Ren.

Damien, Violet, Laney, Talia, and Baron stared. I froze, the door slamming shut behind me. I blinked. No way. They hadn't heard us. Had they? I mean maybe the door was just opened before I came out? I was going to spiral.

"Let's take the curiosity off the table." Baron grinned.

"We heard you," Violet said.

My face warmed.

"That's my cue to exit," I choked out and hurried away. I was going so fast I almost slammed into Sydney. I wove around her and headed out the front door. I put my hand up toward Asher as he turned into the foyer. "Alone time." I heard him ask the others what they'd done to me before I was too far to hear anything more.

I zoomed out onto the asphalt and across the sprawling lawn surrounding the mansion. I hadn't had a chance to see the house from outside. Once I was well away from the front door and anyone that could potentially come out, I turned.

The style was very similar to the last one and I had no doubt that wasn't an accident. Gothic iron windows curving to a point at the top. The front spanned flatter and wider as opposed to upward.

My large window was one of two and the room on the second floor showed movement from within. I squinted. There was a lot of flashes of pink. A slim form crossed the window. That must be where Baron stayed or had placed the others.

But one of the best parts was the sprawling lawn. From out here it wasn't as spooky, instead, there was a quiet beauty. Lending to the calm atmosphere were the fairy lights strung on the various trees. Wandering to the collection of lights behind a tree that had lights wrapped around the trunk led me to a cement bench. Perfect.

I plopped my butt down and tipped my head back. I took a single deep breath, expanding my chest with the force.

A sickly sweet scent reached my nose. I jumped to my feet. There was a vampire. And not one of mine.

"Who's there?" I peered into the dark.

A throat cleared behind me.

I screamed and whirled. I pressed my hand to my chest. Talia stared at me from a few feet away.

"You're incredibly jumpy for a vampire," she said.

"Well, you shouldn't have been so quiet." I huffed. She slowly approached and nodded toward the bench.

"Can I?" I sat, but allowed her some space. She gracefully dropped beside me.

We sat in silence with only the sounds of crickets and wind fluttering the bushes and trees.

"I know you're different."

I looked over at her questioningly. "You feed on vampires," she whispered. "All three of us are never to mention it once we leave. Asher's already ordered it from all of us." Her lips twisted. I wasn't sure if she was upset because she was difficult to read. "He's very protective of you."

"Oh." I nodded, not really knowing how to respond.

"I should not have spoken to you the way I did." The words sounded dragged out of her.

"Did Asher order you to do this?" I asked wryly.

"No." She shook her head. "I think he rather I stay far from you." She winced. "Actually. Could you not tell him about me talking to you?"

I crossed my legs.

"Could you answer a question?" She smirked, flipping her blonde hair over her shoulder. I took it as a yes. "How did you and Asher meet?" I frowned. "It's so weird, thinking about how long their lives have been."

"Yet, time blinks past in a flash." Her eyes took on that far off look. "I knew Asher before, when he was human." I perked up.

Pre-vampire Asher? "We were both employed at the whorehouse." I stayed silent, not wanting to interrupt her, in case she stopped talking.

Her mouth pursed and she turned to look at me.

"He offered me this." She flashed her fangs. "When one of my clients went and infected me with a disease." Her nose wrinkled. "STDs were rampant back then." She said it as if she were talking to herself. "He's always saved me; makes it hard not to want him."

I shifted on the bench uncomfortably. "No, sorry, fuck. I'm messing up what I was trying to say with all of this." Her eyebrows furrowed. "I have never seen him the way he is with you. That's what I was trying to say. Even when he was a human, he's never let his guard down. He's never *cared* for anything more than his brother. When you made a big deal about his past, it made me angry, because I'd never seen him so vulnerable to another." She laughed under her breath. "He uses his sexuality as a shield."

He really did. "It is clear, they care for you more than their lives. That's something big with vampires. And now they're going to the trial in a few nights."

"The trial, right." I kept my confusion from my voice so she could elaborate, but every bit of my body had tensed.

"That Imogen has always been a bitch."

"So, they have a date already?" I tried for nonchalance. In a few *days* based off her comment.

"Yes." She frowned and her eyes widened. "I thought you knew."

I clenched my teeth. How dare they hide this from me? I climbed to my feet.

"No, Cat, don't tell him! He'll think I did it on purpose!" I was already halfway down the lawn.

"I won't let him do anything to you."

"Cat!" she shouted and pulled on my arm. I whirled to face her.

"Nothing will happen to you." I extricated her grip from my arm and left her cussing up a storm.

catalina

I MARCHED INSIDE.

"Enough personal time?" Asher smirked. I glared and headed right for him. His expression smoothed and he put his hands up.

I jabbed my finger in his chest.

"Get the others upstairs, the bedroom."

"What?"

"Now, Asher," I snapped. His eyebrows twitched.

I didn't stick around to watch him do as I asked. Anger made my steps heavier than usual. I reached my room and paced to the window. From here I couldn't see the bench behind the tree. A slim shadow stood on the lawn. I squinted. Talia was still freaking out? I mean I knew how scary they could be, so I understood where it came from, but I wouldn't let them hurt her.

I'd left the door wide open, so I could hear them coming. Tobias was the first one through the door. I thinned my lips and turned to face him.

His eyebrows furrowed and he approached me.

"Is everything all right, Catalina?" he murmured. "Has someone bothered you?"

"Yes."

His eyes narrowed.

"Who," the icy tone would have sent me running before.

"You." I poked his chest.

"At least I'm not the only one that received a chest poke," Asher grumbled as he entered. I glared at him, and he sprawled across the bed.

"Why didn't you tell me." I scowled up at Tobias. He still looked confused. "Why didn't you tell me you were already given a date for the trial?"

His lips thinned.

"Which of your sluts fucking told her," Ren snarled, storming inside. I jumped from the shout. Ren faced Asher who'd sat up. Jax and Bastien entered a beat later.

"Oh great, deflection." I narrowed my eyes.

Ren scowled.

"Back to my point. I'm going."

Tobias's eyelid twitched.

"You cannot go. If someone recognizes you—"

"I'll wear a disguise."

"Your smell—"

"You have to be close to me, and on top of that, I have to be bleeding. I can also wear a perfume, just in case."

Tobias threw his hands up with exasperation. He strode away, like he was too exasperated to continue the conversation. Ren took his spot in front of me. I crossed my arms and quirked an eyebrow up at him.

"Cat." I put my hand up to cover Ren's mouth.

"I am going."

Ren became scarily still.

I cleared my throat and eyed the door behind his too wide shoulder. Bastien stood next to it, watching, but he wouldn't go against my wishes . . . except this had to do with my 'safety'. Was that sound Ren gritting his teeth?

I lunged, managing to get a few feet from Ren. My feet kicked out into the air. Ren swung me to his chest and my back bounced against him. His arm around my stomach squeezed a breath from my chest. I kicked back and smacked his leg with my heel. My slippers went flying. His grip loosened, but he managed to get me to the bed, where Jax grabbed my arm, pinning it on the bed while Ren grappled with my kicks.

I aimed my free hand toward Jax, but Asher caught my wrist and forced me down. Using every inch of strength I had; I writhed to get free.

"She's fucking strong."

As much as I struggled, it only became harder as all three of them pinned me down while the other two watched.

"Bastien!" I cried. A glaze crossed his eyes, and he stepped forward, but just as abruptly, he stopped in place and shook his head.

God dammit, they were liking my thrashing around. I went limp suddenly. All the movement caused pressure in my chest. I'd not been breathing. I sucked in a breath and released it. Their scents smacked me across the face.

A hum sounding too much like a moan for my liking left my mouth. I clamped my lips together and glared over at a smirking Jax. A gentle touch grazed across my forehead. I rolled my head to the side and turned my glare on Asher.

"Are we about to fuck?" Asher grinned.

"In your dreams, you lying blood-sucker."

"Oh, there is no doubt about that, Pet, if I could dream, you'd be the star." He ran his fingertips along my jaw and down my neck. My heart jumped in answer to his touch.

I struggled to beat back my lust. I needed a distraction—now.

"Talking about dreams. I was wondering. Bastien, why can you go into my dreams? Compulsion doesn't work on me and Tobias can't read my thoughts," my words flowed so fast they ran together.

I caught Jax's smirk. I scowled at him.

"What," I snapped.

"You are terribly obvious, Love."

I laughed nervously.

"To answer your question." Bastien approached. "I cannot trap you as I did to Jax. I was able to slip into your dreams, but I could not control anything."

Asher's hand delved under the hem of my shirt, and he started to drag it upward. I pulled against Asher and Jax's grip holding my arms down, but they didn't budge.

My shirt bunched under my breasts, and he released the fabric. His hand slid down to the swell of my belly, his fingernails grazing against my skin. I breathed out, with a steady stream of air. My body was beginning to feel all tingle-y and alive.

I rolled my lips into my mouth and bit down.

"Catalina," Tobias began. His soft, cajoling tone put me on edge. "You will not be coming."

"Sure," I said, laying on the sarcasm.

Asher chortled.

"You're pushing it, Catalina," Asher finally said, his tone rising and then falling like he was mocking me.

"You will listen," Ren snarled.

"I'm not going to argue about it." I sniffled in.

In a flash, Ren tore my pants right down the middle. He forced my knee toward him, effectively baring me in all my exposed glory. I gasped and as I struggled against their hold, all I could hear was Asher's, "I told you."

I hissed up at him and Jax chuckled.

All in the span of time that it took for him to pry open my legs, he struck, sinking his fangs into my inner thigh. The sharp stab was soothed away by his suck. I gasped from the harsh tug of his mouth, my spine arching off the bed. I breathed in, and the scent of my blood permeated the air.

Tobias's grip on my calf became painful. He suddenly cupped the bottom of my knee and yanked up and to the side, so I was fully spread open. Tobias sank his fangs into the meaty part of my inner thigh, closer to my knee. I sucked in a breath, lifting my head in time for Bastien to snarl and suddenly shove his face against my sex.

I screamed and pitched my hips up to rub my sex against his mouth. He met my force, and his fangs pierced me down there. I struggled to suck in a breath. All I could smell was my blood coating the air.

My entire body felt alive.

Jax lifted my arm and sharp pinpricks stabbed into my wrist. The four of them sucked simultaneously and the orgasm throbbed through my limbs. Electrical pulses traveled through my veins and my toes curled. Oh my God, this didn't feel real.

Asher caressed the inner side of my arm. He moved and suddenly, his mouth was against my ear, and I could hear him over the high pitched ringing infecting my ears.

"You make us mad with desire, Pet." His sweet breath

caressed my cheek and that combined with whatever the hell Bastien did down there, catapulted me into a second orgasm.

I screamed so loud it hurt my throat.

Asher's chuckle sounded sinful. His fingertips played along my straining neck.

"Look, Catalina. Watch your vampires feed on you." His thumb grazed my nipple over the shirt. My entire body seized. Their touch and possession engulfed my soul. It devoured me. They fed and took, and I gave. So wholeheartedly, I gave.

Another orgasm throbbed through my senses and took me under. As if I were being tossed in violent waves not allowing me to surface.

Finally, my God, finally, I burst free from the mind-numbing orgasms. I pried my eyes open and watched Jaxon run his tongue across the bite marks he'd made on me. I couldn't move my neck. A stuttering breath wrenched from my lungs.

"Fuck, Kitten," Jax murmured, awe seeping his tone. His eyes flashed red, and he sank his fangs into my arm again.

I screamed and a ringing assaulted my ears. Lights burst behind my eyelids.

"We should do this more often," Asher's voice sounded as if it came from behind a thick wall.

Bastien shoved his fingers into my channel. My scream faded into helpless whimpers, and I gave myself over to the pleasure. My channel throbbed around his fingers, and I couldn't stop writhing. The frenzy swelled, taking me under again.

catalina

TOBIAS EYED me through the rear-view mirror. As he'd been doing the entire drive down to the sea front.

"Imogen cannot see you."

"Tobias," I gasped, exasperated. "That's the twelfth time I've heard it." I scratched at the uncomfortable wig. I hadn't taken a single breath through my nose, because I didn't want to sniff the god-awful perfume Baron spritzed on me. Since I'd been out of the social media fold, I didn't know what was 'in' right now. But I guess it was popular enough that many people wore it.

"And—"

"No one can smell my blood, got it."

Most of Bastien's theories were correct. But a new thing he discovered was that the marker that healed blood-madness was morphed into vampire cells. The way he explained it to me was that humans had red and white blood-cells while vampires had an additional one—black blood-cells.

I'd ask him more about it, if he'd come with us, but he'd had to stay behind, because he'd reverted to his mindless state. Poor timing, but there was nothing to be done about it. Based off their reaction, none of them worried about his absence because Bastien seldom showed. Other vampires just didn't know it'd been because he'd been blood-mad and chained up. He was just known to be a recluse.

Tobias pulled into the busy gas station and parked between two minivans. I looked over my shoulder through the rear window. The car Talia and Baron followed us in slid into the parking spot adjacent to this one.

"Listen to Talia, Pet," Asher murmured and took hold of my face between both of his hands.

"And don't bring attention to yourself," Jax added from his spot in the passenger seat. I turned to Ren.

"Any words of wisdom?"

"Don't do anything stupid."

I pursed my lips. Very fair, very valid.

Ren tapped his fingertips on his thigh. He shoved open the door and held it for me. I scooted out of the car; the romper shorts rode up my legs. Once I was out of the car, I tugged them down. Ren caught my arm and pulled me to his chest. I landed against him with a huff.

All he did was squeeze me tight and press a kiss to my forehead.

I pulled away and nodded at the unspoken warning in his eyes. I hurried to the other car as quickly as possible, making sure to keep my head down. Copper strands of the wig fell against my cheek. I slipped into the backseat of the sports car. A luxurious looking one that I was pretty sure I'd seen in the Crimson's garage.

LED lights framed the inside along the edges of it.

"It's nice right?" Baron sighed, revving the engine. "Can you convince Asher to give it to me?"

"It's Asher's? They didn't lose their cars?"

"Pft, that was the first thing they ordered the humans to retrieve from the place Imogen burned. We managed to save about half of them." Baron smoothly pulled out of the parking spot and revved onto the highway.

"Are we close?"

"Yes, we should be there in a few minutes," Baron answered.

"I should have kept my mouth shut." Talia sighed from the passenger side. "Asher still hasn't even looked at me." Oh, she was talking about her spilling the beans about the trial.

"Well, too late," Baron said. I couldn't agree more. "But we do have a few things to go over." She met my eyes in the rearview mirror. "Stick to Talia's side. She will get you out of there, if things go wrong."

"Wrong?"

They only exchanged a look. The car bumped over a little speedbump, and she revved in front of a hotel. Since it was nighttime, there were lights set up at the base of the huge structure. The red beams cast light across the bottom of the hotel, making the roses surrounding the base of the place seem luminescent. Baron pulled around the front of the entrance where there were people rolling luggage—three-thousand-dollar luggage. Oh, this was for the rich of the rich.

I studied the too-pale bell boy. Baron rolled on past him. He smiled at someone, and I clocked the sharp tip of his incisors.

And vampires. The only two groups that would be able to afford it.

Baron rolled through a lifted gate, with a sign across it, stating that trespassers would face consequences. She revved along the side of the building until it spit her out in the back into a parking lot packed with vehicles.

"A big turn out," Baron muttered.

"How can there not be. You know how many want to see Crimson Coven go down?" Talia scoffed. "Cat, no matter what you see or hear, do not engage. You are an observer."

I nodded. That had been driven into me, repeatedly, by the guys.

"They're giving it all up." She shook her head and turned back around. "It'll be anarchy, if this goes upside down. All for a human." She yanked her hands through her hair. "Or well, a vampire now."

"Don't lessen what she means to them, Talia," Baron said. "If it's as our Sires wish, it is as we will do."

"I just didn't expect war."

"That will only happen, if the trial doesn't go our way." Baron flipped her hair. "And it will."

They went silent. War? At a hotel?

"Why here?"

"One of the Council members owns the hotel. He's hosting the trial." She waved her hand. "Neutral ground and all that." Baron slid between two vehicles. "I'll stay in the car, in case we need to make a quick getaway."

I jumped out of the car and hurried to keep up with Talia's stride. Multiple vampires walked in the same direction we did, toward the glass doors showing the group inside. All vampires —hundreds of them. The chatter and cacophony of traffic caused a conglomeration of noises.

"What did Baron mean about if this goes badly?"

"Imogen thinks you're dead. If she sees you. Crimson Coven is done."

"She can't do anything—"

"It's not about what she can do." She scowled. "You don't understand."

"Obviously," I snapped, having enough of her attitude. "I thought we turned over a new leaf after our conversation."

She sighed.

"You don't understand how *unique* your situation is. If Imogen sees you, there will be questions. We don't want questions." She gave me a pointed look. "They will not give you over. They will fight. Five against everyone else. Even then, we will still be outnumbered. That's why there's an exit plan. If things go bad, we're to get you out of here and out of the country."

The gravity of her words slapped me across the face. They'd choose me over their entire species?

"Where would we even go?"

"If they manage to survive and get out of there. Anywhere outside of the United States Vampire Alliance."

"So, we'd just disappear into another country—"

"Hopefully you won't find out," she interrupted. "Now shh." I slowed, stepping slightly behind her and kept my head lowered as I followed her across the carpeted hallway behind the crowd.

I couldn't believe what she was saying. Why hadn't they been more direct with me? They were putting literally everything on the line.

Two wide doors were propped open, allowing a peek inside. It looked like an area a convention could happen.

I kept my eyes forward, not looking at anyone directly.

It was set up like an actual court, the kind you see on television, except there was a panel-esque set up, with eight vampires seated in black robes behind a semi circle of tables on a raised platform. Carpet covered the floor, and wooden benches were lined in front of a long podium. The first rows were already packed. Talia grabbed my wrist and guided me to the furthest row. The one closest to the door. Excitement and chatter echoed off the walls and a certain atmosphere filled the air.

Vampires were big on theatrics. I ducked my head, keeping my face angled down. Since I was at the end of the row, I only had Talia to my right side.

The large doors slammed shut and the vampires milling around took their seat, offering me a clear view. Asher, Tobias, Ren, and Jax sat behind a long table on the right side of the room, directly facing Imogen's side. She sat alone, hugging her arms, curled into herself.

She was going to feed into the poor-me script.

A young-looking, red-headed vampire sitting to the furthest left of the panel stood, his robes rustled with his movement. The room immediately went eerily quiet.

"Witnesses," he boomed, sweeping his gaze across the crowd. "You are present to spread information of what occurs today as we settle a Coven dispute." He paused. Dramatic, like I said. "Imogen Crimson has claimed unfair treatment and is formally requesting the restitution of all assets owed to her by Crimson Coven. They will each make their case and then we will vote." He waved an arm toward Imogen, the sleeve of his robe fluttering.

"Fred," Talia whispered so low it was practically only a movement of her lips.

Upon him taking his seat, Imogen stood. She approached the middle of the platform and looked up at them, giving her back to us. She'd worn a very basic khaki skirt with a blouse tucked inside the waistband. Her hair was slicked back in a ponytail. She'd made an effort to make herself look plain, like she lacked the necessities needed to make herself look well-off.

"Council members, witnesses. I begin by stating that we all know there is sanctity to a Coven. When one is formed, our alliance becomes only to one another, and yet, they have betrayed that. Betrayed me, and all that a Coven stands for." Imogen went quiet and her voice sounded choked. She sniffled in. I clenched my hands in my lap. I scanned the platform to study the Council members that had been brought together to vote.

No one I recognized.

I kept perfectly still when all I wanted to do was take off running.

"What is worse, is that their betrayal was not even for a valid reason. They . . ." Her voice hitched, like she was holding back a sob. "They betrayed me for a human!"

There were audible gasps from on-lookers. Several vampires in the audience held their hands up to their faces in shock. My lips thinned. Fred shifted in his seat, alarm crossing his face.

"Well, that is highly unusual. Humans are not a matter of importance to a Coven. Do the Crimson Sires still possess the human that is the cause of this dispute?" a woman with curly hair and high cheek bones asked.

"She killed her," Asher spat, standing so fast the chair he sprawled in scraped the ground.

She stared at Asher with impatience. "You have not yet been given leave to speak Crimson Sire, and—"

"I apologize, I don't see the issue with the human's death,"

Fred interrupted the female Council member. I gritted my teeth.

"I was fond of the human. As were the others. She was our chosen Pet." Asher sounded like he was forcing himself not to launch himself.

"Her death at Imogen's hand, as you so state, is still not a crime. There is no reason the female of your Coven, your Sire, cannot remove a human from her Coven, no matter what its status was. They are only humans after all." The woman with the curly hair and tan skin waved her hand. "But we will take it into consideration when voting, despite your speaking out of turn."

I peeked at Talia. *Roberta*, she mouthed.

Well, fuck you, Roberta.

Roberta turned back towards Imogen. "Your Coven members have spoken out of turn, but they seem most insistent. Do you have more you wish to say, other than the written account that was given to us? Or shall we allow them their chance to speak their side?"

Imogen demurely turned her face downwards, in a show of respect for the Council members, her hands laced in front of her. "No Council members. Everything about my grievances and my request for restitution is in the submitted documents." She kept her eyes downcast as she returned to her seat behind her table, hunching her shoulders to make herself look small and vulnerable.

I simultaneously wanted to vomit from her faux respect, and leap over everyone watching and claw her eyes out.

Roberta turned back towards my guys, her face impassive.

"Very well. Your Coven Sire has said her piece. Present your evidence against her claims." She turned her focus on my vampires.

There were murmurs from the onlookers. I caught snippets of words about Imogen. Things like outrageous that this happened to her, clearly within her rights, such a tragedy. My teeth were clenched so hard I wouldn't be surprised if several of them cracked. I dug my nails into the wooden bench.

Tobias stood and gestured for Asher to sit. He waited to speak until Asher had thrown himself angrily back in his chair. "As you have seen in our written report, several key details are missing from Imogen's declaration. For example, she was no ordinary human. Pets are held to a higher level than—"

"But it is her Coven as well. Is it not?" the other female vampire with sharp features asked, raising an eyebrow. Her hair was cut in a short bob.

Tobias's lips thinned.

This did not sound good.

A vampire dramatically shuffled some papers in front of him and set it down. He sat in the third seat, fingers tapping against the surface. Even from this far, he seemed so careless. It was obvious he was preparing to talk, and all the vampires remained silent, waiting.

"Gregor Redford," a female vampire sitting to the other side of Talia breathed.

"He's notoriously ancient and a recluse," Talia whispered in my ear.

"Is it truth that your unique Coven was formed by Imogen?" he asked Tobias.

I gritted my teeth. That didn't sound like the best start to all this.

Tobias's eyebrows winged down.

"It is, but—"

"And who exactly is your Sire, Tobias?" A different vampire asked, cutting of Tobias's answer.

Talia hissed.

"Fucking Wrenhaven." That name. He was the one working alongside her. What was he doing up there?

I widened my eyes at Talia, and she only shook her head.

"Why are *you* part of the Council?" Asher snarled out. "It's a conflict of interest!"

"Answer the question," Fred interjected, ignoring Asher's outburst.

"Imogen." Tobias hissed.

Talia was shaking her head; tension lined her body. I could also tell this was no good. They were only asking leading questions and giving no chance for my guys to defend themselves.

"And from my understanding she is also the Sire of an Asher and Jaxon Crimson. Two of which *are* also Sires to your . . . peculiarly run Coven."

Tobias only inclined his head in answer, unable to dispute their words.

They believed them too powerful. The vampires up there wanted to do away with Crimson Coven because of how they led.

"Well, these unfortunate circumstances are clear reasoning to no longer allow Coven's with multiple Coven Sires," Wrenhaven said, leaning his elbows on the surface of the podium.

"While there may be some truth to your words, we must return to the matter at hand, Wrenhaven. That is a matter to discuss at a later time," Roberta announced.

"Thank you, Council members." Imogen sniffled. This was all a game to her. She just wanted an *event*. She wanted to be in the spotlight, while simultaneously destroying Crimson Coven for daring to reject her.

"However, that is not the only proof that they should be unseated as Crimson Coven Sires as Wrenhaven suggests. There is one more thing I did not include in my initial dispute." She turned to face Tobias. At this angle, her eyes glinted with satisfaction. "They've harbored a blood-mad vampire. Against all vampire Council regulations."

Everyone stiffened. The silence was deafening.

"Bastien Crimson has been blood-mad for decades and they've kept him chained, using him to infect other vampires." An audible gasp crossed the crowd.

I stiffened. The way she said it made it sound much worse. Mingling truth with a lie. I sank my nails into my thigh, making sure not to break skin.

"But that is not the worst of their crimes. They also endanger us as a species, constantly."

"Imogen," Tobias hissed. Jax had stood. He looked ready to pounce.

"No," she cried dramatically, her hands flying up as if to ward them off. "I am done hiding your secrets lest they doom us all." She sniffled.

BASTIEN

I CLUTCHED my head with a groan and the chains around my wrist rattled. I breathed in, smelling the vampire's blood coating the lab. And a human. I whirled toward the female sitting at the chair with her elbows on the counter. She watched me leerily.

"Um, they told me to tell you they couldn't wait for you to." She lifted her fingers and made two hooks with them. "Snap out of it."

"They already left?"

She nodded.

"How long have they been gone?"

She pulled a device from her pocket. "Almost an hour." I yanked on the chains. The edges dug into my skin, making my blood drip to my elbow.

"Hand me the key," I ordered. She only stared at me.

"I don't think I should—"

"Now," I snarled. She jumped and hurried to toss it to me. I caught it and unlocked my chain.

"Wait," the vampire without fingers croaked. I hastened to my area to collect the blood and return it to storage. I didn't answer him. They'd been torturing him to get him to speak but had been unsuccessful.

I'd worked with this type before. Imogen would not have chosen a weak-willed vampire to align herself with.

"Will you really be able to heal blood-madness?" he croaked.

I carefully slid the Petri dish into the ice box.

"Wait." He coughed up blood and it dribbled on his chin. "I'll admit who took me, but you have to tell me, please."

I paused and eyed him. He seemed desperate for my response. I could work with desperate.

"Let's go." I pulled on some leather gloves and went to yank his chains off the hook.

"We will talk in the vehicle." The vehicle I didn't know how to drive.

"You," I pointed at the human girl hovering near the door, watching my every move with cautions eyes. "Go collect one of the two vampires upstairs to drive me."

Her eyes widened on mine, and she quickly avoided them. Many did not like the look of red eyes. They were off-putting.

I didn't grab the contacts to change the appearance. The Council would need the proof I'd been healed. And there was one thing vampires wanted more than bloodshed—a cure.

Catalina had saved this Coven.

catalina

"THEY HAVE EXPOSED our existence to multiple humans. Ones that are not feeders in a Coven." Imogen's voice rang out in the silence.

"Those are grave accusations Imogen, that go beyond your initial Coven dispute." Roberta said, her eyes narrowed.

"I have proof of their wrongdoings." Imogen announced and threw her hand out dramatically. "Here is one of the humans they exposed our existence to." She snapped her fingers. She turned to look to her left where there was a door, expectantly waiting. The door swung open and first there was a flash of long flowing hair and the grin of the vampire who was tugging something behind her. This was giving me flashbacks to Calliope's little show back—

I sucked in a breath as the human being dragged in became visible in the doorway. No! A scream stuck in my throat. Talia grabbed my wrist, stopping me from lunging forward. I turned to look at her, my eyes wide and horrified. She frowned, looked at Peter and returned her gaze to me.

She squeezed my wrist and shook her head, mouthing for me to wait.

I felt simultaneously frantic and frozen. When had she found him? How had she known about him? The how, why, and whens swirled in my head. Talia squeezed my wrist harder, and the pressure pulled me out of my thoughts and back to whatever bull shit Imogen was saying.

The vampire offered the rope to Imogen and glided back through the door she'd entered. I couldn't look at anything. I couldn't look away from Peter's bruised face and bloodied lip. Bites covered the side of his neck. This bitch had left him all bit up and bleeding.

"You are saying that the Crimson Coven Sires were so careless that they let a human know about our existence and sent him back out into the world? I find that difficult to believe. Why can we not simply compel this human to forget as he surely was in the first place?" Gregor drawled, and thank God he'd said that. Yes, just compel him. Then let him go—

"There *is* proof Council members. They did not compel him. They could not. He has some sort of immunity to compulsion."

The Council shuffled, obviously shocked by this.

"Impossible," Roberta spat, shoving her nose in the air, pompously.

"You're welcome to attempt it yourself," Imogen said sweetly. Roberta flicked her hand toward a female vampire standing to the side of the podium. There were six of them. As many as there were Council members. Likely there to step in should there be efforts of retaliation between the disputing parties during the trial.

The female approached Peter. She grabbed the rope at his neck and dragged him close to her face. The frayed edges dug into the back of his neck. Talia forced me back down. If I started something now, it'd all go to shit. She'd kill him once she saw me, just to see my horror. I had no doubt she knew who he was. She was so sick.

"I do not recognize this human. And it is impossible for a human to resist compulsion. Imogen has lost her mind," Tobias said bitingly.

"Such a good brother you are," she said, heavy with the sarcasm.

"That was a lie," Fred interjected, staring directly at Tobias. The crowd broke out in whisperings.

"He can sometimes sense when people are lying. It comes and goes, but it is never wrong," Talia whispered.

We were fucked. It felt like she was about to take off with me.

The female vampire looked into Peter's eyes.

"Stop breathing."

I sucked in a breath. He wouldn't be able to stop himself from breathing. He held his breath. I could tell, he was really, really trying. The vampire continued to stare into his face and I saw the moment he could no longer hold out. His breath whooshed out of him and his face crumpled.

"Is it true. She's dead?" Peter croaked, staring at Tobias.

My heart shattered. It felt like I was about to vomit it up.

I couldn't do this.

The crowd gasped and whispers filled my ears.

"He can't be compelled. This is unheard of!" Wrenhaven shouted. Tobias didn't answer. Peter's eyes filled with tears, spilling down over his cheeks.

The back door slammed open. I turned to find Bastien

entering. He had a hold of a very bloody man. The clothes. This was the guy they'd dragged into the house. The one that had a part in burning Crimson Nights.

Bastien dragged him forward. Blood dripped on the ground, leaving a trail behind them.

"Bastien?" Imogen asked, sounding confused.

The vampire sitting in front of us leaned to the one next to her.

"This is better than a *telenovela*."

"What is this tomfoolery?" Roberta shouted. She glared down at Imogen. "You said he was blood-mad and chained."

"Ah, did she? Well, I will get to that in a moment." Bastien's voice was smooth and calm.

Bastien tossed the vampire forward. He caught his balance and staggered.

"Your eyes," the female vampire with the bob whispered as she watched Bastien.

"Who is she?" I whispered.

"Louisa," Talia answered.

"I have proof of Imogen's treason against Crimson Coven. That she has been behind the attacks on us, sabotaging our lives, refusing to follow our law even after her trial request." Bastien pointedly cleared his throat.

The bloodied, beaten male with fingers missing, struggled to stand.

"I was ordered to oversee that Crimson Nights was burned down. I was also to provide Imogen with any assistance she might need in order to bring down the Crimson Coven."

"Who ordered you to do this?"

His head lowered.

"I am sorry, Sire." He lifted his eyes to Wrenhaven. "I do not betray you lightly. But . . . he has the blood-madness cure."

Wrenhaven hissed and slapped the surface of the wood. A crack opened down to the base.

"This is good," Talia whispered in my ear.

Roberta's glare turned and settled on Wrenhaven. "This is outrageous! Have you helped Imogen circumvent our laws?"

Wrenhaven met her stare, but made no attempt to justify himself.

"Wrenhaven broke the sanctity of our laws." The Council members murmured between themselves. They seemed more upset about Wrenhaven than anything else I'd seen the Council talk about.

He raised his chin with a smirk.

Roberta glared at him and flicked her hand up. Wrenhaven stiffened and his body jerkily stood, the robes dragging around him. He flew over the podium and dropped in an unceremonious pile on the other side of the platform. He quickly got to his feet, brushing himself off with a sly grin. He turned to look at his Progeny.

"I'm sorry, Sire—" Wrenhaven rammed his hand into his chest, and he turned to dust. He brushed his sleeves off.

"Idiot." Wrenhaven sighed. "Yes, I have helped Imogen." He shot her a sneer. "Mistakenly. She clearly was not as capable as she made herself out to be."

Roberta did not look even a little happy.

"All in favor of sentencing Wrenhaven to five centuries of the coffin," she sneered down at him. I didn't know what that meant, but based off the gasps from the others, it couldn't be good.

Roberta raised her hand and all the rest did as well.

Wrenhaven's shoulders stiffened. "We will deal with you later," Roberta spat.

Fergus put his hand out and Wrenhaven dropped to the ground, unconscious. "Bastien, it 'as been centuries," Fergus said with a thick brogue, nodding.

"Now, back to the matter at hand that gathered us today." Roberta began imperiously, obviously trying to get this train wreck of a trial back on track.

"You can do away with blood-madness?" Fergus interrupted, leaning forward, his bulging biceps flexing with his movement.

"I have engineered a cure." Disbelieving silence. "If you need proof, simply take a look at my eyes."

"How did you do this while you were ill?" One of the Council members interjected. They were poking holes—

Bastien remained calm under their questions. "I discovered it before I became ill. Upon moving locations—"

"I found it," Asher said, standing. "We had all his things stored in a different location when he became ill. When the manor was *suspiciously* burned down, we thought it prudent to look through all our belongings." That was a straight lie, but it sounded so believable.

"This is ridiculous," Imogen snarled, standing and slamming her hands down on the table in front of her.

Roberta put her hand up. "Silence. Further outbursts will not be tolerated. This trial has been getting wildly out of hand." She no longer seemed to be on Imogen's side. "It looks to me that the female, Imogen, is simply an upset cuckold."

"It does seem rather unfair to strip them of everything they have accumulated," Gregor said.

"I agree," Fergus grunted.

Bastien had simultaneously turned everyone against Imogen and kept my existence and my differences secret.

"I will gladly keep all Sires informed of my discoveries. Once I finalize it, we can work together to distribute an antidote."

A small smile played on Louisa's lips.

That was why Bastien was so focused. He'd known he could use it as leverage.

"I believe I have heard enough to conclude this trial. Imogen has stated her piece, and the rest of Crimson Coven has as well. I feel no more explanations are needed." Roberta stated.

Fred and the rest of the vampires stood. "All in favor of Imogen's request, raise your hand."

The only one who did was the last member I didn't know the name of.

I drooped. We'd won. I blinked. Not believing it. A smile began to crest across my lips. Now just to get away from here with Peter.

"Your claim for restitution from Crimson Coven is denied and your case is dismissed, Imogen. However, before we disband this session, there is one more thing to vote on. A Council trial is not to be borne lightly, only for the most serious of situations, and Imogen has, for the lack of a better phrase, fucked around." Gregor smiled. "And now it's time for her to find out. I motion she face punishment for her attacks on Crimson Coven. Whatever assets she believes are her due will no longer apply after insulting the sanctity of our Council agreements. I motion her punishment be that she must leave the United States for five centuries."

"Aye," Fergus agreed. "'Tis only fair."

"As the keeper and organizer of our summons records, I will ensure Imogen departures from the States," Roberta said.

My mouth dropped. Thank God for Gregor.

Imogen finally lifted her head. I couldn't see more than her ponytail.

"I respect and will adhere to the Council's decision." Every vampire was absolutely silent. "And I will always uphold the law of the alliance." She turned to smile at the guys. I leaned forward, too focused on Peter, which was why I knew what was coming as it happened. Imogen reached for him and with a quick twist, snapped his neck.

Talia yanked me down and slapped her palm across my mouth, cutting off my scream. His body crumpled forward and landed on the floor with a hard thud.

Imogen's gaze settled on me, her eyes widened, then the corner of her lips twitched up—smug. The crowd stood, cheering and clapping like it was some show. My screams were swallowed by the hand over my mouth. Talia dragged me backwards and my body refused to work. The snap of his neck, the blank eyes. It wouldn't leave me.

She moved so fast that my surroundings blurred, and my tears gathered at the corner of my eyes. The sounds of celebration sounded like a buzz. I regained control of my body as soon as the outside air hit me. I lurched forward, to get out of Talia's grip, but she yanked the back of my clothes.

"Let me go," I screamed and punched her right in the face. Whirling away, I smacked into another body. Hands grabbed at me and more joined. My feet went out from under me and the sound of an engine revved. I screamed, thrashing and hitting, ignoring the hisses of pain from whoever held me.

One breath later, and I smelled the sweetness I could no longer live without.

"Shh, Kitten," Jax murmured in my ear. Another flurry of

movement and my stomach dipped. Jax was running. I couldn't see through the tears spilling down my eyes. He pulled me tight to his chest and the creak of leather told me we were back in the car.

Another body-shaking sob wracked me.

"We have to get out of here," Baron whispered. I swiped the back of my hand across my eyes to glare at her. She stayed at the door, baring me from leaving.

"No, I can't leave him," I screamed, lunging for the opposite door. Ren blocked it from outside. Jax wrapped his arm around my waist, fighting to get me to his chest. He grunted, arms enveloping my waist to drag me back into his lap. I kicked out, slamming my heel into the back of the seats. Asher pushed past Baron and caught my calves.

"You're going to hurt yourself, *Älskade*," Asher said, his voice choked.

"Catalina, I will go get h—" Jax grunted from my elbow connecting with his stomach.

"No. Jax, you need to stay away from Imogen," Tobias said sharply.

Ren opened the door he'd blocked and tossed in the keys.

"Go, take her home. I will collect the boy's body." Ren slammed the door. "You, come with me," he ordered Baron.

His body . . . my stomach lived in my throat. The SUV roared to life, Jax hadn't let my arms go.

Everything was a painful blur. I lashed out, thrashing and fighting to get out of the car.

I dragged my nails down his chest, ripping his clothes and leaving behind bloody gashes on his arms. The car revved, detaching from the curb, leaving Peter behind.

I cried. Jax held me tight, refusing to let me go.

SHE HAD NOT STOPPED FIGHTING until we'd returned home. Now, she lay curled on Asher's lap on the bed.

He cooed to her in a way I didn't know how to. I unclenched my hands only to fist them again. Her sadness physically *ached*. I couldn't handle watching her fall apart.

She was feet away, wailing and I just stood here, as lost as Tobias. Talia poked her head into the room and motioned for me to follow. I scrubbed my face and slipped out of the room.

I hastened downstairs.

"Was he easy to retrieve?" That was my main concern. They would have begun to deal with Wrenhaven's punishment, and we didn't want questions about why we wanted the body.

"They'd dumped him outside."

I sneered. Bastards. If it was another human, I wouldn't give a fuck, but this was Catalina's blood. That made him part of us.

"Ren took him to Bastien's lab." I turned the corner into the kitchen. The three interloping vampires hovered near the table. Their curiosity came off them in waves. They should not be seeing any of this. They already knew Catalina was different, but they didn't know the extent of it. An issue to deal with later. Ren and I could silently dispose of them, if the need arose.

Peter was stretched across the metal surface and Bastien hovered over his arm, setting up an I.V. connected to a bag.

"What are you doing to him?" The little human girl Cat seemed fond of, raced toward them. I grabbed hold of the back of her sweater, stopping her from reaching Bastien. Knowing him, he'd turn, snap her neck and return to doing what he was doing.

All for science. A cold bastard, as much as any one of us, with only Catalina as our exception.

Bastien slid the needle into the soft underside of the boy's elbow and he pulled the little piece on top, sucking the blood into the little tube.

"This will not hurt him." Bastien straightened, looking her in the eyes, and tugged the cuffs of his shirt-sleeves higher on his forearm. "Nor will it change the outcome of him turning. This may help me understand the virus."

"Will he turn like Cat?" I asked, releasing the girl. She stumbled forward and took hold of the boy's hand.

"He may wake as a vampire."

"We have to tell her," I said gruffly, already taking a step away. Bastien grabbed my shoulder, stopping me.

"I did not want to tell her in case my theory is incorrect."

"But—"

"He's right," Tobias interrupted, coming to stand beside me.

"I will take a look at his blood. It will not take long to confirm." He flicked the syringe he held in his hand.

"H-he'll turn into a vampire?" the small human girl asked, squeezing Peter's hand like he'd get up and run away.

For Catalina, I hoped so.

I did not take pleasure in seeing her sobbing in agony.

"Where is my Little One," Bastien addressed Tobias.

"Asher's with her," I answered, stepping to the edge of the table. The slack jawed boy remained still.

"She did not deserve to see her sibling slain before her."

I agreed with Bastien. She did not deserve any of this.

I gritted my teeth, struggling with the foreign throb in my gut.

All I craved was taking her in my arms, but I did not know how to comfort her as she deserved.

catalina

I'D WOKEN with the fall of the sun and continued to stare at the ceiling, as if it had answers. My face felt stiff, and my hair remained a wild mess. All that went round and round in my head were thoughts of Peter. His favorite meals, his favorite shows, how I'd been the one to tuck him in at night. It'd been him and I since I could remember. Even when our parents were alive. They'd often been busy, working to make a living for us, so even back then, it'd been just us.

"I don't know what to do, she won't respond to me."

Asher. He leaned over my face.

I knew what he wanted from me, but I couldn't give it to him right now. It felt like there were ants crawling inside of me.

He held his punctured wrist over my mouth, so I could drink. A blood droplet formed at the opening. I cinched my eyes shut and turned my head away, keeping my lungs shut tight.

I didn't deserve to feed. I'd failed Peter.

"Let us get her bathed."

Tobias' voice. An arm settled behind my shoulder, and I

kept my eyes closed as they efficiently undressed me. "Go turn the bath on."

Those retreating footsteps had to be Asher. An arm fit under my head and the back of my knees. Tobias lifted me and I swayed in his arms.

"Take all the time you need, Love. We will care for you." The sound of the bath became louder, and he lowered me, submerging me until everything but my neck was covered. He reclined me so my back was against a hard chest.

"I have you, Pet," Asher murmured in my ear and ran his hands down my arms to lace his with mine.

Water lapped against my throat. Asher propped me up and I curled my knees to my chest, hunching into a ball.

He poured water over my head and rivulets worked down my face. I blinked droplets from my eyelashes. Tobias leaned over me and swiped his thumb over the liquid working its way down my face.

A little dent formed between his eyes. From behind me, Asher moved, and his fingers worked through my hair. My shoulders incrementally lowered so they weren't hunched near my ears.

"She likes to rub that serum on her face. Hand it to me." Tobias straightened at Asher's order and plucked one of my skin care items off the sink. Tobias pumped the liquid into his palms, and he cupped my face.

"This won't do anything," he murmured, still rubbing the moisturizer into my face with gentle swipes.

"She still likes to do it."

The smallest flutter filled my chest. I hated worrying them, but if I didn't hold myself stiff, I'd go crumple into sobs.

Even though I wanted to remain in the dark hole inside my

mind, them washing me seemed to scrub cobwebs from my thoughts.

I needed to be strong and face Peter's body. To apologize to him, even if he didn't hear me. Everything inside me cringed from the thought. That wasn't my only challenge.

Imogen had seen me. I was sure of it. That meant she would come for me. I'd offer myself to her—happily, but I doubted the guys would sit by and let it happen.

Tobias pulled the drain, and it began to swirl as he opened a towel. Asher braced behind me, but instead of letting him hoist me up, I pushed to stand, keeping my eyes lowered on the wet spots spattering Tobias's dress shirt.

He wrapped the towel under my arms and fastened it.

I carefully stepped onto the towel he'd sprawled on the floor. Jamming my feet in the slippers he placed beside it, I shuffled out.

Asher had already dried and tugged on a silk robe. He patted the bed and waved the brush at me. I sighed and dropped on the edge of the bed with my back to him. He worked a small towel over the tips of my hair. The soothing touches chipped at more of the throbbing ball in my belly. He ran the brush through the top of my hair, taking care to tug gently through the tangles. I settled with the sounds of him brushing. It felt so good. Tension leaked from my limbs, and I closed my eyes.

"Bastien needs the both of you downstairs," Ren's strong voice filled the room. The brush paused and Tobias came out from the bathroom.

"Hand it over," Ren said gruffly. Asher pulled the bristles from my hair and slapped it in Ren's hand. Asher leaned over to kiss my cheek.

"I'll be right back, *Älskade*."

Tobias leaned down and pressed his lips to my forehead. I didn't turn to look at Ren, but he hovered until he took Asher's place. He cleared his throat.

So gently, the bristles returned to my scalp. He dragged the brush down almost too lightly. Like he wasn't experienced.

"I struggle with seeing you upset." He sounded confused. "I didn't think that was possible."

He dragged the brush down my hair, reaching the end of the waves with little tugs.

"Your hair is so long."

Thanks, I grew it myself.

"I understand you have many feelings right now." He sighed. "Okay, I don't understand it, but you have all of us. We will never leave you. Yes, you may be . . . sad? About your 兄弟, but you will never be alone." Was he rambling?

Ren continued to drag the brush through my hair with hesitant swipes.

"It's looking promising, regardless. It took you four days to rise, and the span can last multiple days. Hope isn't lost—" He stopped abruptly. "I don't know how to comfort someone," he muttered the words so low it was even hard for me to hear. But what was he going on about? The span of *what* can last multiple days?

"What do you mean?" I croaked. I turned so fast; the bristles snagged my hair.

I hissed from the sudden pain, and he hurried to untangle my hair.

"These things are a menace."

"Ren," I hissed.

He frowned at me.

"What?"

I stared pointedly. He finally sighed.

"We weren't supposed to tell you, yet. Peter is downstairs, and we think he might change—"

I ran directly to the wardrobe adjacent to the door. The new furniture creaked upon me yanking it open. I shucked off the towel and rifled through the drawer, pulled out underwear and slipped on a bra. I grabbed a yet to be opened package wrapped in cellophane and pulled out the boot cut leggings and the matching baby-tee.

"You need to give—"

I was already out of the bedroom, Ren's voice fading behind me. He cursed, sounding closer. In single minded determination, I stomped down the stairs, taking two at a time. I careened around the corner, crossed the foyer, and went through the kitchen.

Damien and Baron watched me zoom past.

Talia blocked the door.

"What are you doing?"

She fidgeted with her hair.

"You shouldn't go in there."

I narrowed my eyes at her and bunched her hair, dragging her to the floor. She stopped her fist from connecting with my chin. I wanted her to hit me. To feel the pain, so it could distract me. But instead of staying and flailing on the ground with her, I burst through the door and all eyes turned to me.

Tobias, Bastien, Jax, and Asher stood to the side of Peter's head. He lay across the hard table with a sheet covering him from neck to feet. I was at his side in the next beat. I clasped his cold hand, leaning over his face.

His lips were blue-tinted, and his chest didn't move.

"He needs a more comfortable place to lay on." I glared at

Bastien who scratched his temple. "Baron," I shouted. I didn't miss the looks they were exchanging.

Baron leaned through the threshold, obviously close enough to have been listening. "I'm on it, Cat," she chirped and disappeared.

"Thank God you're here," Sydney muttered.

"We didn't want to tell you unless we were sure," Tobias said gently.

I crossed my arms and faced the group.

"You should have told me." I shook my head. "Why didn't it occur to *me*?"

Compulsion didn't work on him, just like it didn't on me.

"Don't be hard on yourself—" Asher shut up when I turned my glare on him. He pursed his lips and backed up. "Nevermind."

My mind was going a mile a minute.

"We aren't sure if he will complete the transition," Bastien said, approaching. "I took a look at his blood and there were," he shook his head and looked almost awed, "very little markers compared to your blood now. That is why while you are human it takes longer for blood-madness to be cured." Because there were less of those cells. "I believe the trigger is being bitten by a vampire. Our saliva begins the reaction." He stopped in front of me, focused on my brother.

"Is there anything I can do?" I pressed my palms against his chest. He covered my hands with his.

He didn't respond and that was answer enough. I clenched my teeth. Lashing out at him wouldn't be fair.

"We have another thing to worry about." I fanned my attention across them all. "Imogen saw me."

They had to kill her.

The tension that swept the room was tangible. She would come to kill me. I was sure the same thought went through their heads. They'd known her much longer than me, but she was vengeful. If nothing else, that was clear.

I leaned over Peter's slack face, my hand hovering over his hair.

We'd get him comfortable and settled for when he woke up. I wouldn't give up hope. Imogen was a problem for another day.

FORTY

catalina

SCREAMING REACHED MY EARS. Sydney? I focused on her words. "Peter's awake." The one time I leave the bedroom we'd set him up in to go shower. I hurried up to the third floor, passing Sydney where she stood at the base of the stairs. She yelped and stumbled back as I zipped past her.

The door was wide open, and I burst inside.

"Peter," I breathed. Then I was by his bed. He flinched and his fangs extended from his gums. He grunted and lifted his fingertips to his mouth.

"What, the fuck?"

I clamped both hands on his face and lifted it up to me.

"Thank God." I sobbed, tears falling from my eyes. "Bastien was right." I brushed the long strand across his forehead back from his eyebrow.

His eyes widened and he gasped.

"What the hell is wrong?" His hand touched my wet cheek, and he lifted his hand close to his face, looking at the red tint staining his fingers.

He groaned and gripped his throat.

"It burns," he hissed. He shook his head. In a sudden move, Peter's eyes turned red, and he lunged.

Bastien shouldered past me, taking the brunt of Peter's attack as he sank his fangs into Bastien's arm.

Bastien scowled.

"I-I am so sorry," I breathed, my hands hovering over my mouth. Peter closed his eyes tight, his nails digging into Bastien's arm so hard it caused blood to trickle down his arm.

"It is okay, Little One, I've fed." I paced from one corner of the room to the other. There were no windows in his bedroom. The bed was smaller than mine, but the wooden frame had swooping carvings similar to mine.

Sydney stood at the threshold of the door nibbling on her lip.

"Is he going to be okay?" she whispered.

Peter gasped, yanking back until he was flat against the headboard.

"Cat?" he croaked. "What's wrong with me?" I rushed back to the side of the bed.

"No, stay back," he choked out, putting a hand out and yanking the blanket up. Why did he need to do that? He had pants on—oh. My eyes widened and I dropped my hands.

"Go. Get out," he hissed.

I helplessly looked to Bastien.

"Go, Little One, I will explain things to him."

Peter wouldn't look at me. I slowly backed up, biting my lip so hard I drew blood. I hovered outside of view of the open room.

"Go," Peter snapped. *I was already out here!* Sydney came running out, tears welling. She slammed the door and ran past sniffling. Oh, he was talking to her. I staggered back, until my back was against the wall. I slid down until my butt was flat on the ground.

I dropped my head with a shuddering breath. Minutes passed and Bastien didn't come out. It would take Peter a while to get his head on straight. I pressed my palm to my mouth to block the building sob.

A loud meow dragged my attention to Binx. I gasped and dragged him into my lap. I knew he was Jax, but for now, he was my therapy cat. I lifted him and pressed his little fuzzy cheek to mine, mumbling nonsense.

So suddenly, I was picked up.

I screamed, flailing an arm out while my other one kept hold of Jax. My grip on him loosened. I looked side to side and could see nothing. But the arms were very present under me.

"Binx," I shouted, but he landed on his paws, padding after me as the invisible form carried me. "Asher, dammit, let me go." I shoved at his chest. Or what I could only assume was his chest.

"You need to feed, Catalina," he murmured.

"I can wait—" I hadn't had one drop. Five long nights of just sitting next to Peter's bed. That was what life consisted of recently.

"No."

"Asher," I hissed.

Damien and Laney looked up at us from the base of the staircase where they chatted with Talia. All their eyes widened, and it looked cartoony.

I clamped my lips tight. Asher's invisible hand slid to my butt and squeezed. I yelped, swatting at his arm and missing.

I hissed.

His steps thudded on the stairs as he climbed and headed toward my bedroom. He was being ridiculous.

He tossed me on the bed, and I bounced a few times. I rolled over and clawed to the opposite side to make my escape, but my ankles were grabbed, and I was flopped onto my front.

My clothes were ripped off my body and my legs were pried apart. A wet tongue traveled up my core. I yelped and became goo. The lick came again.

"Asher," I whined.

Binx jumped onto the bed. He prowled forward, and as I watched he turned into his normal form, cock swinging as he crawled, until his face hovered over mine. His mouth captured mine and he possessed me with a claiming kiss.

He lifted and his fangs burst free. He sank them into his wrist and sucked his blood. I watched, disbelieving. What was he? — Jax caught me with a kiss and his blood filled my mouth. I swallowed, moaning against his lips.

Jax flicked his tongue against mine and his hand curved around the back of my neck, to angle me and deepen the kiss. Our fangs clinked together.

Asher licked me again.

"Such a wet little pussy," he murmured. My channel throbbed, as if pleased. Asher worked his tongue into my entrance. I whimpered against Jax's lips, gyrating up and closer to Asher's mouth who kept a tight grip on the insides of my thighs, not letting me move as I wanted. Jax lifted with a loud gasp, and using his hand behind my head, guided my mouth to his neck as he lowered.

I sank my fangs into his throat. His sweet blood exploded on my tongue, and I moaned, my hip movements becoming frantic. Jax cupped my breast, while I slid my hand downward, until I reached his thick shaft. I clamped my fingers around him and he throbbed in answer.

I swallowed another mouthful of his blood and squeezed him simultaneously. Jax grunted.

The combined ecstasy of the blood filling my mouth and the tongue delving into my sex flooded my system. An orgasm rammed into my gut, and I screamed against Jax's throat.

His hips jerked forward, driving his cock into my hand. Precum slicked the tip, and I rubbed it on his shaft.

An aftershock tensed up my entire body. I licked the puncture wounds on Jax's throat and drooped on the bed, my head falling back.

"You left the door open," I hissed. I peeked at a very nude Asher. "Were you walking around freaking naked?"

"Perks of my ability," he said smugly, crawling to my other side and curling his arm under his head. Jax lay his head on my breast.

Warmth spread through my chest. I buried my fingers in his hair, relishing in the feeling of being cared for.

"Round two?" Asher murmured, taking my jaw and kissing me.

I STEPPED on the back of Peter's shoe. He whirled in the middle of the foyer and pierced me with a glare. I ducked my head sheepishly and took a step back.

"Oops."

"Space, Cat. Space!"

"No need to shout," I mumbled with a huff.

Peter sighed and shoved his fingers through his hair.

"I know you're worried, but I'm fine. Bastien explained everything. What we are, how we're different," he continued rambling away.

I couldn't stop looking away from that tuft of hair sticking up. Getting on my tiptoes, I smoothed the strands down, rubbing until it stuck.

He'd gone silent at some point. I dropped my eyes to his. Here I was, with my arm extended to reach the side of his head, while he glared at me.

I dropped back to the flat of my feet, lips pursed. He sighed and ran his hand over his face. I was just glad he was here and could give me attitude.

"Look, I know you're worried, but you're driving me crazy." He gripped the sides of my arms. "I'm not going anywhere, plus I'm harder to kill now."

My lips twisted. He shouldn't have been dragged into all of this—

"Stop," he said, exasperated. "I'm serious, Catty. Go away." He squeezed my arm and dropped his hands. He focused on the hallway we'd just exited. The one leading to the stairs.

"You too, Sydney. Stop following me around." His tone softened the slightest bit but was no less demanding. He turned and continued toward the kitchen. "I'm going to call your lawyer about my inheritance."

"Okay," I called back, grinning.

A small sigh dragged my attention over to Sydney peeking around the corner.

"He has a temper," Sydney muttered, focused on the direction he'd disappeared.

"It's a new development," I mumbled. Sydney shuffled forward. She wasn't giving up on following him.

"Let me know if he's getting into trouble," I whispered. Her eyes brightened and she nodded. I backed up in the opposite direction of the kitchen. Crossing the foyer, I entered the wide entrance. To the left was another little dining room and a little further down the hall opened to a huge living room with couches set up around a coffee table. Asher reclined next to Jax who had his boots perched on the edge of the coffee table.

"Let's go handle this now. It's obvious she wants to draw us out. If we go, it can be our chance to finish this," Tobias said, leaning forward on the couch across from the twins, while Bastien stood to the side. And on the other side of Bastien, closest to me, was Ren in a love seat. Their discussion cut off.

I jumped onto Ren's lap, curling against his chest. His palm rested on my spine.

"To what do I owe this pleasure?" he murmured, nuzzling his nose into my neck.

I shrugged.

"For being so good," I responded.

"I've never been accused of being good." He chuckled and slid his hand onto my thigh. I placed mine on top of his and turned to look at the rest of them.

"What's happening?" I asked, almost cautiously. Would they be truthful?

Tobias exchanged a look with Bastien and then looked at the twins sitting across from him. He must be reading their minds.

Finally, he faced me.

"One of our Progeny requested a meeting."

"Oh." I sat up. "Why?"

"He said multiple of the vampires he Nested with have been murdered." Nested? He must have read the confusion on my face. "Nests are vampires that have chosen to live together."

"So, like you guys?"

Vampire politics and organization was an interesting thing.

"Yes, but the difference is a Coven always has a Sire. For the lack of a better phrase, we are a Nest of Sires."

And that was what made them so powerful.

"And you are going to check it out?"

"That was what we were discussing."

I pursed my lips, nodding.

"Well, if your vampires are being killed, she obviously wants your attention. Maybe you should give it to her—and take me with you." I cleared my throat, feeling on the spot with five pairs of eyes on me. "Think about it. She saw me. She's pissed and lashing out. She'll probably think you're all going to become uber protective. But if she sees me outside, it could drive her to outing herself—to being rash."

"I don't like how logical this is sounding," Asher mumbled.

"*I don't* want to live forever always looking over my shoulder," I whispered.

Tobias pinched the bridge of his nose.

"She is good at hiding."

"Our Little One is making sense," Bastien said gruffly.

"Weren't you busy following your brother around?" Jax asked me.

"He got mad at me," I pouted. "And ordered me to stop."

Asher laughed.

"You can follow me around whenever you want, Pet."

Jax glared at him.

"Now, to decide which of us will go visit Corbin and what's left of his Nest." Ren curled his arms under my back and legs to tuck me closer to him.

I PLACED my palms on my thighs. Tobias and Bastien stood behind the loveseat. Corbin, one of Ren's Progeny sat on the couch across from me. He peeked at the intimidating vamps behind me. I sank my fingers into my thighs and cleared my throat. We were in the guy's house, and they were treating him like he was on trial.

"I would have been happy to come to you, Sires."

According to what Tobias was telling me on the way down, was that they usually handled any requests like this at Crimson Nights.

They actually seemed pretty irritated at having to make a house call. Ren was outside checking the area. Searching for Imogen. Asher and Jax had stayed behind to look into new locales for Crimson Nights 2.0. Ren and Bastien especially didn't want me to go anywhere without at least one of them since they were the only two that Imogen could not order about.

"Is it true that you may have found the blood-madness cure?" he asked Bastien, staring at him with awe. Word really spread fast.

"What did you need, Corbin?" Tobias interjected.

He licked his lips.

"I believe someone is targeting Crimson Coven vampires. Two of mine have disappeared. Fernando, who leads a nest downtown has also lost a vampire."

"Have you been threatened?" Bastien asked.

He was being purposefully vague, because to me it was clear who was doing this. Imogen was taking cheap shots.

"No." The corner of his lips twitched down.

I peeked over at Tobias.

"He knows nothing, but he thinks it has to do with the trial and Imogen." His eyes suddenly flared, and he whipped his arm out to grab Bastien. "Love, grab him."

I jumped to my knees and reached back to bunch Bastien's overcoat. His suspenders snapped under my grip. Bastien snarled at Corbin and one of his arms swept me behind him. He angled me as if protecting me from the other vampire.

I sputtered the edge of his coat from my mouth and wiggled

my head out from under his arm. Corbin stood at the other end of the room, his eyes wide. Although he remained here, staring in awe, he stood near an exit.

"We will look into the situation," Tobias murmured. "Contact Talia if you come into new information."

"Yes, Sire."

Bastien squeezed his eyes tight and shook his head as if shaking away cobwebs. He shuddered and squeezed me.

"Thank you, Little One."

I reached up and brushed his hair back to cup his cheek. His golden, tan skin complemented the melanin in mine to perfection.

"Anytime."

"I have regained my senses." Bastien nodded to Tobias. "Has Ren contacted us?"

"Not yet," Tobias said as we began to walk to the front door. It wasn't a far walk since it opened into the living room we'd been in. The door snicked behind us.

"You know, you two remind me of each other sometimes," I said, extricating myself from Bastien's grip. They created a barrier in front of me with my back to the door. As always, protecting me.

"That's interesting, considering the differences in our belief system." It took me a moment to grasp what he was saying. Bastien believed in science, and Tobias in God.

"Huh, that's true." I turned from one to the other. "Maybe it's because you're both super *old*." I emphasized the old.

Bastien looked over my head at Tobias.

"I believe we were just insulted."

Tobias chuckled.

I turned to Tobias. I tossed my arms around his neck, his

hands propped on my waist, immediately pulling me tight to him.

"If she's watching, I want her livid," I whispered in his ear. Then regretted it. "Sorry." Inserted foot in mouth. He was her brother. It wasn't fair to put him in this position. His arms squeezed me tighter until I could feel the outline of his cock.

"You never have to apologize to me, Love."

"Do you think she's sending a message?"

His arms squeezed me.

"Most definitely." He nuzzled my ear. "There is nothing she hates more than not being the center of attention. The only time I have seen her avoid making something about herself was when the Coven took on a version of Ren's surname."

"'Crimson' is because of Ren?" I never gave thought to the origin of their names.

Tobias hummed his affirmative.

I sighed, flexing my fingers in his pull-over sweater.

"She'll come for me."

"We will be ready," Tobias murmured so huskily it sent shivers down my spine.

"We need to relocate everyone. Get them away from us. She wants *me* dead. I don't want to put anyone else in danger." I stopped and took a deep breath. His sweet scent filled my nose and the warmth in my belly responded. "Can you do me a favor?"

He remained silent, his gray eyes scanning my face.

"I am worried about accepting, without knowing what it is. I will do anything for you, Catalina, except put you in danger."

"Please, make sure Peter is safe, no matter what happens to me." I could already see the denial forming. "It's not like I'll not be protected. I'll make sure to always be around one of the others. If something happens to me—"

"Nothing will happen to you," he said fiercely.

"Protect Peter. Please, Tobias," I croaked.

He stiffened and a moment later, finally exhaled.

"I will do as you ask."

I would trust his word.

FORTY-TWO

catalina

I LAID with Jax on the couch of the lounging room next to the kitchen. After Corbin's, we were all on edge. They'd even begun to plan where to send everyone away from here tomorrow.

Jax curled around me like I would float away. I combed my fingers through his hair, and he did the same to me, albeit hesitantly. He was terribly sweet, and I hadn't expected him to be.

Baron flounced passed carrying a medium sized box she'd collected from the front porch.

"Catalina, you got a delivery," she sang. "I think it's the Jimmy's."

I was off Jax in the next heartbeat.

"Really, you're leaving me for shoes?"

"Blasphemy! They're not just *any* shoes, they're Jimmy's," I shouted back, reaching the dining room where Baron popped the top of the box open. She froze, her eyes widening. They were beauties, I knew it.

Dark curly hair, opened, glazed eyes, a mouth open in a silent scream . . .

I'd seen this human before. She was the one that Asher talked to at the club in the pink room. Part of my brain couldn't comprehend that I was staring at a head inside the box. I just couldn't compute it.

Baron's hand shook and she scooped out the jar tucked next to their cheek. *Amira & Roberta* was scrawled across the front. She screamed and at the same time a loud bang exploded from the direction of the front door.

The familiar sound of a machine gun accompanied an explosion of glass.

"Go, Catalina. Get somewhere out of the way." Baron shoved me and ran toward the cacophony.

I sagged against the wall. No, I couldn't just go and hide. I needed to make sure Peter was okay. I rounded into the hall and slammed into someone. I screamed, slapping out, but Ren gripped my wrists.

"Cat," he breathed and swept me into his arms as he strode the opposite direction I was going.

"Wait!" I thrashed in his arms. "I need to get Peter." He didn't listen, carrying me into Bastien's lab.

"Cat," he shouted and squeezed my biceps. The pressure dragged me out of my desperation. "Stay here. I will find him."

"I'm not leaving without my brother," I screamed.

"Catalina," Ren roared. "Enough." I clamped my lips tight, yanked out of my panic.

"Go," I said choked. Tobias would make sure Peter was okay too. He'd promised.

I staggered against the wall and slid to my butt. I tucked my shaking hands between my thighs.

They would find Peter. They would protect him. Chanting the words over and over was all that kept me sane.

The door crashed open, stubbing my toe. I ignored the pinch and jumped to my feet. Peter staggered in and pulled Sydney in after him. I slammed the door closed.

"Thank God," I choked and grabbed his arms to scan him. Sydney kept her grip tight on his sweater.

"Where's Ren?" I croaked.

"I don't know. Tobias brought us," Sydney muttered.

Ren had gone to find him. I shoved my fingers in my hair and brushed the waves back from my face.

The door opened and Violet came in and slammed the door behind her. Her shoulders moved exaggeratedly, and she slumped.

"There are a lot of humans with guns." She pressed her hand to the bleeding wound in her chest. Just a little to the left and it would have turned her to dust. Her nails clawed into the wound. She hissed.

"You're hurting yourself—"

"I have to get it out." She plunged her fingers in her chest and her hisses became louder. She lifted a silver bullet and flicked it away from her. She sagged over with a hiss. That little wound weakened her. If they'd shot any of the guys . . .

"Violet," I croaked. "You need to get them out of here."

She shook her head. "The sun is about to be up."

"And what do you think will happen if you, I and Peter pass out while those humans are here?" Her lips tightened. "Exactly. Get them to the car and drive as far as you can before you hunker down from the sun. Sydney will be able to keep an eye on you both while you're unconscious."

"But there's a lot of them—"

"I'll cause a distraction."

"Catalina—" Peter snarled.

I put a finger up.

"No. I am in charge of you. Of both of you." I swept my attention to Sydney. "You need to protect her." His jaw tightened. "We don't have time to argue. Peter, I will be fine. I always am."

I turned to Violet, and she nodded once. I swept my eyes around and grabbed the first weapon looking thing I could use. It was a metal bar. A part of some of Bastien's equipment.

The guys were taking too long, and I wouldn't have left without them anyway. I peeked through a crack in the door. The coast was clear. I gripped the bar tight, carefully opened the door, and inched forward until I could peek into the hallway. No one was there.

"Go out the back and take any of the cars, they always leave the keys in the glove compartment," I whispered and refused to look at Peter. I didn't want him to see the fear in my eyes. Inching out, I left the door semi open so Violet could listen. A large human man stood at the exit, and I purposefully knocked into the wall so he could hear me. He came running after me. I ran into the hallway and kept going until I reached the foyer. Bodies and ash littered the ground.

I huddled behind the turn out into the foyer and lifted the bar. His loud steps echoed as he neared, and I flexed my hands around the metal. I could do this. I was stronger now. It wasn't like the last time.

His boot thumped into view, and I gritted my teeth and swung up. The pipe smacked into his throat and a loud choking gurgle left his mouth. He dropped to his knees. The bar slid from my fingers as I watched him gurgle on his blood. Red dripped down the corner of his mouth.

My stomach lurched. He was suffocating on his own blood. I pressed my hand to my stomach.

I didn't think it could get worse, but Imogen's familiar laugh echoed from somewhere upstairs. I gritted my teeth and turned from the human. A loud slap reached me, and I gritted my teeth, pushing faster until I reached the third level.

I stopped at the top of the stairs and poked my head around the corner. Imogen had four humans with their guns trained on Asher, Jax, and Tobias. She'd forced them to their knees in front of her. Ren lay under chains, hissing and snarling. The ground under him was singed like he'd been using his powers before the silver brought him down.

My chest ached seeing them this way. They looked so pissed.

"Imogen, there is no turning back," Tobias's coaxing voice reached me. She set the tip of a sharp dagger to Jax's chest. "There is no coming back from this. I see inside your head, as much as you try to hide it. You're hurt."

"I am not," she hissed, snarling. She shoved the tip an inch into Jax. His jaw strained but he said nothing, his eyes spitting hate at her. I needed to get her away from them. I backed down a few of the steps. She believed me a coward, and I had to lean into that. I exaggeratedly slammed up the stairs and rounded into the hallway. All their eyes turned to me. I gasped. Imogen's eyes flared.

"Don't shoot her," she snarled.

I staggered back to go up the next flight of steps. "I want her to see what she's caused." Her words followed me as I ran upstairs to where I'd hidden the stake.

catalina

I BURST INTO MY BEDROOM. A second passed and the door banged open as I reached for my hidden stake under the mattress.

She yanked the back of my shirt, right before I grabbed it, and tossed me against the opposite wall. Plaster plumed and I hissed at her. She stilled, eyes widening. She was in my face, grabbing me by the neck to drag me up the wall and pin me.

Oh God no.

"H-how did you change?" I'd never seen her so offput. I swung my fist at her. Before it reached her face, she caught it. With a quick yank that twisted my wrist. I yelped.

"You're the reason they found the cure." Avarice glinted in the gray depths. "You *are* the cure."

She moved toward me so fast it gave me whiplash. I avoided her first grab at me, but she managed to take hold of my bicep. I pulled back in the same motion, my shirt ripped and sent the small buttons all over the place.

"Let me go," I spat. Her eyebrows lifted.

"No."

That was it. Her arm pulled back and she struck like a serpent. Her nails burrowing into my chest, right above my heart. I flinched back, before she dug them further into my skin.

I lashed out and sank my nails into her face, gouging into her cheek. My stomach soured, but I didn't stop as blood trickled from the wounds. While I clawed her face, she sank hers fingers deeper into my chest.

If we continued struggling back and forth like this, she would tear my heart out. Dawn spilled across the window over her shoulder. The shutters should have gone down well before now. She must have had one of her people disable them. I narrowed my eyes at her. It all felt like minutes, but I decided within the span of a second. Holding her hand to my chest, I gripped her hair in my fist and used every ounce of strength I had to ram forward, taking her with me. My feet tangled with her skirt, but I didn't stop.

Gritting my teeth, I wrapped my arms around her and simultaneously shoved us through the windowpane. Glass shattered, raining to the ground with us. Imogen slapped me across the face, and blood burst and tickled my nose. She'd loosened her grip on my chest, so I took the opportunity to scratch her face until it was coated in her blood. She flipped us so I took the brunt of the fall. Pure agony ripped through me, but before she could roll away, I stiffened my abdomen and snaked my legs around hers.

The impact with the asphalt jolted my entire body, and my teeth sank into my tongue. I grunted. She sneered down at me. The sun continued to creep over the horizon. My eyelids became heavy and my body sluggish, but still, I didn't loosen my grip on her.

Imogen rammed her fist into my stomach. A grunt

exploded from my lungs. She lashed her claws at my face, slicing my cheek open. It was enough to allow me to shove her to turn to her stomach. I got on top of her.

I hooked my arms through hers, yanked them back, and rolled so she faced the sky. Her back to my front.

"The sun will kill us," she hissed. I stiffened my hold as she bucked.

I gritted my teeth. Not budging.

"Then this is the end of us," I huffed, tightening my hold. She would never leave us be. I wasn't willing to live fearing my shadow anymore. Keeping my eyes open became harder and harder. I could tell it was the same for her because her struggles tapered off.

The sun crept over both our bodies. The warmth beaming across my cheek soon became agony. She hissed.

"Let me go," she shouted, panicked. I reserved my energy to keeping her on top of me. I struck her shoulder with my fangs. She screamed as I drank from her. Her thrashing slowly faded away. *Focus and stay awake.* A smell of singed meat came from both of us. The sting at my cheek crawled down my neck with every section the sun kissed. I squinted at the sky, struggling to look at the clouds. Everything hurt. I had no doubt the only reason I mustered the energy to stay awake was from feeding on her.

Imogen screamed and the smell of cooked flesh became so intense I had to stop feeding. Her flesh smoked and bits of her body began to flake off.

I gritted my teeth, holding onto her with every bit of strength I possessed.

She suddenly exploded into dust.

I spit ash from my mouth and rolled to my belly. Using my

nails, I dug them into ground and dragged myself forward. We'd rolled too far from the house. I wasn't going to make it.

My eyelids lowered and I went limp with the sun beating down on my body. I was so sleepy.

At least my vampires wouldn't have to worry about her anymore.

tobias

SHE COULD NOT DIE. I gritted my molars and forced myself another step toward the window and the sun. I could see her. She lay in the middle of a field. The sun shining on her. I stopped in place, grabbing onto the wall. I breathed in a gust.

Imogen wouldn't take her from me.

I threw myself out of the window, bracing myself as the ground rushed up. The impact ripped a breath from my lungs. My femur snapped. I gritted my teeth, pushing through the agony.

I staggered to my feet. I could stay up. I could do it. Screams echoed from all around. So loud they seemed to bounce off the trees.

Imogen's dress lay feet from Catalina, empty. The sun beat down on the back of her arms, blistering with raw wounds.

My leg bucked, but I dragged it behind me.

Catalina's arms were stretched out, and she was face down. She didn't move. *I was still too far away.* I pushed through the agony knifing through my thigh and down my leg. I staggered. My cheek facing the rising sun burned.

The scent of cooked flesh singed my nostrils. I focused on the still body. I was close. So close.

Balancing on one leg, I leaned down to grip the end of Imogen's dress to drag it over Catalina's face.

Crouching, I slipped my arms under her and hoisted her up, shoving through the pain. Liquid rose in my throat, and I turned my head to spit blood.

I *would* get her to safety. I half dragged my leg, using the limp limb to keep myself upright as best as possible. Our home loomed nine meters away. At the very least the awning would be enough to get us under cover of the sun.

Catalina's arm's flopped and her head jostled. There best be no harm to her or I'd find a way to revive Imogen just to stake her.

Until now, I'd held on to hope. Maybe the young woman that I grew up with would return. She'd always been selfish, but I would have never anticipated an attack like this. I believed she would attack again, but not in such an underhanded move.

I had given her too much credit.

The sun beat on my skin, and my sluggish movements did not help my injuries. I huddled Cat closer to my chest. I did not know if I would survive this, but I would make sure Catalina had the best chance. The awning of the home blocked the sun from my face.

Blood rose in my throat again and I spat it out. In one moment to the next, my knees gave out. I fell to them, managing to keep hold of my precious bundle. Hugging her to my chest, I hissed through my teeth.

I took moments to gather the last remnants of my strength and lowered her gently. I would not be able to keep going. My body had turned on me. I swept my gaze around. Glass littered the ground, and the door was much too far. I swayed and dropped to all fours. I could not keep my eyes open much longer.

When the sun rose to the highest peak, it would touch us. My movements seemed to be in slow motion. I tucked the dusty dress around Catalina's exposed skin and settled my body over hers. The sun would take me first. At least she would be okay . . . she would survive. The weight on my body became too much to handle and I dropped into nothingness.

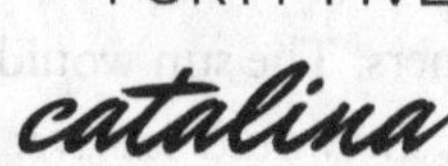

catalina

MY MIND SNAPPED TO AWARENESS, but my body refused to respond as quickly. I almost felt sore. I groaned, squeezing my eyes tight. The last I remembered, I was holding Imogen to my chest and waiting for the sun to turn her to dust . . . until it had, then I'd let go, allowing my body to fall under the pull of the sunlight. Those last moments I'd pinned her against me, I'd believed I wouldn't be waking up, but if it meant the safety of everyone I loved, I was okay with it, yet here I was.

I stretched my fingers into the comforter. Tobias was suddenly leaned over me, staring into my face.

"She's awake," Tobias shouted, his crisp accent gruff. His gray familiar eyes. My stomach soured, and I dropped my head. "Be careful, you're still healing."

"I'm sorry," I croaked. I couldn't look him in the face. I'd murdered his sister. My stomach lurched unpleasantly. She'd been bad news, but I hated all that violence. Tobias lifted my chin with one finger. His gray eyes weren't horrified, angry, or sad. Pure affection reflected in them. "You're not upset with me?"

He scoffed and my shoulders drew higher to my ears, and I waited for him to curse me out—something. His hand slid to cup my cheek.

"Why would I be upset?"

I furrowed my eyebrows. Was this a trick question? It had to be, right? He was messing with me, or something.

"I—" I licked my lips.

"Love," he breathed, wafting sweet breath across my face. I breathed him in and froze from the aroma filling my nose.

My gums and throat burned. I winced and my face stung from making the expression. My cheek felt tender. With each ache, my hunger swelled. I couldn't take my gaze away from his throat. The pop of skin and explosion of blood on my tongue sounded heavenly.

The door swung open, but my attention would not be taken away from Tobias's neck.

"Love?" Tobias said. I lunged at him, attaching myself to his neck. My fangs sank deep. I sucked down blood and he went limp, arms snaking around my waist.

I couldn't get enough. Such sweet blood. I swallowed and with each drink the burn in my body and gums abated.

"You can't take too much from him," Bastien murmured. "He's still healing." His hands flexed on my waist. "Feed on me." I fastened my grip tighter around Tobias. Bastien pulled me again. I whirled to hiss at him. He gripped the back of my hair, bunching it to keep me from feeding on Tobias again. I would have, if he hadn't held me still.

He guided me to his neck. I sank my fangs into the column of his neck. He groaned, craning his head to the side so I could take more from him. The sweet taste coated my tongue, flooding my system, and flaring lust to life. I curled my legs under me and grabbed his shoulder to fit my face into the crevice of his throat. The burning of my gums and throat abated, as if water had doused the flame. I moaned against him. Licking every drop of blood that came. I breathed freely, wanting to taste every bit of him.

"Sorry," a high-pitched voice broke through the seductive haze.

I yanked back.

"Sydney!" I shouted before she shut the door. I withdrew from Bastien's lap and scooted to the end of the bed.

She shuffled from foot to foot right outside the door, her face bright red.

"Sorry for interrupting."

"Peter?" I asked, jumping to my feet.

"He's okay," she said quickly. "He's uh, feeding on one of Calliope's Progeny." Sydney grimaced. She said it almost bitterly. My heart hurt for her. It was obvious she had a thing for him.

"Why is Calliope here?" I hissed. Had she had something to do with all of this? Was she the reason—

"This is the thanks I get for coming to help you lot?" Calliope announced, appearing next to Sydney and jamming her fists on her hips.

"Were you in on it?" I said, unable to hide my suspicion. I took another step forward, eyes narrowed.

"Whoa, relax with those fangs." Calliope eyed me. "Jax called me right before he conked out per the sun. I had one of my humans bring me over via coffin transport."

"What and you came to help out of the goodness of your heart?" I asked leery.

"Of course not." She wiggled an emerald stone ring at me.

"Now, you can't take this away. They traded their most prized possession if I made sure to take care of you in case something ever happened to them." Prized possession? This was the elusive ring they'd had in Imogen's urn that she'd wanted from the start. The entire reason they turned on me? They'd traded that for *me*?

"The damn ring," I huffed. "What's so special about it anyway?" When they thought I was trying to run off with the ring, they'd freaked so epically that I still bore the emotional scars from it.

"The sunlight won't turn me to ash if I'm wearing it." She continued admiring it as I reeled.

They gave it away so easily now—for me.

Elation and anger battled inside my gut. How could they have made such a big deal to the point that they'd kicked me from the house? On the other hand—they cared that much for me? That they would give something with that much power away?

I forced my fangs back into my gums and sank my front teeth into my lower lip, studying Calliope. Her lips twisted as she waited.

"Thank you," I said through a tight throat.

"You sound verrrry thankful," Calliope's sarcasm couldn't be missed. I shrugged. It was the best I could do. She couldn't be trusted in general, but doing something self-serving? I believed that.

She huffed and rolled her eyes.

"Tobias, Talia asked me to tell you that some of Crimson Coven's Progeny will be coming to help clean up and re-install the windows and shutter system." Tobias opened his mouth.

"And yes, she will vet them. Can't have anyone going for all your throats, again."

I didn't like Calliope's smirk. I narrowed my eyes at her, pointedly. She lifted her hands in the air and backed away. "Ren and I are taking care of the dead, so I'll get back to it."

Those two really behaved like siblings. They ignored each other one moment, then threatened to kill each other the next.

"So, we're not leaving?" I didn't take my eyes off the broken glass I'd thrown Imogen and me through. The sheer curtains fluttered from the wind. It would suck leaving. I really liked this place.

"We're not going anywhere," Asher said from behind me as his arms curled around my waist. I peeked up at him. His grin almost split his face.

"You seem happy?"

"The bitch is gone," he whispered in my ear. He nuzzled me closer. "Thank you."

"Oh," I mumbled, red-faced. I preferred not to think about it.

"She no longer has a hold on me or Jax." He shuddered against me. "Knowing someone out there could order us to do whatever they wanted . . ." He exhaled harshly and huddled me even closer to his body. I didn't know he'd felt that way. It sounded like a weight had been ripped from his shoulders.

As much as I hadn't liked killing Imogen, I wouldn't take it back. She was bad news, and she would have eventually used Asher, Tobias, or Jax to hurt the rest of us. Good riddance to her. I hugged his arm curled around my belly.

catalina

I SWIPED the back of my hand across my eyes. One of Calliope's vampires wielded a vacuum, and the loud hum sucked up the ash littering the foyer. Laney and Damien didn't deserve to be vacuumed up. Nor did the humans Imogen brought to attack us deserve to be stuffed in the back of a van to be disposed of. Knowing her, she'd compelled all of them.

"You already informed the people that care for them?" I whispered.

"My emotional Little One," Bastien murmured, smoothing his hand over my hair. During the attack, Bastien had been bound outside, wrapped in chains. He believed Imogen's intention was to take him captive. We would never know for sure.

"There was no one for them—for us," Violet said. "We were each other's family. That's why we came here for shelter." She sounded so sad. I walked over to her and squeezed her arm. She'd lost a lot. Violet refocused on the line up of dead bodies littering the floor. The clean-up had already begun before I'd come downstairs.

Tobias approached with quick steps and stopped in front of me.

"The contractors we hired to build a garage in the back, will be here soon. Is there anything you want changed?"

"A garage for the cars, huh."

"Raining season is no joke," Asher huffed, entering the foyer.

"Priorities," I mumbled, shaking my head.

"We have lived through a lot of loss, Love." Tobias smoothed his hand down the back of my head.

A loud sniffle dragged my attention over to Talia as she careened around the corner. Talia ran at Asher, bloody tears streaming down her face. He yanked me in front of him, using me as a barrier, like Jax had done before. She smacked into me and clung to my neck. "You're not dead," she sobbed into my chest. I glared at him over my shoulder. At least this time I hadn't come out injured.

I stood with my arms at my side, letting her sob into me. She shuddered and let me go, stepping back and swiping the back of her hand across her face. My fangs had burst free, and I kept my lips shut, so it wouldn't be obvious.

"Speaking of priorities, you need to feed more." Asher bopped me on the nose with his fingertip.

"I got it," Ren announced, and suddenly I was tossed over his shoulder. My face swung near his lower back and his shoulder dug into my stomach. I grunted with his swaying strides.

"You could have just asked me to follow you," I grumbled.

"You needed a pick-me-up."

I hesitated.

"Are you making a joke?"

Ren only grunted. As he climbed up the steps, his shoulder dug harder into my stomach.

I smacked his back.

"Put me down."

He smacked my butt in answer.

"No."

I scoffed and clenched my teeth. Oh, bet. I yanked his shirt up and sank my fangs into his side.

Ren grunted and hissed. His blood flooded my mouth, and I swallowed it down. The sweet taste I could never get tired of warmed my stomach, assuaging the burn in my throat.

Ren cursed and he gripped my waist with his two hands. I yanked my teeth out before he tore me off him and made me hurt him. He squeezed me to his chest, trapping my arms as he knocked the door open.

"You want to be rough?" he said gruffly. "I'll show you how rough I can be." That evil smile was the last thing I saw as he turned me on the bed facedown.

His voice sent ripples through my belly.

"Maybe you should," I dared him.

Ren groaned, shuddering against me. His zipper sounded and his hard cock pressed against me.

"Naughty girl," he groaned and clenched my waist harder until he ground against my covered ass. The rough grind elicited shivers.

His palm smoothed up my back, taking my shirt along for the ride.

Taking hold of my hair, he pulled my head back until my neck strained. I tried to move but couldn't. He had me securely stuck.

His fingers delved into the waistband of my slacks, and he tugged it down, until I was bare.

His thick tip prodded my sex and with one pump, he was fully inside me. I hissed a breath out.

"Ren," I moaned and in answer his shaft throbbed inside me. He kept hold of my hair and guided me to the wrist he held to my mouth. I sank my fangs into his wrist and sucked on his blood. My eyelashes fluttered shut. Dear God, he tasted good.

He angled my head to the side and sank into the side of my throat. I moaned against his wrist and his hips jerked forward, grinding inside my sex.

"Ohhh." Asher appeared, sprawling across the bed beside me. Asher's eyes scanned how I was bent over. Ren slammed into me again. Asher grinned. "Sexy."

He ripped the front of his shirt and buttons went flying. The white blouse-like shirt spread open, baring him to me. The dips of his abs were fully on display. My channel clamped on Ren.

"Fffffuck," Ren hissed from behind me and slammed both hands on the bed, corralling me.

Asher's eyebrows raised. "Oh, you like my body?"

I squeezed the comforter.

"Yes," I breathed.

Asher unbuttoned his pants, and his cock bobbed free.

My eyes were attached to his length. Cum beaded at the tip. I rolled my lips into my mouth, hungry for him.

He slid his hand down his pierced shaft. My clit pulsated and Ren grunted.

"Yes, grip me like that." He groaned again. My sex flexed around him. I dropped my head forward, panting. His palm came down on my butt and he rammed into me at the same time.

"Touch yourself," I panted, not taking my eyes off Asher, as Ren continued to fuck me.

The corner of his lips twitched upward.

Asher gripped his pierced shaft, running his hand from the top of his cock, down to the base. His neck stretched and his abdomen flexed, making the muscles on his stomach strain. He was so sexy. I whimpered. Ren withdrew his shaft until only the tip was inside me. He slammed into me so hard I could feel it in my throat.

Every nerve ending spiked with pleasure. I moaned, thrashing under Ren.

I was happy in my little corner of the world and no would take them from me.

catalina

"THIS IS SIMULTANEOUSLY MESSED up and genius." My nose pressed up against the glass pane of the newly purchased van. A sleek luxurious van that could fit a coffin in the back. Because 'vampires prefer to travel via coffin' while the sun was up. Asher had it delivered to Crimson Mansion, as we'd taken to calling it, just yesterday.

That vampire had everything delivered. And I was just as bad. When the others made fun of his obsession with the internet and deliveries, they were not joking. From the sounds of it, per Jax, another shiny thing would catch his attention soon, but for now Asher was all about the car that looked like an incognito delivery van.

I returned my focus to the outside of the renowned blood donation bank. One that had commercials and everything, except the blood didn't go to hospitals, it was distributed to vampires.

"And definitely morally wrong." I slumped in the cushion and turned to Bastien sitting in the oversized single seat beside me.

Bastien cocked his head and blinked. Nothing from his reaction screamed that he understood what I was getting at about it being wrong.

"Nevermind. Can you explain why it's a good thing Roberta Cain is dead?" Ren and Bastien had mentioned it on the drive over, but they never elaborated during their conversation.

Bastien laced his hands on his stomach, as he leaned back. The leather of the seat hissed with his movements.

"There won't be questions about how I came about the cure. Not while her Coven scrambles to hold itself together. Roberta was the Alliance records keeper and her successor will need to take the mantle as well as deal with any that want to leave their Coven. When a Sire dies, it is an opportune time for a vampire to leave their original Coven."

"Records keeper, what's that?" The way they worked politically was so interesting to me. Vampires seemed so lawless, but they tread a fine line with order too.

"When the U.S. Vampire Alliance was formed, all Sires agreed to name her the Historian. In that position she was charged with keeping record of all large events that have vampire influence or involvement. She also delegated summons and trials."

"Why her?" For all vampires to agree on one thing seemed impossible.

"Roberta was two millennia of age."

I gasped.

"That's ancient," I breathed. She made them look like babies. "How did Imogen manage to kill her?"

"Likely by surprise." Bastien shrugged.

"So, her death gives you time."

"Yes, I plan to formulate the medication using Peter's blood—"

"No, use mine."

Bastien's lips thinned.

"I have already discussed it with your brother. We both would prefer to leave you out of this."

We'd see about that. I glowered up at him. He chuckled and his large hand reached out and he patted my head.

"It will not be forever, if there are two of you, then there must be more." I harrumphed. "I will test whether it can be administered via pills or injection, but I will have to figure out how to dilute any traceable scent or gene markers." I trusted him to make sure Peter and I remained safe and anonymous.

The driver side door opened, and Ren slid inside just as the passenger door opened.

"Alistair?" I said, confused.

"Catalina always a pleasure to see your—"

"Watch yourself," Ren snarled. The tension rose in the car, and I bunched Bastien's coat, but he only tapped his pointer finger on his thigh. Alistair burst into laughter.

"Yes, yes, she's all yours, don't worry, Crimsons." He turned to me. "Congratulations are in order, Imogen is dead." He almost sounded impressed, and he returned his attention to Ren. "It worked out for you bastards; it was fortunate she murdered Roberta in plain view of her security cameras. The video is already making its rounds, Cain Coven is in uproar and a little bird told me Wrenhaven's Coven is just as bad. Charles is taking over and vampires are requesting to leave." I remember the smarmy vampire from Calliope's party.

Ren grunted. "Charles finally has what he wanted, he's the Wrenhaven Sire."

"And the Coven is falling apart because of it. Those under him do not respect him as they respected Wrenhaven."

"Alistair," Bastien's roughened voice rumbled. "Let us get to the point."

Alistair grinned.

"Yes, quite correct, Bastien. I will continue to maintain my silence." His gaze focused on me. "All I request is a few batches of the cure, once you have perfected it."

Bastien chuckled. Now, I could see the little games vampires liked to play. The deals, the deceptions, the *quid pro quo*.

"Tobias will be in contact with you," Bastien said.

Alistair nodded once, more serious than I had ever seen him.

"I will leave you to it." Alistair smiled at me. "Catalina." With that, he slipped out so fast, he was gone with my next blink and the door was shut, as if he had never been there.

"Did you plan to meet with him?" I asked Ren, scooting to the edge of my seat and gripping the back of the passenger headrest.

"No," Ren sounded irritated. He turned the key in the ignition.

"What about the blood bags?"

"Fuck." Ren turned the engine off and shoved out of the car.

catalina

THE NEW CRIMSON Nights was close to being ready. I stared through the large window looking out onto the dance floor.

"What do you think?"

Asher asked from his spot on the couch in the middle.

"It's . . . big."

"Like my co—"

"Asher," I hissed and all he did was laugh.

"I'm not lying."

He wasn't. I rolled my eyes pointedly and turned back toward the dance floor.

Talia waved me down. I nodded and mouthed that I would be there. I crossed the carpet and onto the wood floors to get to the door.

"Where are you going?"

"Talia's calling for me."

I didn't hear what he grumbled, because I was already going down the winding stairs to the first floor that spit me out into a slim hall that led to another that cut to the left and right. I took the right to get to the main floor. Talia turned to me.

"I think we can keep the same vibe as the last place. Red accents?" she asked.

"Yes?"

"If you want to be more involved, then you're going to need to be more demanding." She crossed her arms.

A touch caressed my back. I stiffened and sucked in a breath. Asher.

Talia continued droning on, but all I could focus on was how Asher's hand trailed down my back to caress the skin right below my skirt.

"Mmhm," I mumbled.

"Oh, and there was something else I brought up to the Sires. We can't have anyone recognizing you as their prior Pet. There will be questions. At least not before Bastien comes out with the cure." Something he was actively testing, literally on blood-mad vampires he had chained in his lab.

"We need to change both your brother's looks and yours. I vote cutting your hair just because its recognizable."

"My hair," I whimpered, clutching the long strands that flowed to the base of my spine.

"Your hair is lovely, but it's the fastest way to change your look."

"I'm not cutting it."

"Asher was right." Talia winced.

"Asher talked to you about this?" I snapped. Asher's hand on my thigh tensed.

"We're only thinking of your safety, Pet."

Talia gasped, focusing in the general direction of his voice.

"I don't regret taking her side!" She lifted her nose and sniffed. Just as quickly, she pursed her lips, almost leerily.

"I like you," I said to Talia.

Asher hissed. "Not like that, Jesus, Asher."

"Don't they drive you crazy with all that posturing?" she whispered. "And you know, this is stalking, Asher," she said, raising her voice.

"You don't even know the half of it." My words cut off with a squeak. Asher wrapped his arm around my waist and tugged me back.

"And I don't want to know, thank you very much." She shivered. "I'll show you the ropes and we can figure out where you want to fit here. Obviously, we can figure out your schedule around what your vampires agree with," she prattled on and waggled her fingers at me as Asher dragged me backwards until he flattened me to the wall in the hall.

"Ash—"

"Shhh." Asher was so close to my ear my hair fluttered. His hand dragged down, under my skirt. He delved into my undies and sank his fingers into my core.

I gasped as he removed them, and I heard the sound of his lick. He hummed.

"I need a taste." It was so weird not being able to see him as my skirt was dragged up. He curled my leg over his shoulder. I gripped his hair for balance. Violet and Talia were the only ones with us, so I didn't stress out about being exposed. They knew when to keep their distance.

epilogue

CATALINA

I SLOWED on the last steps of the banister and squeezed the grooved handrail. Wood creaked and I relaxed my hold. The back and forth arguing echoed down the hall.

"You can't tell me you don't want to hear it," Asher's voice elevated multiple octaves. "What if she leaves us?"

"Shut up," Ren drawled.

"You didn't see how she froze up when I told her," Asher mumbled. "You, did you apologize? That's what she demanded of Ren. Maybe that's what she's wanting. I don't care what you fucking do, Jaxon, drop on your knees before her and beg her to forgive and accept you. If it's because of you that she's holding back. I swear to the undead I'm going to—"

"Even if she tries to leave, she won't succeed," Ren interrupted Asher.

"Obviously," Asher snapped, sounding heated.

"This is an illogical argument, Asher," Tobias interjected. "You cannot rush her."

My slippers made my steps nice and quiet as I approached. I

stifled my smile as I neared the second living room where they liked to have all their serious talks.

"What are you guys talking about?" All heads swiveled in my direction. A slight pink flush bridged Asher's nose. I turned to Jax, and he only scowled. Then I turned to Ren, and he was smirking.

"Tobias?" He usually gave me answers, but this time, he only rubbed his temple like he was so done with the conversation.

"He's upset because you have not expressed that you love us," Bastien offered.

"I was talking about *me*," Asher said defensively. How had I not shown I cared for them?

"Are you spiraling because I haven't said it?" I teased.

"This is not a laughing matter," Asher sniped. Who would have thought they needed words of affirmation. I pursed my lips, trying to not laugh.

"I mean I stayed after all the stunts you guys pulled. It's kind of obvious what I feel for you psychotic vampires."

He crossed his arms and tipped his chin up, staring me down.

"Then say it," Asher pouted.

I leaned against the threshold sill and cast my gaze across them. They sprawled on the couches. A large clear bottle half filled with red liquid sat in the middle of the coffee table.

"I mean is it really that important?" I worked my nail under the other one, studying them nonchalantly.

"I would like to hear it too," Jax murmured. "She had no problem telling me while I was a cat." He faced me. "I will turn into a cat if you prefer?"

I could only stare.

"Unlike these two, I respect your wishes." Tobias straightened the lapels of his coat.

"Are you quoting another of your books," Ren drawled. "Because I call bullshit."

"Cat," Peter shouted from the foyer. "Just fucking tell them you love them. Dear fucking God, I've been hearing them theorize about that shit enough."

"Language," I snapped, straightening. My face flamed with warmth as all the blood traveled to my cheeks. I cleared my throat, uncomfortable with how the five pairs of eyes focused on me. "And I do." I sucked in a breath. "Love you vampires." I cupped my hand to my ear like someone was calling for me, avoiding looking at the too-still vamps.

"What was that? I'm coming."

"Where are you going?" Asher shouted, sounding much too gleeful.

I hurried away as fast as possible.

Damn them, I wanted to make them suffer—just for a little bit. A smile crested my lips. At least I had the rest of eternity with them.

Visit my website for more book information and be sure to join my reader group and follow my social media platforms to keep up with my releases.

acknowledgments

My entire Crimson Coven hype team, you guys are amazing. Thank you so much for helping me get my book out there!

Special shout out to LeeAnne M, Crystal G, Kyrie M, Becca B, Keisha K, Amber D, Lex U, Rebecca M, Melissa T, Angelica F, and Alexis L🖤

Thank you to my entire family. I love you guys!
Como siempre, gracias a mi mamá y mi papá.

Allie obsessively reads books featuring sexy, possessive heroes and headstrong heroines. So, it's no wonder characters just like that bustle to escape her imagination.

When she's not working away at her keyboard, she can be found in bed with a good book or bingeing Netflix.